DEATH OF A SPY

ALSO BY DAN MAYLAND

The Colonel's Mistake

The Leveling

Spy for Hire

DEATH OF A SPY

───────○───────

A MARK SAVA THRILLER

DAN MAYLAND

Text copyright © 2014 by Dan Mayland.

All maps by XNR Productions

Published by Richard Curtis Associates, Inc.
New York, New York

ISBN-13: 978-0692287613
ISBN-10: 0692287612

Library of Congress Control Number: 2014915980

Cover design by *the*BookDesigners

Printed in the United States of America

Author's Note

———◇———

At danmayland.com, you'll find extras that might be helpful or interesting to have when reading *Death of a Spy* or other novels in the Mark Sava series—maps that may be downloaded or printed, my own photos of places featured in the novels, lists of characters, an annotated bibliography, and a glossary.

DM

If ye break faith with us who die
We shall not sleep, though poppies grow
In Flanders fields.

—From the poem "In Flanders Fields,"
by Lieutenant Colonel John McCrae

GROZNY

RUSSIA

SOUTH
OSSETIA

GEORGIA

TBILISI

ARMENIA

YEREVAN

GANJA

AZERBAIJAN

BAKU

TURKEY

NAKHCHIVAN
(AZERBAIJAN)

IRAN

IRAQ

CASPIAN SEA

0   100 MI

0   100 KM

N

SADARAK

Aras River

NAKHCHIVAN
CITY

MOUNT
△ILAN DAG

ORDUBAD

0   20 MI

0   20 KM

Part One

1

Tbilisi, Georgia

———————○———————

The eldest of all the maids employed by the Dachi, a boutique hotel in charming old Tbilisi, massaged a knot in the small of her back, brushed a lock of hair out of her eyes as she examined her cleaning list, and sighed.

ROOM 405. LAWRENCE PRENTIS BOWLAN.

As far as she was concerned, there were two types of men in this world: those who thought it perfectly acceptable to proposition a sixty-year-old widow as she attempted to clean a hotel room—without receiving any encouragement that their affections would be welcomed!—and those who didn't. Mr. Bowlan, she feared, was one of the former.

Standing with her cleaning cart outside of room 405, she could hear that the television was still on inside the room. She sighed again.

Mr. Bowlan had spent a night at the Dachi the week before, and had been in his room then too when she'd come to clean it. When she'd bent down to collect the *two* empty wine bottles he'd placed by the garbage bin, she recalled how his eyes had lingered on her for longer than they should have. Ten years ago, she might have been flattered; now, it just caused her to consider that the male libido was a particularly tiresome evolutionary trait.

It was one in the afternoon. She'd already cleaned all the other rooms on her list. Steeling herself to the task at hand—he

3

hadn't actually propositioned her the last time, he probably wouldn't now—she knocked three times.

"Housekeeping," she called out, in heavily accented English.

While waiting for a response, she glanced in her cleaning cart and confirmed that she had a second canister of air freshener. Last time she'd needed to use extra because Bowlan's room had smelled faintly of cigarette smoke, despite the fact that smoking was prohibited throughout the hotel.

No one answered, so she gave two more sharp raps. An electronic key card hung from a loop on her apron; after waiting a moment, she inserted it into the lock.

"Housekeeping," she called again as the lock disengaged.

The first thing she noticed upon stepping into the room was not the smell of smoke, but rather...what *was* that smell?

Moments later she saw him. Startled, she jumped back a step, but she didn't scream, at least not in that initial pulse-quickening moment of discovery. She'd been cleaning hotel rooms for the better part of twenty years. It wasn't the first time she'd walked in to find a guest passed out drunk on the floor.

He lay in a fetal heap, facing away from her. She hoped, upon waking, he'd at least have the decency to clean up the urine that was puddled on the tile floor around him. That was what she'd smelled. *Disgusting.* A man his age—Mr. Bowlan had to be near eighty—should know better.

She shook her head and frowned in disapproval as she stepped closer to investigate. Standing right over him, she still didn't scream, even when she perceived that Mr. Bowlan was strangely still, and that his left hand was infused with a strange purplish tint, and that his head appeared to be twisted at an unnatural angle. Maids sometimes did find dead guests. Not often, but it happened. One had to be prepared.

As she stepped around Mr. Bowlan, she gripped the small silver cross that hung from her neck. And that was when she saw his face.

The deathly pale, wide-with-terror eyes would have been enough, but it was the mouth—lips pulled back tight, yellow skeleton-like teeth locked in a cry of pain—that would give her nightmares for years to come.

She screamed.

2
Bishkek, Kyrgyzstan

———————○———————

While the late Larry Bowlan was being poked and prodded by a forensic pathologist at Tbilisi's Central Republican Hospital, former CIA station chief Mark Sava—who happened to have been Larry's boss—was considering that in the all the years he'd been abroad, every apartment he'd ever lived in had come with an exterior balcony.

This was not a coincidence; balconies were common in the sad constellation of post-Soviet states in which Mark operated. And he was quite fond of balconies, of drinking wine on them as the sun set, or sleeping on them when the temperature was right.

His best, he recalled, as he gently rocked his ten-day-old daughter back and forth—he was cradling her in his left hand the way he would a football—had been when he'd been working as a professor of international relations and living in a high-rise apartment in Baku, Azerbaijan, right after he'd quit the CIA. What a view he'd had of the city!

His worst—and there were many candidates—had been a contemptible, bullet-riddled, railingless, bathtub-sized concrete projection in Dushanbe, Tajikistan, that had looked out over a poorly maintained and frequently used outhouse. That had been nearly two decades earlier, back when he'd been doing paramilitary work for the CIA's special activities division.

Those two balconies and others were on his mind now only because he was considering them in relation to the balcony he was standing upon at the moment. When he'd first moved in, it had been a miserable affair. Rusted balusters, a cracked concrete floor, too small to accommodate even a table for one. But his wife had since had the floor redone with hand-painted chrysanthemum-patterned tile imported from Iran, and Mark, after painting the balusters a glossy black, had carefully arranged potted tomato plants around the perimeter.

The green tomato vines cheered him now, as did the pleasant June weather, and the feel of his daughter in his arms. But there was nothing he could do about the size of the balcony, and the fact that it was too close to the street for his liking, so he was thinking that, now that he was married, and a father, and the owner of a successful business—which is to say, happier and wealthier than he'd ever been in his life—it might soon be time to upgrade to a balcony that would more accurately reflect his present station.

Turning his attention to his tomato plants, which were the reason he'd ventured onto the balcony in the first place, he bent down and dipped a finger into one of the pots, taking care not to wake his daughter as he did so. Already dry, he noted—with the hotter weather the things were sucking up water like crazy. So he headed to the kitchen, intending to grab a watering can from underneath the sink.

Upon seeing his wife, his face brightened. "Didn't know you were awake."

"I just got up," said Daria, his wife of six months. "How was she?"

"Way too perky until six, snoozing since then, though."

They kissed, and Mark poured himself a second cup of black coffee before taking a seat across from Daria at the kitchen table. His mind felt a little foggy because he'd been up with Lila since four in the morning. He'd watched competing groups of Russian acrobats perform on a televised talent show while she'd gurgled and burped on his lap, digesting her last feeding. When she'd finally fallen asleep at dawn, Mark had made himself an early breakfast of leftover Chinese food and strong Turkish coffee. It was now eight, and he was tired, but it was an easy, comfortable tired balanced by the caffeine.

Lila started to fuss and Mark rocked her back and forth. "Shh…" he said.

"Is it her diaper?"

He raised Lila up and took a sniff. "Maybe. But I changed it right before she fell asleep."

"She's probably hungry again. Here, I'll take her."

Mark handed Lila over as Daria opened her yellow cotton robe and hiked up her baggy nightshirt. Lila, still looking a little bruised from the delivery, bunched her fingers into tight balls as she began to nurse. With her left hand, Daria held her daughter; with her right, she grabbed her phone, which lay on the kitchen table.

"Yeah, somebody was hungry," observed Mark.

Lila had dark hair that, at least for now, was the same shade of brown as Daria's; Mark hoped it would stay that shade, and that it was a sign that Lila would grow up to have more of her mother's features—a wide pretty smile, high cheekbones, and delicate hands—than her father's.

"Ravenous," agreed Daria.

"That's my gal."

Lila started to gurgle and sputter because she was drinking too much too fast.

"Hey, slow down there." Daria put down her phone and stroked Lila's hair. But when Lila had settled, she picked up her phone again and began to type with one hand.

"Who are you texting?" asked Mark.

"Nazira."

"Hmm."

Daria, who was also ex-CIA, ran a nonprofit organization that helped out orphanages in Central Asia. Nazira, a Kyrgyz woman who had experience running orphanages, was Daria's friend and second in command.

"Everything good?" As Mark spoke, he leaned over and let Lila grip his index finger. "Hey there. You're a hungry girl."

"I'll need to take some time to meet with donors next week, but right now everything *is* good. Nazira might stop by later today to see Lila. She wants to know if we all want to grab lunch after."

"Why don't you two go out? I'll watch Lila."

Until recently, Daria's life had been too tempestuous to allow for lasting bonds of friendship. Mark liked the idea that she now had time to go out for lunch with a friend.

"I don't mind taking her with me."

Daria spoke with just the hint of an exotic, upper-crust accent, with her tongue pressed to her teeth, a result of her spending so much time speaking Kyrgyz, or any of several other Turkic-based languages during her usual workday. That, and she'd grown up as the adopted daughter of wealthy diplomats, so she genuinely was—or at least had once been—a little upper-crusty.

"Either way," said Mark. "Hey, I was thinking. Once Lila starts walking—when do babies walk?"

"Depends. A year, give or take."

"Well, once she starts walking, it might be nice to be in a bigger place." Mark sipped his coffee. "Maybe, you know, I'm not talking now, but in say, six months or so?"

As he spoke, Mark gazed past the kitchen and into the cluttered dining room. When he and Daria had first moved into this apartment a year ago, they'd been reluctant to do much in the way of decorating. Mark, at least, had viewed it as a temporary place to hole up in while they decided where they really wanted to live. Then they'd both gotten so busy there hadn't even been time to think about what that next step might look like. But in the past six months, he and Daria had begun to accumulate a lot more... stuff. Some of it was baby related—a Graco crib Daria's adoptive parents had shipped from Virginia, a diaper genie, a high chair, a bouncy chair, a car seat/stroller combo unit, Boppy pillows and a BabyBjörn—but some of it wasn't. Often they'd take a trip to the local bazaar to pick up a twenty-kilo bag of rice, or fresh vegetables, and wind up also buying house furnishings, like the hammered brass candlesticks on the kitchen table, or the antique Chinese settee in the living room, or the twelve-by-twelve-foot felt *shyrdak* carpet in their bedroom...the place had begun to feel like a permanent home, more than he'd ever intended it would.

"What?" asked Daria. "Move to somewhere else here in Bishkek?"

"Well, we wouldn't have to stay in Bishkek, would we? I mean, there are other options."

Bishkek was in the middle of Central Asia and surrounded by mountains. Mark didn't hate it here, but winters were bleak, dark, bitterly cold, and long. This past one, the sidewalks had been perpetually covered with a dirty slush until late March; it was now June, and the city's many poplar trees had only really leafed out a few weeks ago.

Mark looked to his balcony. From where he sat, a sliver of azure-blue sky was just visible. Inside the kitchen it smelled of coffee and baby, but also of grass and earth and wood fires. No, Bishkek wasn't the end of the world, but he'd never envisioned spending the rest of his life here. If he could live anywhere, it would be—

"What about Almaty?" asked Daria, interrupting his thoughts. Just a hundred and twenty miles northeast of where they were now,

Kazakhstan's largest city was much larger and far wealthier than Bishkek. "I'm there every other week anyway."

"Yeah, maybe." That wasn't the city Mark had been thinking of, but Almaty was at least a realistic option.

"Better hospitals."

"There's that."

Fortunately, there had been no complications with Lila's birth, but that had been at least in part because Daria, after learning that there was never a time when the anesthesiologist didn't stink of vodka sweat and that he was prone to reuse epidural needles, had opted for a natural—albeit painful—delivery. Having better health care options in the future was definitely a consideration.

"But I'd be just as happy staying in Bishkek." Daria paused, then added, "I like it here. At first I didn't think I would, but…"

"Maybe next week I'll price some places. I'm gonna go water the tomato plants."

Mark retrieved the watering can from underneath the sink, filled it, and then walked back to the balcony.

He wore a short-sleeved dress shirt that had developed a hole underneath the right armpit. His charcoal-gray polyester-blend dress slacks were stained in a few places with baby vomit. It had been two days since he'd last shaved.

While pouring water into one of the pots, Mark recalled the intensity of the actual delivery—he'd been in the room—and the outpouring of joy and relief when it was clear that Lila had been blessed with ten fingers and ten toes, and how they'd worried about jaundice, and whether Lila was feeding OK that first day, and…God, his life had changed.

"Hey *myrk!*" called a voice in Kyrgyz. "Watch it with the water."

On the sidewalk below, Mark observed a twentysomething guy in a slim-cut Euro suit and clunky black hipster glasses brushing water off his shoulders.

Mark glanced at his tomato pot. He'd overfilled it; the water was bubbling out of the drainage holes in the bottom, running in rivulets off the edge of his balcony, and raining down to the cracked sidewalk.

He was in an exceptionally good mood, and would have been inclined to apologize had it not been for the gratuitous insult. *Myrk* was what Kyrgyz city folk called the uneducated peasants who lived in the surrounding hills.

So instead of apologizing, Mark said, in Kyrgyz, "Screw you." And when the guy lifted his middle finger without looking back, he repeated the same in Russian, just to make sure his sentiments were clear.

"Nice to see you too," called a different voice from the street.

Mark turned. Behind and below him on the sidewalk was his friend, former Navy SEAL John Decker.

"Watch out for the water," said Mark.

"Making friends in the neighborhood, I see."

Decker wore khaki shorts—perhaps the only person in Bishkek to be doing so, even though it was summer—flip-flops, and a loose yellow T-shirt that accentuated his massive biceps.

"Did you hear what he called me?"

"You ever think of working for the State Department? You'd make a good diplomat."

"What are you doing here?"

Mark was the owner Global Intelligence Solutions, a small spies-for-hire firm based in Bishkek. He and his firm helped provide security for CIA and State Department employees operating out of the embassy in Bishkek, did intel work for multinationals operating in Central Asia, translated communications that had been intercepted by the NSA, and showered cash on local politicians and businessmen in exchange for confidential information.

Decker was Mark's right-hand man and had been running the day-to-day operation of the business for the last ten days while Mark took what amounted to paternity leave. But Decker lived across town in a tiny one-bedroom house with his Australian girlfriend; if some routine problem had come up, he would have just called.

Upon considering Mark's question, Decker's expression changed, as though he'd just remembered why he'd come. "Listen, you got a sec?"

"Sure." Decker proceeded to just stand there, without saying anything, so Mark added, "Why don't you come on up?"

Mark was always struck by how much smaller his apartment looked with Decker—who was a broad-shouldered six-foot-four—standing in it. That Decker was wearing shorts didn't help; his hairy legs cried out for more personal space than Mark's apartment could offer.

"Hi, Deck," said Daria, who was still in the kitchen.

"Hey, Daria."

"How've you been?"

"Great. Wow, you look good—whoa!" Decker turned his head. "Sorry, I didn't know."

"Know what?" asked Mark as he sat back down at the kitchen table, opposite Daria. Decker remained standing.

"You know, that it was chow time."

Daria laughed. "Good Lord, Deck. You can't see anything."

Lila was still nursing, but Daria had exercised discretion when it came to how she'd arranged things.

"I know, it's just that I didn't want to, ah, invade your privacy."

"You're not," said Mark. "Well, actually, you are. Why?"

Decker scratched his close-cropped blond hair and turned to Mark. "Got a call about an hour ago, boss. Didn't want to bother you, but...shit, I'm sorry. I got some really, really bad news. Larry's dead."

3

Daria ran her hand slowly over Lila's head as she looked at Mark. Then she leaned over across the table and touched his hand. "I'm sorry, hon. I'm sorry." She'd never liked Larry Bowlan—he'd always treated her like a china doll that he was afraid he might break, while with Mark it was all business and backslaps. So for her, the news of Larry's death, while unwelcome, was not a cause for grief. But Mark had known Larry for a long, long time. And for Mark, she grieved.

He just sat there, staring through her.

"I took the call from our embassy in Tbilisi," said Decker. "I wrote down the name of the hospital where he's at."

Daria had only been to the Georgian capital twice, and both stays had been brief. But she knew it was a little corner of the world that Mark knew intimately, because it was where he'd gotten his start in the spy business.

Mark shook his head and placed a hand on his forehead.

"How did he die?" asked Daria.

"I think they're thinking he just had a heart attack or something. They're doing some tests at the morgue."

"He passed away at the hospital?"

"No, at the hotel he was staying in. The cleaning lady found him. I mean, Larry *was* kind of old."

"Was he on a job?" Daria asked.

Larry Bowlan had been Mark's very first boss at the CIA. But after Bowlan had retired for good from the Agency seven months ago, he'd come to work for Mark.

"Yeah."

Daria just nodded. Because Georgia was on friendly terms with the United States and a crucial transit hub for oil that flowed from the Caspian region to the Mediterranean Sea, she was certain that the CIA had their own assets in country that they could have used. She was guessing that the only reason they'd hired Mark's firm was that the head of the CIA's Central Eurasia Division—a guy Mark knew well—had wanted to make an end run around the bureaucracy. And the only reason for making an end run around the bureaucracy would be if the job was kind of sketchy. She didn't need, or particularly want, to know more.

"The other thing," said Decker, "is that Larry had already finished the job and filed a preliminary report. So I don't know what the point of anyone killing him would be."

"He liked his booze," said Mark. Larry had only been seventy-two, but he'd looked older.

"That he did," agreed Daria. Bowlan, she gathered, had been something of a bon vivant in his younger years.

"Was there alcohol in the hotel room?" asked Mark. "Did he just drink himself to death?"

"I don't know," said Decker. "But this is the deal. Regardless of how or why he died, we can't just leave him there. I mean, I suppose we can, but…"

"No," said Mark. "He's got a mother who's…" He sighed, and ran a hand through his hair. "I can't believe this. He's got a mother who's in her nineties who he still calls every week. And a brother he sees every once in a while. We can't just leave him there."

"No mother should ever have to outlive her child," said Daria.

"We've got to call his family," said Mark. "Arrange for the body to be transported back, all that crap. Do this right. Damn."

Damn is right, thought Daria. Because she knew who Mark meant when he said *we*.

"Go," said Daria. "You've already arranged to take time off anyway. It'll be easy."

Larry had been Mark's friend and employee. On top of that, now that Larry was gone, she was pretty sure Mark was the only person at his firm who spoke even a little Georgian. She hated the thought of him leaving, but knew that he wouldn't feel right dumping this on one of his other employees, even Decker.

"That's not why I took the time off," said Mark.

He was a good man, thought Daria. Instead of running away when learning she was pregnant, he'd proposed. True, the jarringly quick civil marriage ceremony at the embassy had been less than romantic—but that had been as much her doing as his. He was forty-six, she thirty-four. They'd both spent the better part of their lives operating in the shadows.

She hadn't wanted a fancy ceremony, wouldn't have known whom to invite, or where to have it. But she had wanted a honeymoon, to spend time with him, and their two-week postwedding trip to Tuscany had been absolutely lovely. Then for the delivery, he'd been right there with her, holding her hand. He'd helped prepare her first sitz bath, had brought home-cooked food into the hospital, and hadn't complained once about taking shifts with the baby in the middle of the night. She'd cherished this past week. They'd felt like a family, a real family, not just two battered ex-spies trying to atone—at least in her case, Mark wasn't the atoning type—for past misdeeds.

"I know it's not why you took the time off," Darla said. "But things happen. I understand."

"Damn."

Despite her words, she didn't want him to go. Not *now*. She'd accepted that Mark wasn't cut out to lead a normal life, and that trying to change him would be futile. He'd tried to change himself a few years ago, had tried to quit the intelligence game and teach international relations—and it hadn't gone well; his ties to underworlds in which he'd operated for the better part of his life had proved to be too strong to sever. She'd made her peace with that, and was even proud of him—there was no doubt, he was a hell of a spy. But now was their time to be a family. They'd both arranged to be off for a full two weeks after coming home from the hospital, and after that they were both going to ease back into work, sharing responsibility for Lila.

It would eat away at him if he didn't do what he thought was right by Larry, though. Even if she were able to prevail upon him to stay in Bishkek, his mind would be elsewhere. He'd feel like he was letting down a friend; she didn't want to be responsible for that.

"We'll be fine here. We've got plenty of supplies, and I can sleep when she sleeps." Daria mustered a smile and kissed the top of Lila's head. She loved the feel of her daughter's hair.

"She's only a baby once."

"She'll still be a baby when you get back."

"I can go if you want," said Decker. "But I don't know that I can run the rest of the business from the road."

"I'll go," said Mark. "I have to. I owe it to Larry."

Part Two

4

Tbilisi, Georgia
One day later

———————————◦———————————

"Mark Sava?"

"The same."

"Jim Keal. From the embassy."

Mark pointedly glanced at his phone. It was ten twenty-five in the morning; he and Keal had agreed to meet at ten. Leaving Daria and Lila to deal with the remains of an old friend was one thing; staying in Tbilisi a second longer than necessary just so some guy he didn't know could have a second coffee with breakfast was another entirely.

"Sorry I'm late," added Keal, extending his hand. "Welcome to Tbilisi."

He was about Mark's height and age—a little under six feet, mid-forties—but carried an extra hundred pounds on his frame. His face was freckled, his nose slightly upturned, and his brown hair had a reddish tint to it.

"Thanks." Mark shifted the leather satchel he carried on his shoulder so that he could shake Keal's hand. It had been just over twenty-four hours since Decker had told him about Larry. He'd left Bishkek on a red-eye that had landed in Tbilisi just before dawn.

"So, ever been here before?" Keal asked brightly.

"Yeah."

"Really, when would that be?"

Mark didn't like to be rude, but he liked making small talk

21

even less. He wanted to take care of this business with Larry as quickly as possible. "Can we just do this?"

"Sure, sure, let's do it."

They were in old Tbilisi, where a hodgepodge of ruined and rebuilt medieval churches, sagging latticed 19th-century balconies, subterranean beehive-domed bath houses, twisting cobbled alleys, and architectural anomalies—a puppet theater built like a ramshackle gingerbread house, a peculiar minaret rising above a solitary mosque—hinted at a history marked by equal parts chaos and creativity.

Amidst all this sat the Dachi, a four-story, twenty-room boutique hotel with a baroque-inspired exterior and an interior that had been completely gutted and rebuilt as part of a wave of government-funded gentrification that was rapidly improving—or destroying, depending on one's perspective—old Tbilisi.

The Dachi was where Larry Bowlan had died.

Keal, leading Mark inside, said, "I was talking to the coroner, that's why I was late. Anyway, that blood test they do, where they check for enzymes—you know, that get released if you have a heart attack? Well, they did that test and it came back positive."

"I see."

"I figure after you grab his stuff, we can go over the logistics of transporting his remains."

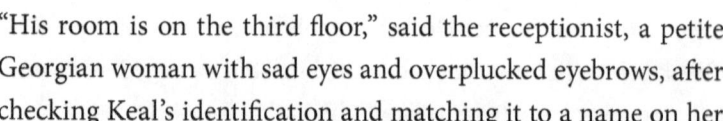

"His room is on the third floor," said the receptionist, a petite Georgian woman with sad eyes and overplucked eyebrows, after checking Keal's identification and matching it to a name on her computer screen. "But first there is the issue of the room charge."

Her English was clear but heavily accented.

Turning to Mark, Keal said, "They wanted to clear the room

and put his things in storage. But I thought it better to leave it all—"

"It's OK."

"It seemed disrespectful to have someone who didn't know him just throw his things into a suitcase, and…since I knew you were coming in a day…"

"It won't be a problem." Mark produced a credit card.

The receptionist prepared the bill, charged Mark's card, then called for the manager. "He'll bring you up to the room."

A tiny glass elevator shot up through the center of a wide spiral staircase. Mark was headed for the stairs, thinking they would be faster, but the manager—a stooped man of perhaps seventy years—pushed the elevator button.

Although it appeared to have been designed to accommodate two, all three of them crowded inside when the doors opened.

"Did you know the deceased well?" Keal asked.

"Yeah."

"Ah, tough one then, coming here. I'm sorry for your loss."

Mark pursed his lips—however heartfelt, that phrase always struck him as inadequate. Also, he hadn't really been thinking of Larry that much, other than to consider that his friend's death had proved to be a major inconvenience. So it felt a little phony to accept sympathy. "Thank you," he said.

The elevator was small enough that everyone was brushing up against each other. Out of habit, Mark kept his hands near his pockets and maintained situational awareness; a casual physical connection could be a feint for a pickpocket attempt, or a knife in the side.

Keal turned his head aside and coughed. "You must have had some friends high up in Washington, huh?"

"I don't know about that."

Keal coughed again; this time Mark could feel the force of it on the back of his neck. He refrained from breathing for a moment.

"At first, this was treated just like any other death of a citizen abroad. It happens from time to time, just part of life, you know? But then we got the cable from Washington that *you'd* be coming, and we were to do whatever we needed to accommodate you. Must be nice."

Mark didn't respond. Larry had been carrying a US passport when he died—albeit not his real one; that was why the Dachi had called the US embassy after they'd found him dead. The embassy had then called the number of the wine exporting company listed on Larry's business cards—which was really just one of many numbers Mark used to backstop his operative's aliases. Mark, in turn, had called Ted Kaufman, who was the chief of the CIA's Central Eurasia Division.

Kaufman had been the one to make sure Mark wouldn't be given any hassles, but Mark didn't want to tell Keal that.

The elevator door opened. Everyone stepped out. The manager led them to a room at the end of the hall and inserted an electronic key into the lock.

Mark stepped inside.

In a small sitting area, a wall-mounted flat-screen television had been positioned opposite a love seat. Relatively new beige carpet covered half the floor; the other half was tiled. Insipid photographic reproductions of oil paintings depicting romanticized scenes from medieval Tbilisi hung from the walls. To the side was a bathroom with a glass-walled shower. Only the high ceilings, framed with egg-and-dart crown molding, hinted at the real age of the building. A room service menu lay on an end table. Morning light spilled in from a partially open casement window.

It smelled of urine. Mark eyed the bed. It was unmade. "Where'd they find him?" he asked.

"On the tile floor, I gather. Outside the bathroom."

Larry's things were scattered around the room: a suitcase sat on a folding luggage rack; a sport coat, dress pants, and a collection of ties hung in an open armoire; his toiletry kit hung from a hook in the bathroom; his small laptop computer and camera sat on a small desk in front of the casement window.

Through the window, Mark could hear church bells, reminding him that it was Sunday morning.

Tbilisi was a city of memories for Mark, not all of them good. But one thing he'd always liked was the church bells. They'd sounded strange to his ear whenever he'd come up from Muslim Azerbaijan, where he'd lived for years and which lay just south of Georgia. Though not religious himself, he appreciated the tenacity that those bells represented. For over fifteen hundred years the Georgian Orthodox Church had survived, despite invasions from Islamist Arabs, Turks, and Persians, and then the atheist Soviets. The bells said *we're survivors, we outlasted you all, we're still here.*

Keal turned to the manager. Speaking Georgian, he said, "You may leave us. My friend here, he knew the deceased and may need some time to grieve. If we need further assistance we'll call the reception desk."

Rehearsing the words in his head before he spoke, Mark said, in barely passable Georgian, "I will only be a few minutes."

He turned from the window. The scene in the hotel room looked depressingly normal. Larry had worked for the CIA for over forty years; he'd run his own stations in Belarus and Moldova, and later had helped Mark conduct risky operations in Dubai and Bahrain. His life had been too colorful for him to die quietly of a heart attack in some unremarkable hotel room. Mark thought his friend should have passed out at a blackjack table in Monte Carlo, or while sipping vodka at a resort on the Black Sea, or in front of a firing squad in the bowels of some prison in the Middle East.

The first thing Mark inspected was Larry's $2700 compact digital Sony camera—it looked like something a tourist might carry in his pocket, but took exceptionally high resolution photos. An 8-gigabyte SD memory card had been inserted into the memory slot; Mark removed it, then retrieved a black 128-gigabyte SDXC memory card that had been hidden in the false bottom of a small box of Band-Aids in Larry's toiletry kit. He inserted it into the camera, then quickly clicked through photos of a Russian military base. As he did so, he looked for gaps in the numbers assigned to each photo—gaps which might indicate that some had been selectively deleted.

There were none.

He powered up Larry's laptop computer, typed in the password, located a hidden file folder, entered another password, then clicked quickly through a series of still photos; they appeared to be exactly the same as the photos on the SDXC card.

The laptop—a small but powerful Lenovo—had also been programmed to wirelessly back up key files online. Mark would check those files against the files on the memory card and the laptop hard drive later. He snapped the laptop shut and slid it, along with the SDXC card and the camera, into his satchel.

Keal was staring at him with a curious expression. "Did you want to pack his belongings?"

"What was he wearing when he died?"

"Ah, I don't know. The coroner will have noted it, probably saved the clothes, I would think. Would you like help packing?"

"No."

Larry had come with one small suitcase and a garment bag. Mark started with the bathroom. In Larry's toiletry kit, he found Coumadin, a blood thinner; Vasotec, a drug used to treat high blood pressure; and Lipitor, a cholesterol-lowering medication. Mark had known about the Vasotec and Lipitor, but not about the Coumadin.

He should have known about the Coumadin, though, because he'd recently grilled Larry about what drugs he was taking and his overall health. Throwing people into the field who were about to keel over from a heart attack was no way to run a company.

So apparently Larry had lied about his health.

Thanks for that.

Mark also found a lighter in the toiletry kit, so after packing up everything in the bathroom, he smelled Larry's clothes in the armoire. The blue sport coat stank of smoke. Which meant either Larry had been hanging around smokers or sneaking smokes himself. Mark didn't care about the smoking—he'd assumed Larry had been overly optimistic when he'd claimed to have quit a few weeks back.

"Where's his passport?" Mark asked, forcing himself to ignore a sudden twinge of melancholy. "And wallet?"

"I have them here." Keal patted the briefcase he'd been carrying.

Mark checked the pockets of all the hanging clothes and found another lighter and a handful of Georgian lari, less than twenty dollars' worth. He pulled down the clothes, and then the garment bag, and dumped everything on the bed. It was when he was stuffing the clothes into the garment bag, thinking that Larry probably had just smoked and drunk himself into a heart attack, that he saw it.

On the wall opposite the door to the bathroom was a waist-high furniture piece designed to accommodate a minibar refrigerator and a microwave. On top of it sat a two-cup coffee maker and a basket filled with tea bags and individual-sized coffee packs.

Above the coffee maker, on the wall, was a painting. Mark gave it a brief look, turned away, then seconds later stopped short and began to stare at it. No, it couldn't be, he thought. He had to be wrong. It was his mind playing tricks on him, just because he was back in Georgia.

At first glance it hadn't looked so different from the rest of the cheap poster-quality photographic reproductions. But it *was* different. This was a real painting. The brush strokes were broad and a bit rough-textured, sharp lines had been softened, and the colors, they were bright and happy. Mark realized that he *knew* all those colors, knew them all by their proper names—cobalt blue, cadmium orange, yellow ochre, viridian…

Up close, the painting looked like a jumble of random brush strokes, but when Mark stepped back a few feet, it came into focus. It was, he was certain, an attempt—and not a terrible one—to paint in the impressionistic style of early Renoir.

He swallowed, blinked, then reached out and touched the frame. It was simple, made of stained pine. "You say they found the body here? Around where I'm standing?"

"I think. They told me they found him just outside the bathroom, so I'd say yeah."

"Which way was he facing? Was he facing this wall?" Mark pointed toward the microwave and minibar.

"I don't know."

The painting depicted a woman sitting in front of an easel, palette in hand, painting a picture of a flower. Mark sucked in a quick breath as he focused on the flower—it was a cheerful Venetian red, a bright shade that might delight a child—and yes, the flower, it was definitely a poppy.

Of course it's a poppy.

The woman's face wasn't visible, just the hint of a high cheekbone, so Mark focused on the way her long dirty-blond hair had been casually tucked behind her small ear. She wore a sleeveless white blouse that flattered her figure and a frilly orange-colored gypsy skirt. Beyond her lay what appeared to be a stand of bamboo and a neglected reflecting pool overgrown with lily pads.

"Are you OK, buddy?"

Mark wasn't. He felt unsettled, blind to a danger he sensed was near.

He studied her slender fingers and the black lacquered paint brush those fingers gripped. He wanted to turn the woman around, and stare upon what he knew was a strikingly beautiful, and kind, face.

Because there was no doubt in his mind. He *knew* the woman in that painting. But the last time he'd seen her was twenty-four years earlier, here in Tbilisi, when Georgia had still been a part of the Soviet empire, and he'd been a young man named Marko Saveljic...

5
Russian Military Base, South Ossetia
Seventy miles north of Tbilisi

———————◇———————

Fifty-six-year-old Dmitry Titov removed the black loafer on his right foot, stripped off his sock, opened the top drawer of his desk, extracted a Kalashnikov bayonet from its scabbard, and began to slice off a callus on the side of his deformed big toe. Ever since a 120mm mortar round had been dropped, fins first, on his foot during the war in Chechnya, that big toe had stuck out at an unnatural angle, causing it to rub against his boot in a way that was a constant source of irritation.

As he tended to his foot, an army meteorologist on his computer screen explained that a high pressure system over Russia would likely dip down into Armenia, displacing a low pressure system that was currently bringing cloudy skies to Iran.

It was a private two-way videoconference, so Titov knew the meteorologist could see the contempt implicit in his blithe foot maintenance. It was an intentionally dismissive gesture that said, *I can get the same information on the Internet from BBC weather, and in fact, I have.*

Titov was the commander of an elite paramilitary unit within the spy organization known as the Federal Security Service of the Russian Federation, or FSB—an organization that, during the Soviet era, had gone by the name of the KGB. But it was a position that afforded him little respect, because everyone knew that he hadn't earned it so much as had it bestowed upon him.

So the meteorologist didn't respect Titov—Titov had been able to discern that much from their brief conversation a minute earlier—and Titov was returning the favor. He also knew this personal weather briefing wasn't designed to inform so much as it was a way for the director of the FSB in Moscow to cover his rear. If the operation that was planned for three days from now went forward as scheduled and the weather didn't cooperate, at least he could say *General Titov was briefed by our top meteorologist and signed off on going forward with the operation. Blame him.*

The meteorologist finished his presentation just as Titov finished slicing a final half-inch-long strip of calloused skin off his toe.

"Yes, yes, thank you, Captain," said Titov, flicking the skin into a nearby waste bin. "Your contribution is appreciated."

"Is there anything else you require, General?"

"No."

Titov clicked the DISCONNECT button on his computer screen and leaned back in his chair. He was tired, especially after that business with the American. His arms felt heavy in a way that they never used to when he'd been a young man. It made him grateful to be sitting in a heated office rather than out in the field, where he'd spent most of his career. How he'd grown to hate the cold. He ran a hand over his balding scalp, and thought about how surreal it was that Bowlan had surfaced at a time like this.

Then again, the Americans were famously incompetent when it came to fielding operatives who were fluent in Georgian. Certainly the CIA operations officers who operated out of the embassy in Tbilisi were a sorry lot. So Bowlan had been a logical choice—his Georgian was excellent, his Russian even better, and the fact that he was white haired and wrinkled had made him easy to dismiss as a potential spy.

The FSB officers who'd stopped Bowlan at the border between South Ossetia and Georgia had just been erring on the side of caution, because Bowlan was a foreigner in a place that saw few. His papers had checked out; he'd been carrying a pocket camera, but none of the photos on them—mainly of local wineries—had raised suspicions. And his cover story had been deemed plausible—he'd claimed to be a supermarket box-wine importer searching for new suppliers.

But when the FSB check had triggered a possible facial-recognition match with a former Moldovan CIA station chief, Titov had been notified. He'd known right away who it was. It had been over twenty years, but he'd never forgotten that face, had never forgotten what Bowlan had done.

Titov's phone, which sat beside a heavy brass double-headed-eagle paperweight, rang. He answered it.

"Someone came for the personal belongings we left at the Dachi."

"Who?" asked Titov.

"Two Americans. One is James Keal. He's CIA, works out of the embassy here in Tbilisi. The other we haven't identified yet."

"Video?"

"You should have it."

Titov clicked around on his computer. He did.

"Where are they going?"

"The hospital. Keal has booked a flight for the body that leaves tonight."

"You have a man there?"

"Yes. And the coroner and morgue director have been cooperative."

"I'd like a confirmation when the body has been accepted for transport."

"Understood."

Titov hung up and clicked on the file he'd been sent. The video camera had been hidden in the smoke detector above the bed.

For the first thirty seconds, Titov watched, unperturbed. It was just two unimposing men cleaning up after a dead geriatric.

But then...

It can't be.

Titov watched as the unidentified one yanked Bowlan's camera out of the suitcase. His motions were quick, and reptilian. There was no hint of a smile on his face. No hint of empathy for the deceased.

The cheeks had filled out, the hair was shorter and now streaked with gray at the temples. But the dark eyes, the sharp chin, those thin lips...Titov knew those lips. Ordinarily they weren't distinctive, but when pressed together into a mean expressionless slit, or curled into a half sneer...

Titov stood watching the video for a few seconds more, transfixed as his breathing accelerated.

Could he be wrong?

No. That was Saveljic.

6
Tbilisi, Georgia

———o———

Mark stood in front of the painting at the Dachi hotel, recalling his first visit to the city when he was twenty-two years old.

He'd loved Tbilisi back then; had loved the cliffs along the Kura River, the foothills of the green mountains that rose up on the west side of the city, the majestic art nouveau buildings that lined the bustling Rustaveli Prospekti, the opera house where he'd seen Verdi's *La Traviata* and Wagner's *Tannhäuser* for four rubles…he'd never been to the opera before, but for that price, why not?

He'd lived alone in a one-bedroom apartment with a rickety wood balcony covered with brilliant purple wisteria vines.

"Hey, are you all right?" asked Keal.

Mark took another look at the painting on the wall. Yes, he was certain that was Katerina, a woman he'd once known, and cared quite a bit about. He had never seen the painting before, but the scene it depicted was intimately familiar to him. And furthermore, he was sure that it was a self-portrait. Even after all these years, he recognized her style.

"I'm fine," said Mark. There was no signature on the painting. Mark pulled it down and checked out the back side. Just blank canvas.

"Shouldn't we leave that there?"

Mark hadn't seen or heard from Katerina in twenty-four years. And as far as he knew, Larry had never even met her—although Larry *had* been in Tbilisi back in the 1990s, lurking in the shadows.

He'd certainly been there when everything had gone to hell. But that was all so long ago. Mark tried to think of some link between that dark past and the present, and drew a complete blank.

"I said"—Keal's voice rose a notch—"shouldn't we leave that there?"

"No." Mark opened his leather satchel and wedged the painting in between his toiletry bag and Larry's laptop. "Did the police inspect this room?"

"I believe so."

"Did they find anything out of the ordinary?"

Keal looked as though he still wasn't happy about Mark having taken the painting. "Not that I know of."

"Did they dust for fingerprints?"

"I don't think so. But when a US citizen dies here, they have to look into the cause of death pretty closely. Someone from the local *and* regional police inspected the room, along with a forensic expert—all this before they even moved the body. There was no sign of forced entry or foul play, though, so my understanding is that they didn't treat it like a crime scene."

"And the room has been unsecured ever since they found the body."

Mark was having difficulty making sense of the idea that one of the last things that Larry had seen on this earth was a self-portrait of his old girlfriend. Katerina hadn't even *known* Larry. Or had she? Had they ever met back then? He didn't *think* so.

"Well, it's been locked. But, yeah, like I said, it hasn't been treated as a crime scene if that's what you're getting at. Because the Georgians didn't think any crime has been committed."

Mark finished packing Larry's things into the garment bag and suitcase, then said, "All right, let's go get the body."

"You sure you're OK? I mean, I get now that you two must have known each other pretty well."

"I'm fine," said Mark, but he wasn't. He couldn't get Katerina out of his head.

They'd met, he recalled, just a short ways away, at Tbilisi University, in a class on the history of medieval Georgia. The professor had been a mumbling septuagenarian…

7

Tbilisi, Georgia
January 1991, eleven months before
the dissolution of the Soviet Union

———————o———————

The American Marko Saveljic was one of thirty-three students enrolled in the class entitled Medieval Georgia: A History, but even on the first day, only twenty-five showed up.

The problem was that the professor lectured in Russian, but with a virtually impenetrable Georgian accent, while chain smoking Troika cigarettes. Indeed, Marko himself might have dropped the class after that first day, had he not taken a seat near the back of the classroom, next to a young Russian woman.

Katerina Kustinskaya was her name—she'd given it when attendance had been taken at the beginning of the class—and at first, Marko had judged her to be out of his league.

He wasn't ugly, but was self-aware enough to know that he wasn't exactly a knockout either. He was of average height, strong but not outwardly muscular, and had an angular face that some women found attractive but that most found easy to ignore. So when he felt Katerina's eyes on him as he sat down, his first thought was that he probably had something stuck to his shirt, or between his teeth; maybe the remains of the pork dumplings he'd eaten before class? Could she even see his teeth? He hadn't been smiling.

He felt his teeth with his tongue, wiped his hand across his lips, and casually glanced at his shirtsleeves and pant legs. Nothing out of the ordinary.

And yet he could still feel her eyes on him. She was trying not to be obvious about it, but Marko had always been adept at noticing things in his peripheral vision.

The professor lectured with his head down, his eyes focused on his prodigious notes, which he'd placed on a podium in the front of the room. Every so often, in between taking a drag off his cigarette, he'd rub his nose. Behind him hung a blackboard and several musty old maps of medieval Georgia.

Marko turned toward Katerina, and met her gaze. She registered surprise, then embarrassment, and turned away.

Marko wasn't as enamored with beautiful women as some men were. He'd discovered that, when naked, he was as attracted to plain women nearly as much as he was to the beauties, and often the plain women were just nicer people. Still, for the rest of the class he was aware of her to his side, aware of her movements. Her eyes were blue, her Slavic cheekbones high, and when she pursed her lips, as though privately questioning something that the professor had said, Marko found it hard not to turn and stare. Every so often he got a whiff of something that smelled like lilacs. He wasn't sure whether it was her perfume or her shampoo, but he wasted quite a bit of time trying to sort it out.

Halfway through the class, he realized that all of his fellow students were scribbling madly in their composition books. All except for himself, and Katerina.

She was dressed in layers of loose bohemian clothing; it was a look that, along with her drowsy eyes, Marko found intriguing.

But she's a Russian, he thought; that much he could tell from her name.

He didn't have anything against Russians. Ethnically, he was a quarter Russian himself. But when it came to communists—many of whom happened to be Russian—that was another matter.

At the end of class, the students began to stand. Marko hesitated, then stood himself. Katerina closed her composition book, prompting Marko to glance at it. It was the same thin-papered hundred-page bound book that most students carried, that Marko himself was carrying. They sold for a single ruble down at the university store. Katerina had drawn some frivolous doodles on the gray cover—flowers and trees and a horse carrying a long-haired girl that bore some resemblance to Katerina herself. But in the left-hand corner she'd taped a picture of Saint Ilia, a man revered by modern Georgians because, in the 1800s, he'd pushed for Georgian independence from the Russian Empire. Now, with the Soviet Union teetering, Saint Ilia had become a symbol of modern resistance against the communists.

Considering that sufficient evidence that she wasn't a communist, Marko turned to face her. At first she turned away, but when he persisted, she met his gaze.

"Tea?" he asked.

What he really wanted was a strong cup of coffee, but that was a luxury he couldn't afford and Katerina, being Russian, probably didn't want to drink.

A pause, then a smile, and a tip of the head. "Da."

8

Tbilisi, Georgia
The present day

———————o———————

Mark had come back to Tbilisi plenty of times since his student days, during the bitter civil wars that had followed the collapse of the Soviet Union, then later—after he'd left the CIA—as an academic.

He hadn't brooded much on the past on those return trips, but seeing the painting caused him do so now, so that when he and Keal drove through the square at the southern end of Rustaveli Avenue in downtown Tbilisi, he didn't see Saint George atop the massive pedestal in the center of the square, he saw Lenin, the man who used to be there. When they passed the old Parliament building, he didn't see floppy-haired teenagers doing backflips off the steps, he saw Soviet paratroopers beating Georgian protestors to death. And instead of the little beggar babies he now saw sleeping in front of al fresco cafés and high-priced perfumeries, he saw swept sidewalks and lines snaking out from government-run stores.

"Where's this hospital?" Mark asked, after they passed the Tbilisi Concert Hall, which now also housed an Elvis-themed American diner that sold cheeseburgers and sushi.

"Vazha Pshavela Avenue."

Which meant they would pass near Tbilisi State University. Mark pictured the old cypress trees out front, the overlook out back where he and Katerina used to build campfires at night, the wide museum-like steps in front leading up to building #1. How many times had he sat on those steps with Katerina?

Katerina. What the hell had that painting been doing in Larry's hotel room?

Although her late father had been a Russian apparatchik who'd been transferred from Moscow to Tbilisi, and her mother a Moscow-born Russian who'd lived on the outskirts of Tbilisi, she hadn't cared much one way or the other about politics of the day, or what had been the sour state of Russian-Georgian relations at the time. She'd only taped old Saint Ilia to her notebook because a few of her Georgian friends had been devoted to the cause of independence and she liked to go along to get along. Art was what really interested her. She liked to paint flowers, children, old people, her friends...and over tea she'd asked Mark if she could paint him. She'd never painted an American before!

Russians had a reputation for being dour and complicated and brooding, a reputation that Mark had thought then—and still thought—was well-earned. But from the day they met until the day they parted, Katerina had been anything but. Her glass had always been half full.

They'd walked back to his apartment that first afternoon. He'd felt awkward, sitting there as she studied him as though he were some kind of exotic zoo animal. Commanding him to turn his head left, then right...she painted mercifully fast, though, and the portrait she'd done of him had been an adequate representation. He'd been sitting on his balcony, wearing jeans and a black sweater, in front of an overgrown wisteria vine that had crept up the side of the building. It had been twilight in January, and cold; the wisteria vine had looked like a cluster of twigs.

In her painting, though, it was sunny and the wisteria was in full purple bloom, cascading around him. And instead of the cheap Russian beer he'd been drinking, she'd painted him grasping what looked like a crystal goblet—filled with what Katerina said was lemonade.

Mark had thought he'd looked a bit like a French dandy, but he'd kept that opinion to himself. He was so mesmerized by the way she spoke, by the way her lips opened when she said *ya*. Russian was so much softer, so much more interesting, coming out of her mouth than when spoken by bureaucrats with bad teeth and worse breath.

They'd had dinner in his apartment that first night—just *khachapuri*, thin bread with melted cheese on top—and a couple of bottles of Georgian wine. They'd listened to The Rolling Stones' *Let It Bleed*, through a little speaker off his Sony Walkman.

God, what a wonderful time that had been. He remembered the smell of beeswax candles and sex—she hadn't been a shy woman, that he remembered with perfect clarity—and resiny white wine, and his nearly empty apartment. He'd had just a pine bed with rough white sheets he'd bought down at a dreary government-run department store on Lenin Square, a single pillow, a kitchen table that was actually an elementary-school desk he'd found in an alley and had cleaned up, two metal chairs, and lots of wine-bottle candlestick holders for when the electricity would go out.

"Goddamn traffic," said Keal, interrupting Mark's thoughts. "It's usually not this bad at this time of day."

Stick with the present, Mark told himself. And stop thinking about sex you had twenty-four years ago when you have a beautiful wife now. He looked out the front windshield of the Ford Mondeo sedan they were riding in, to the line of stopped cars. Glancing in the rearview mirror, he noted just as many were piled up in back.

Keal added, "There must be an accident up ahead."

Mark pulled the SDXC card out of his satchel, slotted it into Larry's laptop, typed in Larry's password, and began to examine the photos more carefully, zooming in as best he could on the various Russian-made vehicles Larry had documented coming in and out of the Russian military base—UAZ Hunter 4×4's, BRDM and BTR armored cars, old Zil trucks, and new T-90 tanks. There were hundreds of images. It seemed like a lot of activity—the T-90 tanks were a worry—but without any baseline to compare it to, Mark couldn't come to any useful conclusions.

The contract Mark had signed with the CIA's Central Eurasia Division had specified that Global Intelligence Solutions— Mark's firm—was to surveil the entrance to a Russian military base located in South Ossetia, a disputed patch of land claimed by Georgia but occupied by Russia.

Via satellite observations, the CIA had detected increased activity at the base. But the Agency hadn't been satisfied with the satellite data; they'd wanted ground-level photos that could lend additional insight into the types of troops that were exiting and entering the base. Because the CIA station chief in Tbilisi had balked at assigning one of his own operatives to the task— the Agency tended to promote the cautious over the cowboys— Kaufman had turned to Mark's firm.

Upon arrival in South Ossetia, Larry had boozed and schmoozed with local vintners, then rented an apartment on the top floor of a six-story building in Tskhinvali, the region's capital. From that vantage point, he'd been able to photograph Russian military vehicles and personnel entering and exiting the adjacent military base.

Was it possible that the Russians had discovered what Larry was up to and killed him? Sure, thought Mark. But that didn't even begin to explain the painting.

He clicked through more of the photos, but there wasn't much to see. They might eventually prove useful to Kaufman, who could have them analyzed by Russia specialists, who in turn could study the uniforms and license plates and armor, and con-trast the level of activity at the base when Larry was there with what satellite data suggested had been the level of activity over the past year. But to Mark the photos said little. South Ossetia was a heavily militarized disputed territory, and it lay just south of Chechnya and several other heavily militarized disputed territories—the Russians had been fighting a series of low-grade civil wars in the North Caucasus for years—so it would have been surprising *not* to see a robust level of activity at the base.

It was only when he got to the end that he noticed that the last photo of the lot was dated June sixth, four days earlier. It was a late afternoon shot of a Russian armored car just outside the base. But Larry hadn't left South Ossetia until the afternoon of the seventh.

"Shit," said Mark. Was it possible Larry had just neglected to take any photos on the seventh? Mark doubted it; Larry had known that the contract with the CIA had specified ninety-six hours of surveillance. Those ninety-six hours would have ended at noon on the seventh.

"Something wrong?" asked Keal.

"Yeah. This traffic."

A hunchbacked old man with a handful of tacky nesting dolls was making his way down the line of cars, hoping for a sale.

Keal waved him off, then said, "We're almost there."

Mark navigated to the folder on the laptop's hard drive where Larry had stored backup copies of all the photo files. No, he hadn't messed up—the photos that had been backed up on the laptop *were* exactly the same as those on the SDXC card. Nothing from June seventh.

Which left one more thing to check: Mark had made sure that Larry's laptop had been equipped with a wireless Internet card with international roaming capabilities—so that Larry would be able to backup offsite, even when traveling to remote locations.

He clicked open the Internet browser, navigated to the online backup storage site for Global Intelligence Solutions, and typed in the password for Larry's account.

A long list of folders appeared, each representing a different job executed by Larry over the past six months. Mark opened the most recent and examined the photos inside it.

There were, he realized, twenty-eight more photos stored online—all from the morning of the seventh—than were stored on Larry's laptop and on the SDXC memory card that had been hidden in the Band-Aid box. Which could only mean one thing—someone had found, and then deleted, the extra photos on the laptop and memory card, but had done so after they'd been backed up online.

Mark began examining the photos in question. All were of the entrance to the military base; none seemed much different from any of the earlier photos. He tried enlarging a few, but the image-editing software Larry had on his laptop was lousy, and the enlarged photos looked grainier than they should have.

Traffic started moving again. Mark glanced at the cars in front of him, and then at the rearview mirror. He wondered whether he was being followed.

Photos of a Russian military base deleted. Katerina's self-portrait. Larry dead. *What was the connection?* He sensed menace, as though a fog of poison gas were gathering at his feet, slowly billowing upward.

He googled *Katerina Kustinskaya Tbilisi*, first typing her name as it would appear in Georgian, then in Cyrillic. He came up with a few hits, but nothing that pointed to the woman he'd known. He dug up what phone records he could for Tbilisi. Nothing.

To Keal, Mark said, "If I were to give you a name of someone, a Russian woman who used to live here in Tbilisi and might still be living here, would you be able to run it for me at the embassy? Maybe come up with an address?"

"I can try. What's the name?"

He told him. "She'd be forty-five years old." Mark searched his memory. "Born in July. I don't remember the exact day."

Keal pulled a pen out of the dash compartment. "Spell it."

Mark did, and Keal jotted down the name as he drove. "You have a photo?"

"No. Kustinskaya might not be her last name anymore, she might have gotten married. But she was a student at Tbilisi State University from 1988 to at least the middle of 1991. You might find some information about her there."

Keal picked up his phone. As he dialed the embassy, he said, "Why am I running this name?"

"She's an old friend I lost touch with years ago." Mark paused. What would he say to Katerina if he saw her again? To be sure, he'd have to ask her about Larry, but...he just hoped this wasn't all leading to a place he didn't want to go.

"Larry knew her a lot better than I did"—Mark thought that was a lie, but wasn't sure—"and it's possible he tried to contact her when he was here. If I could find her, it would be worth asking her whether she and Larry saw each other, and if they did, whether he was feeling OK. I'd like to be able to tell his family everything I can about his last hours."

9

---○---

The parking lot of the cheerless low-slung Soviet-era Clinical Hospital Number 9 was only half full. Keal drove around for a while until he found the open spot that was closest to the entrance. He threw the car into park, turned off the engine, and looked at Mark.

"You ready?"

"Sure," said Mark, but he continued looking out the front windshield for a moment, staring absentmindedly at an overfull garbage can.

He was being pulled in two directions, stretched thin. His marriage to Daria and the birth of Lila had made him feel young; it was as though he were embarking on an entirely new life, shedding his old life the way a snake might shed its skin. He felt more limber, and healthy, than he had ten years ago when he'd been living on his own; even his eyesight had improved, thanks to a LASIK operation Daria had prodded him into getting. But this business with Larry, and Katerina, was pulling him in the opposite direction, back into the past, reminding him that he wasn't so young anymore at all, that his current life was built on layers upon layers of twisted history.

Keal stepped out of the car, and Mark followed suit.

"I'm hoping this doesn't take too long," said Keal. "But it probably will. We're supposed to meet—"

"Mr. Keal?" Mark and Keal turned. They hadn't taken two steps from the car. Walking toward them was a middle-aged woman in a black pantsuit. In her left hand she carried a clip-board. "James Keal, from the embassy?"

"Yes."

"I'm glad I caught you." She introduced herself as the administrator of the hospital's mortuary. "We've already arranged for the transport you requested. So if you could just follow me."

"Huh," said Mark. "You were expecting us then, I take it."

"Yes, yes. The embassy, they called. We're doing everything we can to help."

"Yeah, that's him."

Mark stood behind the open rear doors of a white Ford van. He'd assumed that he'd be required to identify Larry's body in the morgue, prior to having the corpse packed and prepped for transit. Instead, the administrator who'd intercepted them had explained that the body had already been prepared for transport, that the death certificate and other documents were ready as well, and that if they would just follow her inside for a moment so that Mark could pay for the various costs associated with the services that had been provided, they could then complete the process in the rear parking lot.

"Is this the way it's usually done?" Mark asked, as she was charging over a thousand dollars' worth of lari to his credit card. He was assured it was.

Larry had been vacuum-packed inside a clear plastic body bag, and then placed inside a zinc casket that was narrower and shallower than normal, so the corpse wouldn't move around during transport, explained the administrator. Wads of what looked like couch-cushion stuffing had been wedged tightly between his arms and legs and the casket walls. The zinc casket had been slotted inside a wooden box that was marked with the words EXTREME CARE in Georgian, English, French, Russian, and Turkish. The top of the casket had been removed and the lid to the wooden box left open.

Mark stared, transfixed for a moment. He and Larry had been through so much over the years. It was an unsettling twist of fate that it was all ending in the same city in which it had all began. Not a mile away from the hole-in-the-wall cafeteria-style restaurant where Larry had first recruited him.

10

Tbilisi, Georgia
May 1991, seven months before
the dissolution of the Soviet Union

———————◦———————

"Jesus, you couldn't even spring for a place with seats? What the hell is wrong with you, son?"

A man of around fifty, with salt-and-pepper hair and eyes that looked a little rheumy, plopped down a mug of beer next to Marko's red lentil soup and freshly baked torpedo-shaped rolls.

It was true, there were no seats at his favorite lunch spot. Just chest-high tables at which stood men who were eating and smoking; many wore the brown, short-sleeved uniform of Tbilisi's road repair crews.

As Marko eased his soup bowl down the table, trying to give himself a little room, the rheumy-eyed man said, "Your monthly stipend is, what—$1,475 dollars a month? For that Fulbright thing?"

Marko's eyes narrowed. "Do we know each other?"

"Hey, that's peanuts in New York, but over here a buck goes a long way. Hell, you could afford the Daryal once a week." The Daryal was considered the best restaurant in town, meaning it was just OK. "At least there they got chairs. You can call me Larry, by the way. Can I get you a beer?"

Although it was only noon, most of the men in the buffet were drinking beer with their soup.

"No." Marko dipped a piece of his bread into the soup and took a bite, torn between telling the guy to get lost and curiosity. "How

do you know what my monthly stipend is?"

"Oh, I know lots about you, Marko."

Marko took another bite of bread. "Like?"

"Like you bolted from home at seventeen when your mom died, managed a shithole gas station in Piscataway, New Jersey, to put yourself through Rutgers—crummy school, by the way; I went to Yale—but you did manage to score pretty well in math—"

"Who are you?"

"—you figured you'd be an engineer, but instead wound up studying Russian history. Yeah, that's practical. Made no sense to me at first, until I learned that when your mom was a little girl she and her family got run out of Georgia by the Soviets. I'm no shrink, but I'll bet that after she killed herself, you went looking for her in the past, looking for her here in—"

"Who the fuck are you?"

"I already told you—Larry."

"Larry who?"

"We'll stick with just Larry. You got balls, I'll give you that. And smarts—the '78 protests...ha! That was good. The commies actually bought your BS. At first, that is."

Marko frowned.

In 1978, when the Soviets had tried to make Russian an official language of Georgia, massive protests had erupted. In the end, the Soviets had shown uncharacteristic restraint and allowed the Georgians to keep their language; it was a sliver of history that the Soviets wanted Americans to know more about, because they thought it painted them in a forgiving light. To ensure that he would be granted a visa, Marko had emphasized that he would be studying that history.

Larry added, "Of course, you're not fooling me. These interviews you're doing, you're not just focusing on some old protests. You're here to make a list of all the shit the Soviets have pulled in Georgia over the past seventy years, listen to sob stories, maybe weave in your mom's own sob story, and then write all about it when you get back home. Stab the commies in the back. Not that your little project will make a damn bit of difference, but at least your heart's in the right place. But I'm here to tell you that now the Soviets also know what you're up to. There's only a handful of Americans in Tbilisi. They try to keep tabs on all of us—they think we're all spies. Haven't you ever noticed you're being followed?"

Marko didn't respond. He was trying not to appear as unsettled as he felt. Everything Larry had said was true.

Larry said, "They're keeping at least four guys on you. One's your neighbor from across the street. The fat schmuck who never tucks in his shirt and is always so friendly? Here's a news flash, Saveljic—he ain't really that friendly. He just wants to know where you're going."

Marko had been wondering about the weird, aggressively congenial guy across the street. He'd thought it was just a cultural thing.

"Was I followed here?"

"Yeah. By me."

"I meant—"

"I know what you meant. You come here so often they don't bother following you here anymore. Which, come to think of it, is something to remember—if someone's trying to follow you, and you've got the time, boring them into complacency is never a bad option. Here's another news flash. All those notes you've been taking? They'll get around to stealing them eventually. Right around the time you're gearing up to leave. Also, assume your phone and apartment is bugged."

"Are you—"

"I'm a businessman. I buy Georgian cheese and export it to the States—there's a big market for that, you'd be surprised. I'm also in contact with the American government a lot—you know, import licenses and such. So I hear things."

"You heard all that about me because you buy and sell cheese? Gimme a break."

Larry made a little slurping sound as he took a big slug off his beer. "You sure you don't want one?"

Marko was thinking maybe he did. "No. Why do you care about me? Why bother digging up all that?"

"Anyway, so the, ah, we'll call them local authorities, they're onto you. They know you're not doing what you said you came here to do. But if it was just that, I wouldn't alarm you like this."

"I'm not alarmed," lied Marko.

"That little Press Club group you're a part of—between you and me, it's stuff like that that really gets them wound up...especially since you lied to them about what you planned to study while you were here."

The Press Club was an informal organization made up of a ragtag bunch of student journalists, student journalist wannabees, and random anticommunist groupies. Its purpose was to support anticommunist journalism, arrange for student protests, and generally be a thorn in the side of the Soviet bureaucracy. Marko had been attending Press Club meetings for the past month.

He dipped one of the torpedo-shaped pieces of bread into his soup. "I'm not sure what your point is."

"You know how animals that are scared are the most dangerous? Well, God knows these bastard Russians are animals and I'm telling you they're running scared, they can feel the revolution coming. You might think just because that Press Club of yours is made up of a bunch of idiot kids that they don't care, but you'd be wrong about that. They're skittish, they see danger all around them. So you gotta be careful. That's my point." Larry finished his beer and wiped his mouth. "Also, if you think the Press Club could use some financial help, well, I might be in a position to provide it."

At that, Larry got up and walked away as quickly as he had come, leaving Marko, deep in thought, staring blankly at the exit.

11

———————◇———————

His real name had been Lawrence Prentis Bowlan. Fluent in Russian and a handful of other Slavic languages. He'd even picked up some Georgian, and knew a little Arabic. Old-school white-bread CIA elite, a Yale graduate—Larry had lied about a lot back then, but not about that—recruited to spy for the CIA at the height of the Cold War. He'd been able to pull off a pretty good impression of a boozy and brash American, though. As Larry had gotten older, that persona had become less and less of a fiction.

Mark focused on the corpse in the bag again.

After noting that it was indeed Larry, he pressed his index finger down on his old boss's cheek—it felt like rubber; Larry had been embalmed.

"What happened to transporting him in a cold storage unit?" Mark asked in Russian.

A man from the Georgian customs department observed, clipboard in hand, as a hospital orderly began to seal up the zinc casket.

"Oh, but that was not a possibility," replied the hospital administrator, in Georgian. She was dark-haired, maybe fifty, and wore an unobtrusive gold cross necklace. She smiled at Mark with a practiced sympathy reminiscent of an undertaker.

"It was a possibility yesterday." When Mark had spoken with Kaufman, they'd agreed that Bowlan's body should be preserved as it was at the time of death, so that an effective forensic autopsy

54

could be performed back in the States.

"The body cannot be transported internationally if it has not been embalmed. If you were told otherwise, I apologize."

"I was told otherwise." Mark turned to Keal. "Did you know anything about this?"

"Yeah. When I spoke to the coroner yesterday we talked about the cold storage option. He said he'd look into it."

"He must be packed in such a way that the airlines and receiving country will ship him as cargo. Now if you please, I have some forms you'll need to sign."

"What did you do with his blood?" demanded Mark, still in Russian.

"Sir?"

"The blood you took out of his body."

Mark was no expert, but thought it was safe to assume that pumping Larry full of toxic chemicals would shoot to hell any chance of the CIA being able to perform accurate toxicology tests back in the States.

"I took nothing out of his body."

"The coroner, then."

"I'm sure it was properly and respectfully disposed of, sir." The administrator produced a sheet of paper that certified the body had been embalmed, and then a Georgian death certificate, and then something she called a sanitary epidemic certificate. She handed the papers to Keal. "The customs authorities at the airport will need to view these before they will issue an exit permit." Gesturing to the customs official who was now watching the hospital orderly seal up the outer wooden casket, she said, "And he should be able to give you his report shortly, which you will also need."

"May I?" Mark took the forms and read that the official cause of death was a heart attack. "I was told some tests were performed. Before he was embalmed. May I see the lab results?"

"Certainly you may request a copy of the physician's report of death."

"Meaning the autopsy results."

"Yes, but if you are not the next of kin…"

"I'll see what I can do," said Keal.

"I'd rather see them now."

Keal asked the administrator if that was possible. It wasn't.

"I also have received police authorization to release the body," said the administrator. She produced three pieces of paper that had been stapled together and marked up with a multitude of official-looking stamps and signatures.

"What police?"

"The regional police here in Tbilisi. They reviewed the autopsy report and lab tests. To insure that the cause of death was a natural one."

"And they are satisfied that it was?"

"They would not have provided the clearance necessary to release the body had they not been."

Keal and Mark were met at Tbilisi International Airport by a perky first-year employee of the State Department who was on her way to Madison, Wisconsin, to attend her brother's wedding. She'd reluctantly agreed to accompany Larry on a Turkish Airlines cargo flight to Chicago. There, she was to transfer him to a funeral director who would bring him to Cleveland, Ohio, and stick him in cold storage until the CIA arranged for an autopsy. Eventually the body would be cremated and the remains delivered to Larry's mother.

Mark had spoken to Larry's mother the night before. The call hadn't been the emotional disaster that he'd been afraid of, but only because it turned out that his mom, who was confined to a nursing home in Ohio, was senile.

I'm a friend of Larry's, Mrs. Bowlan. And I'm so sorry, so very sorry, to have to tell you that your son has died.

Larry? How is Larry?

After the handover at the cargo terminal, Keal dropped Mark off at the main passenger terminal.

"No word yet on that name I gave you?" Mark asked.

"No. I can look into it when I get back if you like."

"I'd appreciate it."

"What's your number?"

Mark gave Keal a Bishkek number for an automated answering service that would digitize the message and forward it to an e-mail account. "If I don't pick up, just leave a message."

"Got it."

They shook hands. As Keal walked away, Mark reflected that even in a nation like Georgia—which had never fully embraced Soviet-style inefficiency and had only been too happy to get rid of it at the first opportunity—navigating the bureaucracy usually took some doing. It was true, the Georgians had recently done a fine job of ridding many of their institutions of corruption, particularly the police, but even so, the bum's-rush speed with which Larry's death had been investigated, the body embalmed, and then released—in the hospital parking lot!—only served to reinforce Mark's belief that Larry had been murdered.

And probably by the Russians. They were the only players, other than the Georgians themselves, who had the resources to manipulate so many layers of Georgian bureaucracy so quickly.

The only question now was what, if anything, he was going to do about it.

12
Bishkek, Kyrgyzstan

———————o———————

When the phone rang and no caller ID showed up, Daria was pretty sure it was Mark. He'd taken to using a top-of-the-line iPad Mini to route phone calls over the Internet, because such calls were harder to trace and intercept. They also didn't show any caller ID.

She picked up.

"Hey, how're my gals?"

Daria smiled. It was good to hear his voice. "We're fine. Lila, say hello to Daddy." She let Lila stare blankly at the phone for few seconds, then put it back to her ear. "She told me to tell you she misses you."

"How's the diaper rash?"

When they'd spoken earlier in the day, Daria had mentioned that she'd taken a long walk around a nearby park, with Lila riding on her chest in a BabyBjörn carrier. Although still a little sore from the delivery, she was eager to get back to her normal weight—she was sick of maternity clothes and dying to wear a normal pair of jeans—and besides, she hadn't wanted to deal with lugging the stroller down the steep narrow steps that led up to their apartment. She'd also just been restless, and the walk had felt good. All the bouncing around on her chest, though, combined with a wet diaper, had resulted in Lila developing a bit of a rash.

"Not worse," she said. "Oh, and her umbilical cord fell off."

She wished Mark had been there for that milestone.

"Wow, already."

"It was time. Her belly button's a little red. I swabbed it with alcohol, but it didn't seem to hurt her."

"Good to hear."

"How are things on your end?"

"I'm out of here."

"That was quick." Daria hadn't anticipated that Mark would return for at least another day.

"Larry's on a plane to Chicago. Things went faster than I thought they would."

"Well, that's good news. I guess. Is it?"

"No direct flights to Bishkek tonight, but I was able to get a seat on a flight to Almaty. I'll just cab it from Almaty to Bishkek early tomorrow. It'll be faster that way."

Daria detected a note of unease in Mark's voice. "So, the medical stuff…"

"The coroner's report said heart attack. And he was taking Coumadin, which he'd neglected to tell me about. Part of the reason I ask for people's medical history is so that I don't have to worry about them dying on the job."

Mark spoke as if he were just annoyed, but Daria knew better. He'd liked Larry a lot.

"I'm really sorry about all this, Mark. I know how much—"

"Can I ask you a favor?"

"Sure," said Daria. But Mark's tone gave her pause. "What?"

"Open my bottom left desk drawer in our office. There's a couple prepaid phones in there."

"Yeah, I know."

"You been snooping?"

"What do you need, Mark?"

"Activate the blue one."

———————○———————

DAN MAYLAND

A minute later, the blue phone rang and Daria answered it.

"You got a pen?" asked Mark.

"Give me a sec." Daria retrieved one, along with a notepad, from a drawer underneath her desktop computer. "OK."

Mark read off the Internet address and passwords that would be needed to access the storage site where Larry's most recent photo files had been saved. "Larry took twenty-eight still photos on the morning of June seventh. Would you mind taking a look at them? I'd have Decker or some of my other guys do it, but honestly, I trust you on this more than I do them."

"What are these photos of?"

"Vehicles and personnel entering and exiting a Russian military base. In South Ossetia. They need to be enlarged with the equipment we have at home, and I'd rather not wait until I get there. Since you can read Russian—"

"Is that what Larry was doing? Staking out a Russian military base?"

"It was a contract for Central Eurasia."

"For Kaufman."

"Yeah. Langley detected some unusual movement via satellite, but Kaufman wanted eyes on the ground."

"You think Larry was killed." She paused. "What, by the Russians?"

"I'd rather not speculate."

"Jesus." A CIA operation—and probably, from what she knew of the Agency, a senseless and stupid one—was a hell of a thing for Larry to have lost his life over, thought Daria. "What am I looking for?"

"I'm not sure. But someone deleted those files from the memory cards Larry had with him. I assume they did it for a reason. I'd start by checking for identifying words or symbols on the men and matériel in the photos. Look for equipment you don't recognize, new-model vehicles, anything unusual."

"I'm guessing there's going to be a lot I won't recognize."

While in the CIA, Daria had been trained to identify the military insignia of Azerbaijan—that's where she'd been posted—and other countries in the region, Russia included. But Iran had been her specialty.

"Do your best, use whatever online resources you can. This is just a preliminary look, Russia specialists at the Agency will eventually pick these photos apart."

"OK," said Daria, but what she was thinking was, if that was the case, *why the rush*? Was he just upset about what had happened, and fishing for immediate answers? Or was he worried about something else?

"Thanks. I appreciate it."

"You'd...you'd tell me if you were in trouble, wouldn't you? I mean, after what happened to Larry..."

"I'm not in trouble. There's just some weird stuff going on that I need to sort out, that's all."

Daria thought about that for a moment. She reminded herself that she'd known there'd be times like this; she'd known it when she'd accepted his proposal of marriage. "What weird stuff?"

"I'd rather not get into it at the moment."

She debated whether to press him further, then said, "OK. I'll check out the photos and call you back."

13

Russian Military Base, South Ossetia

————————o————————

"He now goes by Mark Sava," said the deputy chief of the FSB's counterintelligence department. "He's worked the region for years, particularly Azerbaijan."

When Dmitry Titov had tried to search FSB files for information about the man *he'd* known as Marko Saveljic, nothing had come up. Nor did the FSB have any information on Stephen McDougall—the name on the fake passport Saveljic had used to enter Georgia. So he'd sent a photo of Saveljic—taken at the Dachi hotel—to analysts at FSB headquarters in Moscow. Facial-recognition software had done the rest.

"Not recently," said Titov. He cradled the phone between his ear and shoulder as he swiped the touchpad on his laptop computer, intending—now that he had a name—to access what FSB records he could on his own. "Or I would have known it."

"Well, until two and a half years ago he was the CIA's station chief in Azerbaijan, worked out of the embassy in Baku. Before that he was an operations officer in Azerbaijan, and before that he was all over the Caucasus and Central Asia."

When Sava had been active in Azerbaijan, Titov had still been in intelligence purgatory, doing penance in Chechnya, just trying to survive. Titov's promotion to his current position—which might have led to him intersecting with someone of Sava's stature—had only come recently, after Sava had left the CIA.

The analyst at FSB headquarters added, "We also believe, but aren't certain, that he served in the CIA's special activities division in the 1990s. He was operating under a different alias at the time, but we have a likely sighting from 1993 in Abkhazia."

Titov's head dipped. So that surly, contemptuous kid hadn't been scared off by his experience in Georgia in 1991. Titov had imagined that after leaving, Marko Saveljic had stumbled back to the United States thankful just to be alive; that he'd been so emotionally and physically scarred that the rest of his life had been a train wreck. Instead, just three years after leaving Georgia, Sava had shown up in the breakaway Georgian republic of Abkhazia, just in time to meddle in what had been a brutal civil war.

Titov stopped typing on his laptop and gripped the phone. "What's his reputation?"

Knowing that Larry Bowlan died looking at Katerina's self-portrait had cheered Titov to no end, but he now realized it had been a terrible mistake to have left that painting in the room. He'd abandoned it, thinking that now that justice had been served, he could let both the painting, and all the memories associated with it, go. But he hadn't considered that perhaps the one person in the world who *could* have recognized that painting would walk into that room.

"He was one of the best the Americans had. When he ran the CIA station in Azerbaijan, he poisoned many—too many—of the wells we tried to dig there. And he had high-level contacts in the Azeri government. His departure presented an opportunity for us to expand our operations in Azerbaijan."

"What's he been doing lately?" asked Titov, although he thought he could guess the answer to that question.

"Private contract work. Mainly for the CIA. He runs a small operation out of Bishkek."

"I see," said Titov.

What Titov saw was that Bowlan, although he'd claimed to be a lone-wolf contractor hired by the US Department of Defense to surveil the base in South Ossetia, almost certainly had instead been working with Sava on a CIA contract. Just as Bowlan and Sava had been working together, again for the CIA, twenty-four years earlier.

"Do you need me for anything else, sir?"

"Yes. Find out everything you can about Sava. Where he lives, who he lives with, who he works with, when he eats, where he eats, when he shits, where he shits, when—"

"I'll need the approval of the director to allocate that kind of manpower to Bishkek."

"Which is why I will call him. In the meantime, make what preparations you can."

If all went as planned, Titov's men would take Sava within the hour, before he left Georgia. An interrogation would follow, to find out whether Sava knew any more than Bowlan had about the upcoming operation. When that happened, Titov wanted to be prepared. If Sava had weaknesses that could be exploited, he wanted to know about them; experience had taught him that without that kind of leverage, Sava would be hard to break.

After the interrogation, of course, they'd have to kill the American; on a purely personal level, Titov would welcome the opportunity to do it himself, but even if he hadn't borne Sava any personal ill will—and he bore him plenty—abducting and inter-rogating such a man, and then releasing him so that he could share his unfortunate experience with the CIA, wasn't practical.

"This American, why does he worry you?"

When it came to dealing with his colleagues in the FSB, Titov was inclined to keep the personal to himself and emphasize the professional—it was enough that Sava was tied to Bowlan, an American spy who'd been snooping around the base here in

South Ossetia just days before the launch of the big operation. But Titov didn't know the extent to which the deputy chief had been briefed on that. So all he said was, "Because it is my job to worry. If the director chooses to say more, that is his prerogative."

14
Tbilisi, Georgia

———————◇———————

Mark suspected he'd picked up a tail.

As he purchased an *International Herald Tribune* from a newsstand inside the terminal, he noted that, fifty feet away, next to a kiosk that sold tacky plastic drinking horns and snow-globe reproductions of medieval churches, a guy wearing jeans and a blue hoodie was seated on a bench, tapping nonstop on his phone. A backpack lay by his feet. Sunglasses were pushed up on his lacquered black hair.

Not so different from hundreds of other guys Mark might have expected to see on the streets of Tbilisi.

But Mark had noted a few anomalies. For one, the guy was dressed as if he were a club-hopping twentysomething. But his black hair was gray at his temples. And he wore a wedding ring. And the camera on the back of his phone was often pointed right at Mark.

Mark had been planning to go through security and wait by his gate, but he had another hour before his flight boarded, so instead he shouldered his satchel, picked up the plastic shopping bag he was using to carry Larry's electronic equipment, and took a stroll outside. As he darted across two lanes of traffic and into the parking lot opposite the terminal, he observed that the guy with the backpack had also left the terminal; he was standing a hundred feet away, near the road that paralleled the parking lot, looking like he was trying to hail a cab.

Mark wasn't shocked. He was often tailed by foreign intelligence services. And if Keal had been CIA, as Mark suspected, well, maybe the Georgians or Russians or whoever just thought—correctly—that Mark was guilty by association. He took heart from the fact that the backpack guy appeared to be operating alone; had he been part of a larger team, someone else almost certainly would have handled the exterior surveillance.

Mark made a show of pulling a pen and pad of paper out of his satchel and pretending to record the license plate numbers of two random cars—let the backpack guy waste time puzzling that out, he thought—then headed back toward the terminal, intending to surreptitiously snap a quick photo of his tail on the way inside. He made it as far as the end of the parking lot, and was preparing to traverse the two-lane road, when he sensed a shadow on his left, and caught a brief whiff of a menthol cigarette.

Out of the corner of his left eye, he saw that he was being overtaken by a blue van, and came to the split-second realization he was being played for a fool. Stopping short, he turned to his right and made eye contact with a broad-shouldered bearded man who was tossing a cigarette to the ground. With one hand Mark threw his newspaper into the man's face and with the other, jabbed a thumb into his eye.

The van came to a quick stop just as someone inside it yanked the cargo door open. Mark jumped in front of the van, smacking the hood hard as he did so, then cried out in pain, and fell to the ground—attracting concerned looks from travelers gathered near the terminal entrance.

"Idiot!" yelled Mark in Russian as he picked himself up off the ground.

The bearded man was clutching his eye, but advancing.

As Mark backed away from the van, he pointed a finger at the driver. "Watch where the fuck you're going!"

The cargo door of the van slammed shut. The bearded man glanced at the van as though confused and not sure what to do, but by now Mark was safely surrounded by the people gathered near the terminal entrance.

———————◇———————

Stupid, thought Mark as he caught his breath inside the terminal. He'd come within a hairsbreadth of being abducted. The guy with the backpack had probably been bait, sent into the terminal with a lousy disguise, and snapping photos with his smartphone to goad a stupid American into trying to flush out a tail.

He massaged the thumb he'd used to poke the bearded guy in the eye. After what had happened to Larry he should have been paying more attention, watching for that van, or something like it, anticipating that someone might try to grab him. If he'd been anticipating instead of reacting, they never would have gotten close.

But who were they? The Russians? Maybe. Probably. Did it have anything to do with this business about Katerina? Mark had no idea. What he did know was that he was getting too old to count on being able to fight his way out of scrapes. He needed to look harder for paths of least resistance. Use his brain to avoid conflict, so that he didn't wind up like Larry.

He took a few more deep breaths—he was still a bit shaken, although he didn't like to admit it—looked around him, and decided that, just then, the path of least resistance led through the passenger-screening security checkpoint. Once he was past that, in the secure zone of the airport, the chance of anyone being able to pull off an abduction was close to zero.

In retrospect, he realized he should have headed straight there in the first place.

———————○———————

After passing through the checkpoint, Mark found a coffee shop near his departure gate and took a seat where he had a wall at his back and a clear view of anyone entering the shop. To his left was a service door exit.

He ordered a double espresso, and downed it right away. When Daria called him back on his iPad, which was connected to the Wi-Fi at the coffee shop, he was sipping a vodka on the rocks.

"I copied and cropped the photos from June seventh," she said, "focusing on any identifying marks I could make out. They were all taken from the same vantage point of the earlier photos, so I didn't worry about the visible buildings or anything else that's consistent across all the dates."

"And?"

"Two Tenth Brigade *spetsnaz* guys, another guy who I believe was VV."

Spetsnaz referred to any number of Russian special forces units. Mark assumed plenty were in and around the base at South Ossetia, especially those from the Tenth Brigade, which was known to operate in the region; VV—short for *vnutrennye voiska*—referred to troops controlled by the Russian Ministry of Internal Affairs. Though they were common too, there were special units within the VV that, if present, would have raised red flags.

"The VV guy, was he North Caucus or—"

"Couldn't tell. I extracted a head shot for him and everyone else that I could, and enlarged and enhanced all identifying marks, so maybe you can make more sense of it. There was another guy who was a general whose last name begins with Golo—it was a side shot, the rest of the name on his uniform wasn't visible. Plenty of Forty-Ninth Army troops too, but that's to be expected."

"Yeah, that's their backyard."

"There was one guy in civilian clothes who got dropped off in a cab. His back was to the camera, but the duffle bag he was carrying had a sticker on it with the letters NAJ. I wasn't sure what it was at first, but I did a little research—that's the code for the main airport in Nakhchivan."

"Nakhchivan?"

"Yeah."

"That's kind of random." Nakhchivan was a tiny scrap of land wedged between Turkey, Iran, and Armenia. Though it was technically a part of Azerbaijan, Nakhchivan was an exclave, to Azerbaijan what Alaska was to the continental US, in that it wasn't physically connected to the main part of the country.

"Yeah, I thought so too."

"I'll put together a full report for Kaufman when I get back, but in the meantime could you shoot me encrypted copies of the crops you made, and write out what you just told me?"

"Already on it. Check your e-mail."

"Thanks. How's Lila?"

"Sleeping."

Mark considered telling Daria about Katerina, but explaining to his wife that he'd just been blindsided by a self-portrait of a former lover was a much longer conversation than he wanted to have at the moment. They'd have plenty of time to talk about all that when he got back home. And he also saw no point in mentioning that he'd almost been abducted, and that, upon landing in Almaty in the morning, he planned to spend a lot of time making sure that no one was still on his tail. He had to make sure he was perfectly clean before coming anywhere near Bishkek. Why worry her about all that? "All right, talk soon."

"Travel safe."

"Always."

———————○———————

Still connected to the Wi-Fi signal at the coffee shop, Mark called Ted Kaufman's secure landline in Langley, Virginia, where it was morning.

"Larry's en route." Mark started to bring Kaufman up to speed on what had transpired over the course of the day. But, as with Daria, he left out the bit about the painting—that angle was far too unsettled, too strange, too raw for him to be able to draw any conclusions from it. He needed to get a better handle on what was going on before he mentioned that to anyone.

He was relaying Larry's flight information, when Kaufman interrupted.

"Hold on, let me get a pen. Actually, screw it. Just e-mail me what I need to know. Talk to me more about these missing photos."

"Daria just put together a preliminary report—"

"Daria, as in Daria Buckingham?"

"Yeah. As in my wife."

"I knew you'd married a trait—"

"Don't go there."

"—but now you've got her working for you? Nice to know. Brilliant move, Sava."

Daria hadn't just quit the CIA the way Mark had. She'd been kicked out because her idealistic streak had led her to do some things that she shouldn't have. Mark had long since forgiven her, but Kaufman hadn't.

"She's just helping out in a pinch."

"She's not the one with the clearance. You are."

"You want the preliminary intel on the missing photos?"

"What have you got?"

Mark started to repeat what Daria had told him.

"Back up," said Kaufman. "Did you say Nakhchivan?"

"Yeah. Why?"

No response.

"Ted?"

"You sure on that?"

"No, I haven't even looked at Daria's crops yet. I'm just telling you what she told me."

"What else could those letters stand for?"

"A lot of things probably."

"But she thinks it's an airport security sticker."

"Yeah. The kind they slap on your bags after they inspect them." Mark waited a moment, then said, "We good?"

He heard tapping on a computer keyboard, then a sigh. Finally, Kaufman said, "Listen, Sava. What if, instead of heading back to Bishkek, you were to hold tight for a bit? While I check something out."

"No can do, Ted."

"I may have more work for you."

"Great. Submit a request for proposal. I'll take a look and price it out whenever you get it to me."

"This might be more urgent."

"I could probably line up someone for you ASAP if you're in a pinch."

"The job I'm thinking of is one you'd be better suited for."

"My plane boards in an hour. I'm heading back to Bishkek, Ted. Tonight. But we can talk tomorrow."

So put that in your pipe and smoke it, thought Mark as he clicked off his phone.

When Mark had been the chief of the CIA's Azerbaijan station, Kaufman had been his boss, so he knew just how far he could push him without seriously damaging the relationship. Besides, while he wasn't just going to forget about what had happened to Larry, Mark knew there was a lot he could do from back in Bishkek. He'd wait for the CIA's Russia specialists to analyze the missing photos. Maybe by then Keal would have come up with contact information for Katerina. He considered trying to hunt her down on his own, but until he had a better grip on the situation, decided he belonged back in Bishkek.

For a moment he started to think about how satisfying it would be to be back home, with Daria and Lila. Then the memory of Katerina burrowed its way into his thoughts.

What if she had left that painting there to send him a message? Was it a coincidence that all this was happening now, right after the birth of his first child? He and Katerina didn't know each other anymore. But had she somehow connected with Larry? Mark couldn't fathom how or why they would have, but that painting…what was equally unfathomable was that such a painting could have wound up in that hotel room if there hadn't been some sort of link between Larry and Katerina.

Mark checked his watch. He still had a half hour before his plane was due to board, so he flagged down the waiter, ordered another vodka on the rocks, and tried to remember as much as he could about Katerina and that spring of 1991. Mostly what he remembered now, though, was how quickly everything had spiraled out of control.

In retrospect, Mark could see that agreeing to help Larry funnel money to the Press Club hadn't been one of his smartest moves. And ignoring the warning lights that started flashing in his mind after Larry intimated that other types of aid might become available if things in Georgia really started to heat up, maybe even weapons—ignoring that danger…well, he'd been young.

Mark recalled that it was shortly after the mention of weapons that Larry had said he wanted to make sure that the Soviets hadn't planted a mole in the Press Club. Money was one thing, but before any weapons were transferred, he needed to be sure the Press Club was clean. Larry had said he'd come up with a plan. Meanwhile, Mark had started paying closer attention to all the members of the club.

Mark had known he was playing with fire. He'd known Larry wasn't just some businessman. He'd known too that he was being watched—the old woman who pottered about in the street in red sandals, sneaking nips of apricot moonshine, who was always full of questions; the same black Volga sedan with a dented fender he'd see several times over the course of a normal day. But he'd wanted to do it, he'd wanted to help fight the communists who had wronged his mother, to be a part of history, to help make history.

Then, Mark found a pill-sized listening device affixed to the underside of the rough pine headboard attached to his bed frame. That was when things *really* had started to go downhill.

Mark thought again of Katerina, tried to bring himself back to that time, to search for clues in the past that might help him understand what was happening to him in the present. Would she have any cause to harbor lingering anger, because of the way things had turned out between them? Was that what this was all about? Mark didn't think so, but the honest answer was that he didn't know. He tried to recall the last time they'd seen each other, when everything had gone to hell...

15

Tbilisi, Georgia
June 1991, six months before
the dissolution of the Soviet Union

———————o———————

Marko was on his way to the Rustaveli metro stop late one after-
noon when a white van that looked like a bread loaf on wheels
pulled up next to him; before he could react, someone shoved him
into the cargo bay.

A figure appeared as the cargo door slammed shut. Marko
scrambled to his knees and raised his fist, intending to strike.

"Easy there, cowboy. This ain't my first rodeo. Don't make it
hard on yourself. Or me."

Larry was sitting on a creaky bench seat that had been repaired
with clear packing tape. He took a swig of some brown liquid in
a clear bottle—Marko suspected it was kvass, *a local concoction*
made from fermented rye bread.

"What the hell, Larry?"

"Hey, Saveljic, you ever hear of a honey trap?"

"What am I doing here?"

"It's when a foreign intelligence service employs someone who
possesses means of persuasion beyond what, say, I would possess.
See, I'm old, and I smell." The van hit a pothole, jolting both Marko
and Larry up in the air. "So even if you were a switch hitter, you
probably wouldn't want to screw me. No honey in that trap. But
a nice young lady? Potentially very effective against a young guy
like you."

"What are you getting at?"

"Your girlfriend's a honey trap. You're trading sex for secrets and you don't even know it. I'm sorry, I should have considered it earlier. Stupid that I didn't."

Marko laughed. The thought was absurd. "No she's not."

Larry spoke slowly and definitively. "Yes, she is. She's using you."

"She's a painter. And a student."

"And a KGB agent who was sent to spy on both you and the Press Club."

"Bullshit."

"You told her about me. You told her that you were being watched. You told her you were helping me help the Press Club."

That much was true, Marko admitted.

"Why in God's name would you tell her all that! Why? Even if she wasn't a KGB plant—didn't I tell you I suspected there'd be one somewhere?—even if she wasn't, why would you share that with anyone?"

"Last night Katerina went to visit her mother. I had trouble falling asleep, I was thinking about what you'd said about my apartment probably being bugged. Even though I'd checked all over for bugs weeks ago—"

"You found one."

"Yeah. Underneath the bed. So when I saw her this morning, I told her about the bug, and yeah, I mentioned that I was helping get money to the Press Club, and that maybe that had something to do with what I found."

Larry shook his head, disgusted.

"I didn't mention your name, or describe you or anything. I mean, what did you expect me to do? You were the one who told me that if I ever found any bugs to just leave them in place, so we don't tip people off that we're onto them."

What, was he supposed to continue to make love to Katerina

while the KGB was listening? *The breach of trust would have been unforgivable. He'd had to tell her something. They couldn't continue to sleep together in that bed.*

"And Katerina. What was her reaction when you told her about all this?"

"Well, she wasn't happy about the bed thing—I mean, that's a pretty sleazy asshole move, even for the Soviets."

"This is a sleazy business, Marko. Did she seem worried?"

"More disgusted than worried."

Katerina had known that the Soviets viewed the Press Club as an irritant; given that Marko was both an American and regularly attended Press Club meetings, she'd already assumed there would be a certain level of surveillance on him. He suspected she would have been more worried if she'd known the amount of money he was funneling to the Press Club, but he'd been intentionally circumspect on that front.

"It's possible she didn't know about the listening device. But that doesn't mean she's clean, Marko."

"You're so full of it. Really, Larry. You don't know what you're talking about."

"The KGB already knows about the conversation you had with her this morning, kid. A conversation that, if I'm not mistaken, occurred outside of your apartment. On the street. Where no one should have been able to hear you."

"You were watching me."

"No, Marko. But someone was watching…" Larry pointed a finger at him. "And listening. And I was watching and listening to the people who were watching and listening to you. I believe I may have intimated that we have ways of intercepting certain types of…let's call them communications." When Marko didn't respond, Larry added, "They know about your conversation with Katerina this morning. They know you've been helping me funnel money to the Press Club. I know this for a fact. She must have told them about it. There's no other explanation. You're completely blown. You fucked up, Saveljic."

"She doesn't care about politics. I got her to go to one Press Club meeting a few weeks ago, and then she never went back."

"Maybe she doesn't care about politics. Maybe she even really likes you. Who knows what they have on her, why she's helping them. They play an ugly game, Marko. But she is helping them, believe it. She's selling you out."

Marko recalled how Katerina had taught him how to speak Russian without sounding like a fool, and all the funny and not-so-funny stories that they'd told each other about what it was like to grow up as a kid in Tbilisi, Georgia, or in Elizabeth, New Jersey—like when Katerina, as a three-year-old, had released the parking brake on the family car and crashed it into the neighbor's fence, or the time Mark had gotten into trouble for climbing onto the roof of his duplex and throwing rocks at a neighbor's window, this when he was six. Katerina liked U2 and Madonna and REM. She'd wept when she'd told Marko about the death of her father. He couldn't believe that she could have been that good an actor.

Larry said, "If I were you, I'd leave Georgia tomorrow. The Soviets have been playing nice with you up until now, but now that they know you're a conduit for resistance money, there's no guarantee they're going to continue to play nice. I'm telling you this because you're an American citizen, and even though you completely botched my operation, I kind of like you, and I don't want to see you get hurt."

The van came to a stop.

Larry added, "If you don't leave and things go south for you, I can't protect you, your government can't protect you." Larry handed him a stack of 100-ruble bills. "This was supposed to be for the Press Club. Use it instead to buy a ticket home. Pretend you got sick, I'll make sure the Fulbright people don't screw you over."

"I didn't ask you to protect me."

"We won't see each other again." Larry pulled open the cargo bay door, doing so in a way that allowed him to stay hidden behind it. "Now get out."

After walking the streets for an hour, Marko came to a decision. He called Katerina from a pay phone.

"What's wrong?"

"You know your favorite place to paint?"

"You mean—"

"Don't say it! Just meet me there."

"When?"

"Now. Can you go now?"

"Yes...OK, yes, but what's wrong, Marko?"

"I'll talk to you soon."

Marko climbed the hill that rose up behind the old city, past the tiny crooked homes and little churches, until it became too steep for buildings and was just overgrown grass and rocks and garbage.

It was dark now, ten o'clock in the evening. The lights of the city twinkled below him, and the sky above was a strange shade of violet. A gentle breeze blew waves through the scrub grass. To his right rose an enormous aluminum statue of a woman who in one hand held a sword and in the other a bottle of wine: treat Georgians well, you will be welcomed with wine; if not, then you'll be fought with a sword. Well, thought Marko, that would be his motto too from here on out.

He climbed until he got to a paved footpath that traversed the top of a long ridge. He turned left, passing the funicular, which had been shut down for the night, and walked until he reached the entrance to the botanical gardens.

Tucked away on the back side of the ridge, in the shadow of a medieval fortress, the gardens of Tbilisi were a welcome refuge from the city. It was a wild place, crisscrossed by little dirt trails and crumbling stone walls. Because the city was on the other side of the ridge, the sound of cars was barely audible, and he could hear little but the wind rustling through the leaves.

During the day, the price of admission was just a pittance—twenty kopeks, payable to a gnarled old woman who, if she was lucky, collected enough over the course of a day to justify her pittance of a government salary. Now, the gardens were closed for the night, but there was no gate. Just beyond the entrance, Marko veered off the path and hid in the woods.

Katerina walked by him twenty minutes later, traveling quickly down the steep gravel path. She wore designer jeans—American style, but made cheaply in East Germany—that Marko had given her. Her loose white poet shirt had frilly flounces at the wrists and reflected enough moonlight that she seemed to glow amidst the trees.

Marko waited in the shadows, watching. Convinced that no one was following her, he ventured out of the woods, stepped quietly onto the path, and began walking in the direction Katerina had gone, keeping to the moon shadows on the path's periphery. Before he got to a terraced section, where there was a stand of bamboo and a reflecting pool overgrown with lily pads, he ducked back into the woods.

Katerina would be waiting for him to approach on the main path, Marko reasoned, so he approached instead through the woods. Though he couldn't make out her expression, he could see that she was pacing, with a nervous energy that was at odds with her usual languid demeanor.

Marko waited, listening to the surrounding woods. The light breeze rustled the leaves of the trees; branches squeaked as they rubbed together. After a time, he made his way silently to the edge of the terrace, picked up a golf-ball-sized rock and, standing hidden behind a tall pine, hurled it into the woods on the opposite side of the terrace.

Hearing the noise, Katerina turned. But Marko wasn't focused on her. Instead he listened to the woods, straining his ears to pick up sounds of anyone else who might be out there.

Nothing.

"Katerina." Marko spoke her name in a loud whisper. She turned. "Marko?"

He stepped out briefly from behind the pine. "Over here."

"What are you doing?"

"Making sure you weren't followed." He spoke in Russian.

"You're scaring me."

"I think we're safe. I was watching the path. Come with me."

"Where are we going?"

"Into the woods, to our campsite." Last week, they'd stayed at the gardens until dark—Katerina had been painting, Marko reading—and then hiked to the edge of the preserve, down by a stream at the base of the hill. They'd drunk wine around a small campfire, and eaten bread and sheep's-milk cheese. "Will you come?"

"Did you bring a blanket?"

"Yes."

Katerina approached him. Her hand was warm. They stole through the woods, picking a path through the underbrush and stepping over downed trees. When they got to the campsite, Marko took off his backpack and pulled out the blanket and two candles. He spread the blanket on the flat section of land he and Katerina had cleared a week earlier; the candles he lit and propped up in rocks that were marked by wax drips, evidence of their previous outing.

Katerina removed her satchel and placed it on the edge of the blanket. "Why are we here?"

"Shh." Marko put a finger to his lips, then took off his shirt.

———————○———————

She wasn't wearing a wire; that much became clear once they were naked. That, combined with the feel of her lips, and her hair brushing against his shoulder, and her breath melding with his own, deflated his anxiety and suspicion to the point where he didn't want to confront her. But he had to, and before they began to make love. Katerina's head rested on his chest, her ear was inches from his mouth.

"Earlier today I told you some things." He paused a moment, listening to the forest, then asked, "Did you...tell anyone else about them?"

His whispered question caused her to stiffen. She lifted her head off his chest. He ran a hand through her hair and guided her head back down.

"What do you mean?"

"The listening device I found. How I've been helping the Press Club. Did you tell anyone—anyone—about all that?"

"No." Her body tensed. Either she wasn't trying to mask her uneasiness or she couldn't. "What are you saying?"

"I'm saying you are the only person I confided in. But now other people know what I told you."

"What other people?"

Marko took a while to respond. "Who do you think?"

"You...you are accusing me?"

"Not accusing, just telling you what has happened."

"Who says that this has happened? Who?" When Marko didn't respond, Katerina said, "The American with the money?"

"Yes."

"He tells you this? He tells you I tell him your secrets?"

"No. He says you told others."

"He lies."

Marko had considered the possibility. He'd known Katerina longer than he'd known Larry.

"Does he?" asked Marko.

"He has to be lying." Katerina lifted her head again. This time, when Marko tried to guide her back down to his chest, she straddled him, cradled his head in her palms and brought her face down next to his. Her bare sex was pressed against his own. He could barely see her face in the dim flickering candlelight. "He has to be," she whispered.

"Get up," said Marko.

"You don't believe me."

He put his index finger to his lips. Quiet.

Katerina didn't resist when he gently pushed her off him. Naked, Marko stood to his full height, walked to beyond the edge of the blanket, and picked up Katerina's bra. Before giving it to her, he felt every inch of the fabric.

"What are you—"

Marko put his finger to his lips again and flashed her a threatening look. When he was convinced the bra wasn't wired with a listening device, he handed it to her. He did the same for all the rest of her clothing. She didn't put any of it back on. It lay in a pile in front of her. Her head was lowered. Marko thought maybe she was crying.

When he finished with her clothes, he started inspecting every single item in her satchel—her art tools, her paints, a few pens, a little makeup kit, lip gloss, a spare sanitary napkin, loose change, *a key that he'd given her to his apartment, a nail file, a schedule of her classes at Tbilisi State, a small pink leather wallet that contained thirty-six rubles, a few receipts, her driver's license, and her internal Soviet passport.*

She faced him, shaking her head, bottom lip quivering, definitely crying now.

It was in the satchel itself that he found it, sewn into one of the side seams, between the outer fabric and inner lining. It was unnoticeable except for a tiny bump. Marko used his teeth to rip the seam open, then fished out the device with his index finger. He held it up for a moment, examining it as best he could in the weak light. It was identical to the bug he'd found in his apartment.

He faced Katerina and held it up. She was looking at him now, but instead of crying, she appeared confused. In front of the blanket lay a fire pit ringed by small boulders. Holding the listening device gently in place with his lips, he picked up two rocks, and sat down in front of Katerina. He showed it to her, then placed it in her hands and stared into her eyes. She shook her head—whether to deny she knew anything about it, or because she was so stricken that she'd been found out, Marko couldn't tell.

He took the bug back, placed it on top of one rock, and then smashed it with the other.

"How do you explain that?" he demanded. After such a long silence, the sound of the rocks smacking together, followed by his own voice—no longer a whisper—was jarring.

A long silence, then, "What was it?"

"What do you think?"

"I don't know."

Marko stared into her eyes, searching. "Guess."

Her eyes began to well up with tears again. "A way for them to listen to us, but I don't know about any of this, Marko! Why are you doing this to me? What have I done to you?"

"*Does there need to be a why? Does there? Life is not a walk across a meadow, Katerina.*" It was a common Russian saying that Katerina had told him her mother was fond of. "*Shit happens.*"

"*Stop it.*"

They faced one another for a long moment. Maybe it was her eyes, maybe it was the tone of her voice, or maybe he was just a sucker for tears. Whatever the reason, in that moment, Marko decided he believed her. He picked up the smashed bug.

"*This is a listening device. Someone planted it in your bag.*"

Katerina took it from him and examined the wires that came off of it.

"*That's the antenna,*" said Marko, as if he really knew what he was talking about. He was pretty sure it was, though.

"*I didn't know, Marko. I swear it.*"

He studied her expression as best he could in the flickering candlelight. "*Do you have any idea who could have planted this?*"

Katerina was silent for a moment. Her head dipped. "*No. I take that bag with me everywhere.*"

"*It was sewn in. They would have needed to take it away from you. For at least a few minutes.*"

"*Maybe at school. Maybe someone took it when I was in class, or eating, and I just didn't notice it. What happens now, Marko? What do we do?*"

Marko had to think about that one. "*We lay low. We live in your dorm, finish out the spring semester, and I stay away from the Press Club and the American.*"

"*And then you leave.*"

It was true. Marko would go back to the States. While Katerina would stay here trapped in Georgia. He hated the thought of that. It would be one thing if she wanted to be a part of the revolution, to see it, to help drive it forward, but she didn't. She just wanted to live, and paint.

"Would you ever want to come with me?"

She cocked her head, incredulous. "To the United States?"

"Yes."

She was thinking hard, her brow furrowed, her eyes wide. "But I don't know that they'd let me leave."

Marko hesitated, and put some thought into what he said next. Worst comes to worst, he thought, even if it didn't work out in the end between the two of them, at least she'd be safe. "If we were married they would."

16

Tbilisi, Georgia
The present day

———————o———————

They'd just been kids, Mark thought, as he finished the last of his vodka and eyed a guy he was pretty sure had been assigned to watch him.

He hadn't realized that at the time. He'd thought that he and Katerina had both crossed that bridge from childhood to adulthood years before. But he'd been wrong, he'd still been crossing it, and so had she. They'd been impulsive, and had confused stupidity with bravery, and hadn't understood real-world consequences, and...

Mark ran a hand through his hair, thinking of that painting again, and of Katerina, and Daria, and Lila, and Larry, and Decker, and all the years he'd spent working for the CIA, and how different his life might have been had he never gone to Georgia in the first place.

The KGB had abducted him later that evening. In front of Katerina. Jack-booted thugs had broken down the door to her dorm room at four in the morning, when they'd both been asleep. He'd been dragged out onto the street, naked. Thrown into the trunk of a car. He could still hear Katerina's screams and the sound of someone slapping her face.

He wanted to rid his mind of that ugliness, to cut that memory and a thousand others out of his brain.

The image of little Lila in her bassinet flashed into his head. He thought of Daria nursing his daughter as morning sunlight streamed in from the kitchen windows. He could smell the fresh coffee, hear it percolating, hear Daria speaking softly to Lila, "Easy there, easy there, you don't have to drink so fast," and it triggered within him a visceral eagerness to get back home with them both as soon as he possibly could.

Because, while he didn't like to think it, Mark knew that beautiful calm, the essence of all that he loved, all that he wanted to protect and keep, could be gone in an instant.

If nothing else, his time in Georgia had taught him that.

Part Three

17

Tbilisi, Georgia

———————o———————

Mark was still at the airport in Tbilisi, waiting in line to board an Airbus jet, when a text came in from what appeared to be KyrgyzTelecom, indicating he qualified for a reduced rate plan. In reality, it was from Ted Kaufman. The message: make contact.

As eager as he was to get home, Mark was also well aware that Kaufman had thrown a lot of business his way. He knew he shouldn't push his luck by completely ignoring his main source of income. So he left the boarding gate, picked up a Wi-Fi signal again outside the airport coffee shop, and used his jury-rigged iPad Mini to call Kaufman's secure landline.

"So that job I was talking about," said Kaufman.

"Throw a request for proposal together, I'll look at it first thing—"

"The thing is, it might be related to what happened to Larry. I would think you'd at least want to hear me out now."

"OK, but my plane is boarding as we speak. It'll have to be quick."

"I have a branch chief who's stationed in Ganja, Azerbaijan. He was running a source, a twenty-eight-year-old woman. Two days ago, she was killed."

Ganja, which lay about a hundred and thirty miles southeast of Tbilisi, was the second largest city in Azerbaijan. The last time Mark had been there it had been a chaotic dump. As far as he knew, it still was.

"I need," added Kaufman, "for you to figure out why she was killed, and whether it was related to what happened to Larry."

"Why can't the branch chief investigate?"

"He's come under some pressure recently. In fact, item one on the agenda would be to bring him an alias packet and see that he makes it out of Ganja without having a nervous breakdown. After you debrief him, of course."

"What pressure?"

"There've been threats."

"You want me to exfiltrate him?"

"It wouldn't be a real exfiltration. As I understand it, he just needs a little hand-holding."

"I'm not in the hand-holding business, and I'm not getting how this has anything to do with what happened to Larry."

"Nakhchivan."

"Still not following."

"This source the branch chief was running was killed right before she was supposed to provide us with the financials for a construction company that had a big project going on in Nakhchivan."

"And that's it. That's the connection. An airport security sticker and a construction project."

"How often does an obscure place like Nakhchivan come up, Sava? And now it shows up on my desk in two separate reports—"

"I don't recall writing a report—"

"You know what I mean. Two references to Nakhchivan, two people dead. I want you to find out why this woman in Ganja was killed. I'll pay double your usual rate. Plus a bonus if—"

"I've been PNG'd from Azerbaijan, Ted. Remember?"

"Oh, shit. No, I forgot about that."

"I've asked you twice to try to get it lifted."

PNG stood for *persona non grata*. Mark had been declared

one by the government of Azerbaijan over a year ago, as a result of an intelligence operation—involving oil politics and Iran—gone bad. Which meant he'd been kicked out of his adopted country and told never to return. Daria had been given a similar shove out the door. That's why they'd moved to Bishkek.

"Yeah, now it's coming back to me."

Baku, the capital of Azerbaijan, had been Mark's *home*. He'd worked there for nearly a decade as an employee of the CIA, and then after quitting the Agency, had stayed on to teach international relations at a local university. Getting kicked out by the Azeris had been one of the worst developments in his life. Kaufman, however, clearly hadn't lost any sleep over it.

"Point being," said Mark, "I'm not going to be able to help you. Sorry."

"What if I was able to get the PNG lifted?"

Mark had been about to check the time on his iPad—he had to get back in the boarding line soon. Instead, he said, "You could do that?"

"Sure. Probably. I think."

"But I thought last you checked, the Azeris wouldn't budge."

"True, but that's because you wouldn't have been going back at the request of the US government. Whereas now you would."

"You never even *requested* that they let me back in?"

"As I recall, I passed along your personal request. That's different from an official request that comes from the State Department."

"I'm aware of the difference, dammit. Thanks for dicking me around, Ted."

"You take this job, I'd be putting in an official request now, I can guarantee you that."

Mark didn't respond right away. He thought again of Daria and Lila. And the frailty of the little life they had together. And then he thought about how much better that frail little life would be if they could all live in Baku instead of in permanent exile in Bishkek. Part of his job as a father was to think of the long term. "Diplomatic passport?"

"No. But I could probably swing an official one."

"That'd work."

"No diplomatic immunity, unless you want to really cozy up with State. I mean, you could try claiming it if you get in a jam, but I don't know that State will back you up."

"Even with an official passport, I'd need a visa for Azerbaijan."

"I can have the embassy in Tbilisi start working on it now. Is that it? Are you saying you'll do it?"

"No. The PNG. It's lifted permanently. I'm not going in for a couple days and then getting tossed out again."

"If you're an approved contractor, working regularly with us, then it will probably stay lifted. But you start pissing people off again—and I'm warning you, the new ambassador in Baku is a bit of a pill—you're going to get tossed again. That's the best I can do."

"Daria gets her PNG lifted too."

"Whoa."

"That's a nonnegotiable."

"You're one thing, Mark. You're one of us and always have been. Daria…"

"People do things in their youth that they regret."

"She wasn't that young, and she doesn't regret shit."

"You know, I got over all that. You can too."

"I don't know that I can even do it. With you, State can say you're working under a government contract. The Azeris will respect that. With Daria, there's no angle."

"Then just say she's working for me and do it all at once."

"I don't know, Mark."

"She's already pitching in on this project. Besides, didn't you have your wife on payroll back in the nineties?" Mark knew he was pushing it, but if he couldn't get Daria's PNG lifted along with his own, then he couldn't justify taking the job.

It was a pretty common practice in the CIA for officers to bring their spouses on board. Often they worked in the same office, and between the two of them got twice the pay for doing what was frequently substantially less than two jobs.

"That was when we were stationed in Moscow and raising two kids. And I needed an assistant I could trust."

"Someone you could trust, but who had no exper—"

"There's no need to go insulting my wife, Sava."

"Just figure it out, Ted. Those are my terms."

18
Bishkek, Kyrgyzstan

———————o———————

Daria was on her way to the neighborhood supermarket that evening when her cell rang.

"Hey," said Mark. "How's it going?"

Because she was using one hand to hold her phone to her ear, it was a struggle for her to push the stroller straight over the bumpy sidewalk. "Fine. Well, not fine, really. She still has a diaper rash and she's cranky." After being up half the night before with Lila and with her all day, Daria was cranky too. "I walked around with her too much. Sorry."

It embarrassed her that, after being around small kids so much at the orphanages, she would have screwed up with her own. But most of the kids at the orphanages were older. And she wasn't responsible for changing their diapers.

"Don't be sorry."

"Our neighbor downstairs said I should try egg whites. As in smear the egg whites all over her butt."

Egg whites! Sure, *why not* baste her baby's bottom as if it were a pie shell? It sounded to Daria like a good way to give Lila salmonella poisoning. Before Lila had been born, she'd researched diaper creams and had come up with three that she thought were the best. None had been available in any of the pharmacies in Bishkek, so she'd had to settle for a Chinese-made brand that she worried might have radiator fluid in it.

"Yeah, let's not do that," said Mark. "Listen, I've got some bad news and some really good news."

Daria checked the time. Mark was supposed to be in flight at the moment. "Where are you?"

"That's the bad news part. I agreed to do a job for Kaufman."

A three-second silence, then, "Mark—"

"It might be related to what happened to Larry, otherwise I wouldn't have said I'd do it. That airline sticker from Nakhchivan that you noticed, it's had some ripple effects."

"You already *accepted* this job?"

"I said I'd see what I could do over the next couple days." Before she could object, he added, "I know, I know, the timing completely sucks."

Another silence, then, "You didn't think to maybe call me first? I mean, dealing with Larry, that I understood. But..." Daria shook her head. She'd known calls like this would come. Just as she knew there'd be times when her work would get busy and she'd need Mark to cover the home front. They'd talked about all that. But she hadn't thought it would start up so soon after Lila had been born. "What kind of job?"

"An investigation of sorts."

"Why do they need you?"

"I guess the guy they have on it now is running into some trouble."

"What kind of trouble? And if he's running into trouble, why wouldn't you?" Upon not receiving an answer, Daria said, "Mark, I don't—"

"Listen, the good news—make that the *great* news—is that the job is in Azerbaijan. I'll be in Baku by tomorrow morning." He neglected to mention that he'd be traveling to Baku, a mere three hundred miles southeast of Tbilisi, via Istanbul, which lay over eight hundred miles to the west. If the Russians really were after him, it would be better to stay moving, and to get out of

Georgia sooner rather than later. And he'd feel safer sleeping on the plane than he would here at the airport, even in the secure zone. True, the Russians also had deep ties to Azerbaijan, but that was Mark's turf as well; if anyone tried to follow him there, he'd lose them in no time.

"OK, now I'm confused."

"Kaufman got our PNGs lifted, Daria. It was part of the deal I struck with him. We can go back to Azerbaijan. We can raise Lila in Baku."

The news was so unexpected that Daria didn't know what to say. But she could hear the excitement in Mark's voice, and he wasn't an easily excitable guy. And she knew how much he loved Baku. She didn't want to be a downer. Besides, they'd talked before about the possibility of moving back to Baku if their PNGs ever got lifted, and she'd agreed she could run her foundation from there, maybe expand into helping orphanages on that side of the Caspian.

But those talks had always been theoretical, because Mark had never been able to make any headway with the Azeris on getting his PNG, much less hers, lifted. "I thought Kaufman hated me?"

"I told him that I wouldn't take the job unless we both could resettle in Baku."

"Oh. Thanks."

A year earlier, she might have greeted the news with more enthusiasm. She'd come to Bishkek not because she'd harbored any particular fondness for the city, or for Kyrgyzstan, but just because it happened to be close to some of the orphanages she'd arranged to help fund. She'd originally viewed the move as temporary, while she did penance for past misdeeds and figured out what to do with the rest of her life. But her penance had become her passion. She took immense satisfaction from interacting with the kids, and working with Nazira, and managing a foundation that was now funded by real donors instead of just money she'd wheedled out of the CIA.

And at the same time, she'd come to like Bishkek. She liked the leafy parks, the nearby mountains, and summer trips to Lake Issyk-Kul. And she sensed that undertaking a major move—Baku was a thousand miles away—on top of running her foundation and raising Lila would be a recipe for stress and anxiety.

"Baku has got so much more going for it than Bishkek. We'll have better schools—"

"And if Lila never says she wants to be president she might even be able to attend them."

Daria was referring to an incident she and Mark had discussed, where a young student in Azerbaijan had been asked what he wanted to be when he grew up and he'd made the mistake of saying he wanted to be president. The student had been told there was only one president, and that the position was taken; the student's parents had been taken to task for having raised a child to would dare utter such an effrontery. As a result of the attention, the child had been pulled from the school.

"She'll be in a private school. We'll have better health care—"

"People in Azerbaijan go to Iran for health care."

"Used to go to Iran. It's getting better in Baku. A lot better. All the oil money, you know? They're building a brand new hospital downtown, and the private clinics, a couple of them are great." Then, sounding a little less flip and a little more annoyed, "I thought we'd talked about this."

"Yeah, we did." But that had been a year ago, thought Daria. When moving to Baku had been a theoretical possibility instead of a real one.

"I thought you said it wouldn't be a big deal, that you could run your foundation from there."

Daria had never been crazy about Baku. It was a big city—over two million people—and surrounded by desert. But Baku was definitely more cosmopolitan than Bishkek and there was a ton more money sloshing around there, which meant far more modern amenities. She had no interest in patronizing the Gucci and Tiffany stores in downtown Baku, but figured it was a pretty safe bet that the mothers who did weren't basting their baby's asses with egg whites. And there was no denying that the health care system in Kyrgyzstan was abysmal. Before Lila, she hadn't given it a second thought. She knew the risks—millions of people around the world dealt with lousy health care systems, she and Mark could too—but what if Lila got sick? Was it fair to put her at risk?

What if they stayed in Bishkek and Lila got really ill in the months or years to come? If she suddenly spiked a high fever, where would they take her? Almaty was two hours away, across an international border.

She imagined trips to the local pediatrician's office in downtown Baku. It would be a clean and orderly place. Instead of an old man who reeked of vodka—she thought of the anesthesiologist who'd inspired her to elect for a natural childbirth—it would be a woman in a white coat who smiled.

"Think they have Triple Paste diaper cream in Baku?" she asked. "It's got lanolin in it. I want it."

"I'll check."

"Either that or Desitin, the maximum-strength formulation, not the rapid relief one."

"OK."

"Baku will be great." She didn't really think that now, but she was hoping she would later, after she'd caught up on some sleep and didn't have to worry about things like Kegel exercises and diaper rashes. "The news took me by surprise, and we'll have to talk about the logistics of the move, but we'll make it work. In the meantime, be safe."

"Yeah, right."

"Just remember, you're a father now."

"I'll call or e-mail when I can. But from here on out, figure I'm on field rules. Maybe I should have started them earlier, but this whole thing's just kind of snowballed."

When Mark was on a job, he typically communicated with her only when absolutely necessary. He did it for the same reason that they'd both used complex anonymous corporate structures to register their respective professional enterprises, why Daria never allowed herself to be photographed with prospective donors to her foundation, why the last name on Lila's birth certificate was Stephenson, and why she and Mark had alias documents in that name as well and had used that name when purchasing their apartment in Bishkek. It was all to create as secure a firewall as possible between their personal lives, and their lives—both past and present—in the intelligence underworld.

When it came to communications, even when they both took precautions, they could never be certain those communications weren't being traced. So when Mark was on a job, radio silence with home was the rule.

"I know the drill," said Daria.

19

Baku, Azerbaijan
The next day

———————◇———————

Baku was booming.

The main airport terminal, which Mark blazed through on his way to the line of cabs out front, was completely new, all flashy curves and gleaming steel and glass—it was three times the size of the old one he'd passed through when he'd been kicked out of the country. The road from the airport, instead of the chaotic potholed mess that it had been just a few years ago, was now an eight-lane, newly paved modern highway that his cab driver navigated at speeds approaching a hundred miles an hour—because he'd been promised a two hundred dollar tip if Mark arrived at the embassy in time for an important meeting. As Mark watched for cars that might be following him—he doubted many could keep up—he observed that the highway was lined with thousands of decorative street lamps, each one of which he guessed cost more than the average Azeri made in a year.

The boom, fueled by massive amounts of oil money, had already been well under way when Mark had gotten the boot, but it still surprised him to see—good Lord, there was even a Trump Tower—how much had changed in the time he'd been gone.

One thing that hadn't, however, was the US embassy on Azadliq Prospect. Constructed during Baku's first oil boom over a century earlier, before the Soviets had driven the Azeri oil industry into the ground, the building itself was grand—much nicer than the nuclear-bunker fortress-embassy that the US had built in Bishkek—but it was set behind high walls, and the utilitarian green-metal entrance door that one needed to pass through to get to it was reminiscent of an underfunded prison.

As Mark jogged up to the entrance, he thought, and not for the first time, would it kill the State Department to slap a fresh coat of paint on the entrance door, and paste up a sign that said something cheerful? WELCOME TO THE EMBASSY OF THE UNITED STATES OF AMERICA! WE'RE GLAD YOU CAME TO VISIT! Because for a lot of people, that grungy door was all they'd ever see of the United States.

At a little guard shack, Mark encountered security checkpoints manned by armed Azeris in blue uniforms. He noted the electric wiring in the little shack was still a mess—the circuit panel still lacked a cover—and the metal detector was the same ancient model that had been there for as long as he could remember.

He handed over his new passport, the one that the US embassy in Tbilisi had brought him, courtesy of Kaufman, just before he'd boarded his flight for Istanbul; it was brown, marking him as a US citizen engaged in official US business.

"Cell phone?" asked the guard, pointing to Mark's shoulder bag. "Laptop?"

"I'm keeping them. Call for approval."

Civilians were required to turn over all electronics, but not people who worked at the embassy.

"You have an appointment?"

"With Roger Davis."

Officially, Davis was the embassy's political counselor; unofficially, he was the CIA's chief of station/Azerbaijan.

Permission to bring electronics into the embassy was denied, so Mark handed over Larry's laptop and camera, along with his own phone, iPad, two charging cords, and an adapter for the iPad that allowed him to connect it to other devices;; in return, the guard gave him a laminated ticket with the number three on it.

A student intern met him at the marine guard checkpoint inside the main embassy building, but instead of bringing him to Davis, she ushered him to the pleasantly cluttered office of the public affairs officer and told him to wait.

He didn't mind the first half hour. Baku was nine hours ahead of Washington, DC. Which meant that when people first arrived at the embassy in the morning, they'd have a mini-mountain of cables to sort through—everything that Washington would have sent during the course of the previous day back in the States. Because Mark had shown up at the embassy at 9:30 a.m., Davis might have been legitimately busy.

After an hour, the public affairs officer—a nervous woman who alternated between chewing her nails while staring at her computer and typing furiously on her keyboard—looked up as though seeing Mark for the first time, apologized for the delay, and asked whether he'd like some tea and cookies. Mark politely declined, but did ask for a phone so that he could call the US embassy in Georgia.

He managed to reach Keal, who'd had no luck finding Katerina. Mark suggested that the Georgian Bureau of Vital Records, or the state pension system that Georgians contributed to, might be able to help, especially if the request came directly from the US embassy. With a name, a birth month and year—July 1968—they should be able to find something. Keal reluctantly agreed to place a few more calls.

After an hour and a half, Mark announced that he needed to visit the restroom—he knew the way, no need to show him—and instead walked unmolested past the public affairs division, where a young foreign service officer was monitoring the Facebook and Twitter feeds of Azeri activists, and into his old office on the third floor.

Roger Davis was reclining in his executive chair, feet up on a six-foot-long oak desk that Mark had bought for the equivalent of twenty dollars when the Azeris had been clearing out a bunch of Soviet junk from Baku's old city hall. Davis was reading *Zaman*, Turkey's largest newspaper, and drinking from a liter bottle of Diet Coke.

"Am I disturbing you?" Mark glanced around the office. It was pretty much the same as when he'd left it. A fraying blue rug, a tall window that looked out onto the little courtyard where he'd liked to eat lunch when the weather allowed, a coffee table, and two wingback chairs. No real decorations, save for a bust of George Washington that sat on the coffee table, a contribution from the station's first chief back in the nineties, when the embassy had been housed in a hotel. Mark did notice the old filing cabinets were gone; in their place was an array of printers, computers, and a row of external hard drives. A laptop sat on Davis's desk.

Davis eyed Mark. "Who let you up here?"

Mark looked around, then shook his head. "Boy, I don't miss this place."

He was telling the truth. He missed Baku, but he didn't miss his old job as station chief. He hadn't been cut out to work behind a desk, to be badgered constantly by bureaucrats at Langley who were more worried about not making mistakes than producing good intelligence.

"I just got back from a team meeting. I have to finish with my notes. So if you could wait just a little longer."

Mark had never met Davis before. But there weren't many CIA

officers out there who lasted long enough to get promoted to station chief. Cordiality among those who had was typically the rule.

"OK." Mark plopped down in one of the wingback chairs.

"The ambassador wants to be here too. That's also part of the holdup. I'll let you know when she's ready."

"I'll wait here."

"I'd rather you didn't."

"Heard they're building a new hospital downtown. Pretty soon Baku isn't even going to qualify as a hardship post. It'll be like Paris."

Davis snorted. "Yes, the Paris of the Caspian. State already downgraded the hardship differential, but they screw with it any more and people are going to be tripping over each other to get the hell out of here. Which might not be a bad thing. People stay in one place too long, they get stuck in a rut. Start losing perspective."

Davis had only been running the station for two months, whereas Mark had run it for five years.

"I'm not here to screw you over, Roger. I'm here because Kaufman asked for my help and I agreed to give it. While I'm here, I'll do my best not to mess with your operation."

Given the circumstances, he thought it best not to mention that he intended to set up his spies-for-hire shop, indefinitely, right in downtown Baku.

Davis put in a brief call to the ambassador. A tall woman—taller than either Mark or Davis by several inches, with wide nostrils and a masculine jawline—showed up about ten minutes later.

The good news, thought Mark, was that she hadn't just bought her post with a massive political contribution. She'd worked for the State Department for the past thirty years, spoke Russian, Turkish,

French, and a bit of Azeri, and knew her policy well. The bad news was that she'd worked for the State Department for the past thirty years. Mark knew her by reputation, but she'd spent most of her career in Turkey and Washington, DC, so they'd never met.

"I understand that Roger here," the ambassador gestured to Davis, "has people he can send to Ganja. I'm really a bit confused as to why we need you at all."

Mark knew perfectly well why he was in Baku, and he suspected Roger Davis and the ambassador did too—because Kaufman didn't have faith in Davis and his team. What he said, though, was, "I'm here because Ted Kaufman asked me to be here. He wants me to debrief and deliver an alias packet to your branch chief in Ganja—I understand the guy's a little anxious?"

"It's nothing we can't handle here on our own."

"After that, I'm supposed to investigate—"

"I read the cable," said Davis.

"My obligations go beyond Ted Kaufman's and the CIA's," said the ambassador. "The media isn't going to set up camp outside Kaufman's home if you cause an international incident."

The ambassador was the direct representative of the president. Part of her job was to make sure no intelligence operation came back to bite the current administration in the rear, or conflicted with the larger goals of the State Department.

"You'd be investigating a possible murder on foreign soil," she added. "Without the consent of the local authorities. That makes me *very* uncomfortable."

"Things have changed since you left," said Davis to Mark. "A lot. The amount of money pouring into this place..." He exhaled loudly, as though at a loss for words. "I mean, every other day we get some wacko-bird from Congress passing through, trying to wheedle some shady deal for their home district, thinking they can just show up and we'll act as their broker! Put them in touch with the *right people*! And that's if we're lucky. It's the ones that try to convince me the northern half of Iran might secede and join Azerbaijan that are really nuts. I mean, you can't believe the level of ignorance."

"Oh, I can believe it," said Mark.

"Point being, the stakes are higher here now. Most people might not have a clue, but they still care what happens here, or think they do. There's a lot of money on the line."

Sensing Davis was just voicing general concerns because he didn't want to run afoul of Kaufman by voicing specific ones, Mark said, "Fine. Point taken. But what does that have to do with what Kaufman has asked me to do in Ganja?"

The ambassador said, "I took the liberty of calling our embassy in Bishkek. People there speak highly of you and the work your firm has done in Central Asia. But the difference here is, well…" The ambassador shook her head in disapproval as her voice trailed off.

"The difference is, I'm being thrust upon you by Washington," said Mark, finishing the thought. "To do a job you don't want done."

"Something like that," said the ambassador.

"Listen, I'm sympathetic to your concerns, but it sounds as if you have a problem with Langley, not me."

"That may be so, but you're the one sitting here in front of me."

"So then veto the investigation. Kaufman will raise a stink and probably drag his boss and your boss into it, but you do what you gotta do."

"You get paid either way," said Davis. "Is that it?"

"Actually, no. I'd bill for the airfare, but not for the job. You know why?"

"Why?"

"Because I'm not a dickhead. My firm delivers good intel at a fair price."

Mark didn't fault Davis for feeling sour about the money; when Mark had run the station, he'd resented the private contractors too. The truth was, even charging the CIA a rate that was more than reasonable when compared to other private contractors, Mark was still making far more than Davis—and a ton more than the operations officers that Davis managed. It wasn't right, it wasn't fair, but that was life. The solution was to fix the CIA so that they could do in-house what they now needed the private contractors to do, but Mark had little faith that would happen any time soon.

Mark turned to the ambassador. "I won't try to work in Azerbaijan without your approval. But if you don't grant approval, we both know it's going to piss off Kaufman. It's your call."

The ambassador paused, then looked at Davis, who shrugged. "I want him sneaking around my station like I want a hole in my head, but my boss wants him here, so that's game-set-match on my end. I'd like daily reports routed directly to me—"

"I'm not guaranteeing daily. It'll depend on where I am and what I'm doing. I'll file timely reports."

Davis rolled his eyes. "Timely reports then. And a restriction on firearms."

The ambassador nodded slowly, considering the matter. "Agreed. No firearms in the station. That's pretty much the rule here anyway."

That had been Mark's official rule too for the last two years that he'd run the station. Azerbaijan had pretty restrictive gun laws; you had to weigh the risk of getting caught with an illegal gun against the potential security a gun could provide. Usually it wasn't worth the risk, but most officers, especially the ones operating under non-official cover, kept a backup hidden somewhere, just in case.

"I'm good with that," said Mark. "Do you have the alias packet for your branch chief ready?"

"I'll need a few hours on that," said Davis.

They discussed logistics for a while longer, then Mark shook hands with Davis and the ambassador and thanked them for their time. He was about to leave when he remembered his promise to Daria. "By the way, you wouldn't know where the best place to pick up decent diaper cream is, would you? It can't just be any old brand, I need Triple Paste or Desitin."

The ambassador wrinkled her nose. "No, I would not."

"Try the new Port Baku mall," said Davis. "I don't know if they have a pharmacy, but if they do it's a safe bet it's stocked with a lot of high-end crap."

Mark collected his electronic equipment and, from the relative safety of the guardhouse, called two cabs. When they arrived, he turned to the armed Azeri guard who appeared to be in charge. "I'll take an escort to my car, if you wouldn't mind."

"You are worried, sir?"

"No, but I'm not exactly the most popular guy around here, so…"

"It will not be a problem. But sir, you're forgetting your computer and camera."

Mark had left Larry's camera and laptop on the counter where the guard had placed them. The memory cards filled with photos of the Russian base were in a Ziploc bag on top of the laptop.

"I'll come for them in a few days." He didn't need them and was sick of carrying them around. That, and he didn't want to be caught snooping around Ganja while carrying photos of the Russian military base. Especially when the photos had already been backed up online.

"I'm sorry, sir. We cannot store them for you. It is only storage for while you are in the embassy."

Mark left everything where it lay.

"Please be careful with the camera, it's expensive. Maybe store everything in a safe inside the embassy. Better yet, talk to Roger Davis. Have *him* store it all for me."

"Sir, I must tell you—"

"Figure no longer than a week, tops. If it's going to be longer than that I'll send someone else to collect them."

"This is not like a locker room, where you can just—"

"Talk to Davis. I've got to go, please escort me out."

The guard did so, albeit reluctantly.

20

Mark hadn't been able to detect anyone following him from the airport to the embassy, but after what had happened in Tbilisi, he wasn't about to take any chances.

Upon exiting the guardhouse, he quickly assessed the two cabs that had pulled up in front: the first was one of the new London-style cabs that the president of Azerbaijan had insisted all be painted bright purple; the other a decrepit Russian-made Lada sedan. The man behind the wheel of the purple cab was considerably younger; judging that the younger driver in the newer car would be the faster ride, Mark climbed in. As he did so, a man across the street, wearing ridiculous mirrored aviator glasses and a brown leather jacket, appeared to glance at him.

"The Four Seasons Hotel," said Mark. "Get me there in five minutes, and I won't need change for this hundred." He slipped the bill into the cabbie's hand and they took off like a shot.

Soon they were cruising west down Neftchilar Avenue, parallel to which ran a promenade that followed the coast of the Caspian Sea. Until recently, the promenade had been a shabby but pleasant place to take a stroll, framed at its western and eastern ends by shipping ports that stank of oil. Now the industrial zones, with their rusted yellow cranes and beat-up container-ship barges were gone, shuffled off to a massive new port south of Baku. In their place were several waterfront parks, one of which was anchored by a massive flagpole that—until Tajikistan built an even bigger one—had been the tallest in the world. The promenade itself, once nothing more than a cracked asphalt path that had run along the edge of a rock breakwater that smelled of rotting fish and seaweed, was now a pristine expanse of white tile that extended all the way down to the water's edge.

Rising up from the hill that lay beyond Neftchilar Avenue, a trio of gleaming flame-shaped skyscrapers dominated the western skyline.

As Mark took all this in, keeping an eye out too for signs that he was being followed, he wondered briefly whether Baku was still the right fit for him. Wondered whether the city had outgrown him. The Baku he knew was one of shady back alleys and pollution and stink and corruption, but this…this place seemed like a shopping mall, a mini-Dubai in the making.

But he was getting older, he reasoned. He was changing himself; he was a father now, and a husband. He no longer took the risks he used to. Maybe it was only right that his adopted city was changing, just as he was changing. They were both cleaning up their acts.

Mark glanced at his face in the rearview mirror of the cab. He saw the crow's-feet around his eyes; the gray that had once been just around his temples was now peppering the hair on the top of his head.

Baku, he had to admit, was aging better than he was.

"Here's fine," said Mark, just before they got to the Four Seasons.

He got out of the cab, shouldered his travel bag, and headed into old Baku. When he'd first come to Baku, the old part of the city had been surrounded by a massive crumbling rock wall that dated from the eleventh century. But once the oil money started pouring in, the Azeris had decided to fix everything. They'd repaired the wall, doing such a thorough job that it now looked new—because it was—and they'd taken the same approach to cultural preservation with the rest of the old city, most of which now appeared to be about as old as the Great Sphinx outside the Luxor hotel in Las Vegas.

The cobbled streets were still narrow, though, and many bottlenecked down to cobbled footpaths that were just a couple of yards wide. The pedestrian traffic was light enough that Mark could focus intently on the footsteps of the few people behind him.

He turned left up a particularly steep alley and passed through a construction site that no one had bothered to rope off, winding his way through a maze of concrete saws and jackhammers and workers hauling mortar. When he reached the top of the alley, he took a quick right. Eventually a newly renovated beehive-domed limestone building appeared, outside of which was a sign that read HAMAM.

There were many Turkish baths in Baku, some of which had been in use for centuries. It depressed Mark that they'd renovated the exterior of his favorite; instead of the sooty stained brown it once had been, it was now a clean light khaki color. But the instant he ducked inside and felt the heat, and smelled the water and the sweat and the ancient wet rocks and the wet wood, and saw the clutter of teacups and papers behind the counter opposite the entrance, and almost tripped on a bucketful of plumbing wrenches and other tools that the Azeri who maintained the bath had left in front of the counter, and when he saw too that the plaster on the arched dome was still crumbling, then all at once Mark felt at home and glad, so profoundly glad, to be back in the city that he loved.

"Mr. Sava!" exclaimed a voice from behind the counter that stood in front of the entrance door. "Oh, but it has been too long.

I thought you were dead!"

"Not yet, friend. Not yet."

———◇———

Hassan—a heavyset Azeri with a bald head and a beak nose marked by a permanent indentation from heavy reading glasses—stepped out from behind the counter. He wore gym shorts and a sleeveless undershirt.

"It *has* been too long," said Mark, embracing Hassan briefly. "How have you been?"

"Well. Very well."

"And your children?"

"My oldest started working here last month cleaning the baths. He works hard."

"I don't doubt it."

"Today you bathe for free, Mr. Sava. To welcome you back. But I fear you must have found another hamam you prefer."

"No, no. I've been abroad, Hassan. Living in a land where all the hamams are dirty and diseased. I went to one and I needed to bathe again when I got home, just to get clean! But it's good to be home. Had I known I was leaving for so long I would have told you, but…"

Hassan waved his hand. "It is no matter. And it is good to see you home, Mr. Sava."

After they spoke of the past year, and of what each of them had done with it—Mark shared that he'd married Daria, and was now a father—Hassan said, "You will take the full treatment, of course." He gestured to the plastic sandals—loaners provided by the hamam—outside the changing room. "You will also take a robe?" Before Mark could say no, Hassan's eyes widened. "Wait one minute, Mr. Sava. I have something for you!"

"I don't—" Mark was going to say that he didn't have time at the moment for a treatment, but Hassan had already ducked into the employee room behind the front desk. A moment later, the Azeri reemerged. In his hand he held a pair of plastic slippers. They were old, and the plastic was partially ripped on one. But Mark recognized them.

"They are yours, Mr. Sava. When you don't return for a year, we took them from the changing room, but I saved them."

"I was wondering whether I'd ever get those back. You are too good to me."

Hassan tipped his head briefly, acknowledging the compliment.

Mark said, "But right now I don't have time for a treatment. I just need a favor."

"Anything, Mr. Sava. What can I do?"

Hassan loaned Mark his spare jacket, sunglasses, and straw cowboy-style hat—the type favored by men who labored long hours in the sun. And he let Mark exit the hamam via an old tunnel that cut underneath the baths and which was used to service the heating elements beneath the hot rooms. The tunnel opened onto an alley behind the hamam; Mark had used the same exit many times in the past, often after the hamam had officially closed—it was one of the ways he'd managed to arrange secure meetings with his potential informants.

21

After satisfying himself that he wasn't being followed, Mark bought a cup of Turkish coffee from a street vendor and walked to Western University, which was housed in a six-story turn-of-the-century building just outside the walled old city. He was waved through the massive oak entrance door by a security guard who accepted his explanation that, although he didn't have a university ID, he was there to meet with the head of the International Relations department.

Once inside, he quickly climbed the wide central staircase to the third floor, eager to get in and out before he ran into anyone who knew him. His brief stint as an academic had been an aberration. When he moved back to Baku, it would be as a spy for hire—and he didn't want to have to explain that career choice to his former colleagues at Western. Nor did he want to lie to them, though, so avoidance, as much as possible, was the best option.

His old office on the third floor overlooked a lonely inner courtyard where a few straggly fig trees were shaded by laundry lines. But the room itself had an old-world charm to it—high ceilings, like his old office at the embassy, carved oak wainscoting, and a fanlight above the eight-foot-tall door.

Mark cracked the door open, then knocked when he saw someone sitting at his old desk, back to the door, tapping a pencil on the desktop and staring at a laptop.

Receiving no response, Mark knocked again, louder this time.

The man held up a finger, typed on his laptop for a moment, as if finishing a thought, then turned. His eyes were puffy, his nose red; a box of tissues sat on top of his desk.

"Can I help you?"

Mark knew the guy, but only from a few casual encounters. He was a mathematics professor, Iranian by birth. One of the few professors at Western, other than Mark, who had refused to take bribes in return for good grades.

"You have a minute?"

They spoke in Azeri.

"Office hours are Tuesday."

"I used to teach here at Western. I believe we've met."

The man turned in his seat. "We have?"

"In the faculty lounge. It would have been over a year ago." Mark entered the room, transferred his coffee to his left hand, and offered his right as he introduced himself and explained that he used to teach international relations. "Listen, this was my old office. When I retired, it was due to a family emergency. I didn't have time to properly clean out my things. I left something here that I need to retrieve."

"From *my* office?"

"It's in the desk. Underneath the bottom drawer on the right. I'd be surprised if it wasn't still there."

"I'm sorry, who did you say you were?" The professor's eyes darted toward the door.

Mark repeated his name. "I worked with Professor Samedov," he said, giving the name of the man he thought still ran the International Relations department. "I'll need to remove the drawer to get my things." He placed his coffee on the desk. "Just briefly. I'll put it right back."

"Professor Samedov retired. At the end of last semester."

"Did he now? I knew he'd been considering it."

"Did you check in with security?"

"Oh, they know me."

"You wouldn't mind if I called them, would you?"

"Not at all."

A cordless phone sat on the desk. A phone line, however, snaked up to the charger base. As though trying to be helpful, Mark slid the base towards the professor. As he did so, he used his index finger to unclip the line—but in such a way that the line was still touching the base.

"While you're calling, if you don't mind, I'm going to retrieve my things."

Mark knelt down, bumping up against the professor's leg, and pulled out the bottom drawer. It was stuffed with books and loose-leaf binders, making it heavy to lift off its runners.

The professor, who now appeared bewildered, grabbed the cordless. "In fact, I do mind. If you were to have made an appointment—"

"I'll only be a moment."

Mark set the drawer down, reached far into the empty space, and removed a small plastic Ziploc bag that had been duct-taped to the interior wall of the desk. A quick inspection confirmed that his alias packet—a custom one that he'd personally commissioned—was as he'd left it: one well-worn Azeri driver's license, a government ID card, and a Western University ID card, all of which displayed his photo, hair cropped short and dyed dark black, next to the name Adil Orlov. There was also a Visa card in Orlov's name that wasn't due to expire for another three months, and ten $100 bills.

Mark didn't need the money; he'd brought plenty with him from Bishkek, but seeing the crisp bills raised his spirits. He slipped the Ziploc bag into his back pocket and replaced the drawer.

The professor was punching buttons on his phone, trying to get a dial tone, glaring at Mark as he did so.

"I'll be leaving now," said Mark. "Thanks for your help."

He scooped up his coffee and downed the rest of it in one long slug. He considered leaving the empty cup on his old desk but decided not to be a jerk.

———◇———

As Mark left the university, intending to check out the new Port Baku mall to see about getting diaper cream—he had time to kill while waiting for the Ganja branch chief's alias packet—he was thinking about where he'd live. Definitely somewhere on the east side of town, where he'd be less likely to run into former academic colleagues. Maybe in one of the new high-rises. He wondered how much a penthouse condo would cost—maybe instead of a balcony he'd have a whole rooftop patio. How about that? He envisioned setting up a little jungle gym for Lila; she'd be crawling soon enough.

But when he pictured himself with Daria and Lila on top of the roof, lounging in the sun, the image only lasted a moment before he began to imagine Lila crawling to the edge, curious, then trying to climb what would probably be a protective wall that was far too low.

A rooftop patio, with a little kid...what was he thinking? But if a rooftop wasn't safe, would any balcony be—

Mark stopped short. *Shit.*

Two men were approaching, both dressed in dark suits with white shirts. He considered making a run for it—he had plenty of avenues of escape, and he'd noticed them in time—but stopped himself because he didn't sense danger the way he had in Tbilisi, and he trusted his instincts.

"Mark Sava?"

"No," said Mark.

"Mr. Sava, we are here on behalf of someone who would like to meet with you."

The one who had spoken, a stocky man with a helmet-style haircut and a thick monobrow in need of a trim, had done so in perfect Azeri. Mark breathed a little easier.

"Who?"

"If you could come with us, please."

"You must be kidding."

A silence ensued. The man gestured to a Mercedes idling on the street.

Mark said, "I'm not getting in your car."

"I am not inviting you. I am ordering you."

"I'm not getting in the car."

"Get in the car."

"No."

The men glanced at each other. The one who had spoken first shrugged, then said, "It's not that far. We can walk."

Mark was tempted to make a belated run for it. But he *still* wasn't getting the sense that these guys meant to do him harm. "Walk to where?"

The man considered, then named a restaurant in old Baku that Mark knew well.

"Who runs this restaurant?"

The name offered matched the name Mark knew.

"How will we get there?"

"Istiglaliyyat, right, left to Kichik Qala, then—"

"OK, I know it, I'll follow you."

From the way they spoke Azeri, the quick answers to his questions, and the easy way the men carried themselves, they almost certainly were Azeris, Mark determined. Probably—given their civil-servant uniformity—from the Ministry of National Security. And the Azeris, while not exactly his allies, weren't his enemies either.

Mark raised his empty coffee cup with his left hand and gestured down the street, drawing the attention of the two men away from his right hand, which he dipped into his back pocket. He palmed his alias packet, and then transferred the empty coffee cup into his right hand, using it to hide the alias packet.

After a minute of walking, they passed an urn-shaped garbage bin. The garbage around downtown, Mark remembered, was emptied every day—but not until early in the morning, just before dawn. He tossed the coffee cup, and his identification, into the urn.

22

———————◦———————

There were few things in this world that intimidated Orkhan Gambar, but his daughter was one of them.

As Azerbaijan's Minister of National Security—the Azeri equivalent of the CIA—*he* was used to doing the intimidating. Thousands of men and women worked under him. When he arrived for work each morning, dropped off by a black limousine in front of the ministry building on Parlament Prospekti, the halls were always silent save for the occasional muted, "Good morning, Minister Gambar." Doors were opened, heads were down at desks.

Deference, that's what he was accorded. Deference and respect. His daughter, however, accorded him neither.

At present, Orkhan was seated in a cool stone-walled basement of a restaurant in old Baku, attempting to conduct a Skype video chat with his daughter. He tapped on his smart phone. "I think I have it now," he said, speaking loudly.

"I still can't see you," snapped his daughter, who was in Paris.

She'd sent him a text late last night, asking him whether he could make time for a video chat today. Of course he could, he'd said, but that had been before this business with Sava had come up, and truth be told, he wasn't good with the video thing.

"I have done everything exactly as you said!" Orkhan insisted.

"Well, it's not showing up—all I have is the audio. Make sure the app knows to use the internal camera on your phone. It might be thinking you want to use an external camera."

It annoyed him that she spoke to him as if *he* were the child. "This app—where do I look for this?"

As his daughter attempted to instruct him, Orkhan grew increasingly frustrated. "This phone, it is broken, I think."

She tried to instruct him again.

"Maybe we could just talk," said Orkhan. "Maybe we don't need the video." He didn't want to be sharp with his daughter, but enough already. Sava would be here soon.

A sigh of frustration and disappointment—*how could you possibly be so stupid?*—then, "OK. We just talk."

"How are your studies progressing?"

"Fine."

When it came to his daughter, Fatima, that was one thing Orkhan didn't have to worry about. She was everything his doltish son was not—intelligent, energetic, and hardworking. She'd applied to, and had been accepted at, the Sorbonne. The *Sorbonne*. It filled him with pride him just to think of it. And this based entirely on her own merits.

"And your job?"

"*Ata*, I have something we need to talk about. It is important, that is why I wanted the video."

Orkhan leaned his head back and stroked his mustache. "What is important?"

"I've decided to apply for French citizenship." A half-minute passed. "*Ata*? Are you still there?"

"You wish to have joint Azeri and French citizenship? Fatima, this...this...well, you know my position, this could be complicated."

"Not joint citizenship."

"Fatima."

"I've given this a lot of thought."

"*Subhan'Allah*, Fatima!" *Glorious is God!*

For seventeen years she had been an obedient girl, but a year ago everything had changed when he'd had her boyfriend, a sniveling long-haired man-child who professed to be a poet—Orkhan suspected the boy had gypsy blood in him—arrested for attending a pro-democracy rally in downtown Baku.

Although Orkhan had made sure that the arrest was made by the local police, not his men, that was when Fatima had started with all her questions.

Why had her boyfriend been arrested when other protestors had not? And what could be done about it? And then, after poisoning her mind with articles she'd read online: why was the legal system in Azerbaijan so blatantly unfair? Why was Azerbaijan saddled with a dictatorship when it was clear that the future belonged to the democracies of the world? And what was her father doing to make things better?

Azerbaijan was not Europe, or America, Orkhan had explained. It was a different culture, with different rules. Be grateful for what you have, be grateful that your father is one of the most important people in Azerbaijan, and remember that with this status comes both privilege and responsibility.

Fatima had not been impressed. She'd declared that the president of Azerbaijan was an oppressor, and that her father was aiding and abetting this oppressor. By the time she'd declared her intention to move to France to study at the Sorbonne, Orkhan had been relieved. Go study, have your silly late-night talks about God and democracy and oppression of masses and such—smoke marijuana even!—get all this out of your system, then grow up, and learn the real ways of the world. In the meantime, we will agree to disagree.

"I consider myself a citizen of the world," said Fatima. "But if I can't be a citizen of the world, I at least want to be a citizen of a country whose ideals I respect."

"That you respect."

"Yes. That I respect."

"And this country is…*France?*"

"I've decided France is a better fit for me than Azerbaijan."

"A better *fit?*" Orkhan gripped his phone tightly. It was a struggle not to throw it across the table. "Your country is not something you change like you change your shoes, Fatima!" He took a moment to collect himself, to steady his breathing. He felt his heart pounding against his ribcage. "Have you told your mother of this?"

"Last night."

"And?"

"She was OK with it."

"Unbelievable."

His wife was in Dubai, on one of her all-too-frequent shopping trips, spending ungodly amounts of money on jewelry and clothing outfits she might wear once if she wore at all. She was like his son—depressingly stupid, and focused on the material things in life.

Which made this ever widening schism with Fatima that much harder. He and Fatima had always been the sensible, responsible ones in the family.

He wondered if she'd even considered the effect renouncing her citizenship might have on his position as minister. If the president found out, well…if Minister Gambar couldn't be relied on to control his own daughter, how could he be relied on to control Azerbaijan's preeminent intelligence agency?

Orkhan said, "Fatima, I know you think what you are doing is right. I know you try to live by your—" He paused as the next word got stuck in his throat. She is young and impressionable, he told himself, don't say it with sarcasm. "Your *ideals*, but I am telling you this as a father, as someone who raised you—"

"I was raised by servants."

"Servants I provided! I am telling you, as your father, that people change over the course of their lives. You are a beautiful girl, with your whole life ahead of you. What you think is right for you now might not feel as right in a year, or ten years, or twenty. So I ask that you wait, and give this more thought."

"It usually takes up to five years anyway, Dad. They don't just let you become a citizen right away."

Orkhan felt a weight lift from his chest. Five years. In five years, he might be ready to retire anyway. If the job and Fatima hadn't killed him by then. "This is good."

"But I'm hoping to do it in three. If I finish my undergraduate degree early, and then do two years of graduate school while working in France, I'll be eligible to apply—"

One of Orkhan's men cracked open the door to the room in which Orkhan sat.

"He is here, sir."

To Fatima, Orkhan said, "Wait a moment." He pressed the phone to his chest, muffling the microphone, then spoke to his man. "Bring him to me."

"He refuses."

"Tell him he doesn't have a choice."

"We have. He still refuses. He said he'd meet you in the courtyard."

Orkhan was tempted to have his men just clobber Sava on the head and drag him into the restaurant. Establish right away what the pecking order was going to be now that Sava was back in Baku. But he worried that if he issued such an order, one of his men might end up with a ruptured testicle, or blind in one eye. Sava may not look like much—physically, he was more than a few years past his prime—but he was a survivor. Orkhan had learned that much about the American over all the years they'd known each other.

"*Zirrama.*" *Idiot.* He muttered this under his breath.

Orkhan stood. As he did so his gut, which had never been a small affair but over the past year had grown to be a bit unwieldy, brushed against the table, causing some of his tea to spill onto the white tablecloth. "I'll be right out. In the meantime, search him." He raised his phone back to his ear. To Fatima, he said, "I need to go."

"Of course you do. The president calls and you must come. He's a brute, *Ata.*"

"Silence, child. Silence. It is not the president."

23

As Mark observed Orkhan Gambar approaching, he noted that his old confederate, and sometimes friend, had grown fat.

Orkhan had always been a big man, but in a powerful, bearlike way. His nose was crooked and huge, configured in a way that most Americans might think ugly but in Azerbaijan was anything but. The nose made Orkhan look like a man to be reckoned with, as did his shoulders, which were broad like a weightlifter's.

But now Orkhan's neck had gone from thick to unhealthy and his midsection from impressively stout to obese. Thirty pounds in just over a year, Mark guessed.

"Minister Gambar," said Mark. "It has been too long."

Orkhan frowned and exhaled loudly through his nose.

"No weapons, sir," said one of Orkhan's men. "Here is his passport and wallet."

Orkhan flipped through Mark's brown official passport. "New," he noted.

"Issued yesterday."

Orkhan gestured to the leather satchel Mark was carrying. "What else is in the bag?"

"Phone, iPad, clothes, toothbrush, razor, and such," said Orkhan's man. "And a painting."

"A painting?"

"Show him," said one of Orkhan's men to Mark.

Mark carefully pulled out Katerina's painting and removed

the shirt he'd wrapped around it. "I picked it up in Tbilisi. Do you like it?"

Orkhan studied it briefly. "No. You have bad taste, Sava. Put it back."

When Orkhan's men looked to him for further guidance, he gave a sharp nod of his chin towards the exit.

His men backed away, leaving the tiled courtyard of the four-teenth-century caravansary—a Silk Road inn of sorts—empty save for Orkhan and Mark. Given that it was approaching lunch-time, Mark assumed Orkhan had ordered the restaurant that now occupied the caravansary cleared for the occasion. High walls, broken up by arched alcoves where traders used to store their livestock and wares, surrounded the courtyard.

Mark said, "I thought it might be you."

"Your powers of deduction are remarkable." Orkhan handed back Mark's passport and wallet. "I am told you married. This is true?"

"It is true."

"And you did not think to tell me this yourself? No wedding invitation? No card?"

"I'm sorry. It happened fast."

"A marriage should not happen fast, my friend."

"Mine did."

Orkhan's expression made it clear that he didn't think much of that.

"And it is with this woman you now have a child." It wasn't a question. Orkhan had clearly been briefed. He pressed his lips together into a disapproving frown. "Ah, Sava...This return to Baku. Perhaps you should have notified me first."

"There wasn't time."

"Always, always you Americans are too rushed. Come, we must talk."

Orkhan turned toward a building in the center of the court-yard. Mark followed behind him, noting that as Orkhan descended the staircase which led to the basement he gripped the handrail tightly, as though worried that he might tumble down the stairs. A fat-fold had developed in the back of his old friend's neck.

"You will perhaps be surprised to hear that Heydar is now at university," said Orkhan, as they descended.

"Congratulations. Where?"

"University of Texas. He studies petroleum engineering."

Orkhan, Mark knew, had been exceptionally keen on getting his son, Heydar, into the University of Texas. The main problem, however, had been the SAT. Mark, because he'd owed Orkhan a favor, had tried to help Heydar prepare for the test.

"I know how hard he must have worked to get in. The SAT is a difficult test."

Orkhan's eyes sagged. "Work, no. He paid someone to take this test for him, and to make his application. This is common, I hear? Now he chases American girls and gets as drunk as a Russian with my money."

"And Fatima, she is well?"

"She studies at the Sorbonne. But we will not talk of her now."

They passed through a long cave-like room with smoke-stained stone walls that arced inward to form an arched ceiling. Gilded couches were arranged on threadbare Persian carpets. At the end of the room stood a massive revolving door made of centuries-old oak and reinforced with thick iron bands. Orkhan pushed his way through it, as though entering a medieval dungeon.

Two place settings had been arranged at the end of a long table. Dim light from chandeliers trimmed with tassels cast reflected light off the water glasses and silverware. On a shoddy modern shelf behind the table, antique earthenware jugs fought for space with a Sony boom box. Mark liked to think of all the spice traders and oil barons and spies and diplomats who had taken shelter in these rooms over the centuries.

"Wait outside," said Orkhan to the man who stood behind his chair, holding his coat in such a way so that it wouldn't become wrinkled. "You will be called when you are needed."

24

———————○———————

Orkhan slumped down in his seat, comforted by the cool cellar air.

"Please." He gestured to the lamb stew in the center of the table. Also on the table was a large bowl of sliced lemons, a pot of tea, and bread.

"No thanks."

Orkhan frowned. "So." He served himself a ladleful of stew.

"How did you know where to find me?"

"You were followed. From the embassy." Orkhan took one of the lemon slices and used his teeth to peel the pulp from the rind.

"Those were your men?"

"No. The men you saw were Russians. My men observed them following you, or they would have picked you up after you left the embassy. Instead we watched."

"Russians. You sure about that?"

"Yes." Orkhan said, "We, and the Russians, did lose you in the old city, but I had men posted at Western University just in case. You had, as I recalled, a strange fondness for the place. Why are the Russians following you?"

"That's a good question."

Orkhan ate the pulp of another lemon slice, then a spoonful of stew. "In any case, I must make a confession: it is satisfying to see you have once again decided to do something useful with your life."

"Teaching international relations wasn't useful?"

"When you were a teacher, they kicked you out of Azerbaijan. Why? Because you were not useful. Now, you work again in your field, you are useful, and just like that you are welcomed back. This is what I see."

"You approved my return?"

"No. I was not consulted."

Bypassing the normal channel of communication through the American embassy in Baku, the US State Department's undersecretary for political affairs had made a direct appeal to the office of the president, asking for Sava's PNG to be lifted. Orkhan felt certain that the president, or whatever underling he'd assigned to deal with the matter, hadn't had a clue as to what they'd approved.

"Hmm," said Sava.

"And now I must admit to some uncertainty." Orkhan reached for another slice of lemon.

"Uncertainty."

"Yes."

"You've developed an affinity for lemons, I see."

Orkhan shrugged. "They are good for the circulation. And I have some circulation problems." He gestured to the bowl. "Please."

"By circulation problems, you mean heart problems?"

"Not big problems."

"You are seeing a doctor, of course."

"Of course. The best."

Mark took a lemon slice.

Orkhan said, "So this new station chief, Roger Davis. Does he work for you, or do you work for him?"

"Neither."

"And your relation to the ambassador?"

"We coordinate."

"You see, this is the cause of my uncertainty."

"I'm a private contractor now, Orkhan. When they need me, they hire me. When they don't..." Mark shrugged.

Orkhan knew perfectly well that the Americans often liked

to hire private contractors to do jobs that should have been handled by the government. His feeling was, if the Americans wanted to pay two dollars for a job that should cost one, that was their business. They had money, they liked to spend it. Just like his wife liked to waste money in Dubai. No problem. But using someone of Mark's stature on a contract basis, that was a different matter altogether. That complicated the chain of command, it complicated diplomacy with the Americans.

Mark added, "It's the new way. Some people in the CIA are looking for ways that the Agency can exercise more operational flexibility. Be less bound by the bureaucracy."

"And you welcome this trend?"

"I neither welcome it nor reject it. I observe it and react to it."

"Bureaucracy is not always a bad thing."

"Not always a good thing either."

"It can help prevent confusion."

"Or create it, depending on who's at the top."

"Enough of this, Sava. On whose authority are you here? Who pays you? This is what I need to know."

"Washington. Ted Kaufman. He's the—"

"Yes, yes, I know. Central Eurasia, CIA. So you and Roger Davis have the same boss."

"We do."

"Roger Davis, and the ambassador, you realize they are fools, no?" Orkhan fingered his lemon rind. "The protestors here, the opposition, they talk of human rights and monitors, always monitors, for elections, but they play the US. They only say these things so your State Department will find creative ways to get money to them. They don't expect to actually change anything, and they won't."

"I realize the situation is complicated."

"I know you do. It is Davis I worry about. The job you have been hired to do. What can you tell me about it?"

When Mark spoke, he chose his words carefully. "It involves a woman in Ganja who was advising us. She died recently, perhaps not from natural causes. I've been asked to look into it."

"This woman, she was Azeri?"

Mark nodded. "You wouldn't happen to know what I'm talking about, would you?"

Orkhan genuinely didn't, which bothered him. "No."

"Pity."

"Azerbaijan is a friend to America. Why do you waste time spying on us?"

"I didn't say we were spying on you. Do you know why the Russians were following me?"

"No. When do you intend to travel to Ganja?"

"Soon."

"If you'd like, I can arrange for transport."

"Oh, I think I'll manage."

"If there are problems, Sava…"

"I will call you."

Orkhan and Mark had worked well together in the past, and Orkhan hoped to do so again in the future. They'd both benefited from the relationship, each often telling the other more than their respective governments would have liked, an arrangement that had allowed both of them to appear particularly well-connected. But Orkhan also realized it was possible Mark had been assigned a job that would put him in conflict with Azeri operatives, in which case his alliance with Mark would be tested.

Orkhan sighed and massaged his temples as he recalled the conversation he'd had with his daughter.

"How have you been, Orkhan?" asked Mark, adding, "It's good to see you again."

"As we get older it doesn't get easier, does it, Sava?"

"No, I guess it doesn't."

25

Russian Military Base, South Ossetia

———————o———————

Titov could sense the resentment, could see it in the eyes of the men who stood before him. Fine. Let them resent him.

Yesterday he'd sent their beloved squad leader back to the main Forty-Ninth Army base at Stavropol, Russia. Some people were too smart for their own good, too questioning, too disrespectful of authority. The squad leader had been such a man; he'd thought himself Titov's better, more capable of leading. The final indignity had come when Titov had overheard him instructing his squad not to bother with their ballistic goggles when packing for the upcoming operation—in direct contravention of orders Titov had given. The insolent fool had forgotten that before a Russian soldier could lead, he first had to learn how to kneel.

There was no insulation or air conditioning inside the windowless steel-walled training warehouse where Titov had ordered the remaining men—all members of the elite FSB paramilitary unit known as Vympel—to assemble. Which meant it was brutally hot. A creaky wall fan offered no relief. Pigeons cooed from the nests they'd built in the steel roof trusses; the floor was stained with their droppings.

The men might not respect him, thought Titov, but now at least they knew to fear for their jobs. And one of the men, the one he'd promoted to be the new squad leader, now owed him, and that was something.

Titov knew he was not the brightest person ever to walk the face of the earth, but he'd served intelligent, powerful men all his life. Time and time again he'd watched them manipulate others to create networks of loyalty. He knew how it was done.

"You will enter Nakhchivan as individuals." Titov's booming voice resonated off the metal walls. He handed each man a sealed manila packet. "Here are your individual travel instructions, a cash allowance that should prove ample, and aliases. You are not to share this information with any of your teammates. Although all of you will enter Nakhchivan via different routes, you will rendezvous tomorrow as a group at the Hotel Grand in Nakhchivan City. There you will be met by a colleague you will recognize. He will arm you, and provide instructions regarding the next steps of the operation. I will be joining you in Nakhchivan in seventy-two hours. Every one of you will leave this base within the hour." Titov considered wishing his men luck, and adding a few words of encouragement, then looked into their eyes and decided against it. "Are there questions?"

There were none. Titov dismissed the men. As they exited, bright sunlight spilled in through the open door. Titov noticed that, waiting near the door, was his liaison to the FSB's counterintelligence department. Multiple layers of FSB counterintelligence, he now knew, had been fully briefed and were assisting with the operation in Nakhchivan. Which was as it should be.

"Do you have a minute, sir?"

"Walk with me to my office." Titov began to walk quickly toward his temporary quarters on the other side of the base. The counterintelligence agent struggled to keep up.

"The American we intended to bring in for questioning."

"In Baku."

"Yes. I'm told we've lost him. Temporarily, of course."

Titov absorbed the news. He wasn't one to shoot the messenger;

he'd *been* the messenger too many times for that. Still, the revelation frustrated him.

"And this American's connection to Bishkek. What news there?"

"He appears to be a careful man. Very careful."

Titov grimaced and cocked his head without breaking stride.

The counterintelligence agent added, "There is no physical address listed for his business in Bishkek, no one of that name is listed in any public records in Bishkek—"

"Did you expect to find him in the phone book?"

"No, sir, but—"

"Are we even certain he operates out of Bishkek?"

"Yes. Six months ago, we received a report from one of our Bishkek-based officers saying as much—that's how we knew to focus on Bishkek in the first place. We've since been able to confirm that, on occasion, Sava interacts with members of the Kyrgyz government."

"And have our men in Bishkek spoken directly to these members of government?"

"I don't know, sir."

"Have we asked these members of government who else works for Sava's organization?" Without waiting for an answer, Titov said, "Incredible. You *must* find out who Sava works with, who he lives with. If he is communicating with anyone, it will be them." Titov knew he didn't technically have the authority to issue such an order himself, but his long association with the director of the FSB was well known. "Where a man lives will tell you where he has gone."

Part Four

26

Ganja, Azerbaijan
The next day

———————o———————

While Baku was fast on its way to becoming a mini-Dubai, Ganja was in no such danger.

Plastic bags, old tires, cans, bottles, and dead birds were strewn all over the rocky bed of the river that ran through the center of the city. Scavengers combed through the garbage. Sewage dripped out of cracked cast-iron pipes left exposed because of low water.

Mark had his cabbie drop him off just beyond the river, then began his surveillance-detection run down a series of noisy, chaotic streets where techno music blared, vendors hawked their wares, and cars careened down narrow pedestrian alleys. He walked quickly, frequently doubling back on his tracks. The strap of his leather satchel crossed his chest like a bandolier. He was hungry—he'd eaten dinner on the train, but not breakfast, and it was now nine o'clock in the morning—so he headed for the local outdoor market. There, men in bloodstained T-shirts stood in front of crosscut tree trunks, using broad-bladed axes to hack up sheep parts, while old women misted beet greens with water from perforated soda bottles, or sold dried fruit and spices—cinnamon, fennel, ginger root, cloves, cumin—out of canvas sacks.

Mark bought a bag of dried apricots. He was finishing the last of them when he reached a two-story brick building, to which

143

was affixed a blue-and-green painted sign that read: GLOBAL SOLUTIONS: HELPING TO EDUCATE THE WORLD.

He walked through the double-door entrance and into an interior courtyard that was protected from the elements by a slapdash roof made of corrugated translucent plastic. To his right, a staircase led to a long upper balcony; empty flower boxes hung from the balcony railing. To his left lay a worn red couch, above which was a bulletin board cluttered with notices in English and Azeri.

Mark took a quick look at the notices—most were promoting upcoming events at the center: an entry-level English course that was starting tomorrow at nine, a talk on how best to apply for visa applications to the US and Europe was being held on Friday at noon, and evidently the American ambassador would be visiting Ganja State University in a month.

From a hallway in back of the courtyard, Mark heard the steady antiphonal rhythm of a teacher posing questions and her students answering en masse. Upon inspection, he observed a young pasty-white woman with dreadlocks instructing a class of about twenty Azeris who ranged in age from early teens to middle-aged.

Mark stood in the doorway, until the students' stares caused the teacher to turn.

"May I help you?" The teacher wore an ankle-length tie-dyed skirt and spoke with a cheerful British accent.

"Sorry to interrupt. I'm looking for Raymond Cox?"

At the mention of Cox, her expression turned sour.

Mark added, "I'm a friend of his. From the US."

"Well, you won't find Ray in a classroom, I can tell you that much."

A few of the students laughed.

"I was told he worked here."

"Depends on your definition of work."

"Would you know where I could find him?"

Her nose turned up. "Try his office."

"And where—"

"It's off the upper balcony. The room that smells. Tell him I want my yoga mat back." More laughs. "Now, if you please."

A foul, acrid smell was indeed leaching out one of the doors that opened onto the courtyard balcony. Mark knocked on it, and heard movement from inside. And then what sounded like someone trying to quietly rack a slide on a semiautomatic pistol.

Mark stepped to the side of the door, outside the potential line of fire.

"Raymond?"

No answer.

"Raymond Cox?"

Still no answer.

"I believe you were expecting me for lunch?" Mark waited for Cox to acknowledge the code. Silence. Raising his voice, Mark repeated, "Raymond, I *believe* you were expecting me for lunch. And if you weren't, I'm going to leave. Now's your chance."

"I can't make lunch. Can we do dinner instead?"

"If we eat by five."

A lock turned and the door opened a crack, releasing a cloud of cigarette smoke. Mark also smelled piss, booze, and something feral.

"Come on in. But be careful—don't let the cats out."

As Mark slipped into Cox's office, he nudged a smoke-colored long-haired Turkish Angora—a popular breed in the region— out of the way. Ray Cox was standing in the back of the room, gripping a snub-nosed pistol.

"You can put that down now," said Mark.

Raymond Cox was a short wiry guy, with brown curly hair that fell to his shoulders but was prematurely receding on top. His curly beard was in need of a trim. He wore a bracelet of braided leather, jeans, and a T-shirt with the Global Solutions logo—an image of a student using the earth as his desktop—imprinted upon it. His close-set eyes darted toward his cat.

"Queenie, get back here!"

Still holding his pistol, Cox darted forward, scooped up the cat, and quickly shut the door. Behind him lay another Turkish Angora, this one white.

"Good Lord," said Mark, taking a look around. "What the hell's going on?"

The office was no more than ten by ten feet. What little light there was filtered in through a gauzy blind that shaded a small window. A bottle of cheap Russian vodka sat on a metal desk, next to a glass filled with water and cigarette butts. Half of the floor was covered with local newspapers. A few pieces of cat shit lay on the newspapers, next to a chipped ceramic water bowl and a small pile of dried cat food.

Cox looked Mark over for a moment, wedged his pistol between his belt and the small of his back, and said, "I had to move out of my house, it was being watched. I figured at least here, there were other people around. I've been waiting for you."

"I see." Mark observed that two yoga mats, one laid out on top of the other, occupied the better part of the floor that wasn't covered with newspapers. On top of the yoga mats lay a blue fleece blanket and a soiled pillow.

"Did you bring my alias packet?"

"Yeah. You got that gun on safety?"

Cox pulled a crumpled pack of Winstons out of his back pocket and extracted a single cigarette with his teeth. As he flicked on a lighter, he said, "You don't have to worry about it."

"I talked to Roger Davis yesterday. He said no firearms were allowed in station. Was that just a rule that applies to me?"

"His ass isn't on the line."

"And yours is?"

Cox took big drag off his cigarette, exhaled, and said, "Take a look at this."

A photo lay face down on his desk. He picked it up handed it to Mark. It showed a row of liquor bottles lined up on a bar shelf. Martini & Rossi sweet vermouth, Chivas Regal, Grand Marnier, Frangelico, Russian Standard vodka, and Jameson Irish Whiskey.

"That might just look like a bunch of booze to you, but—"

"Who sent this to you?"

"Turn it over. Read what's on the back."

Mark flipped it over. In Azeri, it read, PICK YOUR BOTTLE.

Cox said, "It means—"

"I know what it means." The threat was common in the region—pick the bottle you want stuffed up your ass before we beat you senseless, and possibly kill you. "What I asked was, who sent this to you?"

Cox sighed, then slumped down into the seat behind his desk. "That's what's got me worried. I don't know."

"When did you get it?"

"Four days ago. The day after—well, you heard about the source I was running?"

"You got this right after she was killed."

"Yeah. Which is one of several reasons why I think she *was* killed, that it wasn't just an accident. Her body was found in a ditch on the side of a road that leads to the mountains. A farmer said he heard a car honk, and then a crash, but that by the time he got there the car was pulling away. The police are treating it as a hit-and-run."

Mark took another look at the bottle photo, then pocketed it. "Does she live near where she was killed?"

"No, she lives in town, there was no reason for her to have been out there."

"And now you think whoever killed her is coming after you."

"Yeah, I do. Give me my documents."

"First we talk."

"We just did. Who the hell are you, anyway? Nobody ever mentioned you before. Do you work out of the embassy?"

Mark sat down on the corner of the desk. He looked around the dingy office again. "Two yoga mats?" he said. "You really into fitness?"

"The floor's hard. I've been sleeping here the past few days, I didn't want to risk leaving the building."

"Why don't you tell me what you've been doing for the Agency here in Ganja, and about this source you were running. Then we can talk about your alias and come up with a plan for getting you out."

27
Baku, Azerbaijan

———————o———————

Five men—the president of Azerbaijan, the prosecutor general, and the ministers of internal affairs, defense, and national security—sat at an elongated oval table inside the presidential office complex in downtown Baku.

The room had been soundproofed and stripped of all decoration save for two photos that hung on the wall opposite the entrance. The smaller of the two photos depicted the president; the larger, the president's deceased father.

The president, who was an exceptionally tall man, slowly sat back in his chair and crossed his long legs. He unbuttoned his suit—which had been custom made by his personal tailor in Milan—then frowned in a way that caused the hairs on his mustache to stick out.

"Men, we have a problem." The room was silent as the president made eye contact with each of his three ministers. "Dark days are upon us."

Again, silence. Orkhan knew he was supposed to be cowed by the silence, but he wasn't.

Orkhan got along well enough with the president, but the truth was he'd had far more respect for the president's father. Now *there* had been a leader. A strongman in the true sense of the word, a KGB tough who'd not only ruled Azerbaijan when it had been part of the Soviet Union, but who had also been savvy enough to steer Azerbaijan safely through the chaotic post-Soviet period. The son, by contrast, was a bit of a playboy—fond of fine wines and vacations to the Caribbean.

The president nodded to his prosecutor general, prompting the prosecutor general—a bald, gnome-like man who wore rimless reading glasses—to remove a folder from his black leather briefcase, open it, and say, "These are the minutes from the last meeting of the Security Council. All five of us were in this room." He handed out copies of the minutes to each of the three ministers. "No one but the president, his secretary, myself, the three of you, and anyone the three of you may have personally entrusted, has had access to the contents.

"Note," added the prosecutor general, "that portions of the minutes have been highlighted in yellow. They are the sections in which we discussed the status of the ongoing operation in Nakhchivan. Now compare"—he began to pass out copies of another document—"those highlighted sections with *this*."

Orkhan did so. The second document was in Russian. But it too contained sensitive information about the operation in Nakhchivan. And the phrasing was almost identical to the highlighted sections of the minutes. The implication was obvious—someone who had been at the meeting, or had access to the minutes from the meeting, had leaked information to the Russians.

Orkhan was the first to finish. He exhaled loudly, shifted in his seat to relieve a bit of tension in his back, and let the Russian-language document fall to the table. "Where did this come from?"

The minister of internal affairs, the forty-year-old brother-in-law of the president, said, "From the briefcase of a man claiming to be a Russian diplomat. He was staying at the Four Seasons here in Baku. My men took a photo of the original document."

"What diplomat?" asked Orkhan.

The minister of internal affairs gave a name, adding, "He's an attaché with the Russian embassy's economic development department."

"Why wasn't my ministry notified that you were planning this operation?"

"You have been notified," said the president sharply. "Right now."

"Yes, of course," said Orkhan.

"Had I known what we would find, I *would* have notified you," said the minister of internal affairs. "As it happened, I initially believed this to be a domestic matter. He came to our attention when one of my men witnessed him meeting with an opposition leader in the Majlis."

The Majlis was the parliament of Azerbaijan.

"The question," interrupted the president, as though addressing a class of first graders, "of how or why the information was obtained is not nearly as relevant as the fact that it *was* obtained." He drummed his fingers on the tabletop, then added, "I've already issued the order to suspend the operation in Nakhchivan."

The minister of defense said, "I transmitted your order to the ground commanders one hour ago."

"I support that decision, Mr. President," said Orkhan. "Until we can assess the extent of the damage, it is the only prudent course of action."

"Yes, assessing the extent of the damage, that is the key, isn't it?" said the president, his voice rising.

Orkhan, gesturing to the Russian-language document, said, "But I also think we can all agree that there is nothing in this that suggests that the Russians are aware of the true nature of our operation in Nakhchivan, only that some type of sensitive operation is ongoing. Of course—"

The president smacked his palm down on the table. "Of course, of course, Minister Gambar. Of course, you speak too much. Of course, what we must do is find the traitor in our midst and learn the full extent of what this traitor has shared with the Russians. Only then will we be able to fully assess the damage that this traitor has done."

"My investigation will begin immediately," said Orkhan.

The defense and internal affairs ministers concurred.

As Orkhan slipped into his limousine, he assessed his position. The president had demanded the head of a traitor, so a head would have to be produced. The only question was, whose?

Certainly not that of the prosecutor general's, or anyone on the president's staff.

The internal affairs minister was both related to the president through marriage and the one who had—allegedly—discovered the leak. So it was unlikely he was setting himself up.

The defense minister was a possibility, but he'd attended military school with the president, and he and the president liked to drink, and vacation with their families, together.

Orkhan, by contrast, had originally been appointed deputy minister of national security by the president's father, and had only assumed the post of minister when the former minister had died. Though the president had accepted Orkhan, their relationship had always been more professional than personal.

"Where to, Minister Gambar?" asked his driver.

Orkhan considered his options. He hadn't leaked anything to the Russians, so in theory he should have nothing to worry about. In reality, he was pretty sure someone was setting him up.

He searched his pocket for the blood pressure pills his

doctor had prescribed—Lisinopril, 40 milligrams once a day. But he sometimes took an extra or two when he thought he needed it. He'd used the last of his extras yesterday, though, so instead he retrieved a lemon cough drop, unwrapped it, and popped it in his mouth.

"Back to the ministry," he said.

28
Ganja, Azerbaijan

———————o———————

Mark stood by the window in Raymond Cox's office. He'd pulled the blind back just a bit and was peering out to the street.

Cox, who was sitting on his desk, said, "So this source I was running—"

"Start with what you were doing in Ganja in the first place. Why are you..." Mark turned from the window and gestured around the room. "...here? I assume it's not because you really want to help educate the world."

"Global Solutions is a good outfit, actually."

"I didn't say that it wasn't."

Cox took a moment to gather his thoughts, then said, "There's a bunch of local groups, mainly run out of Ganja State University, that are agitating for clean elections. They have just about zero influence, but the government still worries about them."

Mark thought about his experience with the Press Club in Georgia and how depressing it was that, twenty-four years later, the same old fights that were still being fought.

"A lot of the people affiliated with these groups come here for English lessons. They feel safe here, like we're their allies, which we are. I learn what I can about what the government's doing to them, and file reports. Granted, they're reports no one reads, other than maybe a twenty-five-year-old analyst back at Langley, if she's bored. But hey, I bear witness."

"And what *is* the government doing to these people?"

"Oh, the usual harassment and intimidation bullshit. Not a lot of physical violence, but the people in these groups tend to get mugged and robbed a lot more than the general population, you know? At the level it's at, Langley doesn't really give a shit—I'm not here to stop it. Washington just wants to know what's going on so that we don't get caught flat-footed if things get out of hand. Anyway, the local ex-com is in charge of making sure these groups don't ever pose a real threat to Baku, so I was also doing what I could to try to get a handle on his operation."

Ex-com was short for executive committee chairman, which is what the regional governors in Azerbaijan were called.

Cox continued, "He's one of the president's cousins. Local big shot, stuffing himself with *chapka*, that whole deal. The same thing you see in the rest of the country, only here it's worse."

No shocker there, thought Mark. All government programs in Azerbaijan were larded up with *chapka*, which was what the Azeris called kickbacks. If a low-level government lackey wanted to keep his job, he'd kick back some of his salary to his local boss, who would kick back some of his salary to the regional boss, who would kick back some of his salary to the local ex-com, who would then kick back a portion of all his kickbacks to the president.

It was your basic criminal-enterprise pyramid scheme, with the president at the top of the pyramid.

"So I tried for months to recruit an asset that could get me into the ex-com's inner circle, but I wasn't having much luck. I finally got a break when this girl, Aida Tagiyev, shows up for English lessons. On the application she fills out, she says she works for Bazarduzu Construction, which is an outfit owned by the local ex-com. I figured I might learn a lot about him by learning about his business. So I started trying to work Aida."

"What was your angle?"

"She was an accountant for Bazarduzu, so after a few English lessons, I asked whether she'd be able to do the books for the Global Solutions office here in Ganja. She's got a daughter who's less than a year old and a husband who teaches kids how to play different types of lutes or something, and I offered her more than the job was worth by a long shot."

"She do the actual books?"

Global Solutions was a real international nonprofit organization. Cox had just managed to land a cover job working for them.

"Nah, it was bullshit. I took the real books, zeroed everything out, and then made up all the numbers that I fed to her. Tried to make it complicated enough so that she felt she was contributing, but not too complicated. After this goes on for a couple weeks, and we get to know each other a little better, she starts saying how she wished the accounting for Bazarduzu was as straightforward as the numbers I was giving her. That's when I pitched her—you know, help me expose corruption and move Azerbaijan in the right direction and blah, blah, blah."

Mark went back to looking out the window. "If you think all this is bullshit, Cox, why'd you even sign up in the first place?"

"Because I wasn't like this when I signed up."

"She know you were CIA?"

Cox shrugged. "I told her I worked for Global Solutions but was also helping out the United Nations, and that I was involved in a UN project to document incidences of corruption throughout the Caucasus. I don't know whether she believed it or not, but she didn't question it. Anyway, I said that if she was able to get me the financials for Bazarduzu for the past three years, well, that would be worth something—a lot, five thousand dollars."

"And she bit."

"I had to convince her that the data she gave me would never get publicly released in such a way that Bazarduzu could trace the leak back to her, but five grand is a small fortune here. And she really did hate that she had to be a part of the whole sordid kickback system. She wasn't that hard to convince."

"Were you and her…"

"Were we what?"

Mark raised his eyebrows as he turned to face Cox.

"Was I screwing her?" Cox scratched his stomach. "No. She was like most of the Muslim girls around here—plenty flirty, but nothing more. Anyway, the day she disappeared was the day she told me she'd loaded Bazarduzu's financials onto a thumb drive. She was going to dead-drop the drive at a supermarket downtown, after eating dinner with her family that night. It wasn't unusual for her to do a little shopping after dinner, so she was keeping to the routine and all, nothing out of the ordinary."

"Did she make the drop?"

"If she did, it was gone by the time I got there."

"Did she even make it home that night?"

"Yeah, that's where she was when she called me."

"So she goes to work, copies the financials, goes home, calls you, goes out to make the dead drop, and then at some point while she's out, gets abducted and killed."

"That's probably the way it went down. I'm guessing she got caught copying the financials and they decided to kill her."

"Who's they?"

"I don't know. Thugs from Bazarduzu? Maybe the ex-com's men?"

"What about Nakhchivan?"

Cox stared at him a moment. "What about it?"

"In one of your reports you mentioned that Bazarduzu Construction did a big project in Nakhchivan last year."

"Ah, yeah. I guess I did. It was one of the things that came up when Aida and I were talking about what I could expect to see in the financials. She said Bazarduzu supposedly did some big road project there, but she suspected it might just be some big kick-back deal. Nakhchivan is a weird place, and Bazarduzu doesn't usually operate there, so I…well, I didn't think much of it, but I thought it deserved a mention." A pause, then, "Does that have anything to do with why she was killed? Why they're after me?"

Mark thought about Larry, and Katerina—he'd checked his e-mail this morning, but Keal still hadn't come up with any contact information for her—and wondered himself whether what had happened here in Ganja could possibly have anything to do with either of them.

"I don't know. Did you give Aida the five grand you promised her?"

"She disappeared before I could."

"Where is it?"

Cox gestured to an end table that had been pushed into a corner of his office to make room for the yoga mats. "Bottom drawer."

Mark yanked it out. Inside was a manila envelope.

"That's government money," said Cox, as Mark stuffed the envelope into his satchel. "I signed for that."

"You said Aida had a husband. And a kid."

"Daughter."

"Where do they live?"

"On the east side of town. You don't want to go there. That's part of why she was doing this, so she could move them out of that dump."

"I'll need an address."

Cox told him, adding, "Don't say I didn't warn you."

"Where do you live?" asked Mark.

"Alley off Nizami, west side of town. I got some stuff there still, but I took everything important. I'm not going back."

"Safest way to exfiltrate you is through the airport."

"What if they're watching it?"

"You could drive, but if someone's following you, the long trip to Baku would give them a lot more time to act. Ditto for the train. Flying is fast, and fast is usually less risky." Mark decided not to share that he'd opted to take the train from Baku last night, after fishing his Azeri alias out of the garbage and cutting his hair short and dying it black so that it matched his alias photos. Cox might not appreciate that different situations called for different strategies. He added, "I already bought you a one-way ticket to Baku—there's a flight that leaves in an hour and a half, you'll get there right before it takes off—and people from the embassy will meet you on arrival. Once you're in Baku, you'll be fine. In the meantime..." Mark reached into his satchel, pushed Katerina's painting to the side, confirmed that the two large tubes of maximum-strength Desitin that he'd bought at a pharmacy attached to the Baku Hyatt were still there, and fished out a sealed envelope. "Here." He tossed it to Cox. "Your new passport. There's a New York driver's license in there too."

One of Roger Davis's men had delivered the alias packet to him at the Hyatt.

Cox unsealed the envelope and opened the passport to the photo page. He stared at it for a second.

"Make yourself look like that guy," said Mark.

"Ah...OK."

It was a photo of Cox, but it had been altered so that he appeared clean-shaven and bald.

"Get ready." Mark took off his dark gray sport coat, tossed it to Cox, and then pulled a red tie and dark-blue collared shirt out of his satchel. "There's sunglasses in the inner pocket of my jacket. You'll put them on as we're leaving. And find some clean newspaper. Wad some up and put it in each of your cheeks. Not so much that you look like a hamster, just enough to change the shape of your face a little bit. Think subtle."

"I'm not an idiot."

"I didn't say you were."

"And I have good reason to be worried."

"I know you do."

"The people who are after me might have seen you come in. They might have made you."

"How many people come into this place over the course of a day?"

"I don't know. Maybe a hundred."

"Then they would've had to make me prior to when I showed up, and they didn't—I wasn't followed here. We'll leave when a group of students is leaving, I'll be your tail and make sure you're not being followed. We'll catch a cab by the bazaar. I wouldn't worry too much about getting out of here. If the people who killed your source had also wanted to kill you, then you'd already be dead. The bottle threat was designed to drive you out. Since the threat is working, there's no reason for them to interfere anymore."

"I didn't bring a razor."

Mark reached into his satchel again, pulled out a razor, and tossed it to Cox. "I did."

29
Baku, Azerbaijan

―――――――――○―――――――――

Orkhan had never been at odds with the defense minister; indeed, they'd worked well together on many projects over the years. So when he phoned, Orkhan didn't hesitate to have the call patched through to him.

"This matter, Orkhan, what do you know of it?"

The defense minister was a small man—but his deep voice was authoritative and gravelly.

Because he had nothing to hide, Orkhan answered with candor—he wasn't responsible for leaking the information about the Nakhchivan operation to the Russians and, although he'd launched an internal investigation, he doubted very much that anyone who worked for him was.

"And you?" asked Orkhan. "What have you learned?"

The defense minister spoke at length about the internal investigation he'd launched; nothing he said contradicted what Orkhan had already learned from his spies in the defense ministry.

"There is one thing I did want to ask you about," said the defense minister. "And—well, I'm afraid it is a matter of some sensitivity, which is why the president asked that I be the one to call you."

"Oh?"

"I'm afraid it involves your daughter." After an uncomfortable pause, the defense minister added, "A minor issue to be sure, but… you know as well as I that your daughter has consorted with political opponents of the president, taken part in demonstrations—"

"She now lives in France. That is no longer an issue."

"Recently it has come to the president's attention that she may be thinking of renouncing her citizenship. Is this true?"

"The president ordered you to spy on my daughter."

"The president holds you and your family in high esteem. It is a mark of honor that he would order such protection for your daughter."

"No doubt." Orkhan was not shocked by the revelation. Indeed, after the defense minister's son had threatened a bartender at the Baku Hilton with a loaded pistol, the president had ordered Orkhan to watch the young miscreant to make sure he was actually attending the drug treatment program in Dubai that he'd been admitted to. So Orkhan had little cause for grievance now.

"In any case—"

"She is an impulsive girl who changes her mind and her ideology frequently. No permanent decision has been made and, in fact, none can be made for several years—as you may know, French law prohibits it. And I would also add that if I am to be judged on the actions of my progeny, it is only fair that others be so judged as well."

"No doubt, no doubt," said the defense minister. "I only mention the issue of citizenship because it coincides with another issue regarding your daughter."

"And what issue might that be?"

"As I'm sure you're aware, her current employer is a Russian."

"She is a student at the Sorbonne. Because of late she has refused to take money from her parents, twice a week she earns pocket change by helping to care for a two-year-old child. And yes, I am aware that the parents of this child are Russian."

"And I'm sure you're aware of the fact that this Russian is a man of some means."

"Usmanov is a man of means," said Orkhan, referring to the richest man in Russia. "This man is an ant."

"Still, he has ties to the Kremlin."

The hypocrisy of the insinuation was breathtaking, thought Orkhan. Of all the major government ministers, he counted himself as the least likely to be influenced by the Russians. Indeed, he was one of the few ministers who hadn't grown up speaking Russian as his first language. Even now, in private, many of the ministers still spoke Russian to each other—it was like a secret code, a holdover from when the Soviets ruled, a way of affirming to themselves that they were still part of the educated elite, the intelligentsia. Russian, it was rumored, had even been the president's first language.

"Ties," said Orkhan, "which were severed in the 1990s! He's lived in exile ever since. He's a small player who now makes his money facilitating the export of nickel from Russia to Germany."

The defense minister sighed. "You have fully vetted this man?"

"Of course."

"And you are certain that your daughter is not being used by the Russians, and will never be used, as leverage against you? To influence your actions?"

I will remember this, thought Orkhan. "Absolutely certain."

"I will convey your certainty regarding this matter to the president."

30
Ganja, Azerbaijan

———————o———————

Rust-laden water, spilling out of dilapidated gutters and ruined downspouts, had stained the gray stucco tenements that lined the muddy street on which Aida Tagiyev had lived.

Mark could tell that, fifty years ago, all the ramshackle balconies that extended out from the tenements had been identical, but now each was unique in the way each scrap-wood-walled shack in the favelas of Rio, or shantytown hut in Mumbai, was unique. Some were enclosed with old plywood and topped with rusted metal roofs, transforming them into an extra bedroom; others had been covered with paneling, or bricked in. From most, laundry lines hung like bright bunting, suspended between rusting pulleys.

Mark stopped outside a building that had the number 11873 scrawled on it in faded black marker—the address Cox had given him. Out front, a wrinkled old man sat on a wooden chair, in the shade of a straggly apple tree, listening to a soccer game on a small radio. He looked drowsy, but cocked his head when he saw Mark approaching. When he smiled, he revealed a mouthful of teeth—top and bottom—that were solid gold.

Mark extended his right hand. The Azeri responded in kind. His fingers were swollen and calloused. Half-moons of dirt lay under each fingernail. "Hello, my friend," Mark said cheerfully in Azeri. "And how are Kapaz faring today?"

Kapaz was the local soccer team.

"They lead. One to zero. Karim has scored."

As he continued to hold the old man's hand, Mark said, "I'm looking for Rasul Tagiyev, the husband of Aida."

Mark spoke Azeri like a native, albeit one who'd grown up in Baku. He was also dressed for the part—wearing a high-end Turkish-made coat and tie that he'd just bought downtown. It was true his facial features—fair skin, dark brown hair, deep-set light brown eyes, slightly droopy eyelids—were more Russian than Azeri, but after many decades of Russians and Azeris intermarrying, they wouldn't instantly mark him as a foreigner. His left hand clutched a box of rosewater-flavored Turkish delight candies.

"Do you have a cigarette?"

Mark released the old man's hand and patted his sport coat. "Oh, but I wish I did. I gave them up three months ago. Had I one now, it would be yours."

The old man shrugged and adjusted the tuner dial on his radio.

Mark knew the street address for Aida Tagiyev, but Cox hadn't known the apartment number—he'd never visited her home.

Mark asked, "Would you know if Rasul Tagiyev is receiving guests?" He added, "I worked with his wife at Bazarduzu Construction." He held up the box of Turkish delight. "I've come to pay my respects."

Mark figured there was a chance that the old man was a plant. But he'd checked up on Bazarduzu Construction. They employed nearly a thousand people in Ganja alone. So it was entirely possible, likely even, that people from the company would be stopping by. If the old man had been paid to watch the building, all he'd report was that a colleague of Aida Tagiyev's had come to pay his respects.

The old man looked Mark over, then shrugged again. "Apartment 214. He is home, I believe."

"Thank you, my friend." Mark patted the Azeri's shoulder. "Thank you."

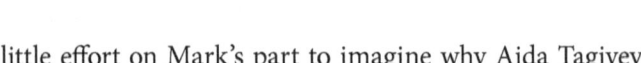

It took little effort on Mark's part to imagine why Aida Tagiyev might have been receptive to taking money from the CIA.

All of the tenement's first-floor windows were protected with jury-rigged metal bars. The ground-floor hallway was cold and damp, and smelled of mold. Though the tiled floors had been recently swept, the ceiling paint was peeling where water had leaked in. What little light there was seeped in from a narrow barred prisonlike window on the first stairwell landing.

The door to apartment 214, however, had been painted a bright green. He knocked—a bit too loudly, he realized, when a moment later an infant begin to cry.

A short, slender man opened the door as far as the security chain would allow. "Yes?"

The single word was spoken with suspicion.

Mark introduced himself as Adil Orlov, a name he'd chosen because Adil suggested Azeri roots, which would explain his fluency in Azeri, while Orlov implied a Russian heritage, which would explain his face. "Would you be Rasul Tagiyev?"

Thick, dark eyebrows accentuated dark troubled eyes.

"I am."

Mark flashed a deferential smile and explained that he worked for Bazarduzu Construction, in the employee benefits division. "I was so sorry to hear of what happened to Aida." And he was sorry. Rasul, Aida, their child…they'd done nothing to deserve this.

Mark held up the box of Turkish delight but it was clear it wouldn't fit through the narrow opening between the door and the frame.

Rasul Tagiyev's eyes began to fill with tears.

"May I come in?" asked Mark.

"Someone already came to collect her things."

"From Bazarduzu?"

"Of course."

"What things?"

"Her computer, her badge. They came yesterday."

"I see. But I am from a different department at Bazarduzu. I am not here to collect anything."

"Aida"— He wiped a tear from his cheek with the back of his hand —"never spoke of anyone named Adil."

"I am told she was a good accountant, but in truth, we did not know each other. I am here because there are financial matters I must discuss with you regarding your wife's estate. Did you know she opted to purchase our company's life insurance policy when she joined the firm?"

Two seconds passed. Mark guessed that Aida Tagiyev had possessed no such insurance; few Azeris did. But it was not outside the realm of possibility.

The baby was still crying in the background, which made Mark wonder whether Lila was awake, and what it would be like to have to raise her in such a place—he envisioned himself pushing a stroller down the rutted street, seeing her clothes drying on lines hung from scrap-wood balconies. What would the schools be like? Terrible, he imagined. He pushed the thought out of his head, and said, "I'm so sorry to have disturbed your child."

Rasul was staring intently at Mark. "You said you were from Bazarduzu?"

"Yes."

He undid the lock. "Come in. I will make us some tea."

———————o———————

Always it was tea, thought Mark as he sat waiting in the cramped living room. He liked to think of himself as a patient man, but that image of himself was always tested when he visited an Azeri for the first time. They prided themselves on being hospitable—the most hospitable people in the world!—and hospitality inevitably involved taking a long time to prepare tea.

As he waited, Mark studied what he could of the apartment. The walls in the living room had been painted a pale green and the furniture looked new. Two handcrafted lutes—one long-necked, one short—were displayed on stands in the corner. Floor-to-ceiling shelving lined one wall. In the center, at eye level, was a cranberry-colored crystal vase etched with a starburst pattern. He stood to examine it.

"Beautiful," Mark said—quietly, so as not to wake the baby again—when Rasul came out with the tea. Gesturing to the vase, he said, "The quality of Czech crystal can't be compared to what they make today."

Back in the Soviet days, Czechoslovakia had been known for making the best crystal in Eastern Europe.

"A wedding gift. From my parents."

"They live in Ganja?"

"Baku."

Rasul set a tray with pear-shaped clear glasses and a teapot down on a low table. His hand trembled as he poured the tea. Also on the tray was a bowl of sour cherry jam, two baklava pastries, and a Snickers bar that had been sliced into bite-sized pieces.

"Thank you." Mark took a sip of tea. It had been prepared the Azeri way—light—instead of the dark Turkish method that he preferred. "Perfect. Do you have any family in Ganja?"

"No."

"And Aida. She was from Baku as well?"

"Yes. We moved last year. For her job. It was supposed to be temporary."

"Will you now move back?"

Rasul shrugged and stared blankly down at his hands, looking as though he just wanted to be left alone but was too polite to say as much.

"Please," said Mark. "Sit a moment."

Rasul sat down on a chair opposite the couch.

Mark ate a slice of Snickers, then said, "About this life insurance. As I said, your wife took out a policy when she signed up with the firm. At Bazarduzu, we consider our employees to be family. We grieved when we heard of your loss. And we want you to know how much we valued your wife's work. We want to do everything we can to help."

"There has been no body, so no funeral, no proper burial, no..." Rasul's voice trailed off. With his right hand he began to use his thumb to touch each joint on each of his fingers, pausing briefly at each joints; it was a habit used by some Muslims, akin to using rosary beads to keep track of prayers. A minute later, he said, "I don't know what to do."

"No body?"

"I saw her at the police station. I identified her, we spoke of funeral arrangements. Then later that day they said she had tested positive for tuberculosis, but she never had tuberculosis, she was healthy."

"Did they show you the results of the test?"

"No, they just said that it was positive and that they were worried about contamination because it was a bad kind so they had to cremate her...I was told it was already done, and that they would bring me the ashes, but then...then nothing."

Mark knew tuberculosis was a problem in Azerbaijan, and that people who weren't visibly sick with the disease could still be carriers. But even if Aida had tested positive, immediate cremation would have been unusual because it was forbidden by the Quran. There was an exception, if burial could potentially cause the mass spread of disease, but drug-resistant TB in a corpse shouldn't have triggered such an exception.

She'd been cremated, Mark concluded, because her body had been evidence. He was reminded of how quickly Larry had been embalmed.

"The police haven't come here?"

"No. There was no reason for her to have been walking on the road to the mountains. I know the police think she was having an affair. But she wasn't."

"Did you tell the police this?"

"Yes, yes, of course, but they said there's nothing they can do, that it was a traffic accident, and she had a disease, and that is that. Is there anything *you* can do? I would at least like her ashes."

Mark sighed. The CIA owed Rasul Tagiyev for what his wife had done for the Agency. But it seemed clear that the police were either in on the killing, or were being pressured to cover it up. "I wish that I could help."

"Please."

"I don't have any influence with the police."

"Bazarduzu, it is a powerful company. They might have influence."

"If I could help you, I would. But I can't. You could try to call Bazarduzu directly. Or maybe write a letter to the president. He might be able to help, but I can tell you with certainty that I cannot. I'm sorry. I wish it were otherwise."

Rasul frowned as he nodded.

Mark said, "Now, about that life insurance."

"Honestly, I wasn't aware she'd taken out a policy."

"It was for five thousand dollars. I was authorized by the company to bring your payment to you in cash. The company knows that this must be a trying time for you and your child, both emotionally *and* financially."

Mark reached into his satchel and retrieved the money Cox had given him. He considered also giving Rasul one of the two tubes of Desitin, but decided that would be weird, and anyway, he wanted to save both for Daria.

Rasul's hand came up to his mouth. "This money. You intend to *give* it to me?"

"It's yours. Your wife designated you and your daughter as the only beneficiaries. The one thing I would suggest is that you accompany me to a bank and that I officially sign the money over to you there. Because once I sign it over to you, then it becomes your responsibility. If it were to be stolen, if any of your neighbors…" Mark let his voice trail off. Rasul knew better than anyone that he didn't live in the safest of neighborhoods. "To avoid all chance of that, I recommend that the transfer be made at a bank. Do you have one you prefer?"

"We keep an account at Ganjabank."

"That would be fine."

"Now? You wish to go now?"

"I wish to do as you wish, Mr. Tagiyev. I am available now, or if now is not convenient for you, I am more than happy to arrange to meet you at the time of your choosing."

"I'd have to take the baby with me."

"Of course. This is no problem."

"Then I can go now."

———————o———————

Mark accompanied a bewildered Rasul Tagiyev and his daughter to the downtown branch of Ganjabank, waited until a bank officer emerged to usher them into a back room, then thrust the money at the young man.

"Here," said Mark. "You don't need me to set up your account. Good luck. I am so sorry for your loss."

"But…" Rasul was flustered. With one hand he held his daughter, with the other he took the envelope. "…don't I need to sign—"

"The relevant papers will be mailed to you shortly. In the meantime, your bank deposit receipt will serve as proof that the transfer from Bazarduzu to you was made."

With that, Mark left the bank, bought a pack of cigarettes—Winstons, like Cox had been smoking—and hailed a cab. Minutes later, he was staring once again at the tenement house where Rasul lived. The old Azeri was still out front.

"Rasul has forgotten the baby's bottle. Can you blame him?" Before the old man could answer, Mark produced the pack of cigarettes and matches. "A gift. For giving me directions earlier."

Mark bounded up the stairs so that by the time he got to the second floor he was breathing heavily. Work smart, he told himself, glancing both ways down the hall. Get in and get out quickly, minimize the risk, and be prepared to run like hell if you have to.

He noted with satisfaction that it took him less than a minute to pick the lock with the improvised set of tools he'd made just before buying the Turkish delight—a thin triple rake and a hook pick, both made from bobby pins and electric tape; thicker versions of the same made from the steel wire used in binder clips; and a tension bar made from a bent pair of tweezers. As a desk-bound station chief, his tradecraft skills had started to atrophy, but they'd grown considerably sharper of late.

In the enclosed balcony, which extended out from the kitchen and was being used as a pantry, he opened the one double-hung window that looked out onto the street; he didn't relish the thought of dropping from the second floor to the ground, but he'd done such a thing before, and wanted to be sure he had an emergency avenue of escape, should it come to that.

He checked his watch—five past two. He'd give himself ten minutes, any more than that and he'd be pushing his luck.

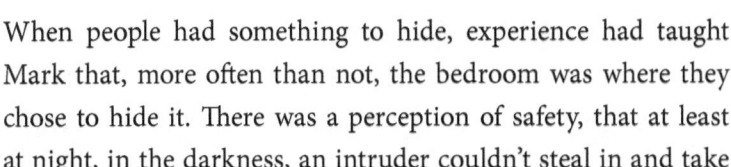

When people had something to hide, experience had taught Mark that, more often than not, the bedroom was where they chose to hide it. There was a perception of safety, that at least at night, in the darkness, an intruder couldn't steal in and take the item without being detected. So it was in Rasul and Aida Tagiyev's bedroom that he began his search.

He could still detect what he perceived to be the scent of Aida, or at least the perfume she'd worn. The smell of rose petals was in the closet, where her dresses hung, and inside the dresser, where her T-shirts and jeans and undergarments were neatly folded. It was a smell distinct from the earthy smell of Rasul's clothes, or the diaper smell of the child.

He searched the closet, under the squeaky mattress, under and inside dresser drawers, behind the mirror that hung on the wall, between the stacks of unused diapers, underneath the plastic bag that lined the garbage bin... He worked methodically, mentally dividing the bedroom into quadrants and searching everything in one quadrant before moving on to the next. When he came upon a small Canon pocket camera that was stashed inside Aida's rhinestone-encrusted jewelry box, he thought maybe he'd found what he was looking for. The SD memory card inside it would be where a spy might think to hide files. But when he slotted the card into the external adapter that was connected to his iPad, it was blank.

It took him four minutes just to finish the bedroom. Another three to search most of the kitchen—in the freezer, underneath a cookie tin, under the small microwave, above the cabinets...in all the drawers. At this rate, he knew he wouldn't have nearly enough time to conduct a thorough search of the rest of the apartment. Rasul could arrive at any moment. He glanced out the window above the kitchen sink. The old man out front was gone.

Think.

Mark reasoned that, if it was here, it would be hidden in a place where neither Rasul nor anyone else would be likely to stumble upon it. So what in the apartment would Rasul be unlikely to use? Mark had already gone through all of Aida's personal effects in the bedroom, but now he searched through the cleaning supplies under the sink—hell, maybe Rasul helped clean, but maybe he didn't—and inside her winter boots and jackets in the closet near the front door, and...

Fifteen minutes after he'd broken into the apartment, he found it—a small unlabeled thumb drive—in the bathroom, inside an over-the-counter medication bottle for menstrual cramping. He slotted it into a USB port on his external adapter and a single Excel file showed up.

He breathed a sigh of relief. It was as he'd hoped.

All that Raymond Cox had told Mark about Aida had suggested she was reliable and organized. The type of person who almost certainly would have been sure to back up any important files in her possession. Mark had been a bit worried when Rasul mentioned that a representative from Bazarduzu had come by to collect her laptop, but reasoned that she would have been unlikely to store such an incriminating file there. Which left an external memory source, or online. And if it had been stored on a memory drive, well, the only place she'd visited between work and where she was murdered was home.

He'd been hoping that whoever had killed Aida had either been too careless or too stupid to think to search her apartment for it. They had been.

31

───────○───────

Mark exited the same way he had entered the building, then ducked into a maze of alleys that cut between the tenements. Once he was sure no one was following him, he made his way to a main road and hailed a cab. From the back seat, he scrolled through the Excel file.

All the text was in Azeri. The heading was labeled BAZARDUZU CONSTRUCTION: ANNUAL FINANCIAL STATEMENT AND SUPPLEMENTARY INFORMATION. Under that was a table of contents that listed BALANCE SHEETS, STATEMENT OF EARNINGS, STATEMENT OF CASH FLOWS, and SUPPLEMENTAL STATEMENTS. Listed as a subset under SUPPLEMENTAL STATEMENTS was GENERAL AND ADMINISTRATIVE EXPENSES, CONTRACTS COMPLETED, CONTRACTS IN PROGRESS...

The total document, including the supplemental statements, was over two hundred pages.

He scrolled down, skimming over each section. ASSETS, CURRENT LIABILITIES, CONTRACT REVENUE... most of the firm's income for the prior year had come from projects in and around Ganja that were listed with considerable specificity in the supplemental statements: repairs to a bridge that spanned the Ganja River, the refurbishing of the train station, road repaving all over greater Ganja. There was one line item, however, that accounted for over forty million manats—almost thirty percent of Bazarduzu's gross revenue from the prior year—that wasn't backed up by *any* supplemental information.

That line item was NAKHCHIVAN.

"Sir," said the cab driver. "We're here."

Mark looked up. They'd reached the downtown.

He paid the driver, walked to a bench opposite a thirty-foot-tall photograph of the president of Azerbaijan that adorned the Stalin-baroque city hall, and spent the next hour searching the rest of the document for more references either to, or related to, Nakhchivan. There were none.

The only useful thing that he did find—under GENERAL AND ADMINISTRATIVE EXPENSES—was a supplemental payroll statement, which linked to a payroll report, which in turn listed every employee of Bazarduzu Construction, their titles and compensation for the prior year, the amount withheld for taxes, their home addresses, their hire dates, and their state social insurance numbers.

Jackpot, he thought, as he scanned the payroll for someone high enough in the hierarchy to know about the Nakhchivan project. Out of over three thousand employees, only four made in excess of a hundred thousand manats a year: the owner of the company, who was also the local ex-com; the vice president; the chief financial officer; and the chief engineer. Between them, the four men had pocketed just shy of twenty million manats the previous year. Most of that twenty million had gone to the ex-com, but targeting him would be too risky, so Mark looked up the addresses of the remaining three.

The chief engineer, he noted, didn't live too far away.

32

———————◦———————

In central Ganja, to the west of the Abbas Mosque, stood what looked like a clone of all the recently restored turn-of-the-century buildings in Baku.

Mark found his way to the back of it, picked the lock on a windowless gray metal door, and let himself into a utility room that housed electric circuit breakers and a row of new-looking hot water heaters. A door off the utility room led to a central hall that ran lengthwise down the building.

Mark couldn't help but compare this place to the tenement he'd just left. Here there were decadently high ceilings, crystal chandeliers, and textured wallpaper imprinted with fleurs-de-lis. A ruby-red silk carpet runner had been unfurled down the center of the parquet floor. An elevator with brass doors beckoned, but Mark took the stairs to the third floor.

From inside apartment 301, he heard what he thought was the faint sound of a television. He put his ear to the door. Definitely a television, and someone was channel surfing. It was just after three o'clock in the afternoon; he'd hoped the chief engineer of Bazarduzu Construction would still be at work. With the apartment occupied, he reconsidered his options, then hiked up to the third floor and stood outside apartment 401, which lay directly above 301. This time, when he put his ear to the door he heard nothing, so he ventured to knock.

No one answered.

Mark pulled out his lock picks, cursed under his breath after a minute of unsuccessful fiddling, bent his thick hook pick to a more acute angle, and finally got the door open. The place he stepped into made his apartment back in Bishkek look like a hovel by comparison. Hand-knotted Turkmen carpets lay on glossy parquet floors, stainless-steel appliances sparkled in the kitchen, recessed lighting illuminated black granite countertops…

"Hello?" he called in Azeri. "Maintenance here!"

Upon receiving no reply, he did a quick search of the five bedrooms—there was no easy emergency egress; he'd just have to risk it—before turning his attention to the toilet in the master bathroom. After unrolling a large fistful of toilet paper, he used a toilet brush to jam the paper into the drain at the bottom of the bowl, lifted up the cover on top of the tank, and then tinkered with the flapper valve so that the toilet wouldn't stop running.

On his way out of the apartment, he made sure to leave the door unlocked.

Ten minutes later, a woman inside the chief engineer's apartment began to cry out in alarm.

Mark listened from the stairwell, then backed down to the ground-floor landing when he heard the door to 301 swing open. A woman ran into the stairwell—on her way, Mark assumed, to investigate the source of the leak. When he heard her open the door to the third floor hall, he bounded up the stairs and let himself into the chief engineer's apartment; in her rush, the woman had left the door cracked open.

"Hello?" he called out, just in case anyone was still inside. "I'm here about the leak."

The place was laid out the same as the apartment above, so he ran down the hall to what he knew to be the first of five bedrooms, determined that it was just used for storage, and then ran to the next, which was set up as an exercise room.

When he poked his head into the master bedroom, he heard water dripping from the attached bathroom. After taking a second to study a photograph of a man he guessed was the engineer, posing with a middle-aged woman wearing stiletto heels, a silver tunic, and a beehive hairdo—likely the wife—he ducked into the adjacent bedroom, which was being used as a home office. The chief engineer was a tidy man, and it didn't take Mark more than a minute to find a bank statement, filed in a cabinet to the left of the desk.

He snapped close-up photos of the statement, then replaced it, just as he heard footsteps and a woman's voice.

"It just won't stop, it just won't stop! Vugar isn't answering, I don't know what to do!"

Mark slowly closed the door to the office, so that by the time the woman passed by on the way to the master bedroom, it was shut. With his ear to the door he listened.

"No, you need to come now! It's not a little leak, it's ruining the ceiling!"

Mark had been counting on the woman taking some time to deal with the toilet—she could have plunged it, or turned off the shutoff valve, or lifted the tank lid and reset the flapper...stopping a toilet from running wasn't rocket science.

He cracked the door open just an inch. She was standing in the middle of the master bedroom, looking toward the attached bathroom, phone in hand, cataloguing—instead of trying to stop—the damage the water leak was causing.

It was the same woman Mark had observed in the photo, but now she was wearing a green velour tracksuit, and her shoulder-length hair was a mess. Mark wanted to shout at her *go back upstairs and deal with the damn toilet.* But after a minute, she just clicked off her phone and sat down on the king bed in the master bathroom, staring helplessly at the bathroom.

He risked opening the office door a little wider. Although she was fixated on the water cascading down from the bathroom ceiling, she'd see him if she turned her head ninety degrees. He thought for a moment; if she *did* see him, he'd claim to be here about the leak. As it happened, she didn't turn, and the sound of falling water masked the sound of his footsteps as he retreated down the hall. He left the apartment, then jogged down three flights of stairs and out the back of the building.

Once he was back on the street, threading his way through the slow-walking sidewalk crowd, Mark used a prepaid cell to call John Decker.

"Hey, how's it going, buddy?" Decker sounded as cheerful as ever. And like he was in the middle of eating a sandwich.

"I need you to make a wire transfer. You got a pen?"

"Ah, hold on." Some chewing, a swallow, then, "So how ya been? Good and all?"

"Yeah, I'm fine. The transfer's gonna be for ten grand."

"Shit, I knew I had a pen around here somewhere."

"I've got extras in the bottom left drawer."

Some rustling and banging, then, "Got it. Shoot."

"It's the International Bank of Azerbaijan, Ganja branch." Holding his phone in his right hand and his iPad in his left, Mark read off the account and routing numbers from the engineer's bank statement, which he'd enlarged on the screen.

"When do you need this?"

"Now."

"You got it, boss."

"Send it from our UK Barclay's overflow account, the one that we set up with just a number. I don't want this traced back to our Bishkek operation."

"Roger that."

33

––––––––––––––––⚬––––––––––––––––

At four that afternoon, Mark observed the chief engineer of Bazarduzu Construction hurrying down the street towards his apartment, carrying a briefcase in his right hand. His eyes looked angry. His thin gray hair was unruly.

"As we discussed," said Mark to his cab driver.

Mark stepped out of the cab and bumped into the engineer, as though he hadn't been watching where he was going. As he did so, he said, "Check your bank account."

"What?"

"I made a deposit today. It should cover the cost of the damages."

"Who are you?"

"A friend."

Mark walked back to the cab, leaving the engineer standing in front of his building, staring at Mark, a confused expression on his face. As the cab driver pulled away, he handed a camera back to Mark.

"Where to, sir?"

Mark slipped him a hundred dollar bill. "End of the street is fine."

––––––––––––––––⚬––––––––––––––––

Mark bought a Turkish coffee and loitered in the park opposite the engineer's apartment, eyeing the people going in and out. After a half hour—more than enough time, he figured, for the engineer to have checked his bank balance—he got up off his bench, intending to go have a chat with the man. But as he was crossing the street, a guy in a Bazarduzu Construction truck pulled up. Guessing that he was there to inspect the damage caused by the overflowing toilet, and that the engineer would be occupied with that for a while, Mark bought another coffee and returned to his bench. As he waited, his thoughts turned back to Daria and Lila. If the engineer knew why Aida Tagiyev had been killed, and what this whole Nakhchivan business was about, Mark thought he might be able to wrap everything up tonight and catch a flight from Baku to Bishkek as early as tomorrow morning.

After an hour, the guy who'd pulled up in the Bazarduzu Construction truck left, prompting Mark to head once again towards the engineer's apartment. This time, however, his plans were upended when he observed the engineer and his wife leaving their building on foot.

Mark, seeing them before they saw him, turned back to the park, and then shadowed the couple to a crowded, dimly lit restaurant where the walls had been decorated with lots of plastic red-leafed maple-tree branches, and an advertisement for Xirdalan beer hung above the bar. In the open kitchen in back, two young men in white aprons and tall white chef hats were cooking *lahmajoon*—the Turkish version of pizza—in a wood-fired oven. Between them, a buxom woman with flour-covered hands fed bread dough through a double roller.

Mark took a seat at the bar and ordered a half-liter bottle of Xirdalan.

"And I'll buy drinks for the couple dining in the back." Mark gestured with his head and put a twenty-manat note down on the bar. "Whatever they want."

The bartender, a slender, dark-complexioned Azeri woman, shrugged. "OK."

The engineer looked up after the bartender delivered the offer. Mark met his gaze, then nodded when the engineer appeared to recognize him.

The offer of a drink was declined, but minutes later, the engineer approached Mark at the bar.

"Who are you?"

"You checked your bank account?"

"Why would you do such a thing?"

The tone was accusing, incredulous.

"I want to show you something." Mark pulled his iPad out of his satchel, opened it on the bar, and clicked on the Excel file. Mark slid the iPad over. "Take a look."

The engineer's eyes widened, and his nostrils flared, as he examined the screen. "How did you get this?"

"Of course, this is just a backup. The original is safe with my colleagues. You made three hundred and sixty-seven thousand manats last year, I see."

The engineer smiled weakly at his wife, who was staring at them from across the restaurant. "You stole this information, I presume?" Without waiting for an answer, he added, "Do you know who I am?"

Although the engineer spoke in Azeri, he did so in a stiff, formal tone that came across as haughty, the way a nonnative speaker might. Educated abroad, Mark concluded, probably in England.

"I know you're a Javadov."

Javadov was the last name of the local ex-com.

"I am."

"You asked whether I stole this. I didn't. You did, though. And then you sold it to me. For the ten thousand dollars that you see in your account."

"I see," said the engineer calmly.

"Do you?"

"I see that you are attempting to blackmail me. It won't work, of course. In fact, I think you would be wise—"

Mark opened his iPad and a photo appeared. "Here we are together, meeting outside your apartment, just after ten thousand dollars was transferred to your account. That's when you passed me the information."

"You embarrass yourself," said the engineer, but he looked stricken.

"Four days ago, an employee of Bazarduzu Construction—Aida Tagiyev—was murdered. Perhaps you heard of her death."

"No."

Mark watched for signs that would suggest the engineer was lying; he saw none.

"She was killed because of the information you see on my computer. Because she tried to steal it and sell it. Now, consider what might happen if it gets out that *you* gave me this information—"

"This girl. Who killed her?"

"Who do you think?"

"I couldn't begin to guess. And no one will believe that I gave you this information. Do you understand that? I am a Javadov."

The clear implication being that his relationship with the ex-com would insulate him from suspicion. Mark wasn't buying it—people in power were usually the *most* suspicious of family members. Kings weren't deposed by peasants, they were deposed by their kin.

"What I understand is that if you don't help me, I will call Bazarduzu and offer to sell this financial information back to them. When I do this, the ex-com will have his men trace the call to my hotel. When they search my room, they will find copies of reports I've written, detailing how I recruited you to spy for me."

"Spy for you," repeated the engineer. "Ridiculous. And in this fantasy, who exactly might you be that I would agree to do this?"

Ignoring the question, Mark said, "There will be photographic evidence and bank receipts. Now, you might be thinking, you can just go to the ex-com now, to neutralize whatever evidence his men might find against you. But know that this photograph of us together"—Mark pointed to the iPad—"is just one of many. I have been following you for several weeks. When you had dinner two Saturdays ago at the Elnur, I was there standing behind you as you walked in, when you picked up your shirts from the cleaners on Vagif Street three weeks ago, I was there, close enough for us to have been talking. All that has been documented by people I work with, photographed, so I could report to my superiors that I was making progress in recruiting you."

The engineer had used a debit card tied to his bank account to make several purchases over the past month, and those charges had shown up on his bank statement.

"I don't think…" The engineer shook his head as though angry, but now he was clearly unnerved. His voice trailed off.

"I'll add another five thousand dollars to your account. But that's my final offer." Carrot and stick. "You have a choice to make."

"I don't want your money."

"I know. Bazarduzu completed a project in Nakhchivan last year. I need to know what that project was. When you give me what I need, all this unpleasantness goes away. No one will know that we ever spoke."

The engineer cast another glance at his wife, looking as though he hoped she'd come to his rescue. He looked down at the bar, and then scratched his head.

"We don't know each other."

"True."

"I can't trust you."

"I work for a respected foreign intelligence agency."

"Who? What agency?"

"And while sometimes the methods of my agency are unpleasant, we don't stay in business by turning our backs on people who help us. If you help me, I will protect you. As I've protected you tonight by making certain I wasn't followed here."

A minute passed.

"I only know a little about the Nakhchivan project," said the engineer.

"I'll take a little."

"What happens then?"

"Then I destroy any evidence of collusion between us and I go away. Permanently."

"This isn't fair."

"I know."

Another minute passed. Then, "It was an airstrip. We built an airstrip. "

"Civilian?"

"I don't think so. It was in a…a remote location."

"Where?"

"Close to the border with Iran and Armenia, but not so close that it could be seen from the border."

"Do you have GPS coordinates?"

"No."

"How do I get there?"

"Go to Unus."

"What's that?"

"A town. There's only one road going north out of Unus. You'll eventually see a fence. It will be guarded. The entire zone is guarded."

"What are they using that airstrip for? What kind of planes fly there? Military ones?"

"I don't know."

"I don't believe you," said Mark.

"It doesn't matter whether you believe me or not. I still don't know."

"You guys got paid a lot of money just to build an airstrip."

The engineer shrugged.

"Why was Bazarduzu chosen to build it?" asked Mark.

"Whoever was paying us didn't want to use any of the big firms in Baku, they would have attracted too much attention."

"Who was paying you?"

"I don't know."

"Guess."

"That was above my pay grade. Someone who needed an airstrip."

Mark clicked open a window on his iPad, revealing recording software. "I will keep this tape I have made of our conversation—"

The engineer let loose an insult that, loosely translated, meant *fuck your ancestors.*

"—until I receive confirmation that the information you have given me is correct. But I must ask you. Is all the information you have given me correct? Think carefully. Your life might depend upon the answer you give."

The engineer glanced at the iPad, looking as though he were tempted to smash it. Mark slid it off the table and into his satchel.

The two men stared at each other for a long moment. Eventually, the engineer said, "It's not near Unus. Go to the town of Ordubad. If you drive north out of Ordubad you will find it."

"Thank you, my friend. The tape I made will be destroyed, along with the rest of the information that might incriminate you, when I confirm this to be true. In the meantime, I will keep all of it safe, as promised. Bazarduzu will not learn of our agreement."

In actuality, Mark would delete the file from his iPad as soon as he left the restaurant, just to be safe. He never kept anything on it or his phone that could be used to incriminate himself or any of his sources. And he frequently restored both to their original store-bought settings, permanently erasing all new files in the process.

"You're not my friend."

"No, I suppose I'm not. Look for the extra five thousand dollars tomorrow."

34

———○———

Mark found a Wi-Fi hotspot at an Internet café and called Kaufman's secure line. "Raymond Cox should be in Baku by now. Davis is going to be looking for a report from me. Can you deal with him?"

"Done. Any idea yet on who killed Cox's source?"

"Lots of ideas, no answers."

"No sign of the Russian involvement you suspected in Tbilisi?"

"This has more of a local feel to it. I'm guessing security was far tighter at Bazarduzu than Cox and his source knew—probably because of whatever's going on in Nakhchivan—and they got caught as a result."

"So the only link between Bowlan's death and Cox's source, assuming there really is a link, is still Nakhchivan."

"That appears to be the case."

"What *is* going on in Nakhchivan?"

Ignoring the question, Mark asked, "Why were you so eager to have someone on the ground at the Russian base in South Ossetia? Why not just continue to have the NRO monitor it?"

The National Reconnaissance Office was the intelligence agency that ran the US spy satellites.

"Like I told you—we wanted better intel on the makeup of the ground units."

"Yeah, I got that. But I wouldn't think that a little extra activity, at one base, in a place like South Ossetia, would have been a cause for much alarm."

A long pause, then, "We've also detected unusual Russian troop movements elsewhere."

"Where elsewhere?" Mark added, "If it's genuinely not relevant, don't tell me." He was comfortable operating on a need-to-know basis—often it was safer that way.

"At their bases in Armenia. And Dagestan." Armenia and the Russian-owned territory of Dagestan both bordered Azerbaijan.

"When was this?"

"Past two weeks. The movement followed a pattern similar to the movement in South Ossetia—never too many men or too much matériel entering the bases at one time, but over several weeks it was substantial. And the movement's all been one way—into the bases, not out."

"What does the NSA say?"

"They got nothing, yet."

"Anyone ask the Russians for clarification?"

"Hell, no. We're not going to let them know we're onto them. What did you find out about Nakhchivan?"

Mark told him about the airstrip. When Kaufman started in with the questions, Mark said, "That's really all I know right now," but added, "I'm going to check it out tomorrow."

Sounding genuinely pleased and grateful, Kaufman said, "Fantastic, Sava. Fantastic."

"But I wouldn't mind having the chance to review some satellite data before I do."

Kaufman agreed to look into it ASAP. Mark was about to end the conversation, when Kaufman added, "By the way, I just got a cable from the guy who runs Tbilisi station. Says you've got one of his men trying to dredge up contact info for some woman who might have met with Bowlan, before he died?"

Mark paused, then said, "Ah, yeah…that's right."

"What's *that* all about?"

"I found…something that belonged to this woman. In the room where Larry died."

"Huh. And who is this woman?"

"I'd rather not get into it."

"I'd rather you would."

"Just tell Tbilisi to run the name."

"They already have. Nothing comes up for someone with that birthdate in Tbilisi."

"They run it through the records bureau and people at the state pension system?"

"Yeah. Tbilisi station sent a cable to me because they wanted to know whether to blow you off from here on out, or whether we should ask Moscow station to try to do a wider search for this woman in Russia, given that she was a Russian."

"Do the wider search."

"What did you find that belonged to her?"

"It's a long story, Ted. When and if I find out anything that you need to know, I'll tell you."

"Sava—"

"Please, Ted. Just do this for me."

Part Five

35

Nakhchivan, Azerbaijan

———————————◦———————————

In the wide valley that lay below, sun glinted off the galvanized metal roofs of little houses that lay interspersed among fields of wheat and sugar beet. There were cows, but few sheep—at this time of year, the sheep would be in the high valleys, up in the mountains. On the western periphery lay a man-made irrigation pond.

Though the valley was fertile and welcoming, the badland hills around it were not. Bare and lifeless, they were marked by alluvial fans, and striped with multicolored layers of ancient rock and clay. Deep bone-dry ravines, scorched from the sun, lay between them.

To the northwest, Mark could see Ilan Dag—the rocky mountain where local legend said Noah's ark first struck land, leaving a deep cleft in the top before landing on the slopes of Mount Ararat, in what was now eastern Turkey.

Wisps of white clouds hovered near the top of Ilan Dag's twin summits. Mark glanced further west, thinking he might be able to glimpse the snow-covered slopes of Mount Ararat now that he'd gained some altitude, but it was too hazy.

It was only eight in the morning; in a few hours, he thought, the haze might burn off.

He'd been driving slowly along a newly paved road, but now he pulled off and parked on the dirt shoulder, a few feet away from a yellow natural-gas pipeline that followed the road. He'd flown into Nakhchivan the night before and checked into a cash-only hotel on the outskirts of Nakhchivan City. For the exorbitant price of forty dollars a day, the owner had been willing to let Mark use his car, a Renault sedan.

His cover story was that he worked for a Turkish firm that made plastic bottle caps. And that he was here to determine the market penetration and makeup of competitor caps in Nakhchivan.

He'd had business cards made up on the fly in Ganja, and then spent the night creating handwritten logs and entering fake data about bottle caps into his laptop. The gray sport coat he wore was a size too big for him, and his striped tie a bit too wide and too shiny—he was a poorly paid bachelor salesman trying to impress, but falling a little short.

On the front seat of his car were a hundred or so bottle caps in a plastic bag, each one individually labeled. Next to the bottle caps was a map, so that if a cop came by and questioned why he was hanging out on the side of the road—a distinct possibility, as Mark knew the cops in Nakhchivan were paranoid—he could grab the map and pretend to be lost.

In the meantime, his real focus was a slender ribbon of a dirt road about a mile away across the valley; after crossing the fields, it slipped behind a craggy hill and then led to the supposed location of the secret airstrip. He was looking for a car—any car—to emerge from behind the hill.

The first batch of satellite photos that Ted Kaufman had e-mailed him had just shown a green valley, surrounded by bare mountains, and ringed by a tall fence. A road—the road Mark was now watching—entered the valley from the south and ended at a small warehouse-like structure.

And that was it. No airstrip.

A second batch of satellite photos, however, taken some six months prior to the first set, revealed that a large portion of the valley had been covered with a long double line of massive tentlike structures, the effect of which was to hide from view whatever had been going on beneath the tents. And the road leading into the valley had been rutted by vehicles that had left tire tracks wide enough to suggest heavy-duty construction vehicles.

Three hours. That's how long it took for the first and only vehicle—a beige sedan—to emerge from the valley. Mark couldn't see who was in the car. He'd refrained from bringing binoculars, or even a decent camera, because having either one in his possession could arouse suspicion.

Surrounded by Iran and Turkey and Armenia, Nakhchivan was around eighty miles long and no more than forty miles across at its widest point. The Azeris were still technically at war with the Armenians—the mutual loathing between those two countries was legendary—and much of the region had just been a secret military zone during the Soviet era, so a siege mentality had developed, a sense among the population that if they let their guard down for even a moment, they would be overrun by the larger, and sometimes hostile, powers that surrounded them. Nakhchivanis were suspicious of foreigners, and people with cameras, and people who asked too many questions. So Mark knew he had to be careful.

He snapped a quick photo with his phone, then enlarged it enough so that he could see the front grill of the car—a Hyundai, he thought, as he deleted the image. Pulling off the shoulder of the road, he began driving slowly toward the main highway a few miles away, waiting for the car to catch up to him. He passed through a little village where roosters pecked at cow dung in the street.

When Mark saw the Hyundai approaching in his rearview mirror, he sped up a bit. The driver and front-seat passenger each wore a suit and tie and looked a bit like Mormon missionaries. The driver, who appeared to be the taller of the two, wore glasses. When the main highway appeared, Mark glanced in his rear-view mirror again and saw that the driver had turned on his right blinker, so Mark turned right.

They were headed toward Nakhchivan City. To Mark's left was the Aras River, which marked the border between Nakhchivan and Iran. To his right, in the distance, lay the snowcapped mountain range through which ran the war border with Armenia.

Wild red poppies grew on the side of the road, reminding Mark of Katerina, and the painting. Keal had left a message for him the night before. Contrary to what Kaufman had said, apparently the Bureau of Vital Records in Tbilisi had been able to provide some information about her—they'd received a copy of her birth record when she'd moved from Moscow to Tbilisi with her family in 1977. There was no current contact information, or any record of marriage or death, but Keal now knew that Katerina had been born on the eighteenth of July, and knew the names and birth dates of her parents; he was forwarding the information to the US embassy in Moscow and would also try searching a few more government databases in Tbilisi.

The highway was lightly trafficked and newly paved. Mark kept to the slow lane. When he passed the surveillance cameras along the side of the road—and there were several of them—he made sure that he was going just under the ninety kilometer an hour speed limit and looking away from the cameras. After a few miles, he reduced his speed enough so that the driver of the Hyundai decided to pass him.

36

Russian Military Base, South Ossetia

————————o————————

Dmitry Titov listened with intense interest as the deputy chief of the FSB's counterintelligence division informed him that a CIA operative had arrived in Nakhchivan last night.

"And what is the source of this information?" Titov removed his new reading glasses. He'd resisted getting glasses for years, but he'd finally broken down last month when he'd found himself unable to read the morning paper.

"The reports officer we turned at the American embassy in Baku."

In order to keep tabs on the Americans in the run-up to the upcoming operation in Nakhchivan, the counterintelligence division of the FSB, posing as Chinese intelligence officers, had recently abducted the wife of a CIA reports officer. As a method of recruiting a source—*we'll kill your wife if you don't spy for us*—it was a bit crude, but had proven to be effective, at least in the short term.

"He shared with you a report that this operative in Nakhchivan filed from the field?"

"No—it was a bit strange in that the intel came from a cable sent by Langley to the CIA's chief of station in Baku, about an operation the CIA is running in Nakhchivan."

"Cable from whom?"

"It had a routing address that we traced to head of the CIA's Central Eurasia Division."

Titov said, "This man is Kaufman, I know of him."

"The cable was short. All it said was there was a singleton on contract leaving Ganja, arriving in Nakhchivan, and to expect no further reports for forty-eight hours."

"Singleton on contract?"

"Probably refers to an intelligence agent operating on his own."

"We don't have a name."

"No."

But Titov wondered whether that was really true.

Sava was reported to be the CIA's most knowledgeable and resourceful asset when it came to Azerbaijan. Titov hadn't given much credence to that assessment when it had been originally rendered, but he'd been forced to reconsider when Sava had disappeared from Baku with such ease.

And now an unknown CIA officer had surfaced in Nakhchivan. The investigation in Bishkek hadn't turned up anything definitive—although FSB men were now looking for an ex–Navy SEAL thought to be an accomplice of Sava's—but Titov wondered whether the Bishkek angle had just been rendered moot.

"The new officer must be reporting directly to Kaufman," concluded Titov. "And Kaufman is keeping Baku station informed. Ask counterintelligence whether they have the means to get the security tapes and flight manifests from the airport in Nakhchivan."

37
Nakhchivan, Azerbaijan

———————————o———————————

Mark had first visited Nakhchivan City in the early 1990s, when he'd been a young officer in the CIA's special activities division. Trade routes into Nakhchivan had been shut down because the war with Armenia had just started. Jobs had been scarce, and people had been hungry. The infrastructure, after all those years of Soviet rule, was in ruins, and there was no oil or gas in Nakhchivan to anchor the economy. What little help there had been had come from Baku, but that had been before the oil boom; Baku in the nineties had been beset by vicious political infighting, corruption, and above all else a lack of money. So they had been able to do little to prop up the struggling region.

Mark had stayed for a month, and had secretly helped funnel weapons to a group of Turks in Nakhchivan City, who in turn were arming the Azeris. When he'd come back to Nakhchivan ten years later as a CIA case officer, to try to convince a Turkish diplomat to spy for the CIA, the city had been in much better shape. Trade with Iran and Turkey had resumed. Roads were being repaired, and the gentrification of the capital had started.

But now...now Nakhchivan City was almost unrecognizable. All the old tenement houses—completely rebuilt. The ancient monuments—restored. The roads—all new. Nakhchivan was favored by the president of Azerbaijan, because his father had been born here. With the oil money now gushing in faster than Baku could handle, a healthy amount had been diverted to Nakhchivan

City, more than any other city in Azerbaijan save Baku.

In the center of this new city stood the thirteen-story glass-clad Tabriz Hotel, the tallest building in all of Nakhchivan. When the Hyundai Mark was following turned into the Tabriz's parking lot, Mark continued straight and parked in front of a pharmacy down the street. Then he jogged part of the way back to the hotel, slowing to an easy walk only when he was in sight of the entrance.

The lobby was a fair approximation of a reasonably upscale business hotel, but it was empty save for the two men in suits who'd been in the Hyundai. They stood in front of the reception desk.

Both were dark-haired, maybe thirty or so. Short-cropped hair, clean-shaven. The shorter of the two wore tortoiseshell eyeglasses. Both carried well-worn leather briefcases. Mark stood behind them, as if he too needed to speak to the receptionist.

"There's a bowling alley and video arcade you can walk to," Mark overheard the receptionist say, in Russian. "It won't be open tonight, but tomorrow it should be."

"We don't bowl," replied the taller one in Russian.

The bespectacled man rubbed his forehead. He looked as if he'd been up all night. "Forget entertainment then. Talk to us about dining options. Not for tonight, for now. The restaurant upstairs, we are tired of it."

"You might try the Goy-Gol on Ataturk. It's not far, you can walk."

"Can you make a reservation?"

"Certainly, sir. But you won't need one for lunch."

The taller man frowned as he tapped the top of the concierge desk. "OK. Thank you."

As the men turned to leave, Mark, speaking Russian, said, "I may join you, my friends, at the Goy-Gol, but don't wait for me to start." He smiled as he patted the bespectacled man on the shoulder.

The two men gave him a look. Mark, betting that they would just think he was being friendly to a fellow Russian, added, "I won't keep you, I must check in myself, I just arrived. What a flight! Go, go. Don't wait for me."

As they were leaving, Mark heard one of them whisper something under his breath to the other. It was just a fragment of a remark, judging by the tone something equivalent to *idiot*, Mark guessed, but in a language he couldn't place. Or maybe they'd been speaking Russian, but Mark just hadn't been able to hear?

"Sir?" said the receptionist.

"I'd like a room." Mark continued in Russian. He gestured over his shoulder to the two men who were walking out the entrance. "Next to my friends."

The receptionist typed for a moment on his computer. "Room 816 is not a suite, but it does have a king bed."

"I'll take it."

Mark handed over his Azeri passport.

Behind the reception counter, a door was cracked open. The receptionist called out "I need the key to 816," and began to enter Mark's information into a computer. After a minute, the receptionist called out, louder this time, "Salman! Room 816. Do you hear?" When this entreaty was met with more silence, the receptionist, looking aggrieved, retrieved a sheet of paper from a printer behind the counter and placed it in front of Mark. "Sign here," he said. "*I* will get your key."

The receptionist pushed open the door behind the counter, revealing two men standing in front of an old tube television. "Salman, you don't have ears?"

"What?"

Mark glanced at the TV screen. On it, he saw aerial images of a bombed-out building surrounded by police cars. The logo on the upper right-hand corner of the screen told him it was the state-run AzTV channel. The program cut to what appeared to be a chaotic press conference hosted by a man Mark recognized as the president of Iran.

The receptionist returned to the counter, and handed a bulky metal key to Mark.

"What's going on?" Mark asked.

"I am sorry to keep you waiting. As you can see, certain employees here are useless. If the Tabriz had to rely on them, the hotel would close."

"I mean on the TV. What happened?"

"Oh, there was a bombing, of course."

"In Iran?"

The receptionist shrugged as he took the sheet of paper Mark had signed and filed it in a cabinet beneath the counter. "Yes! Of course! Someone tried to kill Khorasani. It was his residence that was bombed."

Ayatollah Khorasani was the supreme leader of Iran.

"How?"

"I don't know. Some people say a missile, some a car bomb. Right now there are only rumors."

"When did this happen?"

"This morning, before dawn. But it has only just come on the news. Of course, everyone thinks it is Israel."

"This could be bad."

"Yes, of course. But Khorasani was not at his residence, praise to Allah. He is alive, so I do not think there will be war."

38

Russian Military Base, South Ossetia

———————o———————

It had only been an hour since Titov had ordered the security tapes at Nakhchivan airport to be searched. And already he had his answer.

Displayed on his computer screen was an image of a man who had flown under the name of Adil Orlov, but who Titov knew with certainty was Mark Sava, albeit with hair that was darker and shorter than when he'd been in Tbilisi. First he shows up in Tbilisi, now Nakhchivan. The American was onto them, that much was clear.

"Forward this photo to all our operatives in Nakhchivan," said Titov to his deputy. "Let them know that this man is working for the CIA. He often goes by the name Mark Sava but is now traveling under the name of Adil Orlov. He's also been known to use the name Stephen McDougall. Prioritize a watch on the road to the Ordubad airstrip and all surrounding roads. Next target the main hotels. Get a man in every lobby. Then watch the highways going in and out of Nakhchivan City. Nakhchivan isn't that big a place. Find him. But be careful—he's dangerous."

39

Nakhchivan, Azerbaijan

———————————o———————————

As Mark approached the door to his room at the Tabriz he glanced at the doors before and after his own. A Do Not Disturb sign hung from the one numbered 817. He guessed it was there because the men he'd followed didn't want a maid rifling through their things.

A ceiling-mounted security camera was pointed at him, so as Mark reached into his front pocket for his pick tools, he shifted the travel bag that hung from his shoulder so that it blocked the camera's view of the doorknob.

The lock was a basic four-pin variety, so he had the door open in under a minute. Inside, the room was clean and uncluttered. A bag of potato chips—a local brand—and an open bottle of Georgian wine sat on a table next to the television. Two queen-size beds took up most of the floor space; both were unmade. Large windows looked out over the red roofs of Nakhchivan City and the Aras Reservoir, the Aras River having been dammed up just south of the city. Because the reservoir marked the border with Iran, it was a restricted no-man's-land, a place that lay empty and wild.

He turned from the window and began searching the bathroom. Because the two toothbrushes that lay next to the sink weren't branded, he couldn't tell where they might have been purchased. Same with the little travel containers of shampoo. There were no medications. The two razors were decent Gillette four-blades—but they could have been purchased here in Nakhchivan or practically anywhere else in the world. The waste bin was empty, save for a couple of used tissues.

Back in the main room, he searched the dresser and TV cabinet, but they too were empty. Next to the phone was a pad of hotel paper which he picked up and examined from an angle, hoping that the old spy trick of reading the indentations from the previous note would prove useful. It wasn't—the paper was perfectly smooth.

In the closet, on a luggage rack, he found a single, open carry-on-sized Samsonite suitcase filled with black satin boxer shorts, black socks, and white undershirts. The boxer shorts and undershirts were made by Marks & Spencer, a British firm, but one with worldwide distribution; the socks weren't branded. There were no luggage tags on the suitcase.

Hanging from the clothes bar above the suitcase were two dark blue suits and four white dress shirts encased in dry-cleaner plastic. Mark checked the suit coats; the neck labels had been removed, as had the labels on the rear of the suit trousers, and the neck labels on the shirts.

They were careful men, that much was clear.

He turned both of the jackets and trousers inside out, but found no identifying marks. The suits looked custom made. He could cut away the inner lining, hoping that the tailor had left some identifying marks on the interior. But then the owners would know that their room had been violated.

For a moment, Mark stood there, listening and thinking. He glanced at the shirts again. They hung on paper-encased dry-cleaner hangers. On a hunch, he undid the top two buttons on one of the shirts and slipped it off the hanger.

In light beige lettering, Mark read—in English—KLEINMANN CLEANERS, BEN YEHUDA STREET, TEL AVIV, 03/523-8967. Above the English was text that Mark couldn't read but which Mark guessed was simply the same information in Hebrew.

Hebrew, he thought. *That* was the language he'd caught a snippet of down in the lobby.

40
Baku, Azerbaijan

———————o———————

Orkhan had just gotten off the phone with the director of Israel's Mossad spy agency when his secretary rang.

Sounding flustered, she said, "Sir, they're here for you. Five men, they won't leave, I don't know what to tell them, I—"

"What five men?"

"From the Interior Ministry. They have a warrant they say is signed by the president."

"A warrant for what?"

"Sir, I'm sorry."

"A warrant for what?" Orkhan repeated, though he knew the answer. He was going to be arrested and accused of leaking information about the operation in Nakhchivan to the Russians.

"For you, sir. For your arrest."

"I see."

His secretary was calling from the Ministry of National Security in downtown Baku, but Orkhan was at his home south of the city, seated on the periphery of an inner courtyard that extended out from his ground-floor office. Ten years earlier, he and his family had moved out of the densely populated part of the city and into this mansion. It was a move he'd come to regret. At the time he'd thought being in the desert highlands, with the other wealthy Bakuvians, in a fenced compound with a pool he'd never use and a state-of-the-art security system, was where he belonged. But he missed his old neighbors.

Still, he enjoyed his courtyard patio, particularly when it was sunny and hot, as it was today; even though he was wearing a suit and tie, he welcomed the heat. It sank into the dark fabric of his suit and deep into the knotted aches in his shoulders. The heat slowed him down, calmed him, helped him to think more clearly. A fountain in the center of the courtyard made a pleasant burbling noise.

First Mark Sava shows up, then a Russian spy is found to have evidence of the Nakhchivan operation, then someone tries to drop a bomb on the supreme leader of Iran, and now the interior minister was trying to arrest him.

Orkhan had a feeling that the confluence of all these events was not coincidental. Something big, and almost assuredly unpleasant, was about to happen. But what?

He eyed the guard standing at attention near the French doors that led to his office. He had a total of eight men here at his house. All loyal, all related to him by blood. There was a reason he had elected to work from home today; he'd suspected this was coming.

"This warrant," he asked. "It has been signed by the president?"

"I saw the signature myself. What should I tell them?"

"Tell them the truth. If they wish to find me, I am at my home."

Silence. Orkhan considered the public humiliation that was now being inflicted upon him. Five men, marching into *his* ministry.

He'd leave immediately, but two of his men would remain behind to challenge the warrant, to make the interior minister's men wait, to buy time.

"Are you sure—"

"One more thing—record the names and positions of the five men now attempting to serve this warrant. This violation will not be forgotten. Is that clear?"

"Perfectly, sir."

41

Nakhchivan, Azerbaijan

---○---

Were the two men he'd been following really Israelis? Had he *really*, Mark wondered, heard a snippet of Hebrew?

If they were Israelis, Mark guessed they'd immigrated to Israel from Russia and had been picked for this job because of their fluency in Russian. Assuming they were Israelis, though—what were they doing visiting a secret restricted area in Nakhchivan?

Mark could guess at part of the reason. Relations between Azerbaijan and Israel were surprisingly good, despite the fact that Azerbaijan was a predominantly Muslim nation. Because of all the regional sensitivities, neither country could publicly admit how close the relationship was, but Israel got around forty percent of its oil from Azerbaijan and Azerbaijan was buying Israeli arms—drones, antiaircraft and missile defense systems—at a rapid clip. In a leaked cable, the president of Azerbaijan had once compared the Azeri-Israeli relationship to an iceberg, where ninety percent was below the surface.

So if a couple of Israelis were traveling incognito to a secret restricted zone, Mark knew the likelihood was high that it was because the Israelis and Azeris were cooperating on some project, probably military in nature, they didn't want the rest of the world to know about.

The only question was: what was it? An airstrip that couldn't be seen from the air? Or had the engineer from Bazarduzu Construction been lying? Mark recalled the briefcases each of the Israelis had been carrying. He suspected answers to his questions lay inside them.

———————————○———————————

Mark stopped by his room at the Tabriz, stuck his iPad Mini in his back pocket and his permanent phone and two prepaids in his front pockets, placed his leather satchel in the closet—he hesitated to leave the painting unattended, but didn't want to carry anything that would slow him down—and then exited the Tabriz on foot, intending to intercept the Israelis at the Goy-Gol restaurant and steal one of their briefcases.

His plans were disrupted, however, when a gaunt young man with eyes set too close together followed him out the door of the Tabriz—without even making much of an effort to be discreet about it. He looked too fair skinned to be a true Nakhchivani, but just as in Azerbaijan proper, the long Soviet rule had left a lot of Nakhchivanis with Russian blood in them.

Crap, he thought. He was hoping the guy was a Nakhchivani, because it would be bad news if the Russians had found him here. Whatever the case, he'd have to deal with the guy behind him first, and quickly, before the Israelis were done with their lunch. He exhaled, and pictured the layout of the city in his head, and where the Goy-Gol was relative to places he that might best ditch a tail. *The path of least resistance*, he told himself. *Find it.*

He began walking, at a fast clip, south down Heydar Aliyev Prospekti. His tail followed about fifty feet behind, not bothering to use pedestrians or vehicles as cover. Just past a mosque, Mark stepped into a virtually empty Soviet-era park that was several hundred feet wide, and equally long. There were no roads in the park, so he didn't have to worry about being overtaken by someone in a car.

At the end of the park stood a ten-sided eighty-foot-tall 12th-century mausoleum that was decorated with the word *Allah* rendered in Arabic. Mark headed for it, but instead of going inside, ducked around the structure and began to sprint in a line he calculated would keep the mausoleum between him and his tail for the longest time possible.

That line took him through a tulip garden and then down a steep grassy embankment. At the bottom, he turned sharply to his left and, using the embankment as a blind now instead of the mausoleum, sprinted along the edge of a large public square that overlooked the Aras Reservoir. When he reached the southeast corner, he vaulted over a decorative waist-high metal fence and began to run down a steep hill overgrown with wild lilac bushes and evergreen trees.

But before disappearing into the vegetation, he cast a quick glance back up the hill—and that was when he really began to worry. A man—shorter and older than the one who'd originally been following him—was climbing over the fence. Mark ran, dodging branches, then hit a road, and sprinted south as fast as he could, downhill, searching for escape routes and improvised weapons, thinking this was exactly the type of situation he was too damn old for.

Behind him he heard footsteps pounding on pavement. By now, Mark was breathless and his chest was heaving.

"Stop!" The word was spoken in English, but with a heavy Russian accent. Glancing behind him as he ran, Mark saw yet another guy, this one young and lithe, built like a cross-country runner.

A line of parked cars came up fast on Mark's right. He made for the first, as if he planned to run right over it. Instead he hit the front grill with his right foot, pivoted a hundred and eighty degrees and instead of stopping, charged. As they collided, Mark tried to slam his fist into the man's throat, but only half succeeded. Momentum carried them both onto the hood of the car. As they fell, Mark threw another punch to the throat and this time connected.

A hundred feet away, a car was speeding toward them. Another car appeared from behind, the engine revving far louder than normal. Mark cut left, but the guy who'd been following him from the Tabriz had caught up and was trying to outflank him.

The Tabriz guy produced a pistol and fired two low shots— he appeared to be aiming for the legs—but missed. Running for all he was worth, Mark eyed the wooded hill that paralleled the road. Running back to it now would be crazy, but he was boxed in and there was nowhere else to go. His only option was to try to lose the men who were after him in the lilacs and evergreens that covered the hill.

The slope was steep, and Mark was tired. He climbed up maybe twenty feet, then turned sharply to his left. Below him he heard bodies crashing into the woods. Above him, from the edge of the public square by the mausoleum, he heard shouts, people issuing orders—in Russian—to the people below.

Dammit all.

A small army was chasing him. Why, though? What had he stumbled upon that that was so important?

He estimated that the odds he was going to get caught were approaching a hundred percent. He cursed under his breath, took a few more steps walking as quietly as he could, rolled under the low branches of a tall pine tree, and pulled out one of his prepaid phones.

42
Bishkek, Kyrgyzstan

————————o————————

Daria tested the water in the small plastic baby bath with her index finger—it was warm, but not too warm—and then slowly lowered Lila into it for the first time, the small umbilical-cord wound on Lila's belly button having healed over to the point where Daria thought it was OK to submerge it. She squeezed out a little baby shampoo onto a yellow duck-shaped washcloth and began to clean her daughter.

Lila cooed and her mouth formed what Daria imagined was a smile, even though she knew babies weren't supposed to really be able to smile with happiness at that age.

"You like that, don't you?" Daria was on her knees in front of the bathtub. The baby bath was inside the larger tub. She tickled Lila's belly a bit. "Bath time is fun for Lila!"

After washing what little hair Lila had, she moved on to her daughter's feet, then hands.

She wondered whether her own mother—her birth mother, that is, the one who'd been murdered in Iran when Daria was just a baby—had ever washed her like this, ever loved her like this?

But of course she had, Daria told herself. She'd been feeling close to her mother of late, closer than she'd ever felt before. She thought now of what it would be like to be separated from Lila by death, the way she and her mother had been separated, and a wave of emotion swept through her—longing for Lila, sympathy for her mother, sadness for what might have been…

Lila made another cooing sound.

"Mommy's thinking crazy thoughts, isn't she?" She tickled Lila's tummy. "Tell Mommy not to worry so much."

She was bound to worry, though, especially with Mark gone. It had been two and a half days since they'd last talked. She had no idea where he was. She wondered whether it was going to be like this for the rest of their lives—with Mark always taking off and her sitting at home, anxious, tending to Lila.

That would suck.

Their agreement—partially spoken, partially unspoken—was that they would share responsibility for Lila, each pitching in as needed. It wasn't that Daria minded taking care of Lila now, far from it, the joy she felt was sometimes intense, but in the back of her mind she wondered whether Mark thought…

"You're worrying again," she said out loud. "Stop worrying." Then, "OK, let's finish up this bath."

When Lila was all clean, Daria lifted her onto a white baby towel that she'd spread out on a terrycloth bathmat.

"OK, let's get you dry."

Daria's phone, which she'd left on the kitchen table, chirped once. She finished drying Lila and swaddled her in the towel. On the way to the changing table, she passed by the kitchen and glanced at her phone.

The text message was from a number she didn't recognize. She tapped the screen. At first glance, she thought the actual message was blank, but then she realized that there was a single x in the upper left-hand corner.

"Oh, no," she said. "No, Mark, no…"

43
Baku, Azerbaijan

———————o———————

Orkhan sat in the rear seat of his armored black Suburban. Accompanying him were two bodyguards, both second cousins by marriage; his driver, who was one of his many nephews; and his personal assistant. They had just pulled out of Orkhan's driveway and were now speeding down from the hills above Baku.

"Sir, where to now?" asked the driver.

Orkhan considered. His spies in the Interior Ministry were already investigating what the interior minister was up to. But if he allowed himself to be caught before his men got to the bottom of this—if it became widely known that he'd been imprisoned and had fallen out of favor with the president—then all but his most loyal men would abandon him.

No one would abandon him, however, until the warrant was served.

"First to Nardaran. We'll pay a surprise visit to the ayatollah, to see whether he knows anything about this bombing in Tehran." Nardaran, which lay twenty miles northeast of Baku, was the most religiously conservative town in Azerbaijan. Orkhan, though not a particularly observant Muslim himself, maintained good relations with the local ayatollah by making sure the donation boxes at the mosque were full; in return the ayatollah informed on Muslim extremists.

Orkhan's cell rang. He checked the ID; it wasn't a number he recognized, so he handed the phone to his assistant. "Answer it on speaker, find out what they want. If it's for me, tell them we're already in Nardaran and that I'm in a meeting."

Orkhan's assistant, a burly man with a fat neck and a short beard, answered the phone.

"Orkhan?" said the caller.

"Who is this?"

"Where is Minister Gambar?" The voice was a whisper.

"Nardaran. Speak louder."

"I need to talk to him. Now."

"He is in a meeting."

"Interrupt him. Tell him it's Mark Sava."

"Sava?" Orkhan asked.

"Orkhan, pick up. I've only got seconds, I'm about to be taken."

Orkhan grabbed his phone back and took it off speaker. "Talk to me, Sava."

"I have information for you, but first I need your help."

"What information?"

"About your operation in Nakhchivan."

Two beats, then, "What do you know of this? And why didn't you tell me what you knew two days ago in Baku?"

"No time now, Orkhan. I have seconds. Send help."

"What is your location?"

"Nakhchivan City, near the Momine Khatun mausoleum. Can your men track me from my phone?"

"Yes, but—"

"I'll leave it on as long as I can. I'm in a tight spot."

"Mark, what—"

"They're here."

"Mark?" Orkhan took the phone away from his ear and stared at it for a moment. He put it back to his ear. "Mark?"

The connection had been severed.

44
Nakhchivan, Azerbaijan

———————o———————

Mark stuffed the prepaid he'd used to call Orkhan into his underpants. He pulled the second prepaid from his pocket just as someone grabbed his ankles and yanked him out from under the tree he'd been using for cover.

Two more men ran up. Mark noted that both carried MP-443 Grach pistols—a graceless but effective weapon favored by the Russian military. They kicked Mark repeatedly in the stomach and chest—he felt at least two ribs break—until he almost blacked out.

The word *motherfuckers* kept looping through his brain.

In Russian, "Drop the phone."

In English, Mark said, "I don't understand you!"

The response came in Russian-accented English. "Phone, you shit. Drop!"

Mark let the prepaid in his hand fall to the ground just as the Tabriz Hotel guy showed up.

While patting him down, they found and removed his wallet, iPad, permanent phone, and keys, but missed the prepaid he'd used to call Orkhan. Someone yanked him up. Mark just hung like dead weight.

"Walk!" one of them commanded.

Mark refused to do so—instead he pressed his legs close together, which helped him keep the prepaid lodged in his nether regions from falling out.

All four men pushed and dragged him back down the hill to a black Kia sedan that was idling on the side of the road. They heaved him into the back of the car, stuffed a canvas sack over his head, and pushed him onto the floor.

"Head down!"

Mark was in the process of complying when someone kicked his head to the floor. He felt a pistol on the back of his neck. A man climbed into the rear seat.

"You raise head, I shoot. You fight, I shoot. Understand?"

"Up yours."

Another kick. "Eyes to ground. No question."

———————○———————

They drove for maybe a half hour, during which time a boot was always jammed against the back of Mark's head. The left side of his chest, where he'd broken a couple of ribs, hurt where it was pressed up against the floor of the car.

Even with the sack over his head he could detect the sun streaming in from the rear right-hand side of the car. It was late morning, so he calculated the sun would be shining from the southeast, which meant the rear right-hand side of the car was facing southeast, which in turn meant the front of the car had to be facing north.

They traveled over land that was flat, or nearly so, for most of the trip—until the end, that is, when they drove up a steep, winding slope for a few minutes before coming to a stop.

"Get out."

Mark just lay there.

"I say get out!" A kick, then, in Russian, "Grab him."

Mark clenched his arms to his chest and crossed his legs, preferring to endure more immediate pain than get out of the car of his own accord and risk dislodging the prepaid. When they tried to grab him, he let his body relax so that he was dead weight again. Three guys muscled him out of the back, then dragged him across what felt like a long stretch of pavement. He listened for other cars, or people, but heard none.

He was stuffed through what he guessed was a revolving door and into a carpeted and air-conditioned space.

"Where do they want him?"

"Downstairs. Guard him until General Titov gets here."

"He knows we made the capture?

"Yes, yes, as soon as you reported from the city we told him. He will arrive later today."

They were speaking in Russian, as though Mark wasn't there.

"He wasn't due until tomorrow."

"Yes, I don't understand it."

"Is the prisoner hurt?"

"Not very."

"Why won't he stand?"

"Because he's a cocksucker."

They lugged Mark down several hallways, down a flight of stairs, then into an elevator. They descended. When the elevator opened, Mark smelled something metallic, or...he couldn't quite place it. The air seemed particularly dry and cool, though. Through the canvas sack, he perceived a dim light.

Footsteps of men walking on gravel echoed off the walls. They dumped him on what felt like a bed with a saggy mattress. Springs squeaked beneath him as the bed settled. Mark rearranged himself so as to remove pressure from his broken ribs.

"OK, cocksucker, welcome to your new home."

Someone laughed, then said, "I need a drink."

"The bootlicker forbids it."

A top being unscrewed from a bottle. "Screw Titov."

45
Bishkek, Kyrgyzstan

———————o———————

Daria called John Decker.

"Mark's been taken!" Cradling her phone between her shoulder and her ear, she was stuffing supplies—diapers, baby wipes, a digital thermometer, breast pads, a pacifier, a changing pad, and the crummy Chinese-made diaper cream—into Lila's diaper bag.

"What happened?"

"I got the emergency text." Daria crammed in another diaper and then struggled to zip the bag up. Lila had woken up and was crying in her bassinet.

"What text?"

"We'd agreed on a system. If he was ever in a situation where he thought he was about to be captured, he'd let me know, if he could. So that I'd know what happened to him, but also so that…" Daria didn't want to say the words aloud. "Anyway, I'm packing now."

"So that whoever had taken him couldn't use you and Lila against him."

"Yeah." Threatening to harm, or actually harming, a prisoner's family was a common way of conducting an interrogation. So she and Mark had taken some basic precautions. "We agreed on certain signals. I just got the worst one. Can you track a cell phone?"

"Here, yeah, we've got some connections, but not in Azerbaijan. The NSA could."

"Deck, I don't know…"

Lila was crying louder now.

"Where'd you last have a location on him?"

"Baku."

"He went to Ganja after that, I wired him some money. If I push hard enough I should be able to get through to Kaufman. If he's not a dick, he'll leverage Agency resources to figure out where Mark called from. Forward me the text Mark sent you."

"OK. Make Kaufman do this, Deck. He owes Mark."

"I'll try."

"Don't try, do it! If Kaufman screws Mark over on this, I swear I'll come after him myself. You can tell him that too."

"You know, you could always go to the embassy for the time being. No one could get to you there."

Daria was in her and Mark's bedroom, slipping her alias documents into her purse next to the snub-nosed Glock that was already in there.

"Just find out where Mark is, I'll handle the rest."

46
Nakhchivan, Azerbaijan

———————○———————

Mark heard footsteps on gravel, then, "Welcome, General Titov."

For the past several hours Mark had been thinking of Daria, hoping that she'd gotten his message, and that she and Lila were someplace safe. He'd also been wondering whether he was too far underground for his prepaid to transmit a signal.

Now he had the sense that someone was staring at him. No one spoke for a good minute.

Then, "Uncover his head."

The canvas sack was yanked off. Mark blinked as his eyes adjusted. He was in what appeared to be a mine. But it wasn't a dirty mine, where coal or iron ore was being extracted. Instead the ceiling and walls appeared to be made of grayish, translucent crystal.

"It's salt," said a man in Russian-accented English. He stood behind Mark. "It keeps the air clean, and dry. People who have lung trouble come here to breathe. We're on the women's side. It's nicer."

Which explains all the beds, thought Mark. There were maybe a hundred of them, lined up in two perfectly straight rows down the length of a long cavern. The beds were all metal framed. Polyester blankets imprinted with a floral pattern were spread over each one. A string of dim, bare-bulb lights ran down the apex of the cavern's low arched ceiling.

"Turn around."

That voice—Mark had a sense that he'd heard it before, but he struggled to place where. He turned.

DAN MAYLAND

A man sat, or rather slouched, on a bed about six feet away. He was of average size, but muscular in a flinty, weathered way. His eyes were blue, cheekbones high, lips thin, forehead prominent, gray hair crew-cut short. He wore gray slacks, shiny black wingtip shoes, and a too-tight short-sleeved collared dress shirt that accentuated his muscular torso and arms. In his right hand was a big black semiautomatic Grach pistol; he held it lazily, resting it on his right thigh in a way that said he wasn't the slightest bit afraid of anything Mark might do.

"Why do they call you bootlicker?" Mark asked in English.

"What?"

"Your men. Why do they call you this? Whose boots do you lick?"

Turning to the guards behind him, Titov snarled in Russian, "You idiots! You talk in front of him? He understands Russian."

"He lies, sir," said one of the guards. "No one said—"

"Leave us!"

Mark studied his captor. Switching to Russian, he said, "Have we met before?"

Instead of answering, Titov took a manila folder that lay beside him on the bed and tossed it to Mark. "Open it."

The folder hit Mark's shin and fell to the ground. Mark leaned forward to pick it up, forcing himself not to wince as a bolt of pain from his broken ribs shot up his side.

Titov shifted his gun arm slightly, so that the barrel was aimed at Mark's head. "You haven't changed much, considering the years," he observed. "Not so much, at least, that I wasn't able to recognize you when I reviewed the tape."

Mark pulled a large glossy color photograph out of the envelope. It was grainy—a single frame grabbed from what he guessed was a video—but he had no problem recognizing himself. He was at the Dachi hotel in Tbilisi, in the room where Larry Bowlan had

224

been found dead. And he was looking at Katerina's self-portrait.

He studied the photo, then Titov. "Recognized me from what? From when?"

"Katerina, you can't really see her face, but her hair, her figure, she looks beautiful there, no?"

Ordinarily, Mark tried to control an interrogation—even if he was the one being interrogated—by trying to assess what the interrogator wanted to hear and tailoring his answers accordingly. But in this case, he hadn't a clue as to what Titov was after. Or why he was after it. Which meant he was in danger of giving a wrong answer.

He observed the tension in Titov's jaw, saw that the pistol that rested on his thigh was now gripped a little tighter.

"Answer my question," said Titov.

"I don't like the tone of your question. Did you kill my friend?"

"Friend? What friend?"

"Larry Bowlan."

"That pig? Yes, of course I killed him. He was foolish to have come back to Georgia. I gave him an injection of sux—you know this drug?"

Mark did. Succinylcholine—sux for short—was a muscle relaxant that induced complete paralysis, including in muscles needed to breathe. In hospitals, it was given to patients just prior to inserting a breathing tube attached to a mechanical ventilator; outside of hospitals, it was used to kill people, mainly because it was hard to detect in toxicology tests. Mark recalled that the Mossad had been caught using sux to assassinate a Hamas operative in Dubai a few years earlier.

Titov added, "I watched him suffocate to death while looking at Katerina's painting. His brain was working just fine, but he couldn't breathe. He looked like a fish out of water." Titov made a fish mouth with his lips. "Urinating all over himself. I enjoyed this very much."

Mark eyed Titov. "What does Katerina have to do with this? Where is she?"

"I took a risk killing—" Titov stopped in midsentence. For the first time, he looked genuinely surprised. "What did you ask me?"

"What the hell does Katerina have to do with this?"

Speaking slowly, as if incredulous that Mark had dared to pose such questions, Titov said, "Where *is* she?" Titov stood. Gesticulating with his Grach pistol, he said, "You mean to tell me you don't..." He shook his head. "I don't believe you."

"I knew a woman named Katerina Kustinskaya twenty-four years ago, when I was a student in Georgia. I haven't seen or heard from her since."

Titov leaped forward and swung his pistol down hard. Mark blocked the blow with his forearm and dove into Titov, who clobbered him on the back of his head with the pistol and sent a knee up into Mark's face. Mark stumbled, then felt the barrel of the pistol on the back of his head.

You sonofabitch, thought Mark. *I'm going to pay you back for that.*

"Don't you dare move," said Titov, as he maneuvered himself behind Mark while keeping the pistol barrel tight on Mark's skull. Then, in a manic voice just short of a shout, he said, "This is the end of your time on this earth. No God will save you. Your pleas for mercy will go unanswered. After you die, and your blood stains the earth, you will be buried in a trash heap. No one will mourn you, no one will care."

Mark felt the barrel of the pistol lift off the base of his skull.

Titov said, "Now do you remember who I am?"

47

Tbilisi, Georgia
June 1991, six months before the
dissolution of the Soviet Union

———————o———————

Marko Saveljic had never used heroin of any kind before, hadn't even smoked it, but he'd seen enough doped-up vagrants on the streets of his hometown of Elizabeth, New Jersey, to know that it was possible to take the drug in doses that left one reasonably functional.

But the KGB thugs who'd kidnapped him, just hours after he'd discovered the listening device in Katerina's art bag, clearly hadn't been aiming for him to remain functional. After an initial interrogation and beating, the results of which evidently hadn't been satisfactory because it had been followed by a second inter-rogation and beating, they'd spent weeks—two? three? Marko had lost all track of time, but a glance at all the needle marks on his arm told him that it had been awhile—injecting as much heroin in him as his body could take, as often as his body could take it. Sometimes the initial rush of the drug had been so strong that he'd started choking before floating down into that warm painless netherworld...

But the night before, the injections had abruptly stopped.

When he'd been high they hadn't bothered to beat him. Perhaps because it was pointless to inject someone with a powerful painkiller and then try to inflict pain. But now he knew that, while he felt no pain when high on heroin, the pain was magnified ten-fold when coming off it.

When they started interrogating him again, he tried to answer their questions, he really did, but the problem was he had no good answers. So they beat him again, and again, sometimes with a rubber truncheon, sometimes with their fists.

He told them now as he had before all about his meetings with the American named Larry, and about funneling money to the Press Club, he told them everything he could remember, every little detail, but that wasn't enough. They were convinced he actually worked for the CIA, that he knew more.

He even tried to make up things about the CIA, to tell them what they wanted to hear, but he didn't know enough about the CIA to make his lies believable.

They gave him breakfast—water and stale salted crackers—but he threw everything up as a jaw-rattling fever and intense stomach cramps came upon him. He felt like he needed to shit, but his body hurt all over, hurt too much to squat over the bucket that sat by his head and which was already full with his excrement.

He moved his cheek a few inches, so that it lay on a new, cooler patch of concrete. Maybe they were done with him. Maybe they'd finally realized that he had nothing left to tell them.

A door opened. Light spilled in. Someone kicked him.

"Get up." This in Russian.

Marko couldn't get up.

A hand clasped his hair, yanked him to a kneeling position, and pulled him in the direction of the door.

Outside, four men wearing black ski masks stood around a fifth who was kneeling in the dirt, face uncovered, arms handcuffed behind his back. All the men with the ski masks were armed.

"I want them facing each other," said the man who, even with the ski mask on, Marko recognized as the leader. He recognized the blue eyes, and the slope of the muscular shoulders, and the pattern of scuff marks on his black boots.

Someone pulled Marko a few more feet forward, until he was facing a young man with shoulder-length brown hair, swollen lips, and teary, bruised brown eyes.

The leader gave Marko a sharp kick in the thigh. "You have been unhelpful. This is what we do to bitches that are unhelpful." He removed a black semiautomatic pistol from an exposed shoulder holster, aimed it at the back of the head of the unnamed prisoner, and in Russian said, "This is the end of your time on this earth. No God will save you." The prisoner began to shake. "Your pleas for mercy will go unanswered. After you die, and your blood stains the earth, you will be buried in a trash heap. No one will mourn you, no one will care."

And then, just like that, the trigger was pulled. The bullet traveled through the back of the prisoner's head, out the front of his nose, and into the dirt between Marko's knees. As the prisoner slumped forward into Marko, he drooled blood on Marko's shoulder.

"OK, now it's your turn," said the leader to Marko. "Are you prepared?"

The strange thing, thought Marko, was that, yes, he was prepared. He was so tired, and in so much pain, that he was ready for it all to end.

48

———————————o———————————

"You," said Mark, now recognizing the eyes, and the voice—even the slope of the shoulders—of the man who'd tortured him all those years ago. He'd never known the Russian's name. He did now.

Titov.

Mark had been sure he was going to die that day, but instead he'd just heard the click of a firing pin descending on an empty chamber. In the weeks that followed, the Russians had executed five more men in front of him, some old, one even younger than the first had been. His captors—whose names Mark had never known—hadn't told him where the men had come from, or why they were being executed. Mark had hoped they were criminals who'd been given the death penalty, and that the Russians had just been carrying out executions that would have occurred anyway, but he'd never known for sure.

Titov had gone back to sitting on the bed. "So all that time, you were lying. You *were* working for the CIA. As you are working for them—or with them—now. Don't try to deny it. I know about your operation in Bishkek, about your Navy SEAL friend, the work you do for the CIA there. I'll know even more soon."

As Mark stared at Titov, horrified to be face to face with him again and to hear him mention the city where his wife and daughter resided, he recalled that his imprisonment in Georgia had taught him an important lesson—that the only way to avoid being completely controlled by monsters was to stop caring about what they might do to you. He'd gotten to that point in Georgia, when he'd accepted—and even welcomed—his own death, and he'd carried that feeling with him throughout much of his career with the CIA. It was at the very heart of what had made him a good CIA officer.

With Lila in the picture, though, he'd changed. Even if his own life wasn't worth worrying about, his daughter's certainly was, and her fate was tied in some small way to his own. He couldn't provide for her and protect her if he was dead.

At least that's what he'd been telling himself—until now. With Titov standing in front of him, bragging about how he'd been poking his nose around Bishkek, Mark felt a nearly overwhelming urge to rip the Russian's throat out, consequences be damned.

Mark eyed Titov for a moment, then said, "When I was a student in Tbilisi, I was helping Larry Bowlan, and Bowlan was working for the CIA. I knew nothing about operations outside of the one I was involved in. I told you everything I knew back then, but you were too stupid to realize I was telling the truth."

The insult didn't appear to affect Titov. "You came back to Georgia within two years of leaving. You were spotted in Abkhazia."

"By then I *was* working with the CIA. But when you knew me I was just being used by the CIA, by Bowlan."

"After we kidnapped you, Bowlan searched for you. He sent men to rescue you. He wouldn't have done that if you were just someone he was using."

"He did." Bowlan had leveraged his connections to Georgian rebels to put together a proxy hit squad that had hunted down and decimated the KGB in Tbilisi. All of Mark's captors had been slaughtered; Titov had only survived because he hadn't been there at the time.

Mark and Titov stared at each other for a while.

Titov asked, "What happened to you, after you escaped?"

"Why do you want to know?" Mark didn't understand why they were talking about his distant past instead of the secret military zone in Nakhchivan, or the buildup of Russian forces in the region, or why Titov had killed Larry Bowlan five days ago. And he still didn't understand what any of this had to do with Katerina. There were too many questions.

Titov didn't answer.

Mark asked, "Why do you care about all this ancient history?" The two men stared at each other for a while, then Mark said, "I went back to the United States, kicked the heroin, and joined the CIA. Larry Bowlan recommended me, made sure I was taken care of."

"I mean before that, after Bowlan rescued you, but when you were still in Georgia."

"Nothing. I just left Georgia."

"You are so full of lies, Sava."

"I didn't finish my Fulbright, I didn't do anything."

"You just left." Titov words were undergirded with sarcasm.

"The people who freed me—"

"You mean the people who killed my men."

"—dropped me off on the streets of Tbilisi. I tried to go back to my apartment, but I'd been away for over two months and it had been cleaned out and re-rented. You know what I looked like, you know what you did to me. I could barely stand. I was going through withdrawal. I needed a fix but I didn't have the slightest idea where to get one. So I sat outside the door to my old apartment and just... did nothing. The landlady tried to get me to leave, even threatened to call the cops. Your men got to her, I know, that's why she would barely look at me. I told her I'd leave, but only if she let me use her phone. I tried to call Katerina, but I couldn't get through to her. I walked out onto the street—Katerina's apartment was over a mile away, and I didn't think I could make it there, but I was going to try, and that's when Larry Bowlan picked me up."

49

Titov found it impossible to gauge whether Sava was lying or not. Even as a twenty-two-year-old, Sava had been difficult to read, and his stories had always shifted. Though he might not have been a spy at that point, he'd certainly acted like one. If the kid had just broken down and pled for mercy, the interrogation might not have gone on for as long as it had. But Titov had always sensed that Sava had been keeping something in reserve, even if it had just been his dignity. He'd been determined to completely break the kid, to strip him of everything, but he hadn't been able to do it. Sava had held on. He'd been barely conscious half the time, but had still found the energy to spit—literally and figuratively—in people's faces.

"What happened after Larry Bowlan picked you up?"

Sava's eyes looked dead. His mouth formed neither a smile nor a frown. "Of course, as you know, I was addicted to heroin."

Titov didn't bother responding. He had many regrets, but what he'd done to Sava wasn't one of them. After Sava had been set free, and the KGB in Tbilisi left reeling as a result of Bowlan's death squad, Titov had been demoted to protection duty in Chechnya. Those had been bleak days, and they had become bleaker still when the Soviet Union collapsed. The very existence of the KGB had been called into question, and it had taken many long years for both Titov and the KGB to rise again.

Sava said, "Bowlan took me to a house. In the countryside. He helped clean me up. He fed me. Got me some heroin too, not much, but enough so that I wouldn't experience any more with-drawal symptoms while still in Georgia. The idea was that he'd patch me up just enough so that I'd be let on a civilian plane. And that's what happened. A few days after getting to the safe house, I was driven to the airport. Someone from the embassy accompanied me. I was still a wreck, but at least I could walk. The story was I got mugged in Tbilisi. Anyway, I made it home. Kicked the heroin addiction first, then got a call from Bowlan asking whether I wanted to join the CIA."

"And you said you did?"

"It would appear so."

"And you never tried to talk to Katerina again?"

"No."

"Why not?"

"It was safer that way."

"You said you tried to call her right after you got back to Tbilisi."

"I did."

"What changed?"

"I had time to think about it. Time to realize that maybe she'd be safer if I stayed away from her. I didn't want you doing to her what you did to me."

"What makes you think we would have hurt Katerina?"

"You used her, didn't you? You and your men planted a lis-tening device on her to get to me."

It seemed surreal to Mark that they were having this conver-sation about something that had happened such a long, long time ago, so long ago that it hardly seemed real anymore.

"We might have."

"We both know you did. And I knew that if I didn't walk away from her you'd try to use her again to get to me. So I let her go."

Titov tapped his thigh with his pistol. "Still, not a *single* call. Not even a note. You must not have thought much of her."

"Wrong. I thought I loved her."

Titov stared into Mark's eyes. They were as dead when he spoke of love as when he spoke of torture. Either the American was an exceptionally good liar, or he honestly didn't know about what had happened.

"Did Bowlan try to stop you?" asked Titov. "From contacting Katerina?"

"No."

"Really?"

A silence. Titov wasn't sure whether Mark was trying to remember or had decided to ignore the question.

"He might have," said Mark eventually. "We discussed my predicament, and how best to proceed."

"How to proceed."

"You're asking about something that happened over twenty years ago. And you know the condition I was in. My memory of that time is foggy. Why did you kill Larry Bowlan? And what was the painting of Katerina doing in his room?"

"Ah yes, the painting. Let us talk about it." Titov's voice rose a notch. "Because if you really left Georgia when you said you did, without bothering to contact Katerina, you would not have been able to recognize it."

"Not true."

"The painting does not even show her face, Sava, so you could not have simply recognized *her*. And I happen to know that this painting, she made it *after* you were captured! So if you never saw her again after you escaped, then there is no way you would be able to recognize this painting." Titov let Sava think about that for a moment. "That is how I know you lie. No, what happened is that after you escaped you paid a visit to Katerina. You saw this painting. It was still drying, no? And Sava—I *know* what you did when you were there."

Titov glared at Sava, daring the American to deny the truth.

The elevator door at the end of the cavern opened. One of Titov's men appeared. He wore a combat headset and carried a short-barreled automatic rifle. "Sir, we have a problem."

Situated on the edge of the badlands ten miles northwest of Nakhchivan City, atop an old salt mine, the Babak Sanatorium was housed in a grand old prewar building that had originally been built to accommodate asthmatic Soviet pensioners seeking refuge from the damp, cold hinterlands of central Russia. More recently, it had been restored by a group of overly optimistic Turkish investors hoping to lure aging pensioners from Turkey and Iran to the restorative air of the mine.

The venture had failed—it turned out the appeal of traveling to a police state and paying top dollar to sleep in a salt mine was limited—and one month earlier, the FSB had bought the property from a Turkish bank. One week ago, Titov had begun quietly transferring his men and matériel from South Ossetia into Nakhchivan, using the sanatorium as his base.

Now, upon exiting the elevator that led from the mine to the ground floor of the sanatorium, Titov was greeted by one of his men, a twenty-five-year-old Muscovite who was the son of the FSB's Saint Petersburg director.

"How many are there?" asked Titov as he half-walked, half-jogged around a dormant fountain that stood in front of the elevator.

"Six cars, fourteen men."

"Where are they now?"

"Nine have taken positions around the perimeter of the sanatorium, five are at the front door."

"Weapons?"

"Makarov pistols and a few Uzis. No heavy armor."

"What do they want?"

"To search the premises."

Why was this happening? The advance team from FSB coun-terintelligence had paid off the local police. The sanatorium had no close neighbors; it was surrounded by badlands and desert. *Sava.* Somehow he'd led the Azeris here. Titov didn't know how the American had done it, but the fact that they'd shown up so soon after Sava's arrival wasn't a coincidence.

"What have you told them?"

"We asked if they had a warrant to enter. They said no, but that they intended to enter by means of force if we didn't allow them entry."

"Do you believe them?"

Titov had reached the front lobby. Though it had been ret-rofitted with shiny ceramic tile and gaudy chandeliers, there was no furniture, which gave the room an empty, sterile feel. Through the glass doors he saw one of his men arguing with what appeared to be an Azeri police officer.

Titov ducked into a room off the lobby where ten different LCD monitors hung from walls; each displayed a live CCTV feed from different points around the sanatorium. They confirmed what he'd already been told: the sanatorium was surrounded.

Titov had confidence in his men; they were highly trained, and the tunnels were filled with arms that—although earmarked for the upcoming operation—could be used now to mount a robust defense. But once the fighting started, the Azeris could call in rein-forcements, the army even. The tunnels would be inspected, the weapons would be found. Their cover would be blown.

Titov grabbed a radio headset, confirmed that the transmitter was set to block intercepts by rapidly changing frequencies, then called out a series of codes. He listened as each of his men responded, then instructed one of them to relay a message to the man who was dealing with the Azeris at the entrance—*continue to stall.*

Titov pulled off his headset, but held one of the earphones to his left ear so he could monitor any ongoing communication between his men. Then he picked up a satellite phone off the desk and dialed the direct number of his boss, the director of the FSB.

His call was answered on the second ring.

Titov quickly explained the situation. When the director began to berate him, Titov interrupted. "It is not the risk to me that is of concern. It is the risk to the operation. What I need now is for you to authorize the early activation of my second unit."

Titov had split his operatives into two groups—spies with paramilitary skills, and paramilitaries who had also been trained as spies. The former had come to Nakhchivan weeks earlier and were now with him at the sanatorium. The latter—with the exception of Titov himself, who had originally trained as a soldier—had just entered Nakhchivan the day before.

"You can't contain this failure even if we dispatched your second unit this very minute. The men who are threatening you now are no doubt in touch with the authorities in Nakhchivan City as we speak. There's no point trying to protect your cover—it's already been blown."

"I can draw the Azeris inside, make them think they are safe, and then quickly neutralize them once the second unit arrives. If you can arrange for the operation to launch tonight, then the level of confusion will be such that the Azeris won't know what hit them, they won't have time to react."

The director cursed.

"Battles don't always go as planned, sir," said Titov. "You and I, we have always improvised. That is why we are here today, why we survived for so long. Will you do it?"

"I will put the matter to the president. Whether the Iranians are even capable of moving up the timetable, I don't know."

"And my second unit?" When the director didn't answer, Titov said, "Sir, we can't wait until after you speak to the president to activate them! By then the battlefield will have changed. Our options will be more limited."

Another pause, then, "Activate them now."

"Thank you, sir."

"But first tell me—how did the Azeris discover your location?"

Titov hesitated—he didn't want to tell the director about Sava. "I don't know."

50

───────○───────

Mark observed as his Russian guard appeared to listen to something that was being transmitted over his radio headset.

"Yes, sir. Immediately, sir." The guard turned to Mark. "Put your hands behind your head. Walk to the elevator."

Mark stayed seated. The Russian repeated himself. Mark still wouldn't move, so the Russian—speaking into his radio headset—asked what he should do.

After listening for a moment, the Russian said, "If you don't walk, I am to shoot both of your feet, then your arms, then drag you to the elevator. This is your choice. Walk."

So subtle, the Russians, thought Mark. But he knew a real threat when he heard it, so this time, he stood.

"Quickly!" The Russian prodded Mark in the back with the barrel of his AKS-74, an automatic rifle with a folding stock that, like the Grach pistol, was favored by the Russian military. When they reached the elevator, the guard said, "Lower your left hand. Right hand stays on your head. Then press the elevator button."

Mark did as instructed. The elevator door opened.

"Step inside," said the Russian. "Press level six."

Mark pressed levels one, two, and three, but the Russian couldn't see that because he was still outside the elevator.

"OK, now what?" asked Mark.

"Both hands behind your head. Face the back wall."

Mark complied, the Russian stepped into the elevator, and

the door closed. The barrel of the AKS was now pressed against the left side of Mark's upper back.

Noticing that Mark had pushed the elevator buttons for the wrong floors, the Russian cursed, then jabbed Mark in the back, hard, with the barrel of his rifle, causing a spike of pain to shoot through Mark's chest.

"You think this is funny!"

"No."

Another hard jab, this time to the kidney. More muttered curses. "Piece of shit. Cocksucker."

The business with the elevator buttons had just been a hunch—if the Russian was in a rush to get to the sixth floor, Mark figured it couldn't hurt to slow him down.

The Russian cursed yet again as he punched the various elevator buttons, trying to reset them.

When the elevator doors opened on what Mark guessed was the first floor, he heard two things: one was the sound of the Russian frantically hitting the elevator buttons; the second was the sound of men, maybe fifty feet or so away, arguing in Azeri—one wanted the other to step back from a door, while the other was yelling about someone not having permission to enter.

Mark felt the pressure from the gun barrel on his back lessen slightly as the Russian repositioned himself. Sensing that his captor was distracted, Mark took advantage of the unexpected opportunity—maybe the only one he'd have. Twisting violently, he grabbed for the rifle.

A shot rang out. Mark felt a sting by his hip but his left hand already had a purchase on the AKS and he was pushing the barrel away. More shots were fired, but they went wild into the elevator walls. Glass shattered. Mark kicked at the Russian's crotch with his right foot and tried to bite the Russian's trigger hand.

A blast of automatic rifle fire, lasting several seconds, sounded from what Mark could now see was a reception area of sorts.

"Drop the weapon!"

The command was spoken in Azeri.

The door to the elevator began to close, but before it did so there was a popping sound, like a water balloon bursting as it hit pavement. Mark felt something wet on his face. The Russian's grip on the rifle relaxed. Mark ripped the gun away and fired a single round into the Russian's leg. But then he realized his shot had been unnecessary—that the rear of the Russian's head was mostly gone, and that the water-balloon-popping sound he'd heard had been the man's skull exploding.

Mark threw out his hand and pushed the OPEN button just before the elevator began ascending to the next level. Two men in rumpled civilian clothes stood ten feet from the elevator, Uzi machine pistols aimed at him. One of the men wore plastic sandals. Mark let his AKS rifle drop and held up his hands.

"Your name!" shouted the older of the two, in Azeri.

"Mark Sava."

"It's him," said the second.

"Come with us," said the first.

"There are more Russians here," said Mark.

"How many?"

Mark considered how many he'd encountered, how many he'd heard. "At least six, maybe more. Some might be on the top floor. That's where this guy"—Mark gestured to the corpse on the floor—"was taking me. Be careful, they're all armed, mostly AKS-74 rifles, a few short-barreled carbines too."

51

————————◦————————

Outside the sanatorium, a white Ford van with tinted windows screeched to a stop underneath the large portico in front of the main building, just beyond the reception area where Mark stood.

"Go," said one of the plainclothes Azeris, ushering Mark along. "Quickly."

Five more men rushed into the sanatorium. Two appeared to be local cops; the rest were dressed in plainclothes, but carried themselves like trained soldiers.

Mark was directed to the front passenger-side door of the van. He yanked it open, then did a quick double take. Behind the steering wheel sat Orkhan Gambar. A Makarov pistol lay on the dashboard and an Uzi rested on the floor of the van, between the passenger seat and driver's seat.

Concealing his genuine surprise at seeing Orkhan—Mark had hoped Orkhan would send help, but hadn't imagined he'd deign to show up in person—he said, "I don't think I've seen you drive in what, ten years? What happened to the chauffeur?"

Orkhan was wearing what he always wore—a dark suit with a pressed white button-down shirt—but he'd removed his tie. The way he was seated, his considerable girth had stretched his shirt so that his ribbed undershirt was visible between the buttons. The bags under his eyes sagged more than usual. His Turkish nose appeared especially enormous.

"Get in," said Orkhan.

Mark did, wincing because of the increased pressure sitting

put on his ribs. "What are you doing here?"

"I received your call, of course. We tracked your cell phone signal to this sanatorium but then it disappeared. What happened?"

"They were holding me in the salt mine below the sanatorium. Were you already here in Nakhchivan when I called?"

"No. But I was near the military air base at Sumqayit."

Mark still didn't understand why Orkhan, who commanded an army of men, would have seen fit to drop everything he'd been doing and immediately hop on a flight to Nakhchivan. He said as much.

Orkhan said, "There have been some developments. In Baku. It was better that I leave. And I also think we must talk. What are my men walking into?"

"Russians."

Mark repeated the information he'd already relayed to the Azeris inside the sanatorium, prompting Orkhan to lower the driver's-side window of the van and call to the Azeri who stood guard in front of it.

"Go! We will take care of ourselves out here. Coordinate with Salimi on the interior assault."

"Yes, sir."

"Do you have reinforcements coming?" asked Mark.

"No."

"You should."

Orkhan shook his head, "Not a possibility. But if I include the two of us, we have fifteen men to their six. It should be enough."

"I said they had *at least* six, and those Russians in there are professionals."

Orkhan let out a weary sigh. "My wife's brother-in-law is the only man I trust here in Nakhchivan. He was the one who assembled this team—with men *he* trusts. They are good men, experienced men, but even if they were not, the army is not an option. The Interior Ministry forces are not an option. Because of complications I don't wish to discuss, most of my men in the National Security Ministry are not an option. So there will be no reinforcements. There is no one else."

"You're in trouble, my friend," said Mark.

Orkhan leaned across Mark and pulled open the glove compartment. Inside was another Makarov. He grabbed it by the barrel and offered the grip to Mark.

Mark asked, "Do you want me to join the search inside?"

"No. You are helping with exterior security. If I tell you to shoot someone, shoot them. And after my men secure the interior of the building, you will help us interrogate the prisoners. I am hoping you will know the right questions to ask."

As Mark took the pistol, he assessed their position. The roof of the portico provided cover from the sanatorium's upper-level guest rooms. And they had a clear view of the front reception area, the glass doors of which had been shot out. An assault from the road, or from the rear of the sanatorium, was possible, but he and Orkhan would have some time to react to either. The van itself afforded them some protection, and mobility. It wasn't a terrible position. "OK," he said. "We talk."

"You're bleeding."

Mark glanced down to his right hip. Beneath it, his shirt was sticky, and not from sweat. He inspected the wound. The shot had just grazed one of his modest love handles. It wouldn't bleed for long.

"I'm fine."

"You said you had information for me. What is this information?"

Orkhan sat grim-faced as Mark told him that Russian forces had been massing not only in South Ossetia, but also at bases in Armenia and Dagestan.

"Who told you this?"

"The CIA's Central Eurasia Division has been monitoring the situation."

"So your boss, this Ted Kaufman in Washington. He told you."

"Yes."

"And you believe him."

"Yes."

"The Russians are preparing to invade us," concluded Orkhan flatly. "This much is obvious."

Mark had certainly considered that possibility—why else would the Russians be secretly massing forces at all their bases closest to Azerbaijan?—but an unprovoked attack on Azerbaijan would trigger an international outcry. Which the Russians might be prepared to weather, as they had when they stole Crimea from Ukraine, or when they seized disputed territories in Georgia. But if the Russians were to interfere with all the oil flowing to the West via the BTC pipeline, or with the natural gas that was slated to flow to Europe from Azerbaijan via the proposed Trans Adriatic Pipeline, *that* the US and Europe would be hard-pressed to stand for. There was too much money at stake. Mark explained his thinking to Orkhan.

"Yes, but these Russian dogs, you have dealt with them for decades, I know. But you don't know them like I"—Orkhan tapped his chest three times with his index finger—"know them."

Mark recalled his time with Titov back in the 1990s. But he also recalled his time with Katerina, and all the other Russians he'd known over the years, many of whom he still counted as friends. "I think I know them well enough, Orkhan."

"Then you should not be shocked by what you see happening now! The Russians have never accepted the loss of Azerbaijan, or Georgia, or Kazakhstan, or Kyrgyzstan, or Ukraine, or—"

"I get it," said Mark. What Orkhan was really saying was that some Russians, including the Russian president, considered all the former Soviet states to be within Russia's rightful sphere of

DEATH OF A SPY

influence. "But an *unprovoked* invasion of Azerbaijan…I don't see it happening."

"Oh, it will not be unprovoked. We must speak of Nakhchivan. What do you know?"

"I was told an airstrip was built, in secret, in the south. Our satellite data picked up the construction phase, but nothing shows up now. What's going on there?"

Orkhan exhaled loudly through his nose. Then he dipped his hand into his inner suit-coat pocket and produced a lemon-flavored cough drop. As he unwrapped it, he said, "Would you like one? I have plenty."

"No."

Orkhan sucked on his cough drop for a while. "And it is the CIA who has hired you to investigate this restricted area?"

"No, the Russians hired me."

Orkhan flashed him a look.

"It's a joke."

"Not funny."

"The CIA noticed Russian troop movements in South Ossetia, so they hired my firm to investigate. When the man I sent got murdered—he was also a friend—I was pulled in to figure out who killed him and why. My investigation led me here."

"And who did kill him, this friend of yours?"

"A Russian general named Titov."

"He is the commander of the special forces unit of the FSB known as Vympel," said Orkhan matter-of-factly. "Promoted last year. His qualifications are questionable, but the director of the FSB is his *krisha*."

Krisha was the Russian word for roof. In the Russian mafia, it meant the person to whom one paid—often unwillingly—protection money. In the Russian FSB, which often competed with the mafia in the protection racket game, it meant much the same thing.

Continuing, Orkhan said, "Titov first started paying his *krisha* when they served together in Afghanistan and Titov was dealing heroin on the side. His *krisha* was his commanding officer. This is common knowledge, everyone knows it."

"I didn't."

"This is because you waste too much time with women and children, of course. As his *krisha* rose, Titov rose with him, played enforcer for half a dozen criminal enterprises the FSB was running in Moscow. They are all criminals, these FSB people. You are saying Titov killed your friend because of what your friend learned in South Ossetia?"

Mark hesitated. He didn't want to bring up all the stuff about Katerina. "I think so. By the way, I know that whatever project you have going on here involves the Israelis. I tailed a couple of them from the restricted area back to the Tabriz Hotel earlier today."

At that Orkhan laughed. "Well, at least you make this easy, Sava. I will confide in you. At this point I have no one else I can confide in."

"What has happened, Orkhan?"

"The Russians have gotten to people in my government. I see now that, in preparation for attacking with troops, they first attack from within. As we speak, my own government is hunting me. I have lost the confidence of the president. Also, your information is correct—the restricted area is an air base."

"Why doesn't it show up now on our satellite photos?"

"Because it was built in such a way as to prevent it from being detected by satellites. Most of the facility is underground. The aircraft must slip into an entrance ten meters high and twenty meters long and there is an exit as well. Both the entrance and exit are shielded by overhangs covered with earth. They are invisible from above."

"This was a joint project with Israel?"

"Yes."

"You have pilots that can use this airfield without killing themselves?"

"Pilots? No. There are no pilots."

"Drones," said Mark after a time, understanding.

"Yes."

"Israeli-built drones."

"Yes. Herons, but the new stealth models. Of course. You can guess the rest, I'm sure."

Mark's pulse quickened. "The Israelis are using the drone base to spy on Iran from Azerbaijan." Israeli-made drones couldn't get to Iran from Israel—the distance was too great. But all of Iran would be in range from a drone base in Nakhchivan. "And in return…" Mark had to think about that, but only for a moment. "And in return, you get to use Israeli drones to spy on Armenia. And Nagorno-Karabagh."

Nagorno-Karabagh was the disputed bit of territory over which Azerbaijan and Armenia had been fighting for over twenty years. It was currently occupied by Armenia.

"Of course."

"And the Russians found out about the operation?"

"Almost certainly, yes."

"And because they favor Armenia over Azerbaijan—"

"Sava, listen! It is true the Russians don't like that our oil flows to Israel and the West, and they worry about deals we are making to send even more oil and gas to Europe, bypassing Russia. And the Russians do not want to see us gain an advantage over their Armenian pets. But that is not why they will invade. They will invade simply because the Russians are like the Armenians—when they live someplace for a little while, they begin to think that place is theirs. They forget who the land really belongs to. The issue with the drone base is secondary. It is merely an excuse."

DAN MAYLAND

Mark didn't agree with Orkhan's blanket characterization of the Russians and Armenians, but knew it was pointless to argue. He said, "But if the Russians really are gearing up to invade—"

"It appears they are."

"—then they need to come up with a better excuse than just the presence of a drone base. Do you think—" Mark had been staring outside the van as he spoke. He squinted, then said, "Hand me the binoculars."

A pair of binoculars protruded from a pocket on the driver's side door. Orkhan handed them over. "What is it?"

Mark adjusted the focus. A white minibus, visible in the flat desert that lay beyond the badlands, was approaching.

Orkhan cursed.

Mark focused on the Turkish lettering on the side of the van. "NATURE TOURS AND AVIARY EXPEDITIONS. KARS, TURKEY," he read, adding "Nakhchivan does get birders…but I don't think—"

"Bah! These fools are not here for birds."

"No, I don't think so either."

Orkhan picked up the walkie-talkie on the dashboard and informed his men that they were about to have company. "Have someone close the first gate, now! Tell them the sanatorium is closed. And get two more men outside. Fire on the bus if it tries to pass through the gate."

Moments later, a Nakhchivani cop burst out of the sanatorium, sprinted to his police car, and took off in the direction of the metal gate a hundred yards down the road.

The cop reached the gate and swung it closed just as the minibus pulled up to it. The driver of the bus engaged in what appeared to be a heated conversation with the cop. Through the dirty windows of the minibus, Mark counted twelve passengers. All men.

He studied them all as best he could. Some gray hair, but collectively they were much younger than Mark would have

250

expected a group of birders to be. And they weren't chatting with each other the way they should have been had their plans to visit the sanatorium been suddenly dashed; they all sat stone-faced, staring straight ahead.

One of the men inside the minibus lifted the underside of his wrist to his mouth and spoke a few words.

"Yeah, we definitely have a problem," said Mark.

Moments later, gunfire erupted from the upper floors of the sanatorium. The Nakhchivani cop fell to the ground as the minibus lurched forward and crashed into the gate.

The gate held. Orkhan fired on the minibus, which backed up twenty feet, then surged forward. This time the gate burst open. The men inside were smashing out the windows with their guns. When Orkhan ran out of ammunition, Mark raised his pistol, and, shooting past Orkhan's face, fired three shots at the driver. He missed.

"Go!" Mark pointed west. They were outnumbered, and about to be outgunned and overwhelmed. "Cut the corner!"

It was possible to avoid the gate and approaching minibus by driving down a long scrub-covered hill, at the base of which lay the road.

Orkhan steered the van up and over the curb that lined the circular drive in front of the sanatorium, but as he did so, the van's front tire on the driver's side blew out and the metal wheel rim smashed into the concrete curb, sending a violent jolt through the van.

Orkhan struggled to steer as the van careened down the hill. Mark swiveled in his seat, looking back. Several seconds passed—then a police car appeared at the top of the hill.

"They've got a car." Mark had to yell so that he could be heard over the rattling of the van. "The cop they shot at the gate—they found his keys."

Orkhan tried to speed up, but the van swerved dangerously. The police car began descending the hill at what Mark estimated to be over twice the speed of the van. He could see two men in the car.

"What do we have for ammunition?" Mark checked the magazine of his Makarov. He had seven shots left. He opened the dash compartment.

"There's nothing," said Orkhan, adding, "We had to move fast with what we had…" Orkhan's voice trailed off as he focused on keeping the van upright as it skidded down a steep section of hill.

The paved road appeared in front of them. Through his binoculars, Mark focused on the two men in the police car. The one in the passenger seat was leaning out the side window, holding an AKS rifle, waiting to take a shot. When they reached the road, Orkhan tried to speed up. The flat tire ripped away from the rim. Sparks flashed from the wheel well, and the metal rim ground jarringly along the pavement.

Paralleling the road was a deep ditch. Mark gauged that, in about a hundred feet, when the van rounded a gentle corner, he and Orkhan would be out of sight of the police car for at least a few seconds.

"Slow down as soon as we round the bend. Just enough so that I'll be able to jump out without killing myself."

Mark climbed out of his seat and squatted on the floor behind Orkhan, next to the van's cargo door. With his right hand he gripped his Makarov; with his left, the cargo door handle.

Orkhan looked skeptical. "And then what?"

"Then I deal with them."

"You are not so young anymore, Sava! Perhaps you should stay with me in the van."

"Screw it, I'll be fine."

"I'll wait for you."

"Don't. I'll take care of them, and we'll meet back in Nakhchivan

City. Send a man to the Blue Mosque." Mark wasn't trying to be heroic. Splitting up would help confuse the enemy, and Mark would rather take his chances on foot, hiding in the hills and waiting for the right moment to slip back into Nakhchivan City. The alternative—rattling loudly along in an easily identified and barely functional van, out of ammo, and trying to fight off a Russian posse—was a lousy option. Orkhan, however, too fat and out of shape to handle running through badlands, had no choice. "If things go bad for me, call Ted Kaufman. Tell him what you told me. He may be able to help you." Mark recited the number for Kaufman's cell.

Orkhan recited the number back while looking around for a pen in the dash compartment.

As the van entered the curve, Orkhan slowed down. Mark yanked open the cargo door, took a quick look down the road to confirm that the men in the police car couldn't see him, and jumped. He hit the road running, but his speed was still too fast for his legs to handle, so he wound up diving into a somersault roll. The instant he came out of the roll, he slammed into a large waist-high boulder on the side of the road, just above the ditch.

Crawling, he forced himself to move forward as he slowly caught his breath. His chest felt as though someone had taken a sledgehammer to it. His broken ribs were burning—he'd connected with the rock right around where they'd been hurting.

He'd planned to hide in the ditch beside the road, but the boulder was large enough to provide decent cover, so he hid behind it.

Seconds later, the police car appeared, roaring toward him at top speed. When it was within fifty feet, Mark ducked his head out from behind the rock. He forced himself to ignore the pain, took quick aim at the guy in the passenger seat, squeezed off three quick shots—one of which he thought might have hit home—then fired three more shots at the driver.

When the car barreled past him, it already had begun to swerve off the road. It hit the ditch, bounced high, then rolled.

Mark charged toward the car; along the way, he picked up the AKS assault rifle that had been thrown from it, confirmed that the magazine was full, tossed his Makarov into a ditch, flipped the safety on the AKS to automatic fire, unfolded the stock, and lifted the rifle to his shoulder.

He was having trouble breathing, which he attributed to being out of shape. Slow it down, he told himself. He felt light-headed. It was a struggle to suck in enough air.

The police car had landed upside down. Both men inside were lying on the ceiling, which was now the floor, of the car. Their bodies were immobile, and twisted into unnatural configurations. Mark approached the driver's-side door and tried to take a few deep breaths to gather his strength, but it hurt his chest when he tried to breathe too deeply, so he took several shallow breaths and then smashed out the window with the butt of his rifle. He dragged the driver out onto the dirt, then fell to his knees.

What the hell is wrong with me? The sun was bright in Mark's eyes. *Don't pass out.* He took a second to gather his strength, then focused on the Russian.

Blood ran freely from the man's left eye, temple, and mouth. He was lifeless, shot through the head. On a lanyard that hung from the Russian's neck was a name tag that, in Russian and Turkish, read VICTOR PETROV, BIOLOGICAL RESEARCH INSTITUTE, ST. PETERSBURG UNIVERSITY and under that, in smaller print next to bird-themed logo, NATURE TOURS AND AVIARY EXPEDITIONS, KARS, TURKEY.

Mark coughed a bit, spit in the dirt, searched the driver, and extracted a black Grach pistol from a shoulder holster. He checked the clip—five bullets left—so he wedged it between his belt and the small of his back and then walked around to the other side of the car. He smashed out the passenger-side window and examined the second Russian. He detected a bullet wound to the chest—he'd been trying for a head shot and had evidently missed—but the guy appeared to be dead anyway. Mark searched him, finding an identical Grach. After removing the magazine, which he slipped into his front pocket, he tossed the pistol into the ditch that paralleled the road.

OK, Mark thought. You're safe for the moment. Now concentrate.

He coughed again, then doubled over because of the pain in his chest. God, why was it so hard to breathe? He stood slowly and felt around his wounded ribs. Everything was hot; he thought maybe he was bleeding there, that maybe he'd been shot and just hadn't noticed, but the fabric of his shirt was dry.

Assess the situation. You're armed, but you've got angry Russians above you.

Mark glanced back toward the sanatorium. The roof was just visible. Could they see him? Had they watched the crash?

Behind him, were the badlands; in front, the low desert valley that led to the Aras River. His plan had been to run through the badlands, lose the Russians, then make his way back to Nakhchivan City, maybe call a cab when he got to the main highway, but God, he felt awful, and—

Mark felt for his prepaid, the one he'd stuffed down his pants. Gone. There would be no cab.

Damn.

Maybe Orkhan had stopped after all, or wasn't that far away, he thought. He felt an almost irresistible urge to lie down right where he was, but instead forced himself to slowly jog down the road, in the direction Orkhan had gone. He'd only made it a few yards, though, when he glanced behind him.

A man was sprinting down the hill in front of the sanatorium. He was maybe a half mile away, but headed straight for the crash site. Mark rounded a bend in the road. No sign of Orkhan. He looked southeast, searching for a pass, or a gully, between the badland hills. He saw one, took a few shallow breaths as he steeled himself to the task, blinked as he wiped some sweat out of his eye, and began to run.

52

———————o———————

Orkhan reached the main highway and turned left toward Nakhchivan City.

He glanced in his rearview mirror. Several cars were approaching—he was traveling far slower than the speed limit—but none from the road that led to the sanatorium. As the cars buzzed by him, the occupants inside stared with alarm at the disabled van. Shortly thereafter, a cop car passed, going in the opposite direction. Orkhan sounded his horn repeatedly and brought the van to a stop. The cop executed a quick U-turn and raced up behind the van.

Orkhan collected his cell phone and handheld radio, but left his Uzi on the floor. As he stepped onto the pavement, the cop called to him.

"Get back in the vehicle."

Instead of obeying, Orkhan strode forward. The cop put his hand on the grip of his belt-holstered gun. Orkhan, his face twisted into a snarl, ignored it.

"Stop!" ordered the cop. Then, gun drawn, "Step back to your vehicle."

Speaking slowly and deliberately, as if issuing a threat, Orkhan said, "You will take me to Nakhchivan City." Showing zero concern that the cop might shoot, Orkhan reached into his back pocket and produced his government identification. He held it up in front of the cop's face.

"Sir, I—" The cop suddenly focused on the identification.

"And you will take me there now," said Orkhan.

The cop swallowed hard. He glanced at the gun he was pointing at Orkhan and then lowered it. "Are you—"

"Yes. I am that Orkhan Gambar. Your minister of national security. And you will either do as I say—immediately—or I will have you arrested and shot."

53

Mark glanced behind him. The Russian he'd seen running down from the sanatorium was no longer visible, but couldn't be more than a few minutes away. He also noticed the rubber treads from his shoes were making faint impressions in the dry ground, so he jogged to a dry rocky streambed where his footprints wouldn't show up; he was too light-headed to keep his balance on the uneven terrain, though, and he twisted his ankle and fell, which in turn caused the muscles around his rib cage to spasm.

As he lay on the rocks, curled into a fetal position, he considered the last time he'd broken his ribs, back in 1997 when he'd been hit by a car in Tajikistan. He didn't remember it hurting this much. A little pain, which he'd alleviated by self-medicating with vodka over the course of several days. He'd only been twenty-nine years old, though. His body had been much more flexible, much more—

Get your head out of your ass and move!

He pulled himself to his knees. Using the AKS as a cane, he rose to a standing position and continued along the dry streambed, pushing himself as fast as he could.

Which wasn't fast at all. The harder he tried, the more his injured ribs burned and the more difficult it was to breathe.

The Russian would be here soon, and he wouldn't be able to outrun the guy. Something had gone seriously wrong with his body. Had Titov drugged him? Or had that hit he'd taken when he jumped out of the van done more damage than he'd thought?

Mark stopped, because he didn't have the energy to go any further. He had to find cover, and now, but there was no cover to speak of. The assault rifle felt so heavy. He wanted to let it slip from his hands. Instead, he let his whole body slip to the ground. The sharp rocks hurt his knees.

He raised the rifle and aimed where he expected the Russian to appear. But after a minute, he grew too weak and he let the gun fall to the rocks. He'd have to use a pistol, he thought, just as another coughing fit wracked his body.

His chest muscles spasmed again. When the spasm subsided, he pulled the Grach out from behind his back and spit. What sprayed onto the bleached river rocks was bloodred.

At that moment, the Russian appeared at the entrance to the canyon. His eyes and rifle were fixed on Mark. Mark tried to raise his pistol, intending to shoot, but found that he couldn't do it. As the world began to spin, the Russian became a blur. Mark slumped back and hit his head on the rocks. The sun was bright in his eyes, too bright. He tried to suck in a breath, but it was so hard. If he could just sleep for a moment, he thought, he might be able to regain his energy.

54

---○---

"Minister Gambar, to what do we owe this pleasure? If I had known—"

"I need a room. With a secure phone."

"Certainly, sir."

"Your office will do."

Orkhan had instructed the cop to drop him off at the gates of an unassuming government building in downtown Nakhchivan City. He'd shown his identification to the guard just inside the front entrance. Thirty seconds later, the chief of the local Ministry of National Security outpost—a man whose appointment Orkhan had personally approved—had appeared, breathless.

"Right this way, Minister Gambar. Is there a problem?"

Looking straight in front of him as he walked several feet ahead of the chief, Orkhan, his voice cold and pitiless, simply said, "Yes, there is a very big problem."

---○---

Orkhan sat in a leather office chair, behind an oak desk that, he noted, was larger and nicer than his own back at the ministry building in Baku. He made a mental note to have the desk shipped to him, when this was all over.

On the desk was a phone. Orkhan set it on speaker, then dialed the president's direct number.

"I'm afraid the president is not available, Minister Gambar. May I ask where you are?"

"The president is available. He is always available to his minister of national security. And no, you may not ask where I am."

A long pause, then a nervous, "Just a minute, please."

He was kept waiting. Orkhan imagined that even if the apocalypse were raging, the president would find time to emphasize his power over his supplicants by wasting their time.

Five minutes passed. Then the line clicked. "Orkhan."

Orkhan leaned back in his chair. The phone was still on speaker. "Mr. President."

"You have news for me about the traitor?"

"I know you signed the warrant for my arrest, Mr. President. I know you believe I am the traitor. Let us dispense with the ruse, shall we?"

Orkhan could hear the president breathing. He imagined that he was smoothing his mustache. What a petty, frivolous man. He had inherited the ambition and arrogance of his father, but not the great man's foresight, or—Orkhan feared—ability to manage a crisis.

"I'm not clear on why you called, Orkhan."

"The Russians are preparing to invade us."

Orkhan had no love for the Americans; they were as vicious as they were self-righteous. Nor did he harbor any fondness for the Chinese; their superiority complex notwithstanding, they were just a pack of xenophobic grubby small-thinking merchants. And the effete Europeans were simply insufferable. *Why France, Fatima?* But it was the drunken Russians he truly loathed. They were as violent as the Americans, as sure of their own cultural superiority as the Chinese, and just as boorish as both—no small feat! No, Orkhan did not like the Russians one bit. The fact that his father had spent five years in a Siberian gulag didn't help either.

"What?" The president sounded genuinely surprised.

"They are massing men and matériel at their land and air bases in Armenia, South Ossetia, and Dagestan. They have infiltrated Nakhchivan with spies—"

"Nakhchivan has *always* been infiltrated with spies."

"Not like this, Mr. President. I fear the same for the mainland. You need to alert the defense minister. We must move troops to the northern border crossings immediately."

"Who tells you this?"

"An American source."

"You have always been too taken with the Americans, Orkhan. Either they are playing you, or you are trying to play me."

"No, Mr. President, it is *you* who is being played. I tell you this information so that you will have an opportunity to defend our country. There is a reason, too, why I am being set up by the interior minister. It is because the interior minister is in league with the Russians and wishes to get rid of me before the Russians attack. Because the Russians know that I will fight them! And that I will tell you to fight them!"

A long pause, then, "Odd that your recommendation to move troops to our northern border should come at the precise moment the Iranians appear to be determined to attack from the south."

"The Iranians? Why would—"

"Come now, minister. Have you been hiding in a cave today?"

"If you're referring to the bombing in Tehran, I assure you I have been monitoring—"

"Monitoring! Oh, well if you have been *monitoring* the situation, then this might interest you." The derision in the president's tone was evident. "An hour ago, the president of Iran held a news conference. The Iranians are now claiming the attack on their supreme leader originated from a secret drone base in Nakhchivan—yes, *that* base, Minister Gambar, the Iranians know of it! They allege that we collaborated with the Israelis to build this base and supply it with Israeli-made stealth drones, and that we let the Israelis arm some of the drones for the purpose of carrying out assassinations in Iran. They claim to have the remains of an Israeli drone they shot down!"

Orkhan, blindsided, took a long time to respond. "But none of the drones *have* been shot down. And even if one had been, it would not have been armed."

"They claim to have proof, that they have the drone that fired on the supreme leader's house—"

"They lie. If the residence of the supreme leader was bombed, then the Iranians did it themselves just so they could blame us."

"How do you know this? How do you know the Israelis didn't arm one of their drones behind our backs? How do you know that they really didn't try to kill the leader of Iran?"

"Because I trust the Israelis."

"You trust them. Well, good for you, Minister Gambar."

"And I don't believe they would ever be so reckless."

"Me, I cannot afford to be so trusting. Either way, lie or not, the Iranians claim that they shot this drone out of the sky after it fired upon Khorasani's house in Tehran. And they have a wreck, which they displayed on television, of something that looks like an Israeli drone. And they say that, in retaliation, they intend to take possession of the airfield in Nakhchivan—yes, you heard me. Iranian troops are already massing. They appear to be preparing to *invade* Nakhchivan. Did you hear me? The Iranians are planning to invade! And now—now!—you talk to me of the Russians. Of moving troops north. You are at best a fool, Orkhan, and at worst a traitor."

"But the Russian base in Armenia, and—"

"Military intelligence has detected nothing of which you speak." The president's voice rose a notch. "The Interior Ministry has detected nothing of which you speak! I don't know why you passed information about the drone base to the Russians, Orkhan—"

"I did nothing of the sort."

"But I know I have a nation to defend, and that you are not helping me do my job." The president didn't speak for a long time. When he did, he just said, "Where are you?"

"Nakhchivan. Within the hour, I will board a plane back to Baku. After that I may be found at my desk in the ministry."

Orkhan heard a click. The president had hung up on him.

Without even pausing to think, Orkhan hung up the phone on his end just long enough to reset the dial tone, then entered the number for Ted Kaufman. If the president was too corrupt or stupid or both to defend Azerbaijan from the Russians, Orkhan would see whether he could get the Americans to do it instead.

Part Six

55
Baku, Azerbaijan

———————o———————

When Orkhan Gambar touched down at the airport in Baku, his plane was met on the tarmac by a convoy of Azeri military vehicles, mostly armored South African–made Hummer knockoffs. As he descended the air stairs, he was greeted by a general from the Ministry of Defense.

The general, a diminutive man whose uniform hung loosely on his frame, was accompanied by thirteen armed soldiers. His right hand gripped a single sheet of paper. He and Orkhan had worked together a decade ago to shore up Azeri defenses on the border between Iran and Azerbaijan.

"Minister Gambar." The general frowned, then said, "These certainly are strange times we live in."

Orkhan stepped forward. "Strange indeed."

"I want you to know I did not ask for this assignment." The general held out the sheet of paper. Orkhan grabbed it unceremoniously and began to read.

"You understand," said the general, "I have no choice in the matter."

It was, as Orkhan had suspected, a warrant for his arrest. He was being accused of treason. In the lower right-hand corner was the presidential seal, underneath which was the large, fussy signature of the president.

"Do not worry yourself, General." As he spoke, Orkhan continued to scan the warrant. "When this matter is resolved, I assure you I will not hold *you* personally accountable."

Underlying Orkhan's words was a hint of venom, and malice, suggesting that he would, in fact, hold the general accountable.

"Thank you, sir."

A moment passed. The general appeared unwilling or unable to do what he needed to do next.

"Well?" said Orkhan.

"If you'll come with me, sir. Please, ride with me in my car."

"And where will we go?"

"Gobustan, I'm afraid, Minister Gambar."

Orkhan nodded. The news was unwelcome, but not unsurprising. Gobustan was a miserable prison that lay in the desert south of Baku. Many of Azerbaijan's political prisoners were housed there. The cells were filthy—Orkhan knew this from experience, having conducted several interrogations inside the prison—and many of the prisoners were drug addicts, or infected with AIDS.

The general added, "I'm sorry. The order came directly from the president."

Orkhan, looking behind him to the bodyguard who was carrying his suit coat in such a way as to prevent it from becoming wrinkled, said, "Follow me to Gobustan. Along the way, inform my wife as to what has transpired."

56

Nakhchivan, Azerbaijan

———————○———————

Mark felt a sting on his chest and opened his eyes. He was on his back, staring up at a light. To the side of the light stood a jowly man with bloodshot blue eyes and a deeply wrinkled forehead. Gray chest hair tufted out around the top of the man's button-down shirt, which was open at the collar.

Someone cursed, then said in Russian, "He wakes, give him more."

Mark tried to remember where he was and what had happened to him.

Dammit that hurts...

He tried to put his hand to his chest—that's where the pain was coming from, it felt as though he was being poked with something sharp and cold—but someone pulled his hand away and held it down.

"Don't move!"

Mark coughed. It was still hard to breathe, the air just wouldn't enter his chest. He felt consciousness slipping away from him again but he willed himself not to pass out. He tried to lift his head up, but someone pushed it down.

"Immobilize him!"

Strong hands pinned down both of his arms, then someone wrapped a rubber tube around his left forearm. Seconds later, the jowly man pulled out a needle. Mark tried to pull his arm away, but couldn't. The struggle made him need to breathe more deeply, but he couldn't—the air he needed just wouldn't fit in his lungs. He felt as if he were drowning.

The jowly man hovered over him a moment. Mark smelled acrid underarm sweat, felt the needle enter his forearm, and then seconds later, the rush.

Those bastards. They were doing it to him again.

He struggled, but the hand on his arm held firm. He felt a burning sensation; moments later, it was as if something were pushing its way up his arm, and then his body began to feel light. It was an entirely new sensation, one he'd never experienced before.

Russians were talking. "OK, we try this again. Hold him. One, two—"

Mark felt a prick on his chest and then an awful sensation of metal slipping into his body, as though someone were slowly pushing a knife into him. He screamed, or thought he did. The sounds in the room melded with the air. It was as if he were floating. The surface beneath him no longer felt hard. His head was sinking; he tried to lift it.

He heard something that sounded flatulent, like a balloon that hadn't been tied properly and was rapidly losing air.

"It's done. Keep his arms pinned until he passes out."

The hand on his forehead lifted. Mark raised his head. His vision was blurry, but he could see well enough to make out the grotesque horror that had been inflicted upon his body. Protruding from the left side of his chest was an enormous needle, part of which was encased in plastic. Blood ran from the incision point down the side of his chest. Attached to the top of the needle was what looked like the cut-off fingertip of a rubber latex glove. The fingertip was affixed to the end of the needle with a rubber band. The whole contraption looked sinister, the work of a crazed mind.

The needle looked as though it had been inserted close to his heart.

Get that thing out of my body.

As Mark tried to raise his head a bit higher, the flatulent sound started up again. And that's when he realized that *he* was making the sound, or rather his body was. The fingertip on the end of the needle gave another belch as air escaped from it.

Mark lowered his head. The drug that had been injected into his arm was overwhelming him. He allowed himself to hope that he'd been hallucinating.

No, he thought, as he slipped into unconsciousness. What he'd just seen and heard had been far too real.

57
Baku, Azerbaijan

———————○———————

As they were passing through downtown Baku en route to Gobustan Prison, the general who had arrested Orkhan received a call on his cell phone. He answered it, listened a moment, said, "Yes, yes, of course I'll hold." And then, a minute later, said, "Of course, Mr. President. It's just that I—"

Orkhan reached into his shirt pocket, pulled out the last of his cough drops and popped it into his mouth. He breathed deeply through his nose, enjoying the sensation of lemon scent rising through his nasal cavities.

"—yes, yes, Mr. President. No, no problem. I will bring him there at once." The general clicked off his phone and turned to Orkhan. "We will not be going to Gobustan."

"No?"

"No. The president wishes to see you."

Orkhan took a moment to digest this new bit of information. "I see. Did the president say what he wanted?"

The general looked worried. "He did not." A moment later, he said, "I truly am sorry about all this, Minister Gambar."

Orkhan sucked on his cough drop as he wadded up the wrapper and let it fall to the floor. "I'm sure you are."

———————○———————

Several upscale waterfront restaurants had recently sprung up on the shores of the Caspian south of Baku. At one, the president of

Azerbaijan sat outside at a circular table, beneath a bright cerulean-blue umbrella. The air smelled of seaweed, and salt, and fish. Just offshore, oil rigs sparkled in the waning sun, as did the tower cranes that stood atop all the man-made islands under construction. Gentle waves surged up and down through the rock-pile breakwater.

Before Orkhan could get within a hundred feet of the president, he was stopped and frisked by the president's bodyguards, a process that resulted in the confiscation of his phone. That minor indignity was compounded by the fact that, when Orkhan was brought to the president's table, a large meal of what appeared to be beef tenderloin, served with a red wine reduction sauce of mushrooms and shallots, sat in front of the president. The rest of the table was bare.

It was dinnertime. Orkhan was hungry.

"Minister Gambar. Good of you to come." The president skewered a piece of beef and stuck it in his mouth.

"Mr. President."

"You were right. About the Russians." The president spoke with his mouth full. His fork clattered to his plate, and he nervously wiped his mouth with a napkin that lay on the table. "Dubov just held a press conference."

Dubov was the Russian foreign minister.

The president, his voice laced with equal parts anxiety and derision, continued, "He warns the Iranians not to attack, that Russia would see this as an unacceptable encroachment on the Russian sphere of influence. He spoke of troops at their base in Armenia. In South Ossetia. In Dagestan. You were right. The Russians, they have prepared for this."

Orkhan considered the president's words. "*Sphere of influence.* He dared to say that, did he? The dog."

"They have no shame."

Orkhan drummed his fingers on the table. "And the Russian ambassador. What does he say?"

"That Russia is willing to offer military assistance if Azerbaijan should need it. Generous of him."

"Should we need it," repeated Orkhan. Now it was clear. Now he knew the Russian plan. But it was happening even faster than he thought it would.

He looked out to the nearest of the man-made islands under construction in the Caspian. The islands were to be Azerbaijan's answer to Dubai. There would be luxury hotels, a Formula One racetrack—there were even plans to build the tallest skyscraper in the world. Orkhan had never liked the thought of turning Baku into a mini-Dubai, but he liked even less the idea of the Russians putting a stop to it. No one would want to invest in an Azerbaijan dominated by Russia.

"The Russian ambassador tells us not to worry, that Russia will not tolerate an Iranian incursion into Azerbaijan. That Russia is bound—by the treaty of Kars—to protect the territorial integrity of Nakhchivan."

"That old communist treaty has nothing to do with this."

"He adds that he is deeply concerned that we would not be able to adequately defend ourselves against an Iranian invasion." The president swallowed hard and took another bite of his steak, as if to communicate that, while the matter they were discussing was indeed troubling, things were not yet so dire that they merited interrupting dinner. His darting, nervous eyes suggested otherwise. The president was scared, and it showed.

"And, of course, he speaks the truth," said Orkhan. "We would not be able to adequately defend ourselves."

"I tried to send word through the Iranian embassy that we are prepared to shut down the drone base, shut down everything, and accept Iranian monitors. But the Iranians have closed all diplomatic channels. They don't want to hear the truth, they don't want to negotiate. Instead they say nothing and are moving troops to the border."

"We could hold off the Iranians for a few days, perhaps. But if the fighting spilled past Nakhchivan into the heart of Azerbaijan…the border is too long, and of course, if we were drawn into a fight with Iran, the Armenians would take full advantage of our weakness."

"You think I don't know all this!"

"It was not meant as a criticism, Mr. President. Simply an observation."

As the president took a sip of water, his hand trembled. "You have been free with your *observations* of late, Minister Gambar."

"I speak as I do only because I hope to prevent the catastrophe I fear may be unfolding." Orkhan leaned forward in his seat. "This is what happened, Mr. President. The Russians found out about our drone base in Nakhchivan, and that the Israelis were using it to spy on Iran. How they found out I don't know, but it doesn't matter. What matters is that the Russians decided to tell the Iranians about it. Why? Because the Russians knew the Iranians wouldn't stand for it. But instead of encouraging the Iranians to attack the base, the Russians came to the Iranians with a proposal—agree to *pretend* that the Israelis have attacked their supreme leader from this base, and that they are prepared to invade Nakhchivan as a result, and then Russia will do their dirty work for them."

"The Russians will invade us to save us," said the president.

"Yes."

"From the Iranians."

"Yes. Of course, they will not call it an invasion. They will call it offering assistance. Coming to the rescue. Just as they rescued Crimea. But the Russians don't expect to shoot their way into Azerbaijan. They expect to be let in. By you, Mr. President."

"By me? Why would I do such a thing?"

"Because your interior minister—your brother-in-law—will advise you to let the Russians into Azerbaijan. He will offer forked-tongue counsel, will say the wise choice is to work with the Russians rather than oppose them, will try to convince you that the Iranian threat is real when it is not, and will claim to have assurances from the Russians that they will leave within days, as soon as the drone base is dismantled, that this really is about protecting Nakhchivan from the Iranians. And all that will be a lie, Mr. President. The interior minister is betraying you, and our nation. The Russians are waging *maskirovka*, disguised warfare, just like they always do."

"I see," said the president.

"You doubt me."

"I doubt everyone."

"Have you spoken with the interior minister since the Russians offered aid?"

Ignoring the question, the president asked, "And what do you think the Russians will do if I refuse them entry?"

"They will enter regardless." Orkhan remembered when the Soviet tanks had rolled into Baku in 1990. He'd been there, he'd helped tend to the wounded and bury the dead. He knew it could happen again. "And they will claim to have been invited. It won't matter that we and others will know they are lying—the propaganda, the cyberwarfare they will wage, the *spetsnaz* forces who will throw off their uniforms and pretend to be Azeris in support of the Russian presence, it will be enough to confuse the situation, to silence voices of opposition. Will our border troops even resist them? I don't know, but if they do, the Russians will likely threaten—through secret back channels, so they won't look like bullies—to invade the mainland with troops from their bases in South Ossetia and Dagestan. Of course, since Russian tanks in South Ossetia would have to pass through Georgia to get to us, the Russians would be sending a message to the Georgians as well."

"If the Russians were to learn that we intend to fight them, that might be enough to get them to reconsider."

"I suspect instead they would simply add more troops to the

DEATH OF A SPY

incursion, believing that we will back down in the end. Whereas if they think they can take us by surprise, and that they won't be resisted, then they will likely use as small a force as possible so as not to alarm the international community. What we must do is fight their deception with deceptions of our own, Mr. President. What we do is we lure the Russians into thinking they can enter Azerbaijan unmolested, and the second they cross the border, we do everything we can to see that they are slaughtered. That is the only message the Russians will understand. Then in public, we claim it was nothing more than a minor skirmish with the Armenians, so the Russians can back down without losing face."

"And if the Russians don't back down? If they send more troops?"

"If they are truly committed to taking Nakhchivan, they will."

The president stared at his hands. "There are few ethnic Russians in Nakhchivan. And any sizeable Russian troop reinforcements would have to go through Georgia *and* Armenia. It will not be easy for them to mount a real invasion."

"If we give the Russians Nakhchivan, they will take it. But if it becomes clear that they will have to pay a steep price, they may decide it is not worth the cost. That is our only hope." He paused. "It would help if we were not alone in mounting a defense."

"If the Turks were to intervene—"

"Forget the Turks. A year ago, maybe. Not now."

Turkey and Azerbaijan, both Turkic-speaking countries, had historically been close. But Azerbaijan's deepening military relationship with Israel had come at a time when Turkish-Israeli relations were at a nadir. The Turks had wanted the Azeris to back away from Israel, as a show of solidarity. The Azeris had refused.

The president pursed his lips into a worried frown, then said, "Yes, I fear you are right."

"And even if we should ask, help from the Turks might not be enough."

"I can't pull all our troops from the south. Some must remain. As must some troops in the north, by the border with Georgia and Dagestan, in case you are wrong and the Russians do intend to invade the mainland."

"The Russian goal is to spread us thin. That is why I have made some preliminary inquiries with the Americans, Mr. President."

"Inquiries with whom?"

Orkhan explained about his conversation with Ted Kaufman. "And?"

"The Americans have much to lose, should the Russians invade. Even though our oil does not flow through Nakhchivan, they will know the Russians could use an occupation of Nakhchivan to bend us to their will. They do not want to risk letting Russia control the flow of oil and gas out of the Caspian. And the Americans are a bloodthirsty lot. They enjoy fighting. But they have grown cautious of late. So I cannot say for sure. Of course, for assistance to be rendered, the request must come directly from you."

"This is a dangerous game we're playing, Orkhan. What if the Americans do render assistance, but the Russians respond with more force, and then the Americans even more still? The Turks may yet get involved, and then the Armenians. And the Turks and Americans are part of NATO and the Armenians and Russians and Kazakhs and—"

"Yes, yes, but—"

"—have their own mutual defense agreement. These agreements, they lock countries into war. And then maybe instead of a little skirmish at the border, you have NATO against Russia and their most devoted lackeys, and before we know it we are fighting World War III."

"There is risk involved with any course of action we take, Mr. President. But right now the most immediate risk is that part of our nation is about to be overrun by Russia. Call the Americans. If you won't, I will, but it would be better if the call came from you."

58
Bishkek, Kyrgyzstan

———————○———————

Daria was in her Volkswagen Jetta, approaching the bridge that led from Kyrgyzstan to Kazakhstan, when her phone rang. Darkness had fallen. After driving around the outskirts of Bishkek, and then stopping to have dinner at a little hole-in-the-wall restaurant she'd never been to before—a place no one would think to look for her—she'd resigned herself to driving to Almaty, where she planned to spend the night in a hotel.

Behind her, Lila was sleeping in a rear-facing car seat that Daria had special ordered from a department store in Europe because she hadn't been satisfied with the options in Kyrgyzstan. She answered quickly, before the ring tone could wake Lila.

It was John Decker.

"What have you got?" Daria kept her voice low.

"Kaufman just called."

Decker explained that the CIA believed Mark had been abducted somewhere in Nakhchivan. But that no one knew for sure where he was now.

"This can't be happening. We just had a kid, John. We were happy." Daria stopped herself from saying anything more because she knew she'd start crying if she did.

"Mark's a tough guy, Daria. I wouldn't—I mean, I wouldn't go panicking about this or anything."

"I'm not panicking," she snapped. "I'm worried, there's a

difference."

"I didn't mean panic, I just meant…anyway, there's another angle to all this. Have you been listening to the news?"

"No." Daria had kept the radio off so that it wouldn't bother Lila.

Her spirits sank as Decker told her about the bombing in Tehran, and the Iranian response, and the Russian reaction.

She said, "And Mark is in the middle of this shitstorm. That's wonderful. Just fucking wonderful."

"It gets worse. Reading between the lines of what Kaufman told me, the CIA's not going to just roll over and let the Russians, or the Iranians, invade Nakhchivan."

"Of course they won't. Crimea was one thing, but they'll be afraid that if the Russians start having their way with the Azeris in Nakhchivan, next up will be the oil."

"Whatever the reason—"

"Oh, that's the reason."

"Kaufman tells me he's been ordered to assemble a team that can serve as a liaison between the Azeri ground forces and any, uh, any military assets we might just happen to have in the area." Decker let that statement hang for a while, then added, "Should it come to that. I guess the situation is kinda fluid."

"I'm not sure I'm following."

"If the Russians or the Iranians attack Nakhchivan, the Azeris would have a hard time holding them off, assuming they even dared to try."

"One of the many reasons Mark needs to get the hell out of there."

"Yeah, well, Kaufman—and I guess people way above him—are thinking if we could just give the Azeris a little boost, maybe it would turn out differently, you know?" Without waiting for Daria to answer, Decker said, "The thing is, they need at least one person on this team who's fluent in Azeri, and there just aren't many people on the CIA payroll who fit that bill, and I guess the CIA isn't thrilled about tasking one of their own to something that, well…"

"Has the potential to be a serious cluster. So they want someone they can disown if things go south."

"Something like that."

"If communication is the issue, there are certainly plenty of Azeris who speak English."

"Kaufman wants a translator he can trust. And he's not going to trust someone that the Azeris serve up. Daria, listen, Kaufman asked me to ask you whether you'd do it."

For a moment, Daria was dumbstruck, even though in retrospect she realized that, from the way Decker was talking, she shouldn't have been. She'd sworn off that underworld of secret operations, sworn off contributing to deaths of others. She'd done too much of it already. "But…Kaufman hates me."

"He doesn't like you much, that's for sure. But there aren't that many people like you out there, Daria. You speak fluent Azeri. You worked for the CIA, but don't now. All qualities they're looking for."

"The CIA fired me, Deck. They don't trust me worth shit, and I don't trust them."

"Yeah, but Kaufman trusts you more than he would a random Azeri guy pushing some crazy Azeri agenda. And he thought that maybe—because by helping to hold off the Russians and the Iranians you'd be helping Mark—you might go for it. This could be your opportunity to get back on the Agency's good side, Daria."

"I don't want to get back on their good side. I don't give a crap about them. They're a pack of amoral liars. If it was up to me, I'd shut them down."

"I'm just the messenger, Daria."

"Not to mention, I've got Lila."

"I completely understand. So I'll tell Kaufman no?"

Daria glanced back at Lila. She seemed content now, occasionally kicking her legs or raising her arms a bit. Leaving her at this stage in her life, even for a little while—Lila had never even fed from a bottle—was unthinkable. Helping out Ted Kaufman and the CIA, that too was unthinkable. As was helping Azerbaijan or the United States kill twenty-year-old conscripted Russian soldiers.

But so was not even lifting a finger to help Mark.

Ever since she'd received the text from him, Daria couldn't help but think that she was letting him down in what could be his moment of greatest need. And by letting Mark down, was she also letting Lila down? If Mark were to—she tried not to even think the word *die*, but there it was—if that should happen, and she had done nothing to try to prevent it, how would her daughter judge her in the years to come? How would she judge herself? What wife would do such a thing?

Yes, the deal with Mark had been that, in the event he ever sent such a text, Daria was to focus on keeping herself and Lila safe. Protect what remained of the family. But Mark was part of the family. By helping him, she would be helping Lila.

"Daria, you still there?" asked Decker.

59
Nakhchivan, Azerbaijan

———————○———————

When General Dmitry Titov had arrived at the restaurant atop the Tabriz Hotel an hour and a half earlier, the dining room had been nearly full with dinner guests. But now it was empty save for himself, three of his men, two overly solicitous young waiters, and an officious pear-shaped supervisor in an ill-fitting suit who was bossing the waiters around.

Which meant it was almost time. Titov's men had killed all the Azeris who'd stormed the sanatorium—except for one who may have escaped with Sava—and then had hastily cleared out all the weapons and communications equipment, anticipating that the operation would be approved for tonight. As soon as it had been, Titov had come to the Tabriz.

Because the Tabriz was the tallest building in all of Nakhchivan City, boasting unparalleled views of most of the downtown from the top floors, it was of both strategic and tactical military value. As a result, the Russian army intended to occupy it; Titov himself had made the recommendation.

The risk, however, was that as soon as the Russian army crossed the border, the Azeris would think to fortify the Tabriz, particularly the upper floors. So Titov had further recommended that he and his men secure the top floors early, just before the invasion started, so that the Russian army wouldn't encounter any unnecessary resistance when they finally did arrive.

Titov continued to peck away at his dinner—chicken served

with a pomegranate walnut sauce, boiled potatoes, and wild herbs that had been picked in the mountains the day before—until he observed a cook leaving via the single elevator that serviced the restaurant.

It was nine-thirty. The kitchen had closed a half hour earlier. Titov guessed there was another cook still in the back, cleaning up. Perhaps a dishwasher too. He didn't want to take more life than necessary, but considered it likely that everyone else in the restaurant would stay until the last diners—in this case, he and his men—had left.

He downed the last of his beer, then nodded to a short man with a lazy eye who sat across from him.

One of the waiters, who'd been watching from nearby, approached the table.

"Another beer, sir?" he asked Titov.

"Please."

"Where is the bathroom?" asked the lazy-eyed man.

"This way, sir," said the waiter. "Come, I will show you."

Titov's man followed behind the waiter—until they passed under the security camera that was affixed to the ceiling above the door to the men's room, at which point he reached underneath his baggy tracksuit jacket, withdrew a silenced snub-nosed pistol, calmly shot the waiter twice in the back of the head, then fired three more quick shots into the rear of the security camera.

The sound of the camera being blasted apart attracted the attention of the second waiter and the pear-shaped supervisor. As they turned toward the sound, Titov shot the second waiter twice in the back, then once in the head, before aiming his pistol at the supervisor, who by now had noticed the dead waiter by the security camera.

As the manager dropped to his knees and began to pray—*Allahu Akbar*—Titov shot him.

Addressing his two remaining operatives, who had remained seated, Titov said, "The kitchen." He drew his finger across his throat and made a clucking sound. "Go."

Soon, two quick spitting sounds came from the kitchen, followed by the clatter of metal pots falling to the floor.

To the man with the lazy eye, Titov said, "Go get the gear."

Many of Titov's men had dispersed, first to cut the telephone cables that led from Nakhchivan City to surrounding Azeri military installations, and then to rendezvous at the northern border to assist with the invasion. Those who had accompanied him to the Tabriz had checked in using their fake Russian passports—they were traveling as businessmen negotiating a deal for the import of crop fertilizers—and had taken three rooms on the twelfth floor, directly below the restaurant. Their luggage had been loaded with weapons and communication equipment.

"Yes, sir. And the prisoner?"

"Him too. We'll set up a communications station there." Titov pointed in the direction of a baby grand piano. Most of the restaurant was carpeted, but the red marble floor around the piano might offer some protection from small arms fire coming from below, should it come to that.

The operative who had disposed of the cook in the kitchen was standing in front of the elevator door.

"You," Titov pointed. "Station yourself in the stairwell on the twelfth floor. Alert us when guests enter and leave their rooms. Don't interfere with them unless you have reason to believe that they intend to interfere with us." To his remaining operative, Titov said, "You, make sure the roof is clear."

He assumed the Azeris on the lower levels would eventually realize that something was amiss on the restaurant level. There was the broken security camera. And the employees who had never left. But the Azeris were lazy, and lacked personal initiative;

it was likely that by the time anyone was sent to investigate the anomalies, it would be too late—the invasion would already be well under way.

60

———————o———————

Mark first became aware of sounds—a faucet running, a door closing, clipped words spoken in Russian. He was comfortable, and warm, and enjoying the sense of weightlessness; he sensed that the sounds posed no threat to him, that they were there purely for entertainment.

But then, some errant synapse fired in his brain, and he thought, *Lila is hungry, she needs to be fed...*

Lila, where was she? He wanted to check the bassinet at the foot of the bed, but he couldn't see; it was too dark in his bedroom. Lila had to be there, but...now he couldn't hear her, couldn't even hear her breathing. He couldn't hear Daria breathing either. Only this strange intermittent tapping sound, as though a mouse were scurrying around between the walls.

The lamp, where is it? To your left on the end table. Mark opened his eyes, froze for a moment, then shut them again. He forced himself to remain perfectly still.

Your breathing, control your breathing, if you breathe too fast he'll know you're awake.

He focused on what he had just seen, tried to reconstruct the picture in his head.

Seated five feet away was one of Titov's operatives—the tall gaunt one with narrow-set eyes who had followed Mark out of the Tabriz Hotel earlier in the day. He was tapping on some sort of tablet computer device.

Mark recalled the attack at the sanatorium, and trying to escape with Orkhan, and collapsing in the desert. But after that, nothing.

No, not nothing. An image of a needle flashed across his mind—they'd slid it into his arm—and then an enormous stainless-steel needle, this one plunged into his chest. What in God's name had that been?

Control your breathing. Don't show anger.

Breathing, thought Mark a moment later. *He was breathing easily.*

And he didn't feel drugged up any more. He focused his thoughts on his chest. There was pain there, pressure, but it was bearable. In the left side, he felt something foreign, pressing against his shirt. He sensed tape on his arms. Holding an IV line in place?

Think.

Broken ribs, jumping out of the van driven by Orkhan, slamming into that rock on the side of the road. He'd been having trouble breathing, he'd spit up blood.

But he could breathe now, which suggested the needle in his chest—now that he thought about it, he realized it was right about where his left lung should be—might have been there to help him. To drain away blood so that he could breathe again?

Which would mean the Russians had saved him. But why? It certainly hadn't been an act of mercy.

So that Titov could continue to interrogate him, of course.

In his mind, Mark tried to study the scene he'd glimpsed when opening his eyes. He'd focused on the Russian, but what else had he seen? He recognized the décor of the room they were in. It was…institutional, like…

The Tabriz Hotel. That's where he was. He recognized the slate-gray carpet and the heavy ivory-colored window shades and the black lacquer table and the floral-patterned bedcover. There was more, though. He was seated, but not in a normal chair; he'd glimpsed footrests—he studied the mental image in his head—and a bit of a wheel by his foot.

A wheelchair. That was how they'd gotten him into the hotel, they'd just wheeled him through the front door. An invalid taking a nap.

So he was in a wheelchair, at the Tabriz Hotel, the Russians had treated his punctured lung, and he was being guarded by one of Titov's men. Mark wasn't sure of his strength—he wanted to try flexing his arms, or stretching his legs, to give himself a better sense of his physical condition, but he didn't want the guard to know he was conscious.

A blanket had been draped over his lap and forearms. He risked briefly tightening the muscles on his arms and concluded that, while some of the tape he felt against his skin may have been there to hold in place IV lines, it was primarily there to secure his arms to the armrests.

61
Above Nakhchivan

———————o———————

Daria felt another flutter of nerves in her gut. She couldn't take her eyes off the live video feed. It was playing on a military-grade tablet computer that an Army Ranger had hung on the seat back of a civilian Airbus jet, a jet she'd boarded in Bishkek a few hours earlier. Up until now she'd been trying to convince herself that this was all just a big bluff, that the Russians would never be so bold as to take real military action, that they'd just use the threat of occupying Nakhchivan as a means of extracting some concessions from the Azeris.

But this, this was no bluff. The tanks were coming, and they were coming fast.

She'd agreed to serve as a liaison between the Azeri ground forces and an undercover team of US special forces provided that, if all went well when it came to stopping the Russians, they'd then be tasked with helping her to locate Mark.

The quid-pro-quo arrangement hadn't sounded reasonable at the time, and it felt even less so now. It still hurt to pee, and her breasts were leaky. She was glad she'd bought a decent pump before the birth; at least she'd been able to leave her friend Nazira—the only woman Daria would have considered asking for help—some breast milk to feed Lila. But she'd only been able to pump enough to last for maybe twelve hours, and she worried that Lila wouldn't take to the formula Nazira would have to use after that.

The last of no less than fifty latest-model T-90 tanks had left the gates of the Russian army base in Armenia a minute ago and were now hurtling south toward Nakhchivan at nearly forty miles per hour, chewing up the asphalt roads and sideswiping parked cars. The tanks were being followed by mine-clearing vehicles, armored cars, transport trucks, a satellite and cell phone jamming station, and tracked vehicles mounted with sophisticated Buk surface-to-air missile systems. A batwing RQ-180 stealth drone that had flown across Turkey from the US air base in Incirlik was now circling high above Nakhchivan, relaying it all via an encrypted satellite feed.

"What's their distance to the border?" Daria asked.

"Call it seventy clicks," said one of the Rangers. "At the speed they're going, they should be there in a little over an hour."

Daria calculated in her head. Say they landed as planned in ten minutes. Five minutes to meet with their Azeri counterparts at the airport and transfer themselves and their gear into whatever vehicle was provided.

As though reading her mind, Decker, who was sitting next to her on the plane, wearing a tactical chest rig over an armored vest, scratched his head with both hands and said, "Even driving fast we're talking, say, forty-five minutes to get from the airport to the assembly point at the border...but they won't need us unless things get so screwed up that the drone operators can't tell the good guys from the bad guys. And that won't happen right away. So we should make it in time. Barely."

Daria nodded. They'd gone over this. Before seeing the Russian tanks, though, it had all seemed so theoretical. Even signing the boilerplate legal forms that designated her adoptive parents as Lila's guardians should something go wrong—maybe it would be better for Lila to be raised in Virginia, in a nice home—even that hadn't made it seem real. Nor had dropping off Lila with Nazira, although that certainly had been one of the hardest things Daria had ever had to do in her life. It had felt unnatural, and wrong. Almost as unnatural and wrong as it would have felt doing nothing to try to help Mark. But it hadn't made her experience the kind of fear she felt now, watching the tanks advance.

Fear and disgust. This game that the Russians were playing; it was so pointless. People would die, likely on both sides, and for what? Because old men in Moscow wanted something they weren't entitled to have, and old men in Washington, DC and Baku were willing to sacrifice the lives of others to prevent them from getting it?

Knowing that the entire American ground presence would consist of just three Rangers acting as spotters for air support, her as the translator, and Decker as her bodyguard and a backup spotter in case one of the Rangers went down, didn't make her feel any better.

"If things go to hell, medevac is all on the Azeris," Decker had said when they'd boarded the plane back at Manas Air Base north of Bishkek. "Point being, don't get hurt."

A light footprint, so that the United States could deny they'd even been there, that was the idea. Just enough to get the job done and no more. Then the Azeris could take credit for having mounted a surprisingly robust defense.

The Rangers—who'd just downed multiple cans of Red Bull and, in the case of at least one, Adderall—were unplugging battery chargers that they'd set up in the back of the plane. They wore camouflage fatigues with no identifying marks on them. Decker was inspecting a scuffed-up pair of four-tube night-vision goggles.

"We're all charged up," said one of the Rangers as he handed a bunch of batteries to Decker.

"Thanks, buddy." Decker inserted one battery into his night-vision goggles and then another into his SOFLAM—a Special Operations Forces Laser Rangefinder Designator—which was about the size and shape of a small slide projector and could be used to guide smart bombs to targets.

"Give me your goggles," Decker said to Daria.

She handed them over, and Decker slotted in the battery.

"Thanks."

"I'll be carrying a couple spare batteries if you need them." Decker tapped an ammo pouch on the combat vest he was wearing. "Which you won't, but just in case. How's the vest?"

Decker had given her an armored vest, which she was wearing over her black sweatshirt. In retrospect she wished she'd just worn one of her old T-shirts. "Hot. And too big."

Decker nodded. "It was the smallest they had."

"It'll do. Better than too small."

"These grid maps suck," said one of the Rangers, looking at his tablet computer.

"Best they could do on the fly," said Decker. "I don't think anyone anticipated we'd be paying a visit to this shithole."

62

───────○───────

Mark bit down hard on his tongue, intentionally severing the side of it, then coughed. He opened his eyes slowly, coughed again, and looked around, as though confused. "What...?"

The Russian agent, who was wearing what looked like a small Bluetooth headset, raised his pistol, pointed it at Mark's head, and said, "He wakes."

"Help," said Mark, speaking Russian. "I need..." His voice trailed off.

"What is it you need?"

"Where am I?"

The Russian sighed. "Just be quiet."

Mark coughed again. "Water."

"No."

"I can't..."

"You can be quiet. Everybody can be quiet."

On the table to the right of the Russian lay a pack of cigarettes and an old-style Zippo lighter. Using one hand, the Russian tapped out a cigarette, stuck it between his lips, and lit it with the Zippo.

The blood flowing out of the cut in Mark's tongue was pooling in his mouth, mixing with saliva.

"I can't...breathe." Mark spoke in a pained whisper. "Oh, God..." Mark coughed again, and this time spit up blood, which rolled down his chin and dripped onto the bright-orange fleece blanket that covered his lap and forearms.

The Russian let loose a string of expletives.

Mark began to make croaking noises, as though he could barely get air into his lungs. Then he spit up more blood and coughed again, trying to make it sound like he was choking on his own blood, or vomit.

The Russian relayed what was happening into his Bluetooth, then said, "How should I know? Am I a doctor?"

"I'm drowning," said Mark.

Ignoring Mark and speaking instead into his headset, the Russian said, "All I know is what I have told you." Then, "OK, OK. Two minutes."

Mark rolled his eyes back into his head and kept up the labored breathing.

The Russian stood, Grach pistol in hand. "OK, sick man. We are going on a little trip."

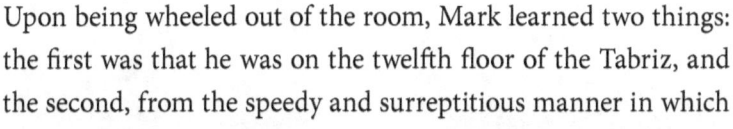

Upon being wheeled out of the room, Mark learned two things: the first was that he was on the twelfth floor of the Tabriz, and the second, from the speedy and surreptitious manner in which he was transferred to the elevator, was that the Russians didn't fully control the twelfth floor.

The same could not be said, however, for the top floor.

When the elevator doors opened, arranged in front of a waist-high decorative garbage bin-*cum*-sand-filled ashtray were four corpses, piled atop one another. The armed Russian who stood near the bodies spoke into his radio headset. "They've arrived." A pause, then, "Yes, sir." To the Russian who was wheeling Mark around, "Follow me."

In an alcove attached to the main restaurant, a black baby grand piano, a lonely little fish tank, and several circular tables had been pushed aside to make room for a large rectangular table that had been placed in the center of the red marble floor. General Dmitry Titov sat at the table amidst a jumble of communication equipment: two army-green radio stations, several tactical headset systems, smaller commercial headsets, a satellite phone, two laptop computers, and a tangle of extension cords and assorted wires.

An AKS-74 rifle, equipped with a thermal night-vision sight, also lay on the table. Titov put his hand on the grip.

Mark coughed up more blood and wheezed.

"How long has he been like this?" asked Titov.

"Since he woke up."

"Open his shirt."

Mark didn't resist as the Russian agent who'd been wheeling him around stripped the blanket off his lap and then ripped open his shirt.

63

———————○———————

Titov sighed.

The elderly medic who had performed the operation on Sava was in the field, supporting the Vympel commandos who were operating near the northern border. Though Titov and the agents he had with him at the Tabriz were all trained in first aid, this situation with Sava's lung was beyond their ability to address.

The American really was a mess. And that flexible plastic tube sticking out of the side of his chest was just repulsive. At this point it might be a kindness to kill him, thought Titov, but he'd delayed doing so for a reason.

"Can you talk, Sava?" Titov spoke loudly, as though addressing someone with a hearing problem.

Sava didn't answer.

"Maybe he should be lying down," said Titov. "Maybe the tube is getting crimped."

"You want me put him on the ground?"

"Do it. But give me your weapon, just in case."

The Russian operative handed his Grach, grip first, to Titov, then pulled out a long double-bladed combat knife from an ankle holster. He pressed the tip into Sava's throat. "You try to fight, I cut. Understand?"

Sava took a few quick, shallow breaths, as if trying to get the air he needed to respond. "Understand."

The agent cut the surgical tape away from both of Sava's forearms, hoisted him out of the wheelchair, then laid him on the red marble floor. Sava rolled to his good side and lapsed into a coughing fit. Blood dribbled out of his mouth.

"Leave us," said Titov to his man. "Help Sergei with guard duty." When they were alone, Titov pulled Sava's leather satchel off the communications table. He flipped open the top flap and removed the painting of Katerina.

Standing over Sava, holding his pistol in one hand and the painting in the other, Titov said in English, "You had collapsed lung. Broken ribs, other things. Very big problems. We operate to relieve pressure, lung is better—very good doctor, I work with him in Chechnya for very long time, he heals my shoulder once when I am shot."

"I need him...now."

"Not possible. You can breathe better now, no?"

Sava pushed himself up, so that he was on his hands and knees.

"Stay down."

"This position...it's better, there's not so much pressure." Sava spit out more blood, then glanced down his shirt. "What the hell was that needle you stuck in my chest...and what is... what is that plastic tube with the rubber thing stuck to it...doing there now?"

Titov watched Sava warily.

"Needle was to let air out, and create path for plastic tube. Once plastic tube goes in chest, needle comes out. Rubber tip from glove at end of plastic tube makes air not go back in." Switching back to Russian, Titov said, "I wish to speak about the painting." He walked around to the front of Sava, and let the painting fall to the floor near Sava's face. "You saw her *and* this painting after you escaped."

"I was in the desert after I escaped...I saw nothing, I passed out and then your men caught me."

"Not today, idiot! In 1991. After you escaped from me in Tbilisi with the help of your criminal friend Bowlan. You must have seen this painting then. Otherwise, you would not have recognized it three days ago. And I think I know why you are lying to me about it now. But I want to hear it from you." Titov waited a moment, then added, "I tried to help you with this injury to your lung, Sava, but it was only a temporary measure. You are going to die here. If not from your wounds, then…" Titov tapped his Grach pistol against his thigh. "I think you understand what I mean. As we Russians say, life is not a walk across a meadow." Speaking those words caused Titov to think of his mother. She'd buried two husbands and a daughter before she'd died of heartache and cancer. It was hard to complain about his own lot in life, or to feel pity for Sava, when he thought about all the pain she'd borne. "It is time for the truth." Titov stared at Sava, waiting for the American to respond. When he didn't, Titov asked, "Are you dying *now*?"

"No. Thinking. Trying to remember."

"Remembering what?"

"That phrase, *life is not a walk across a meadow*. I've heard it before."

Titov wondered whether Sava was losing his grip on reality. "It was a line in a poem from *Doctor Zhivago*. That is why you know it. The truth, Sava."

"Did you know Katerina and I used to visit the botanical gardens?"

"What botanical gardens?"

"In Tbilisi. We went there the last night we were together, just before your men kidnapped me. But we'd been going there for weeks before that. There was one day, it was early spring, if you'd been there you would understand."

64

Tbilisi, Georgia
May 1991, seven months before
the dissolution of the Soviet Union

———————○———————

Marko and Katerina had stationed themselves near the center of the preserve, next to a stand of bamboo that was ringed by English ivy. All the redbud trees, which had been bright pink the month before, were now fully leafed out. Songbirds were calling out from their high perches up in the cedars. Katerina was seated on a small folding camp chair, in front of an easel and canvas, painting a brilliant red poppy flower. The reflecting pool beyond her was covered with lily pads and formed the backdrop to her painting.

Marko sat cross-legged on a blanket beside her, reading and smoking.

After a half hour of silence, he put down his book and, in Russian, asked, "What do you think about Ioseliani?"

The book he'd been reading—or at least trying to read, it was in Georgian and he was having difficulty with the language—was about the Mongol invasion of Georgia in the 13th century. But he couldn't focus on the distant past when so much was going on right now. Jaba Ioseliani was a modern-day criminal-turned-paramilitary who was, at present, advocating for Georgian independence from the Soviet Union.

Katerina had been concentrating on her poppy. "What do you think about him?"

"Well, I like his politics now, of course."

Stifling a yawn as she dipped her brush into a dollop of Venetian red paint, she said, "Then I like him."

"But I worry that he doesn't care about democracy, that he'd be just as bad as the communists if he ever had his way. I mean, he's not a communist, but..."

As Katerina painted one of the poppy's petals, she offered, "I too would prefer democracy."

"You just say this to please me."

"And does it?"

Katerina professed to have no love for communism, but Marko knew that mostly she simply didn't care. She preferred to talk about Renoir—do you think he really was happy, or just trying paint in a way that would inspire happiness in others?—or if not Renoir, then she'd gladly engage in long conversations about Manet or Corot or Matisse or Cassatt or Picasso. She didn't like Picasso, but one of her art books had paintings from his blue period that she knew Marko liked, so she'd try to use Picasso as a way to lure Marko in...or if not conversing about painters then she'd gladly discuss American movies or U2 or sex or cats—she wanted a cat, but the university wouldn't allow her to keep one in her dorm room...

"You should come with me to the next meeting," said Marko, referring to the next meeting of the student Press Club.

A gentle sigh. "And what would I do at this meeting? My mother and brother made me promise not to take part in any of the protests."

Marko had never met Katerina's mother, or her brother, because Katerina worried they might not approve of her dating an American. They were, she'd explained, more traditional in their views than she was.

"Going to a meeting is not the same as going to a protest. At the next meeting, we're discussing the kind of government we would like to see for Georgia once the Soviets are gone. I mean, a

democracy, yes, of course. But will there be a president? A prime minister? There are many questions to resolve."

Katerina tilted her head, smiled, and then leaned down to where Marko was sitting. When she spoke, she breathed into his mouth. "OK. We'll go together then."

"Really?"

"Really."

They kissed. Katerina went back to her painting and Marko went back to struggling with his book on Georgian history. After an hour, though, Marko took a break to light another cigarette. It was late in the day, nearly five o'clock, and the way the sun was filtering down through the trees and dappling Katerina's dirty-blond hair struck him as exceptionally beautiful. So he reached for his backpack, unzipped the top flap, and pulled out a small point-and-shoot camera.

65

———————◇———————

Mark told Titov all that he remembered of that day, then said, "The painting is a reproduction of a photograph I took of Katerina a month before your men captured me. I didn't visit her after I escaped. I wasn't lying to you." Katerina has always been beautiful, but she'd been exceptionally so that day and Mark had wanted to capture it. "It was one of my favorite images of her, and she knew it. That's why she used it to paint her self-portrait."

Mark let his voice trail off as he rested his forehead on the floor. He was sure that was what Katerina had been thinking. He felt connected to her right then.

"So you really don't know."

"Don't know what?"

Instead of answering, Titov said, "I am glad I had the opportunity to kill that scum Bowlan, but now that you have told me this story, I confess that it is with regret that I must kill you, Sava. Come, I will make this easy. But first you must move to the carpet. I cannot have the hard floor here getting wet, not with all the electric wires."

As Titov bent down next to him, Mark considered asking the Russian to explain whatever the hell he'd just been talking about, and why he cared so much about Katerina, and why he'd really killed Bowlan. But then he thought of Lila, and Daria, and concluded that he didn't have time for that luxury. His first priority had to be staying alive.

The second Mark felt Titov's hand under his armpit, he pushed up off the floor with everything he had, slammed the back of his head into Titov's chin, and then twisted and threw a punch into Titov's neck, aiming for the windpipe. Titov took a step back, trying to aim his Grach at Mark, but he stumbled on an extension cord that led to the communications table.

Mark dove for Titov's gun hand and simultaneously kneed him in the balls. Then he bit the base of the Russian's thumb as hard as he could. He felt the skin break, and bone separate from tendon.

When Titov's grip loosened on the Grach, Mark snatched it, fired a quick shot directly into Titov's chest, pivoted, lurched to the communications table, stuck the Grach in his belt as he grabbed the AKS rifle, and fired on automatic as he stumble-sprinted toward the Russian operative who had been guarding the elevator but who was now running for cover.

To the left of the elevator, an open metal fire door led into an emergency stairwell. Mark ran to it, slammed it shut, and took cover behind the cinder-block wall to the side of the door. One of the Russians pinged the door with bullets. Beneath Mark, in the stairwell, a man called out in Russian, "Sergei! Is that you?"

Responding in Russian, Mark said, "Yes, the American, he's escaped!"

As he spoke, Mark took a step forward. He didn't have a clear shot at the Russian below him and he didn't know how many men there were in the restaurant. He glanced up. The stairwell rose one more level and ended at a door that led to the roof.

The Russian below him called out, "Thirty-seven, nine! Identify!"

It was a code of some sort, Mark assumed. One that required a proper response. Instead, Mark fired a single shot down the stairwell and headed for the roof.

He twisted the doorknob, encountered resistance, flicked the firing mode to semiautomatic, fired two shots at the latch, then kicked at the door, but it held firm. He fired two more shots, and this time broke through.

66

Titov groaned as he lifted himself off the floor. It wasn't the burning in his chest—that was minimal, he'd been wearing body armor—but the thought of what had just transpired that really pained him.

Sava.

He should have known the American would pull something like this. But Sava's lung really had collapsed on him. He really *had* to be hurting. Just not as much, evidently, as Titov had thought.

"Vlad!" called Titov.

"Here, sir!"

Titov stumbled into the main room. His right thumb was dripping blood. He thought his nose might be broken. And his balls were killing him. He observed Vlad—a twenty-year veteran of the FSB—on one knee, back pressed against the wall adjacent to the stairwell entrance, AKS rifle pressed to his chest, finger on the trigger. The bullet-riddled stairwell door was open.

"Where did he go?"

"The roof, sir."

"Who's hurt?" Titov was tempted to admonish his operative for having let Sava run past him, but to do so would have only emphasized Titov's own lapse.

"Sergei's down."

"Dead?"

"Maybe."

Two piercing beeps sounded from the communications table. That would be the command center at FSB headquarters in Moscow, Titov knew. He cursed.

"Sir?"

"Keep watching the stairwell. I have to take this."

Moscow had told him they would let him know when the Russian ground forces were about to cross the border. Shortly thereafter, Titov could expect to see Russian tanks rolling into Nakhchivan City and a Russian helicopter on the roof of the Tabriz. Russian ground troops would clear the hotel from the bottom up while Titov's men and a *spetsnaz* platoon from the helicopter would clear from the top down. Once the hotel was clear, the Tabriz would serve as the main communications center of the Russian occupation.

But now the roof was not secure. *That* had to change.

He jogged back to his communications table and answered his satellite phone.

"We are at the border. Prepare yourself," said the voice on the other line.

"Understood," said Titov.

As he hung up the phone, Titov heard screaming. At first he was confused as to its origin, but after a moment realized it was coming from the roof.

Titov took a step toward the window that overlooked the parking area in front of the Tabriz. An Azeri armored car had just pulled into the lot. Sava was yelling, thirteen stories down to them, at the top of his lungs. The Azeri in the armored car appeared to be listening to him.

Titov could make out some of the words. *Russians, taking over, restaurant, killing Azeris...*

67

———————○———————

At first it wasn't even a fair fight, thought Daria.

"JDAMs," said Decker, with whom Daria was communicating via the radio headset she was wearing. "Probably five-hundred pounders. Anything more would be overkill."

She was in northern Nakhchivan, crouched in a decades-old trench that overlooked the Armenian border, peering out of a small hole that had been cut through a low stone wall that ran parallel to the trench. The Russian T-90 tanks had seemed so large and menacing, their diesel engines so loud, that it had been hard for her to imagine anything could resist them. They'd stopped at the border fence, but only to demand that the Azeri troops let them pass. A man claiming to be a Russian general had stood in front of the tanks with a bullhorn.

We come in peace, to help defend the southern border of Nakhchivan from an Iranian attack. Open the gates now or we will drive through them. You have one minute.

A minute had passed. The gates had remained shut. So the tanks had advanced, pounded through the gates as if they were made of paper, and then—before a single shot had even been fired by the Azeris—the first two tanks in the Russian column had been blown to hell by a single B-2 stealth bomber circling some fifty thousand feet above. Daria could see the two tanks now, smoldering. She felt awful for the soldiers who'd been inside them. Because one thing she knew for certain—this invasion loosely disguised as assistance certainly hadn't been their idea.

The Azeri general who commanded the defense stood by her side, dressed in desert camouflage.

Boom! Then two seconds later, *Boom!*

Two more Russian tanks that dared to cross the border were destroyed. And then two more after that. It was clear to her that the Russians hadn't been prepared to encounter anything close to such resistance. The advance, which had been thrown into disarray after the first two tanks were hit, halted.

Below Daria, on the Azeri side of the border, were some thirty Azeri military vehicles, most of which were Russian-made: T-90 tanks, but older versions than the Russians were using; armored personnel carriers topped with antiaircraft machine guns; and a few surface-to-air missile systems. The trenches closer to the border were packed with heavily armed troops, as were the surrounding hills. The Azeris were waiting for the Russians to advance further before engaging them. Daria wasn't sure that was even going to happen.

One of the Rangers' voices sounded on her headset.

"Tell the Azeris to expect incoming! Someone's lighting up the friendlies!"

Daria passed along the message to the Azeri general standing next to her. Moments later, an Azeri armored personnel carrier was hit by a missile that streaked down from a neighboring hillside.

Turning to Daria, the Azeri general said, "We have Russians behind the lines. I need you to relay these GPS coordinates to your team."

The general read them off; as he spoke Daria translated the numbers into English for the Ranger she was linked to via a secure radio connection.

Seconds later, there was an explosion on a nearby hillside.

68

---○---

Alarms began to sound all over Nakhchivan City. Army trucks rumbled through the streets.

The Azeri soldier Sava had called down to had radioed for backup. Titov and his men had disabled the elevator right after Sava had pulled his stunt, so the Azeri infantry men sent to investigate Sava's claim had been forced to trudge up the stairs. After two were shot, the rest had fled, but minutes later, what Titov guessed was an entire infantry platoon had pulled up to the hotel and raced inside.

So the Azeris were coming; it was just a matter of time.

And the minute Titov saw the antiaircraft lighting up the sky to the north, he knew something else had also gone wrong. The Russian MiG fighter jets that had been assembled at the air base in Armenia weren't supposed to be part of the incursion unless the Azeris used the few MiG fighter jets they had stationed in Nakhchivan to attack the advancing Russian ground forces. The MiG made a distinctive sound, audible from many miles away, but Titov couldn't hear any in the air.

In fact he couldn't hear any fighter jets in the air.

Which meant there should be no need for antiaircraft fire at all. But there *was* antiaircraft fire, so something had to be up there, way up high, where it couldn't be heard. The randomness of the antiaircraft fire suggested that whatever it was couldn't be seen by radar any more than it could be heard.

Which meant the Azeris had, at the last minute, found someone to help them. The Turks, perhaps, or more likely, the

Americans. FSB counterintelligence would eventually find out who—their mole in the US embassy probably already knew—but by then it might not matter.

Titov's satellite phone began to ring. Ignoring it, he walked to the emergency stairwell.

One of his men was still positioned to the side of the door, waiting to shoot up the stairwell should Sava show himself. Before seeing the antiaircraft fire lighting up the sky, and hearing what sounded like aerial bombs exploding, Titov had planned to order his men to take the roof. But given what was going on at the border, he'd decided on a different course of action.

He slung an AKS assault rifle with a strap on it over his shoulder, stuck two extra thirty-round magazines in the pocket of his armored vest, pulled his combat knife from his ankle holster, and affixed his night-vision goggles to his head, but with the dual tubes flipped up.

"I recommend you step back, sir," whispered the operative guarding the door. "The stairs are not secure. If you—"

"Dammit."

Titov was trying, using his knife as a lever, to pry the top hinge pin from the bullet-riddled metal door that led from the restaurant to the stairs. The door was thick heavy steel, designed to stop fires from penetrating the hallway; though it was pockmarked with bullet holes on one side, there were no exit holes on the opposite side.

Titov's throbbing right thumb was useless because of Sava's bite. He transferred the knife to his left hand. It took him a couple of minutes, but eventually he managed to work all the pins out. He pulled the door off its hinges.

"I'm going up," said Titov. The metal fire door had been overengineered; as a result, it was exceptionally heavy. With his useless thumb, he struggled to keep it off the ground. "Cover me."

"Sir, I wouldn't recommend that."

"I said, cover me."

Titov stepped into the stairwell and eyed the door that led to the roof. Sava appeared to have attempted to shut it, but because the latch had been shot up, it remained cracked open an inch. As Titov slowly climbed the stairs, lugging the door up with him, he considered the layout of the roof.

Sava would be positioned so that he had a clear shot of anyone trying to access the roof from the stairwell. Because of the way the door opened, that meant the American would have to be somewhere to the right. So what was to the right?

A big air-conditioning condenser, that was what.

With that in mind, and using the fire door as a shield, he bounded up the last remaining steps, kicked open the door to the roof, and burst through it—holding the fire door between himself and where he thought Sava would be.

69

─────────○─────────

Mark had been faking exhaustion when he'd been with Titov in the restaurant, but he wasn't faking it now. He was seated, leaning up against one of several large rooftop air-conditioning condensers. While the condenser probably wouldn't stop a bullet, it was at least a decent blind and might also help mask the heat of his body. The rifle he'd taken from Titov was equipped with a thermal sight, making it likely the rest of the Russians had been issued similar equipment. But the heat was also making him sweat; he felt light-headed, and his heart was beating faster than it should have been.

He was trying not to move any more than he already had, so as not to disturb the flexible plastic tube protruding from his chest. Although he could still breathe well enough, his left lung ached, and he worried that he'd further damaged it when fighting Titov. He desperately wanted to rip the tube out—it felt as though he'd been shot in the chest with an arrow—but knew better than to act on his instinct.

An involuntary shudder swept through him. He thought of Daria, and how they'd strolled through the streets of Florence on what had passed for a honeymoon, recalled how they'd started most mornings taking long breakfasts, him downing double espressos, she with her cappuccino... He'd been uncharacteristically calm, and happy, and content to just let time pass; he'd never been to Italy before and maybe because of that, because he had no history there that could have come back to bite him, he hadn't been constantly looking over his shoulder. As his thoughts turned back to the present, he pictured Daria back in Bishkek with Lila, holed up somewhere safe, he hoped, and he steeled himself to the task of guarding his position and holding onto consciousness. At least the light show he'd seen in the northern sky suggested that the Russians were encountering—

The door to the roof burst open.

Mark fired two quick shots at someone who appeared to be using a metal door as a shield. The man made it to a second air-conditioning condenser and dropped the door in front of it.

"Enough, Sava!" cried a voice in Russian, a voice Mark recognized. "You are surprised I am alive, no? Well, there is this thing they make now, armor that can stop bullets. You wear it like a vest. Perhaps you've heard of it?"

Mark didn't respond to the sarcasm. Instead, he focused on the sounds around and below him, listening for evidence that Titov was advancing, or was just talking to cover the approach of another assailant.

"Ceramic armor, Russian kind. Very good quality. I recommend it to you."

Titov spoke flippantly, but in a way that seemed to border on mania.

"You've got big problems," said Mark. "The Azeris are coming. There will be more than your men can handle."

"You don't know my men, Sava. And my own reinforcements will also be coming soon. *Spetsnaz* GRU from our base in Yerevan, the very best. If I were you, I would not be so confident."

Mark wasn't feeling the slightest bit confident. And *spetsnaz* GRU troops, elite special forces culled from the military intelligence branch of the Russian army, were no joke. "There is fighting in the north. Heavy fighting." He tried not to sound as drained as he felt.

"I have seen it."

"That does not bode well for you."

"I do not know what it bodes, nor do you. All I know is that I have been ordered to secure the roof of this hotel, so one of our helicopters can land here. If you are still alive when it arrives, that will mean I have failed. But still, the men inside the helicopter will kill you."

"The hell they will."

"There will be too many of them, even for a slippery person like you. So either way, if I kill you first or they kill you later, it is the same for you." A long silence, then, "And if these men don't come, well…yes, you are right, that will mean the invasion has failed, in which case things will not be so good for me, you understand? If you don't kill me, well, the Azeris will."

Mark didn't answer.

Titov said, "So, Sava, will you try to kill me now?"

Mark still didn't answer.

"Katerina was my half sister, by the way. I don't think you knew that. We shared the same mother, but had different fathers—my father died when I was two, then my mother remarried and had Katerina. She was ten years younger than me."

The words just hung there in the thick air. The heat from the condenser stuck in the back of Mark's throat, making it difficult for him to swallow. The fact that Katerina and Titov were related was a shock, but less of a shock than what Titov's words implied.

"*Was* your sister?" said Mark. When Titov didn't answer, Mark asked, "What do you mean *was*? What happened to her?"

More sirens sounded from down below. Mark heard tires screeching in the front lot of the Tabriz. He glanced north, but couldn't see any more evidence of fighting.

Titov said, "Some might say I killed her. I resisted that thought for years, but now I've come to accept that yes, in a way I did kill her."

"What did you *do*?" Mark took a deep breath and decided he didn't feel as lousy as he'd thought. He certainly still had the energy to kill Titov.

"She didn't know about me. She just thought I worked at the embassy."

Mark tried to remember back that far. He thought, yes, Katerina *had* talked of an older brother. He recalled her saying that her mother and brother supported the Soviet Union, and that she was afraid they wouldn't like him, because he was an American. So she'd never taken him to meet them. Mark had been too absorbed with Katerina to care.

"What didn't she know about you?"

"When I was twenty-one I was pulled from university in Moscow and sent to the war in Afghanistan. After the war, the commander of my tank battalion was recruited to work for the KGB. He brought me with him."

Remembering what Orkhan had told him, Mark said, "You dealt heroin in Afghanistan. Your commander was your *krisha*, and still is. He is the director of the FSB. That is why you are here."

"This is true. I am not proud of everything I have done, but I will not deny it. Katerina never knew I was a KGB officer, though. She just thought I was in the army, and then worked at the embassy in Tbilisi."

A thought suddenly occurred to Mark. "Did Katerina know about your history with heroin?"

"No."

"The painting of the poppy—it wasn't a message?"

"I wondered the same thing once, but no. I don't see how she could have known. I look at a poppy and I see seeds that can be made into a drug. She sees a pretty flower." Titov let a weary sigh escape. "It was a mistake for me to have come to Tbilisi, where Katerina was, where my mother was. But I did not choose the posting. And, of course, I didn't ask her to get close to you, do you understand? I didn't intend to use her like that. But when she told me she was seeing an American, well, of course I was going to investigate who this American is, and why he was in Georgia. She was my sister. And when I investigated, I learned things about you. I learned that you associated with bad people at the university, people who would cause trouble, so I made sure you were watched closely, and then I saw you met with this Bowlan man who we knew was CIA...I should have told Katerina to break it off then. I should have told her you were dangerous."

"Not to her I wasn't."

"But I made a mistake. I told my superiors about Katerina's relationship with you. And they insisted that we use her to learn more about you, and what you were doing with Larry Bowlan. You understand, being in the KGB, this was a very good job for me. I alone was supporting my mother, helping to pay for Katerina to go to school."

"You—*you* were the one who planted the bug on her?"

"So, yes, I planted this listening device on her. And this was my mistake. Because if I hadn't involved her in my world, she would never have been targeted."

"What happened to her?"

"She was killed the same day that you were freed."

Mark felt his heart rate quicken as he anticipated what Titov was going to say next.

"You see," said Titov, "your friend Larry Bowlan, he didn't just arrange for those Georgian criminals—"

"They were Georgian patriots fighting an occupation."

"Ioseliani and his men were criminals!" Titov's voice trembled. "Bowlan didn't just arrange for those Georgian *criminals* to attack and kill the men who were holding *you* prisoner. He also arranged for them to kill..."

Titov stopped in midsentence, unwilling or unable to finish.

"Katerina," said Mark. "You're saying Larry Bowlan arranged to have her killed?"

Could Bowlan have done it? A man Mark had considered a friend for twenty-four years?

The answer, Mark knew, was *yes*. If Bowlan had thought Katerina was a willing agent of the KGB, and not just the unwitting half sister of one, he could have done it.

"Yes. That criminal son of a bitch Bowlan and his gang of criminals had her killed! Because of her association with me. For years I looked for him…"

Mark was too old, and too weathered, to cry anymore, but if he'd been twenty years younger, he might have now. In the years right after leaving Georgia in 1991, whenever he'd thought of Katerina, he'd imagined her living a happy life somewhere. Falling in love with someone who was kind to her, painting for pleasure, taking joy in beauty, aging with grace. Maybe even thinking of him every so often. Their relationship had been transitory, but in the end, what relationship wasn't? What mattered was that, for a time, however brief, they had loved each other.

He wanted to bridge the gap of time, to go back and comfort her, to let her know that he was sorry about what had happened, and that he wished her well.

"Our mother never recovered, you know," said Titov. "The death of Katerina was too much for her to bear. She only lasted a year."

Mark let his head hang as he recalled the lethal efficiency with which the team of Georgian men who'd rescued him had dispatched his Russian captors. It sickened him to think that Katerina had met a similar fate. It was such a shitty, mean thing. Why God or fate had allowed him to survive for so long, when others more deserving had long since passed, was beyond him.

He realized he was breathing quickly, almost to the point of hyperventilating.

"The painting," Mark said. "Where—"

"I found it in Katerina's dormitory room. It was still wet, she must have just finished it before she was murdered. I gave it to our mother. She lit a candle next to it every day until she died. When I inherited her house, I stored the painting in the attic over all the years I rented the place out. I thought I was saving it because I couldn't bear to throw it out. But now I know it was so that I could bring it to the Dachi hotel, so it could be the last thing that son of a bitch Larry Bowlan saw before *he* died."

She'd been one of the innocents, thought Mark, collateral damage in a cold war that had already gone on for far too long, a war that had already destroyed far too many lives. Her death hadn't even helped to end that war; it had been utterly pointless.

Titov was quiet for a long, long time. Mark listened to the shouts and sirens in the city, and the sound of sporadic gunfire below them.

Just when Mark was beginning to wonder whether Titov was through talking, the Russian added, "Life is funny, Sava."

Mark closed his eyes, leaned his head against the warm condenser, and let both his pistol and assault rifle rest loosely in his lap. "Yeah," he said. "Yeah, it sure is."

70

———————◦———————

Mark heard two sharp beeps. After a time, Titov, sounding as though he was speaking on the phone, said, "I understand. Thank you for all you have done for me."

Titov was then silent for several minutes.

Below them, the sound of gunfire grew louder and more frequent. An explosion, maybe a door being blasted open, echoed up the stairwell.

"What's the news?" asked Mark.

"Do you know what I planned to do when I retired, Sava? No, of course you don't, but I will tell you. Manager for a hunting and fishing lodge. A big one, the best in eastern Russia. Of course, I would prefer to own such a lodge myself, but I have always known my place, and I know that ownership is not possible for a man like me. But I am very good at helping people for whom ownership is possible. And that would not have been such a bad life." Titov paused, then said, "There will be no helicopter. Our troops are retreating back to Armenia. The attempted incursion never happened. I was never here."

Mark smiled grimly, relieved, but too battered and weak to take much satisfaction in the news.

"Was this your work, Sava? The Azeris could not have stopped us on their own. They had help, from the Americans, I think."

Mark considered that if he hadn't investigated Larry's death, and found out about the drone base, and told Orkhan about the Russian military buildup and Titov's paramilitary operation in Nakhchivan, then Orkhan would never have thought to ask the Americans for help—Mark was certain that was what had happened—and then Nakhchivan might have fallen to the Russians, and the Russians might have used their position in Nakhchivan to bully the Azeris for years to come, and to make an example of Azerbaijan so that other former Soviet states would know what was in store for them if they dared to resist a resurgent Russia. In that sense, he'd stopped one very important domino from falling.

But that was false reasoning, he knew. By that standard, Titov himself had stopped the domino from falling by killing Larry and inviting a deeper investigation. Or Orkhan had stopped it, by coming himself to the sanatorium. One could even say Katerina had stopped it decades ago by saying yes when Mark had asked her whether she wanted to go out for tea, for without Katerina, Titov and Mark would never have crossed paths.

In the end, Mark didn't believe—despite superficial appearances to the contrary—that any one man or woman had much control over the fate of nations…whether that man was a president, a spy, or just a young woman who wanted to paint like Renoir.

Mark said, "If you surrender yourself to me now, I will try to see that you live."

The torture Mark had endured as a young man, and the executions he'd witnessed—even when he tried to consider that bleak, awful time from a distance, to imagine what it would have been like to be in Titov's shoes—even then he didn't believe Titov's actions had been necessary evils. No, Titov had inflicted far more unnecessary pain than any decent human being should have been capable of inflicting. He might have been Katerina's half brother, but he didn't have her kind soul.

Still, Mark wasn't out for revenge. He'd do what he could to see that Titov wasn't hanged in the streets by an angry mob.

"Being kept alive is different from living, Sava. You of all people should know this."

Mark didn't answer.

Titov said, "The Azeris are not a particularly forgiving lot. I'm going to stand up now."

Mark stiffened, and readied his assault rifle. "Put your hands above you. Leave your weapons where they are."

"You know, I have a different idea, Sava."

Mark lifted an eye just above the air-conditioning condenser he was using as protection. In the dim light of a half-moon, he could see Titov's silhouette at full height, completely exposed, holding his pistol at his side. The night-vision goggles he wore on his head were flipped up. Mark knew what Titov was asking of him, but he didn't want to do it.

"Stand down!" called Mark.

"Do it, Sava!"

Titov fired a shot above the condenser. Mark's ears rang.

"Stand down!"

Titov fired again.

Ignoring the pain in his chest, Mark rolled out from behind the condenser, flicked the safety switch to semiautomatic, and fired a single round at Titov's chest. When the Russian fell back, Mark advanced quickly, shot Titov's gun hand, and then kicked the Russians' assault rifle aside.

Titov's eyes were wide open, as was his mouth. For a moment, he appeared to be incapable of breathing. But then one breath did come, and then another.

"You fool! I told you I was wearing armor."

"I remembered."

Titov closed his mouth and took several short, sharp breaths through his nose. "Please. If not for me, then for Katerina."

Mark slowly raised the rifle, aimed for the center of Titov's head, and pulled the trigger twice.

Speaking now only to himself, he said, "For Katerina then."

71

Nakhchivan, Azerbaijan
Six hours later

———◇———

Daria hadn't been certain whether the American the US Rangers were whispering about was really Mark.

Certainly when classified reports began to come through about a man, possibly American, who had single-handedly stopped a group of Russians from taking over the Tabriz Hotel, she'd hoped it was him. And when Decker had called Kaufman, and received word that Mark had made contact and might be able to meet them at the airport, her hopes had soared. But until she actually saw him step out of the Azeri armored car and onto the airport tarmac, carrying the leather satchel he'd left Bishkek with, she hadn't been sure.

"Mark! Mark! Over here!" Daria started jogging toward him. He turned, and when he saw that it was her, his face registered disoriented confusion. He gestured to the two Azeri army officers standing on either side of him that it was OK.

"Daria?"

His face was haggard, the circles under his eyes unusually dark, and he sounded exhausted, and confused. He appeared to be trembling, or maybe shivering.

"Oh, Mark." She'd been so, so worried.

They embraced, but Mark's body stiffened when she wrapped her arms around him, as though he were in pain.

"You're hurt," she said.

"I'm OK."

"No, you're not." Daria had felt something when they'd embraced, something protruding from his chest. She put her hand out to touch it. "What is that?"

"It's nothing."

His voice sounded gravelly, as if he'd been smoking too many cigarettes.

"No it's not."

"Had a little lung issue, but it's going to be OK." He coughed. "Orkhan's got some doctors lined up for me, one should be here at the airport. Daria, what are you doing here?"

"I came to look for you."

Daria told him about receiving his text, and of the deal she'd struck with Kaufman, and the role she and Decker had played in helping to fend off the invasion.

"I don't know what to say. Thank you." Then, "But where's Lila?"

Daria wasn't sure whether the question was just a display of fatherly concern or an implication that she should have stayed home and worried about caring for their daughter, even if it meant he might not return.

"With Nazira. They're staying at Nazira's cousin's place in Tokmok... Lila's safe, don't worry." Daria had just talked to Nazira ten minutes earlier. Lila had taken well to a bottle, and accepted the formula.

"Good." Mark's eyes closed for a moment. "Good." He inhaled deeply, then said, "I got the diaper cream."

"What?"

"Desitin, the kind you wanted, they had it in Baku."

"OK." Daria wasn't sure whether he was delirious, trying to be funny, or just telling the truth. But she couldn't care less about diaper cream just then. "What happened to you, Mark? You look like you've been through a war." She observed the way his shoulders slumped, as though he barely had the energy to stand. "Here, let me take that."

Daria lifted the strap from the leather satchel he carried and slung it across her own shoulder.

"I've got something else in there for us. We don't have to hang it up, but I couldn't throw it out, and I didn't know what else to do with it."

"What are you talking about?"

"I've had a strange few days, hon. I…" his voice trailed off as he gently shook his head.

Daria studied him, concerned.

She knew her husband well enough to know that when things got tough for him, he typically closed up. His eyes would go dead, in a mean sort of way, and with ruthless emotionless efficiency he'd do what it took to get the job done. It was a disconcerting aspect of him that Daria both admired and feared, but she also knew it was the reason he'd survived for so long.

At the moment, though, he had an expression on his face that she hadn't seen before—one that, if she hadn't known him so well, she would have sworn was *sadness*.

"Hey." She leaned into him, gently this time, careful not to aggravate his wounds. His head dipped toward hers, their breath intermingled. "You going to be OK?"

"Yeah, of course."

"You're sure about that?"

Mark lifted his head. At first his smile was clearly forced, but then his eyes seemed to relax, and he looked at her as though seeing her for the first time, and a genuine smile—albeit crooked and tough—appeared. "Yeah. You, me, Lila. We're *all* going to be OK."

Epilogue
Baku, Azerbaijan
Six months later

———————○———————

"But you grow skinny, Minister Gambar! Surely this is too much. A man like you must eat."

Orkhan Gambar lay naked, face down on a masseur's table in his favorite Turkish bath in downtown Baku. The masseur—an enormous Azeri with a belly suggestive of a sumo wrestler—was in the process of massaging Orkhan's upper thighs and buttocks.

"Two more kilos. I must lose two more kilos," said Orkhan. He was still fat. If not by the standards of his masseur, then certainly by the standards of his daughter and his personal physician. But he had made considerable progress. "I must follow the treatment."

"This treatment, I don't agree with it."

The masseur ground his palm into the back of Orkhan's lower right buttock, leaned all his weight into it, held the position for several seconds, then released it and gave Orkhan's posterior a smack. The pasty mass of flesh jiggled.

"My daughter. I made her a promise. She said, maybe if I am not so fat, she will be more respectful to me. I told her this was no way to talk to her father, but I also think that maybe she has a point. And that maybe she says this out of concern for me."

Orkhan was in a good mood because the minister of the interior had finally been executed at Gobustan Prison the day before, the last of the United Nations monitors that had been overseeing the dismantling of the drone base in Nakhchivan had left, and the Russians were signaling through back channels that they would leave Azerbaijan be, provided the Azeris limited the volume of natural gas they sent directly to Europe.

"Daughters," said the masseur. "I have a daughter. Always this talking back to their fathers. They learn things on the Internet that are not good for them."

Orkhan grunted in agreement. "It is much easier when they are younger," he observed.

"You speak the truth. Arm."

Orkhan extended his right arm and the masseur began to knead it roughly.

"For example, I know this American," said Orkhan. "Now, it is easy for him. He and his wife just moved to Baku with their baby daughter, a very nice girl, I have met her. But she is so young, she cannot even talk. She does not know what her father does for a living. And I cannot say what he does, but it is not always nice, you understand?"

"Of course, Minister Gambar."

"Yes, well, when this little girl gets older and finds out what her father does, then he will have trouble!"

Orkhan closed his eyes, as he began to really relax. He considered how nearly every day Sava, looking stupid and emasculated, pushed his little girl in a fancy stroller—the men Orkhan had assigned to watch Sava claimed it cost over four hundred dollars!—on the promenade by the Bay of Baku. What kind of man does this?

"Maybe this American will stop doing what he does?"

Orkhan laughed, then coughed up some phlegm, and spat. "No, I don't think so."

Acknowledgments

———————◦———————

The more I write, the more I realize how lucky I am to be lifted up, with such regularity, by people who are in equal measure intelligent, constant, and kind.

With that in mind: I am deeply grateful to my agent Richard Curtis for his wise counsel, editorial advice, and for role he played in publishing this novel. I also can't thank Christina Henry de Tessan, my developmental editor, enough; her contributions to the Mark Sava series, and to this novel in particular, have been invaluable. Tim Gifford, David Mayland, Scott Stone, Heather Cathrall, John Vickerstaff and Mark Burstein all read early versions of *Death of a Spy*; the novel is far better as a result of their corrections and suggestions. Mike Lindgren did a brilliant job proofreading the book.

Christopher Lane deserves special thanks for bringing the Sava series to life in his outstanding audio versions of the novels. With foreign accents galore and place names like Nakhchivan, I know these aren't easy stories to narrate, but he makes it seem as though they are.

XNR Productions of Madison, Wisconsin did their usual great work with the maps for *Death of a Spy*. The Book Designers of Fairfax, California designed the cover—which I absolutely love—as well as the interior of the book.

While researching Death of a Spy, I traveled to the regions in which the story is set and interviewed a wide range of people. The contributions these individuals made to the novel were enormous, but given the political realities of the situation, to name these people here—many were government officials—would do them no favor. I am, nevertheless, indebted to them. I would also like to thank the many reporters, scholars, and ex-CIA officers who, through their books, lent insight to this novel. An annotated bibliography can be found at danmayland.com.

Finally, many thanks are due to my wife, Corinne, and my children Kirsten and William—for their enduring love and support, but also for serving as my sounding board of first resort.

Contents

Dedication

As always to my husband—a supremely useful person to have around during a pandemic.

And to the amazing scientists, nurses, doctors, and every single other person who has lived through the shittiness of COVID-19. You are all absolute heroes. Thank God our reality doesn't echo this one!

Books by Evie Mitchell

Nameless Souls MC Series
Runner
Wrath
Ghost
Shield

Elliot Security Series
Rough Edge
Bleeding Edge
Knife Edge

Capricorn Cove Series
Thunder Thighs
Double the D
Muffin Top
The Mrs. Clause
Beach Party
New Year Knew You
The Shake-Up
Double Breasted
As You Wish
You Sleigh Me
Resolution Revolution
Meat Load

Trunk Junk

Thor's Shipbuilding Series
Clean Sweep
The X-list
Reality Check
The Christmas Contract

Dogg Pack Series
Puppy Love
The Frock Up
Pier Pressure
Bad English

Archer Sibling Series
Just Joshing

Connect with Evie Mitchell

Website
www.EvieMitchell.com

Newsletter
www.subscribepage.com/z2p2x3_copy

Amazon
www.amazon.com/author/eviemitchell

Bookbub, Instagram and Facebook
@EvieMitchellAuthor

Facebook Group
Evie Mitchell's Greedy Reader Book Club

Ghost

Ghost

I do my best work in the shadows.

Trained to be a killer, it's all I've ever known. All I've ever cared to know.

I embrace pain and destruction, turning everything I touch into ash.

I'm a ghost. No past. No present. No future.

Until Ava.

This woman sparks a hunger in me, a dark, dangerous desire.

If I don't fight it, it could destroy us both.

The devil knows I'd burn the world for one taste.

God have mercy, 'cause I won't.

Trigger warning: This is a darker series than my other books and contains some violence. Happily ever afters are still guaranteed, but this is a gritty series so proceed with caution.

Prologue

Ava

Day 500 – Post the Dark

I'm not one for capturing my thoughts, but Audrey pointed out the benefits of recording our history for the future. She wants them to know what we went through and who we were. Ordinarily, I wouldn't give a shit—but Audrey is a scary bitch when she wants to be, so here I am, sitting on a goddamned chair at a goddamned desk writing my goddamned thoughts.

Are you happy, Audrey? You better be.

I'm Major Ava Whitwick—or at least I was. I guess titles and surnames don't matter much anymore.

The world didn't end with a bang but a whimper. A virus that closed borders, spreading far and wide. Mistakes happened, and over the course of three years, the shitshow simply escalated until finally, the world as we knew it ended.

There'd been a vaccine trial. Some kind of attempt to stop the virus. Three vaccines were tested for distribution, but before they could immunise the population, something cataclysmic occurred. Entire cities went dark. Power grids shut down. The internet cut off. Communications were blocked. All went silent.

I'd been military, stationed up in Far North Queensland

1

when shit started going south. When they'd started locking down the bases and referring to the women as commodities and breeders, I'd got the fuck out. The military has taught me to read the room, and this room had said to get the fuck out of dodge.

I'd left, taking enough firepower to kit out a small army, and driven two days straight through rogue militia areas, bumper-to-bumper traffic jams, and panicked crowds down to southern New South Wales.

Down to my sister—Charlotte.

Lottie had holed up with a group of eleven women in their university. While the rest of the students and staff had returned home, these women had somehow convinced Lottie to stay.

At first, I'd been fucking pissed—desperate to get Lottie out of there and away to a safe house. But then I'd met the women and learned of their plans, surveyed the space, and been persuaded to stay.

Big. Fucking. Mistake.

Three months ago, The Purge—a militia group filled with sadistic misogynistic women-enslaving abusers—had stormed our haven. We'd driven their scouting party back, but they had taken two of our women in the battle.

With no choice but to find safety elsewhere, we'd reached out to the Nameless Souls Motorcycle Club. The club had welcomed us with open arms—no surprise, considering they were a bunch of horny men and we were eleven semi-attractive women.

I'd been ready to fuck shit up, kill the lot of them if required. Only, they'd turned out to be mostly decent people who appreciated the skills these women could contribute to their

2

club's survival.

Which brings us to now. While most of our group had stayed at the club's commune, a small group of us were moving between the Nameless Souls' other two remaining chapters. We'd been tasked with educating them about farming and showing them how to produce their own biofuel. It was a fucking dangerous journey that put us in harm's way but would have long-term benefits for the entire community.

Plus, I'd heard there were coffee beans in Queensland. God knew I'd slaughter a village for a decent cup.

The journey had already seen one of our number injured, but it had also brought hope. Those two women who'd been taken by The Purge? There'd been a potential sighting. A slaver cage fight only hours from where we stayed, where women were offered as prizes.

We'd discussed it and agreed that it was worth me leaving to recover our friends.

I just hadn't expected *him* to follow.

Chapter One

Ava

"Do you have your knife?"

"Yes."

"And your gun?"

I grinned. "Yes."

"And your other gun?"

I rolled my eyes. "I'm good, Lottie."

My sister twisted her hands nervously in front of her, her wide blue eyes filled with concern.

"Are you *sure* you have everything?"

"Yes, for the millionth time." I reached out to cup my sister's face, pressing my forehead to hers. "I'll be back. Afghanistan, Iraq, that time in the Congo—I came back, didn't I?

Lottie nodded, her small body hitching with a suppressed sob.

Hold it together, sis.

"Don't worry. These bastards have nothing on me." I reassured her.

She wrapped her arms around me, clutching me to her chest.

"It's not the bastards I'm worried about—it's the idiots with guns. I just—promise you'll come back?" she asked against my shoulder.

I squeezed her tight. "Promise. You won't even notice I'm gone."

Audrey—our fellow survivor, and the most intelligent person I'd ever met—interrupted our moment.

"I'm out." She shook her head, her straight black hair whipping around her head in the strong breeze. "Ava, good luck. Don't get killed or I'll find a way to clone you and kill you again."

I grinned. "I don't doubt it."

I stepped back from Charlotte, giving her a moment to compose herself as I wrapped an arm around Audrey, offering a quick hug. "Don't run into any trouble while I'm gone. And be nice to Pope, he can't help being a doofus."

She grinned, her dark eyes dancing with amusement. "No promises."

Shit. We're dividing again.

We'd already been forced to leave the majority of our number back in the Nameless Souls' compound down in Adaminaby. This mission had me torn. I needed to see if I could get my missing women back. But the constant fracturing of our group meant I couldn't keep them all safe. I fucking hated it.

But if it means we find Jules and Lilith then it'll be worth it.

The hair on the back of my neck prickled in a way I was becoming far too familiar with.

"That fucker's behind me, isn't he?"

Lottie glanced over my shoulder, her grin instantaneous. "Yep."

"Fuck."

I'd been able to ignore the infuriating man when we'd been back on club grounds, back in Adaminaby. But we were on a journey to support the other chapters of this motorcycle club.

Ellie—our biochemist—had worked out a way to make biofuel. And, unfortunately for her, that made her a fucking attractive asset to have in the After.

I'd fight tooth and nail for their safety. Which meant when this little jaunt between club safehouses had been proposed, I'd had no choice but to deal with the creepy fucker behind me.

I purposefully kept my back to Ghost, hyper-aware of his attention but determined to take the time to farewell the women I'd taken responsibility for. In addition to Ellie, Lottie, and Audrey; there was Jo, a mechanic whose sisters we'd left back in Adaminaby. She was older, like me, seasoned with the kind of pragmaticism I appreciated. Then came Kate, the daughter of the former club president, and our botanist. The woman had a backbone like steel and a face like an angel.

I accepted her hug, then stepped back, picking up my trusty backpack and offering a jaunty salute.

"See you in a few weeks. Make sure the Cunnamulla crew have a cold beer waiting for me."

I turned on my heel, heading for the waiting SUV, Ghost already in the driver's seat, his gaze blank as he watched me walk towards him.

Bastard.

I threw my pack in the back, pulled the door shut and looked ahead to where the gate of the compound was slowly opening.

I felt his gaze rest on me for a moment.

"We sitting here all day or leaving?" I asked.

After a beat of silence, he put the car in gear, the damn thing shuddering as it rocked across the gravel and dirt of the courtyard.

I wanted to look back, wanted to see if Lottie was waving,

or if Audrey was yelling some last-minute piece of advice.

Instead, I faced forward—determined to ignore the pang, determined not to give in to the little doubts that whispered in my ear asking if this was the last time I'd ever see my girls.

Not today, Satan.

Behind us, the gates closed with a final, loud bang. Ghost shifted gear, our SUV bumping down the road sending us on our way to Dubbo.

Chapter Two

Ava

I popped my feet up on the dash, adjusting my sunglasses as we drove along the empty roads, no soul in sight. Nature had begun to reclaim the road, while long-dead cars pepper the shoulder, rusting where they lay.

Silence had dominated our trip for the last two hours, and while I wouldn't normally have an issue with my own thoughts, my body twitched with nervous energy.

I glanced at the big guy beside me, taking him in. Despite being built like a mountain, the motherfucker had the extraordinary ability to blend. Upon first meeting him, I'd assumed I'd always be able to hear him coming. He'd quickly proved me wrong.

He shifted in the driver's seat, the sunlight highlighting his features.

Ghost wasn't what I'd call traditionally attractive. His features were far too brutal for such a weak description. He had a blunt face, unyielding but cruelly beautiful, each feature seeming as if carved from stone. His eyes were dark pools of secrets, revealing no thoughts or emotions he didn't want you to know. The breeze from the open window whipped at his hair, the strands overly long—and I got the sense if we'd met in the Before, that he'd have had it shaved into a buzz cut.

Dark bristles shadowed his jaw adding to the rough edge that hung over him like a cloud. He wore a plain black shirt and dark wash jeans over his thunderously muscular body. His feet were encased in thick fuck-you boots, and I had no doubt he had at least fifteen weapons hidden on his person.

For some reason, his readiness for violence turned me on.

Audrey once commented that he looked like Ares, the God of War, violent and physically untamed. While I could see her point in his physique, his utter void of emotion had me likening him to Hades, God of the Underworld—cold and unrelenting, stern and pitiless, forbidding and aloof, dwelling in the shadows, administering final judgement on those unlucky enough to cross his path.

All his blunt edges and general fuck-off vibes should have rendered Ghost unattractive—and it would have, if it not for his lips. Those lips had no business being on a face like his. They were too full, too sensual. Hedonistic promises that no mere human could resist.

The entire package is far too tempting.

I crossed my arms, finally giving in. "Okay, truce."

Ghost glanced over at me, raising an eyebrow above the dark lenses of his sunglasses.

"I can't deal with your silence. I know that's your 'thing'"—I made quotation marks with my fingers—"but, dude, I need more from you if we're about to go into battle together."

He turned back to the road, his mouth pressed into a single line. It made me want to kiss him until those freaking lips parted and I could taste his—

Stop it, Ava! He's annoying as fuck. You don't need the mess he's got written all over him.

I sighed as I reached for the map that sat folded in the console between us. With an exaggerated flick, I opened it. Tracing a finger along the worn paper, I followed the lines marking the roads we would soon travel.

"You know, it makes me nervous that we still use roads." I gestured at the long stretch of bitumen in front of us. "It's like a sign that's pointing this way saying, 'kill me here.'"

For a moment Ghost remained silent, his big bulk tensing.

"It's the fastest route."

I rolled my eyes, ignoring the kick in my gut at his gravelly voice. "Sure. But that doesn't mean it's the safest."

He nodded once.

"Wait." I pressed a hand to my heart, feigning shock. "Did you just agree with me?"

He glanced my way. "Don't let it go to your head."

I snickered, settling back in my seat, fingers once again tracing our route. "What are you thinking?"

"We go off track about an hour outside Dubbo, find a safe house, and stow the vehicle. Settle in until it's dark, make our way on foot into town. Do some recon, then we'll decide what comes next."

I nodded. "That works for me."

He fell silent.

"What?" I asked, sensing an unspoken question.

"There's gonna be more girls there. More women than just your two." He paused, adjusting the car slightly to avoid a tree that had fallen across the road.

"And?"

"We can't save them all."

My gut tightened, the map crinkling in my hands. "I know that."

"You knowing that is different to you being okay with it."

I swallowed, looking away. "I get it, Ghost. The world is fucked. What I would have done in the Before is different to what I'd do now. My focus is on protecting mine."

"And what's *yours* exactly?"

"Those under my protection—in this case, Jules and Lilith. Same as you."

Ghost's cheek twitched. "We get in, we get your girls, and we get out. No arguments."

My gut churned, a bitter taste lingering in my mouth.

"No arguments," I agreed.

We rode in silence, the landscape ever-changing as Ghost drove.

"You're ex-military."

His statement surprised me. In the short months since my girls had joined the Nameless Souls, this was the first time he'd ventured to speak to me without prompting.

"Yeah. Army."

He nodded once as if my answer explained everything.

"You?"

His lips twisted, his expression darkening. "Not Army."

I looked him over with a practised eye. "The guys said you were special forces but you don't act like it."

He raised an eyebrow.

"Too big for the Airforce—unless you were support crew and, dude, you are *not* a follower." I tapped my chin. "Too much of a loner for the Navy. Which leaves intel. Am I right?"

He didn't answer.

"Had to be a spy. Which shadow org was it?"

"Does it matter?"

I shrugged. "Not any more. Not since the world ended."

Ghost slowed the vehicle, frowning at something in the distance. "Didn't matter before either. Left it years ago."

"With Hazard, right?" I asked, referring to the Nameless Souls' Adaminaby chapter President.

"Mm." He slowed the car, his eyes narrowing as he stared at something on the road ahead.

I sat up, dropping my feet from the dash. "What is it?"

"Movement."

I scanned the horizon, my eyes locking on a glint of light up ahead.

"Fuck. It's people." I looked around at the empty paddocks. "Bastards or...?"

"Don't plan to find out. We're not stopping."

I unbuckled, crawling into the back seat to unzip a duffle bag and pull a sniper rifle out. I adjusted the scope, using it to pinpoint the figures as we sped along the road.

"Three," I said, quickly taking stock of the threat. "They're armed. Two men, one woman." The familiar churn of impotent rage burned in my gut. "She's chained."

"Most women are in the towns."

Over my fucking dead body.

My finger hovered over the trigger. It would be so easy to punch a bullet through the windscreen freeing me to follow it up with one shot for each abuser.

"No," Ghost said, his hand coming up to rest on the rifle. "We don't have time, Ava. We can't take on a stray if you're gonna get your people back."

With great reluctance, I agreed.

"I fucking hate this world."

Ghost's answer was to put his foot down, picking up speed. I adjusted my scope, keeping watch as we raced towards them. For a moment one reached for his weapon.

Just give me an excuse you piece of shit.

His friend shook his head, mouth moving. They watched as we raced by, leaving them in our dust.

"Well, that broke up an otherwise monotonous drive." I crawled back over the console, settling into the front seat. As I clicked my seat belt in, Ghost jerked the wheel, taking us off the road and into the thick brush of the adjacent paddocks.

"What are you doing?" I asked, death gripping the oh-shit bar.

"Taking the longer route." He flicked me a glance, his dark eyes flashing with some kind of emotion—amusement, maybe?—before wiping clear once more. "You're right. A less occupied route would be preferrable."

A funny little frisson of something warm unfurled in my belly.

Seriously, Ava. Grow the fuck up. Mess isn't in your plans. Keeping your people alive is.

I hardened the fuck up, crossing my arms and settling in for a bumpy ride.

"Next time, you should listen to me earlier, Ghost-boy."

Chapter Three

Ava

The ride had been hellish. Where there had once been farmland, the fields had long since disappeared falling fallow and hiding fences, equipment, and rivets from view.

"Next time," I said, dusting my hands on the legs of my jeans. "I'll drive."

Ghost didn't answer, as equally filthy as me from digging the vehicle out of a sand trap.

"Are we close? 'Cause I'm gonna need food soon. And it's starting to get dark."

The sun sat low on the horizon; the day still warm. Supposedly we were getting close to summer, but I could no longer tell days or seasons. The concept of time now felt foreign. There was simply morning, noon, and night, heat or cold, rain or shine. And somehow, that felt okay to me.

"We're about an hour out," Ghost said quietly as the car bumped through another field. "There should be some houses coming up soon."

I nodded, rubbing at my gritty eyes.

I needed food and a nap before we hit the town. A shower too, if I was lucky.

The car turned slightly and I looked up, seeing the familiar shape of a roof on the horizon.

Ghost reached into the glove compartment pulling a gun free. He handed it to me silently.

I checked the safety then rested it on my thigh, adrenaline overpowering the exhaustion.

"Are there likely to be bastards?"

Ghost shrugged. "Haven't heard of any passing through this way, but doesn't mean they're not around."

Bastards were the mutation the world hadn't expected. The original virus had been transferred by body fluids—even the smallest spit droplet if inhaled could end in infection. It'd been a mutation of rabies, turning people into raving, dangerous individuals before finally killing them.

When the world had started going dark—overnight, cities disappeared off the grid—there had been rumours of a new, more dangerous strain. I'd kept my eyes open and mouth shut, hoping it had been stopped. It wasn't until we'd left the south and begun moving through central New South Wales that we ran into our first horde—a pack of bastards not dissimilar to zombies in their mindless quest to bite, tear and destroy.

I palmed the gun, searching the horizon for movement. Under the dying sun, all remained quiet. A few kangaroos looked up from their graze, their ears twitching as they watched us pass.

"Looks okay," I murmured as Ghost pulled up to the house.

"Let's check inside."

The stench hit us before we'd even made it out of our vehicle.

"Fuck," I cursed, lifting a hand to cover my nose as I slammed the door shut again. "What is that?"

Ghost's expression was grim, his gaze sharp as he watched the flies we'd disturbed swarming the yard. "Smells like dead body. Or bodies."

I nodded, gaze still trained on the house as he set the car into motion. A twitch of an upstairs curtain caught my eye. I lifted the gun as a pale man looked out, his expression blank as he watched us pull away.

I expected gunshots but we were left alone, the SUV bumping along the rough dirt as we began to plough through the fields once more.

"Do you think he killed someone?"

"Probably a slaughterhouse."

"What? Inside the house?"

Ghost shot me a side-eye. "Cannibal. Or a victim of."

"Shit." I twisted to look back. "Should we—"

"No." Ghost cut me off. "We don't have time to care."

His tone grated on me. "I know, Ghost. I was simply asking the question."

He didn't answer, once again his silence a third party to our relationship.

Ghost drove us through two farms, putting distance between us and the potential cannibal. At the third homestead, he finally slowed the vehicle, his hands gripping the wheel.

I appraised the location, nodding in approval. High on a hill, not too far a walk from town, the farmhouse sat tucked into a grove of trees—offering it protection from the road. The dwelling itself felt old and unused. Weatherboard shutters hung at odd angles, windows haphazardly open, the front door askew. There were three outbuildings—two sheds and a small open sided feed shelter.

"Looks abandoned," I noted, scanning the surrounding buildings for movement. "That shed looks like a good place to stow the car."

16

Ghost slowed us to a stop, the car still running.

"Cover me," he ordered, pulling a weapon from the console. "If anything happens, leave."

I opened my mouth to protest but the fucker was gone before I could utter a word.

"For fucks sake," I muttered, unclipping my belt, and pulling the rifle from the backseat. "He legit thinks I'm useless. Well, motherfucker, you just wait."

Twilight had fallen, allowing Ghost to disappear into the long shadows.

"Honestly," I grumbled as I clicked off the safety, picking out landmarks and surveying the shadows. "This man thinks his shit don't stink. Well, dude, I have news for you, you motherfucker. I am more than capable of taking care of shit."

I waited, rifle at the ready as I scanned the yard.

Ghost materialised from the shadows giving me a sharp nod.

I lowered my gun, poking my head out the door. "Does that mean we're good?"

He nodded, reaching for the driver's side door.

"You know, this silent treatment is really getting on my nerves."

Ghost switched the idling car off, quiet descending.

"You'll get over it." He swung his backpack over his shoulder, heading for the house. With an exaggerated eye-roll, I followed, rifle in one hand, bag in the other.

A thick layer of dust coated the surfaces of the home, the furnishings slowly disintegrating as time and nature tried to reclaim the house.

Ghost led me into the kitchen, his bag dropping beside the butcher's block island. He rummaged in it for a moment then pulled out two packets, tossing them to me.

I held them up, squinting in the dim light.

"Chicken Italiano or beef casserole. Sounds delicious." My tone may have been sarcastic but my mouth was watering. It'd been a long day of travel with nothing but an energy bar to keep us going.

"I'll stow the car."

And as his name suggested, the fucker faded back into the shadows, once again a ghost lost to sight.

I sighed, pressing my palms into the two packets on the bench-top, cracking the heating component in their bottoms to cook our meals.

With the rifle still slung over my shoulder, I clicked on a light and explored our temporary accommodation. Wood flooring creaked under my boots, tiny puffs of dust blooming with every step.

It's gonna be a long night if we stay here.

The ground floor of the house consisted of the main living areas including dining room, kitchen, and lounge. Faded pictures still hung on walls, the images of people living lives in the Before.

I followed the pictures up the stairs, opening doors and finding moth-bitten mattresses, dusty books, and the occasional broken trinket.

"Eureka," I muttered when I opened the bathroom door. Not expecting much, I twisted the tap, delighted when the old pipes groaned in protest. After a moment, thick dirty water spurted from the faucet, stuttering with a splash into the basin. After a little while the water changed from dark brown to a perfect clear.

"Oh, baby, come to mumma." I tried my luck, twisting the hot water on and hoping against hope that it might be at least tepid.

"Damn," I sighed, twisting the basin taps off after a few minutes. "But one out of two ain't bad."

I twisted the shower taps on, watching as the water ran thick with sludge and grit before washing away the dirt caked onto the tiles. I stripped, needing to scrub the filth of the day off my skin. Naked, I cleaned the remaining debris from the shower floor then stepped in, sighing as the water ran over my heated skin.

An ancient bottle of shampoo sat on a ledge.

"God, if you are listening, I wouldn't mind a little sudd-i-ness in my life."

A few squirts of the caked nozzle had thick creamy soap pooling in my waiting hand.

"Honestly, this is heaven."

"I agree."

Chapter Four

Ghost

Ava spun around, nearly losing her footing.

"Jesus, Ghost." She pressed a hand to her chest. "You scared the shit outta me."

The woman had temptation written all over her. Long muscular legs, a lean, strong torso, delicate but deadly arms. I appraised her naked body—clinically at first—looking for vulnerabilities.

Instead, I found my own.

An unfamiliar need punched my gut, my body reacting to hers as my gaze followed the water flowing from her crown, down her dark, wet, soapy hair, across her full breasts, and down, down, down to the tempting curls at the juncture of her thighs.

She offered me a smile, spreading her arms wide. "Like what you see, biker boy?"

Fuck.

My voice sounded like gravel. "Don't leave your back to a door unless I'm watching it for you."

Ava rolled her eyes, then deliberately turned away from me, confirming my suspicion that her back was just as tempting as her front.

20

I want to fuck that ass.

"I'm not an idiot, Ghost. I know how to protect myself."

If that were true you wouldn't have let me see you naked.

I gritted my teeth, my body tight and aching. "Then do a better job."

I turned on my heel, leaving her to her shower as I fought the urge to join her. The image of Ava's naked body had burned itself on the back of my eyelids. I wanted nothing more than to taste the water that had dotted her skin.

Lock it down.

Distractions were how people ended up dead. Live or die—my life didn't matter, but my club needed me and I'd promised to keep Ava safe. Nothing would stop me from delivering on that promise.

Not even the woman herself.

In the kitchen I found our meals, ripping open the chicken to stab at the pale meat inside. The thing tasted like shit but it was food, and any food in the After was good food.

Above me the water shut off, the floor creaking ominously as Ava moved about the bathroom.

Food, rest, travel, recon. Decide options once we get the lay of the land.

I recited the agenda, fighting the temptation to dwell on Ava's naked body.

Food, rest, travel—

"Right." Ava entered the room, rifle slung over one shoulder, a ratty towel wrapped around her hair and piled atop her head. "Food and rest. Are we still on to recon tonight?"

Not for the first time, her words matched my thoughts perfectly. The only other person who had ever done so had been Hazard, but I'd left him back in Adaminaby with the rest of the chapter.

"Yeah."

"Cool. You want to rest first, or should I?"

"Sit. Eat," I told her, nudging the hot rations her way. "I'll rest now."

She shrugged. "Suit yourself."

I settled in a corner of the small kitchen, leaning my back against the wall, my gun at my side as I closed my eyes. I knew I wouldn't sleep; I'd been trained to go weeks without rest, my body and mind still functioning at their peak. But such an admission would reveal far too much.

I listened to Ava's packet crumble as she scraped it with her camp spoon, her body shifting slightly on the rickety chair. Outside, the noises of the night had taken over. I focussed on that rhythm, paying attention to any changes that would alert me to an unwelcome visitor as my breathing evened out, giving the appearance of rest.

Some time later, Ava's soft voice broke the silence. "I wonder what happened to them."

I opened my eyes, finding Ava standing before a series of frames on the wall, her torch lifted to light the wedding picture. I pushed up, coming to stand behind her.

The woman in the picture wore a white dress and a smile so broad I wondered if I'd ever felt even a tenth of that joy. The man had dressed in a blue suit, his adoring gaze on his bride.

Idiots.

"Dead."

Ava jumped, losing hold of her torch, the light flickering as she tried to catch it.

"Motherfucker! Seriously, I'm gonna put a fucking bell around your neck. Jesus fucking Christ, Ghost. A little

22

warning next time." She stepped back, flicking hair out of her eyes. "Did you say dead? How do you know? Or are you just being a morose motherfucker?"

I paused, unsure if this woman needed more shit piled on her shoulders.

"The car is stored in the third shed with the red door." I glanced back at the wedding photo. "Don't go in the green barn."

Ava caught my look, her face pinching. "Bastard or...?"

It had looked like murder-suicide, but then the bodies were badly decomposed and I hadn't stuck around to do a thorough analysis of the scene.

"Does it matter?"

She turned back to the photo on the wall. "I guess not. Not anymore."

Perhaps in the Before the death of the farmers would have been news but this was the After, a time of death and destruction where the only thing that mattered was your own survival.

"Rest," I told her, reaching out to take the torch. "We'll leave in an hour."

Chapter Five

Ghost

"This isn't what I expected," Ava said, as we stood on the roof of an abandoned building surveying the town. "I guess I thought it would be like Farmer's place—early to bed, early to rise. No extra power wasted. This is...."

"Sodom and Gomorra?"

She laughed. "That's a pretty apt description."

The residents of the town of Dubbo had reduced their footprint to a few blocks of houses, most centred around the old gaol which seemed to have been converted into a safe hold. They'd erected a wall around the inhabited areas, lights and fires burning as music pumped out of various bars, men mulling about here and there as rats scavenged for food in the dirty alley ways.

"Or perhaps *Lord of the Flies*," Ava murmured as two men burst out of a bar, tumbling into the street, punching each other as if their lives depended on it. A crowd gathered, placing wagers.

"Not many women."

My body tensed, not liking the feel of this place. "Stay close," I ordered.

"Well, duh, Mister obvious." She touched the rifle at my

shoulder. "Keep or stow?"

As much as I loathed having to hide the weapons and hope some lucky dick didn't stumble across them, their presence would draw more eyes than I wanted.

"Stow."

We searched the dark areas around the wall, finally settling on an abandoned fibro shack, storing the larger weapons and our bags in the roof.

"We get separated, meet me here. If you can't get here, get to the farm house."

Ava nodded, checking the safety on her pistol before tucking it into the back of her jeans. "Though if you're not back after twenty-four hours then I'm leaving you."

"Good."

She shot me a grin. "You like being left behind?"

"If I'm not here after twenty-four hours it means I'm dead. There's no point waiting longer."

Her eyebrows rose and for a moment she looked as if she were going to say something. Then her face cleared and she shrugged.

"Noted. You ready?"

I followed her out into the street, both of us keeping to the shadows as we made our way to the wall.

"Up and over or main gate?" Ava asked.

"Wall."

The main gate would no doubt be full of fuckers ready to take advantage of the fresh meat wandering in.

Better to slip in unannounced.

I boosted Ava up, following behind as we scrambled our way over the haphazard wall.

"Cars, barbed wire, sheet metal, I'm surprised there's not

a—oh, wait no, there's the kitchen sink." She pulled a loose tap handle off, tossing it at me with a chuckle. "Wouldn't keep a bastard out for more than fifteen minutes. These people are idiots."

I caught the handle easily, slipping it into my pocket, and continued to follow her up the junk heap, silently agreeing with her assertion.

Bastards couldn't climb. The virus ravaged its host until they were more animal than human but it had three weaknesses —climbing, swimming, and decay. The disease ravaged their extremities, causing fingers and toes to curl into mangled claws, their arms following suit as the virus attacked their muscles.

The infection was a form of rabies, making the host ravenously mindless and violent. They didn't hunt humans so much as anything that moved. Some of it was hunger, most of it seemed to be mindless rage caused by the virus. It was a hell of a way to die.

A car door gave way under Ava. I caught her, setting her back on solid ground as we continued to pick our way up the wall. It could hardly be described as climbing. The wall was nothing more than a heaped rubbish pile on a slight curve. The bastards would swarm this easily.

I give them less than six months before the town is overrun.

On the other side, Ava and I faded into the shadows, sticking close to buildings as we walked through the town, getting a feel for the ebb and flow of Dubbo.

"There," Ava said, leaning into me. "I think that's our best bet."

Rough but clean, the bar had a certain clientele hanging about that looked like the kind of people who'd talk—for the right price.

"Stay close."

Ava rolled her eyes. "No, Ghost. I'm gonna go rogue and become a dancer. Jesus, dude. It's not my first rodeo."

I ignored her, leading us across the street.

I knew she had training. Had seen her putting Hazard through his paces back at the compound. Her sniper skills were fucking exceptional.

But the fuck if I could stop myself from acting as if she needed me to protect her.

That's because you want her.

Desire had no place in a mission.

I shoved the thought away as we made it to the pub entrance.

"Ready?" I asked, hand on the door.

"Let's get this over with."

Chapter Six

Ghost

Dimly lit, the lights were obviously running on a generator as they blinked, ebbing and twitching every now and then, casting a menacing glow across the bar.

The inside felt as rough as I'd expected, and not just because it needed a clean. The clientele were a mix of rough travellers and dirty locals—each with the gritty suspicious gaze of those that had survived the initial days after the Dark.

Twelve men, plus one barman. Exits are at three and nine o'clock. Tables are secured to floor but chairs are free movement—possible weapons. Four men at back table, three with knives, one with gun. Three by window—no threat. Four at centre table—possible issue if continuing to drink. Knife in boot, back pocket and on table. No guns. One man by door—fuck.

I moved us through the room to the bar, keeping my side to the danger sitting alone by the door.

This is a complication we didn't fucking need.

Ava leaned against the bar, her body at ease as she perused the bottles of liquor on the shelves behind the bar.

A viper waiting to strike.

"Be with youse in a sec," the barman called, pulling drinks for another table.

I gave him a chin lift in acknowledgement.

"So," Ava murmured as she settled in. "Who's your friend by the door?"

I leaned my back against the bar, keeping my stance casual as I surveyed the room, alert for threats.

"Caught that, did you?"

"I would have missed it if he hadn't moved for his knife. Rookie move."

I swallowed a grin.

"So." She bumped her hip into mine. "Who is he?"

My dick responded to her innocent touch. For a minute all I could see was her naked boy, my body demanding I strip her and fuck her right here, right now, claiming her while these fuckers watched.

This is how people get killed.

I cleared my throat. "He's a Kincaid."

She turned, an eyebrow arched in question when I didn't offer more.

"Sorry, am I meant to know what that means?"

I narrowed my gaze on one of the men as he stared at Ava's ass. He caught my glare, quickly looking away.

Fucker.

"Ghost? You gonna answer me?"

"Mafia. Cartel. His dad runs the family. The kid by the door is the youngest brother."

"Of how many?"

"Four, last I heard."

She glanced in the bar's mirrored splashback, considering the Kincaid.

"Friend or foe?"

"Depends on the day."

"Noted."

The barkeep trudged up, interrupting our conversation.

"What can I—shit." The guy stared at Ava. "She's not collared."

Ava tilted her head to one side. "Excuse me?"

The old guy reached under the bar pulling a small basket free, leather dog collars lay inside. He took one out, tossing it to me.

"Cuff her or she'll cause a riot."

I shook my head. "No."

"Cuff her," the barkeep hissed. "Or I'll do it myself."

Ava bristled. "Over my dead—"

The Kincaid interrupted her.

"Do it." He dropped on an empty stool beside her. "Last woman who refused they had to scrape off the bar floor." He pointed at a dark patch on the wood boards. "Fucking waste of a woman."

I reached for the collar, holding it out to Ava.

"Your choice."

She gritted her teeth, turning to present her back to me. She lifted her ponytail away from her neck, revealing delicate skin.

"Just do it."

I wanted to press a kiss to her neck, to mar her pale skin with my mark.

"How's that?" I asked as I finished buckling the collar. "Too tight?"

I caught some loose hairs, gently pulling them free of the collar, my body throbbing with need as I breathed in her scent.

"Let's just drink and get the fuck out of here."

The barkeep nodded in approval. "What can I get you folks?"

"Two of whatever he's having." I nodded at the Kincaid.

"Coming up." The barkeep pulled a tap, filling two tall glasses.

"What do I owe you?" I asked, reaching for the gold in my pocket.

Kincaid slapped a hand down on the bar. "Put it on my tab, Pat. I got this." He shot me a grin that didn't reach his eyes. "Anything for an old friend."

I considered him. Black Irish, they'd have called him back in the Before. Dark hair, dark eyes, pale skin. He had the unmarked skin of a young man, but the dead eyes of someone who had survived the worst life had to offer. I put him at mid-twenties, and while inexperienced, he was no less deadly than his brothers who I'd had the misfortune to tangle with in the Before.

Ava accepted the offered glass, taking a sip and coughing at the taste.

"Jesus," she spluttered, voice hoarse as she held the beer away from her. "What the fuck is this?"

"Potato-hooch," the Kincaid said with a grin. "Best this place has to offer. Don't worry, you get used to it."

"God, if this is the best I don't want to know what the shitty stuff tastes like."

The fucker leaned in, ignoring my warning glare as he held out a hand to Ava.

"'Cause I know this fucker won't introduce us, I'm Sean. The youngest Kincaid."

She considered his hand for a moment then took it, giving a firm shake. "Ava."

"Ava," he repeated, as if he had the right to speak her name. "A pretty name for a pretty lady."

I snorted, reaching for Ava's half-drunk glass, smoothly

31

swapping ours out, ensuring one of us would remain sober tonight. If she noticed, she didn't comment.

"You know, I'm not sure I know what a Kincaid is."

Sean pressed a hand to his chest. "I'm wounded, truly wounded that my good friend here hasn't revealed all."

I snorted again, watching the card game at the centre table.

"They were organised crime in the Before," I explained. "Now? No fucking clue."

"Surviving like the rest of you," Sean said, his expression sobering. "We're distributors now. Connor's made sure of it."

"Connor?" Ava asked, taking another sip of her beer.

"My oldest brother. The head Kincaid."

I raised an eyebrow. "What happened to your father?"

"Dead. Got the virus just as the Dark happened. Connor himself had to put him down."

Ava winced. "I'm sorry for your loss."

He shrugged. "I'm not." Sean lifted his glass, taking a long drink. "Now, what brings you to this part of the world."

"Could ask the same of you," I commented mildly. "Dubbo's quite a way from cartel headquarters in Queensland."

He shrugged but a tension had crept into his limbs. "Action and adventure, my friend. New horizons and all that."

I placed a hand on Ava's back, leaning over her. "So, it doesn't have anything to do with a little rodent we both know?"

The Kincaid froze, his body alert. "Rodent?"

"A certain Mouse, perhaps?"

Sean's expression blanked. "What do you want for the info?"

I nodded at the room at large. "Safe place to stay. Access to the circus. Backup if we require it."

There were only four things which made people talk in the After—food, gold, fucking, or info. Though I wasn't above adding torture to the list if required.

"Seems like a fair trade for information," his tone sarcastic.

I shrugged. "What I know might just help you find her."

Sean hesitated for a moment then shrugged. "Fuck it. Share your wisdom and I'll get you what you need."

"Safe place first, then information."

The Kincaid rolled his eyes. "Ever the suspicious fucker, isn't he? Fine, drink ye gut rot, I'll be back to escort you to your palace."

He downed the last of his own beer, pushing away from the bar, heading for the exit.

Ava watched him with a bemused expression. "Why would he be searching for a slip of a girl back at your compound?" She tilted her head back. "And how did you know he was looking for Mouse?"

"It's my job to know."

"Is the club protecting her?"

"Fuck no. Girl's more work than she's worth."

"So, you'll just hand her over as if she has no choice."

"Hazard will allow her a choice. But she's Kincaid's property. Has been the moment she was born."

Ava tilted her head to one side. "What does that mean?"

I shrugged. "Not my story to tell. Ask the Kincaid or wait till we return to the compound."

"That's likely months away," Ava pointed out.

I lifted my glass to my lips. "Yep."

She narrowed her eyes on me. "You're enjoying this, aren't you?"

"Yep."

She let out a frustrated sigh. "Fine. What's next on your list, biker boy? Cards or beers for the back table?"

She'd also clocked the three men then.

Good woman.

"Back table. Locals but poor. Let's see if a few beers and a little bribery might get them talking."

Chapter Seven

Ava

The gut rot brew wasn't sitting so crash hot in my belly but I pushed through, only slightly leaning on Ghost as we followed Sean through the streets. I could feel the hungry looks from some of the men we passed, each of them assessing me as a potential fuck.

I haven't felt this uncomfortable since that tour in the middle east.

Back then I'd been a warrior in the military patches of a foreign country. Here, I was simply a woman.

The world ends and women get screwed over—fucking typical.

We'd spent the last few hours working the three men in the pub for information. Each round of beers we'd purchased had loosened their tongues a little more until we'd gotten the info we'd been searching for.

The circus was in town. The first round of fighting was due to start in two days. And the whispers of fuel being shipped in weren't rumours—The Purge had an airfield outside town which received regular deliveries in exchange for live-streamed fights.

Not to mention the export of women.

My feet slipped, my world wobbling as the hooch hit me.

Ghost's hands gripped my arm, holding me steady as we followed Sean through the dark streets.

"Here we are. Like I said, it's not anything pretty on the outside but the inside?" Sean lifted his fingers to his lips executing a chef's kiss. "Perfection."

Ghost—per usual—didn't comment as Sean led us up a small flight of stairs to a brick and tile building. Old and a little run down, he pushed the door of the non-descript residence open.

A delicious scent tickles my nostrils as we walked through the doors into a fantasy land. The building held an immaculate front parlour, complete with plush, generously comfortable furniture, wood and bronze furnishings, and five body guards strategically positioned around the room.

"Where are we?"

"It's a brothel. The safest place for a woman in Dubbo."

Ghost and I exchanged a look as Sean led us through the parlour to a back staircase then up two flights. Ghost supported me, my drunk ass enjoying his attention as I pulled the collar free.

Fuck it. I need to get him out of my system. Tonight, I'm gonna fuck this man.

"Here we are," Sean said with a grin, shoving open a door to a cave of wonders. "Misty, I'm home!"

The decadent room held nothing but soft furnishings, silks, and sweetly scented candles—it was a room so incongruent with my experience in the After that my brain didn't know how to process it. My drunk mind likened it to a cloud, or perhaps a dream.

"Sean, darling," a sultry voice greeted. "I see you've brought me some new clients. Or are these two looking for a position at my fine establishment?"

36

I stared at the woman before me, her overt femininity jarring. I'd long fought to stamp out the appearance of vulnerability in the women under my care by teaching them to be hard and sharp. We were all vulnerable in one way or another, but to present that physically was a sure way to die. I'd told them time and again that there wasn't any place for soft edges and pretty things if we wanted to survive.

This woman flew in the face of all my claims.

Misty wore a diaphanous robe that revealed as much as it hid. The corset had her breasts pushed up until they nearly spilled over the cups, her nipples slight shadows that played peek-a-boo with the material. Her legs were encased in soft silk stockings tied with pink ribbons to match the robe. I hadn't seen anything like her since the Before, and to see it now when we were surrounded by grit and death was discombobulating.

Discombobulating? You've spent far too much time around Audrey.

"They're friends, Misty," Sean interrupted my thoughts. "Just passing through and needing a safe place to rest their heads for a week or so." He moved to her, pressing a kiss to her cheek even as he slipped gold into her palm. "You be kind to these two. The *full* treatment."

She smiled, her perfect pink lips parting to reveal a perfectly straight set of teeth. "Of course, Sean. And you be sure to tell that brother of yours just how wonderful I've been to take care of these two."

Sean backed away as Misty approached us, her hips swaying sensually as she moved.

Perhaps it was the juxtaposition between the harsh world outside and the decadent room we'd stepped into, or maybe it was the strong alcohol fizzing through my blood, but I found myself wanting to reach out and touch her, to see if her skin really did feel as soft as it looked.

It can't be. No one is that soft in the After.

"Welcome to the Den," she greeted, her voice a purr. "I'm Misty, owner of the Painted Lips." Her hand lifted and she reached out to lay it on Ghost.

"No," I barked, my voice raw. "He's mine."

Ava, what are you doing? No messes, remember?

The claim stopped her movement, her hand hovering above his chest.

"Ah, I see." She cocked an eyebrow at Ghost. "And what about you, handsome? Is this woman yours?"

I tilted my head back expecting him to claim me as I'd claimed him. Instead, he remained silent, his face blank, eyes dead.

See? He doesn't want you.

My cheeks flushed as hurt and embarrassment burned in my gut.

Fuck you, biker boy.

"I'll take that as a no." She lay a hand on my wrist, pulling me gently away from Ghost.

"You can leave us," she told Sean. "I'll take it from here."

With a grin and a wink, he left, shutting us in the plush room with the brothel owner.

Misty considered me, her expression understanding and warm as she glanced from me to Ghost and back.

"Come, lovely girl. Let's get you clean and comfortable." She cupped my cheek, her eyes dancing with mischief. "And perhaps something... more?"

She leaned in, her lips catching mine in a kiss before I could stop her. I noted clinically that she was as soft as she looked as she licked at my lips, encouraging me to open to her. I made to draw away, only the tiniest bit regretful that no part of me was attracted to any part of her.

It would make life easier.

Behind me, Ghost sucked in a breath, halting my retreat.

A spiteful, dark part of me wanted him to ache with the same unfulfilled desire I felt for him. I wanted him to feel half of the agony his silence had churned within me.

I allowed Misty to kiss me as she moved closer, her hand snaking under my shirt to fiddle with my belt.

I relished the feel of Ghost tensing behind me, hoping like hell he was feeling even a tenth of the fucked up need I did.

Her fingers unzipped my pants, her hand slipping down the front of my jeans. A fraction away from cupping me, she yelped, pulling back.

"No," Ghost grunted, holding her wrist, his expression fierce. "No."

My body ached, the arousal that hadn't been present for Misty flared at his possessive tone.

"Then replace my lips with your own," Misty invited, stepping back. "I'm doing nothing for her."

She drew me to him, pressing my hand to his chest, directly over his heart.

Ghost's gaze met mine, a wildness in his eyes that had my body responding.

I moved in, a wet heat pooling between my thighs, little fires igniting everywhere my skin touched his.

"No," he choked out, his hands settling on my hips. "Ava, stop. We need to focus on—"

"Touch me or get the fuck out and let her do it," I told him, sick of denying what I wanted.

39

No—what I *needed.*

With a muttered curse, his head lowered, his lips capturing mine in a brutal kiss. There was no finesse, nothing but possessive passion and desperate, demanding need.

I groaned, my mouth opening to allow his tongue to tangle with mine, delighting in his taste.

More. I need more.

"There's a shower through the backdoor, condoms in the bedside table, and ropes underneath. Ring the bell if you desire food or drink." Misty let out a bell-like giggle. "Have fun you two."

A door opened and shut behind us, the madam sealing us in her den of iniquity.

Ava, what have you done? You need to stop this.

But I didn't want to. My head might recognise what a fucking stupid idea this was, but my body wanted him. God, it had been so fucking long since I'd had anyone touch me. Fuck, I hadn't even touched myself in months—always on alert, always desperate to ensure everyone I cared about was safe.

One of Ghost's hands shoved my jeans down to my thighs, my underwear following. His foot kicked mine wide, his other hand running gently over my hip down to tangle in my curls.

He braced me as his mouth continued to fuck mine, his blunt fingers stroking the sensitive skin of my labia, teasing at my slit.

Ava!

I rocked against him, desperate for more, desperate for him to touch all of me.

Ghost bent me back, his thick fingers parting me as he began to stroke in a way that felt as if he'd done this a million times before. There was a surety to his movement, a firm knowledge that he was bringing me pleasure.

My body arched, my mouth ripping free from his, a gut-wrenching groan tearing from deep in my soul.

"Fuck," he muttered, nipping at my neck, his lips sucking the sting away. My thighs were now slick with the evidence of my desire. "Ava."

He fucked me with his fingers, slipping first one then another into me, his thumb setting a counter rhythm on my clit. Ghost played my body like a master musician determined to land every note. Desperate gasps and harsh demands ripped from my throat, as he finger-fucked me to a lusty, delicious climax.

"You fucker," I groaned, collapsing against him, my body craving more. "Fuck you, Ghost. Seriously, fuck *you*."

"Soon," he promised, pressing a kiss to my lips. "First I'm gonna taste this pussy." He lifted me into his arms, my jeans and underwear falling away as he stepped across the room to lay me on the large bed, following me down—not allowing me even a moment to recover. His hot breath brushed against overly sensitive skin then his mouth fell, his tongue flicking repeatedly against me searching until he found my clit, a rumble of pleasure slipping from his throat.

I tried to close my legs, tried to limit his access but Ghost was determined. His hands pegged my legs open, his mouth demanding as fuck as he ate me with a single-minded focus I found incomparable.

This was a mistake. This was a glorious, delicious, much needed fucking mistake.

With a curse I arched my hips up, pressing myself to his face, one hand fisting his hair as I rode his tongue, breaking apart as Ghost's mouth worshipped my clit.

I slumped back on the bed, attempting to catch my breath

as he surged up, hands unsteady as he shoved his jeans down, weapons spilling across the sheets. With a rough grunt, he fisted his cock, his gaze locked on mine as he roughly pumped his dick.

I grinned, arching my back, my hands sliding up my sides to cup my breasts, offering them to him.

"Come here," I said, pinching my nipples with a groan. "Come all over me, Ghost. I want you to spill on me. I want you to mark my skin. I want—"

He lost control, his cock splashing hot cum across my breasts, up my neck, down my belly. His hand dropped, scooping a small amount to rub into my clit, his expression fierce before he leaned down, capturing my lips as he fingered me to another climax.

He easily rolled when I shoved him off. I flopped back on the cloud of a bed, relishing the sweet spark of desire that still ran through my exhausted body.

Ghost lay beside me, his fingers tracing little designs on my skin.

It's almost like he can't not touch you.

"I'm gonna need a shower," I told him, my eyes still closed. "And it had better be hot. Your cum is *not* staying on me."

A strange sound came from his side of the bed.

I opened one eye, offering a raised eyebrow. "I'm sorry, was that a laugh?"

He grinned and the expression was so stunningly gorgeous, so unexpected, that I couldn't help but reach out and trace the curve of his lips.

"You look different," I whispered, aware that we were crossing all sorts of lines.

Crossing? Babe, you obliterated the lines the moment you let him kiss you.

"So do you."

I huffed out a laugh, then sobered pushing upright, the moment broken. "Go find us some food while I shower. It's the least you can do."

Ghost watched me move, his expression growing increasingly guarded until his emotional trap door snapped shut, locking away anything he might have let me see.

Something in me hitched, knowing what was coming and preparing myself for the oncoming hurt.

And that's why he's a mess. Don't get attached, Ava. The man isn't a keeper.

"Ava, I—"

"Well—" I interrupted, shoving myself off the bed and climbing to my feet. "Glad we got that out of our system. You going for food or what?"

He watched me with those dark, blank eyes.

"Ghost? Food?"

Finally, he nodded.

I shut myself in the bathroom, leaning against the sink as I listened to him moving around the bedroom. A moment later the door opened and shut, leaving me alone.

I closed my eyes, sucking in a breath.

Alone. Just like always.

I turned to the sink, staring at myself in the mirror.

"Pull it together, Ava. You're the person people need. Not the one who needs people."

I just wished I believed that.

Chapter Eight

Ghost

I lay awake beside a slumbering Ava, listening to her soft breath, relishing the feel of her exhale as it brushed my arm. The only thing missing was my scent on her skin. She'd cleaned me off in the shower last night.

You're a sick motherfucker.

The sun had risen long ago, the light creeping through the window blinds. I knew we needed to move. We needed breakfast and to do more recon. We needed to work out a safe house in case this one wasn't sufficient. We needed to scope out the circus and establish if Ava's girls were being held there.

Instead, I was nursing morning wood as a result of her breath touching my skin.

You sorry fucking excuse for a human being.

I slipped a hand under the bed sheet, reaching down to fist my cock.

The first time I'd seen Ava she'd looked like shit. Pale, nursing a wound, but determined as fuck to stand her ground and ensure those under her protection were safe.

She'd shot the mirror off my bike and I'd gotten a fucking hard on.

As we'd helped the women pack their shit, readying to move them from the university where they'd holed up into the club's compound, one of the guys had asked the question that had been burning on my tongue the whole day.

"How did you survive this long?"

The same answer had been repeated by every single woman in the room.

"Ava."

Which had me asking, if she was their shield, who had her back?

The answer had been simple—no one. The woman was their last line of defence. Which made it my duty to ensure she didn't have to make that sacrifice.

Hazard had called me an idiot, laughing that the she-devil wasn't worth the effort.

"If she's determined to get herself killed, let her. She's a decent sort but there are easier ways to get your dick wet."

It wasn't about getting off. This ran deeper. There was an integrity to Ava. An authenticity in her actions, a care that attracted me.

She was everything I'd never—could never—be. I was made to kill, not care. I had no business wanting, no business touching a woman like her.

But fuck if that didn't make me want her more.

Her breathing changed.

"You better not be touching yourself, you dirty fucking perve," she muttered, eyes still closed. "If you've come on me while I've been sleeping I will have cause to cut it off."

"Good morning, Ava."

She blinked awake, her gaze immediately falling to where my cock tented the sheets.

"Fuck," she muttered, her tongue darting out to lick her lips. "It's bigger than I remember."

I didn't bother telling her it was likely a reaction to the fact I now had her taste memorised and the devil knew I wanted more.

Give me a sign, Ava. Let me touch you. Let me make you come.

She stretched, the sheets sliding down to catch on her nipples, my mouth watering at the sight.

"Fuck, that hooch is hitting me hard. Never again, Ghost. I get that one of us needed to keep their head but next time, big boy, you're taking one for the team. I feel like a rat died in my mouth and a lumberjack took up residence in my forehead." She draped an arm over her eyes. "God, I'd kill for a half-decent painkiller."

I rolled out of bed, digging through my pants until I found the small tin.

"Here."

Ava took the offered tin, giving it a shake. "What is it? Crack?"

"Aspirin."

Her eyebrows shot up. "Wait, seriously?"

"Let me get you some water."

"Where did you even get painkillers? These things are impossible to find."

I shrugged, filling a glass in the small sink in the bathroom. "Had them since the Before."

"Well, praise be to Jesus and biker boys who don't get migraines." She took the offered glass, downing it with a grimace. "Thanks."

I'll burn the world down before I let anything happen to you.

The truth settled in my soul, the first real emotion I'd felt in

CHAPTER EIGHT

decades.

She's mine. Fuck the world. Ava is mine.

She sighed, smacking her lips together. "So, breakfast?"

Chapter Nine

Ava

Breakfast was an experience.

The Painted Lips had not one, not two, but four gourmet chefs—all of whom had become experts at cooking over wood fires.

Succulent breakfast bowls were presented with sprigs of herbs and garnishes of fresh edible flowers—it was as if entering the Painted Lips took you back to the Before.

Like Narnia only with fucking.

"It's all about atmosphere, darling." Misty lifted her tea cup, taking a dainty sip. "The people walking through my doors are paying for the fantasy. And that starts with the presentation."

She turned the page of her newspaper, settling the tea cup back in its saucer with a delicate click.

"I didn't realise you guys still have news." I pointed with my fork at the paper.

She snorted. "This old thing? No, formal news has gone the way of technology and medication." She gave a small shrug. "But it's nice to have some familiarity in your day. Some traditions just stick with you. This is my indulgence."

I glanced around the kitchen, taking in the shining brass pots and pans, the kitchen hands as they bustled about prepping for the coming day, and Misty's outfit—a perfectly pressed and pristine white wiggle dress.

Indulgence? This whole place is one indulgence after another.

Ghost, never one for small talk, continued to glare at Sean who'd joined us at the table.

The cheeky Kincaid sent me a laughing look. "How'd you find your night?"

Hot. Sexy. Frustrating as fuck?

"It's a different world," I answered honestly, scooping another forkful of the delicious breakfast mix. "But not sure how practical all this will be to move when the bastards come."

Misty and Sean froze.

"The wall will stop them," she said, a small frown line creasing her brow. "We've been told they can't climb."

Ghost snorted into his bowl.

"What my partner means to say is that we've had some experience with the bastards. They can't climb but they can scramble. Which is what your wall allows."

Sean and Misty exchanged glances.

"Excuse me," she said, rising gracefully from the table. "I have a few matters to take care of."

Sean watched her walk away, a dark look on his face.

"You've scared her."

"Good. Scared means she might live." Ghost's unexpected comment landed on Sean in a way I hadn't expected. Instead of being angry or frustrated, the Kincaid nodded, his expression thoughtful.

"Alright, Ghost," he said a moment later. "I've held up my end of the bargain. Tell me about Mouse."

Ghost took his time chewing, his face carefully blank.

"We'll be here until the circus finishes." He looked up, his

49

expression void. "That means one piece of info for each day we require your protection."

The Kincaid's jaw tightened, a muscle jumping in his cheek. "Fine. One piece. Where is she?"

"Somewhere safe."

Sean slammed his fist on the table. "Fuck you, you MC piece of shit. Tell me or I'll—"

Ghost stood, his hand shooting out to grip Sean's neck. With barely any effort, he lifted him up and across the table, twisting to shove him into a wall. Sean's hands clawed at Ghost's arm.

"Listen to me, Kincaid," Ghost said, his tone deadly. "Ever talk to me like that again and you won't be leaving with bruises. Get me?"

Sean attempted to nod, his eyes wide, lips turning blue as Ghost continued to apply pressure to his windpipe.

I raised the final forkful of my breakfast to my mouth, wondering if I could steal more before we needed to head out for the day.

"Mouse is fine. She's safe with the club. She's happy. She's fed. She's protected. If you're a good little boy, tomorrow I might even tell you what she does around the place." Ghost let Sean go abruptly. The Kincaid fell back against the wall, his body crumbling as he spluttered, sucking in long drags of air.

"Now, sit your fucking arse back down and tell me what the fuck is going on with the circus. What do we need to know?"

Sean sat back at the table, his expression wary as he tried to control his stilted breathing.

"Darling," I said, turning to Ghost as I channelled my inner Misty, giving Sean another moment to recover. "Was that really necessary?"

Ghost crossed his arms over his chest, a shadow of amusement briefly touching his eyes before vanishing like a vapour.

Frustrating as fuck.

"Yes."

"The tournament starts tomorrow," Sean ground out, rubbing his throat. "Today you need to sign up at the show ground. There's three different types of battle."

"And women?" I asked.

"The women who are prizes are kept in a secure cage in the circus. Fars I know, there's not many ways to get access to them beyond winning one as a prize. The Purge keep a tight rein on access."

I nodded, mentally taking notes.

"There are four options when entering—food, fuel, women or gold. Each are needed to buy your way in. Without them, you're relegated to a spectator. And the spectators are just as vicious as the fighters."

"What about prizes? How many women do you get if you win?"

"It's a one-to-one ratio. Wager one, get yours and another back. Want more? Gotta wager more."

"Fuck," I muttered, shooting Ghost a look. "We need another woman."

"Or gold. Or food. Or fuel. Up to you," Sean said with a shrug. "Either way you need to find something additional to barter."

"What's the buy-in price?" Ghost asked, his breakfast forgotten.

"Women—has to be of breeding age or a kid. Gold is subjective depending on how the fuckers feel. Food is standard—one car load."

I nodded. "Anything else?"

He shrugged. "Just don't die."

Misty bustled back in. "Now, that's done, should we get Ghost and Ava outfitted?"

I blinked. "Sorry?"

She paused at the table, pressing her hands together. "How do I put this delicately?" She tilted her head to one side. "You're both lovely people and obviously enjoy a bath but your clothes... they're rather...."

"Rank? Smelly? Ready to be burned?" Sean offered.

"In need of a wash," Misty finished, shooting him a disapproving look. "And if you're going to the circus, no doubt you'd like a little camouflage. I have just the thing." She crooked her finger at us. "Follow me."

Chapter Ten

Ghost

For years I'd worked for the government in a shadow organisation, a special forces officer on paper, a hitman in practice. The org hadn't been listed on any website, hadn't been more than a whisper around the halls of Parliament House.

I'd been recruited as a kid, plucked from my home—chosen for my rage and fists. The organisation had taught me how to silence the noise in my head. How to extinguish every part of me that could feel emotion, hurt, pain.

Those weaknesses were what got you killed.

I'd assassinate men and women at far range, taking them out with the flick of a finger. I'd hunted my targets, slitting throats as I felt the heat of their blood on my hands, all while their dying breath faded on my cheek.

I'd worn everything from jumpsuits as I parachuted into combat zones to leather fucking harnesses as I tracked targets through sex clubs.

I'd run on less than an hour's sleep for two months, never pausing as I evaded an arms dealer in South Sudan. I'd been tortured, beaten, and dumped in a mass grave in Moscow.

But this? This had to be the fucking worst mission I'd ever

agreed to.

"No."

Ava slapped hands on her hips, glaring at me. "But—"

"I said no." I crossed my arms, returning her glare.

"It's a fucking outfit, Ghost. I've worn less clothes exercising."

Not around me.

"We're going to sign up, not to attract the kind of attention that—"

"If you wanna live beyond the next five minutes then you better keep your fucking mouth shut," she warned, pressing a finger into my chest. "You do *not* want to finish the misogynistic bullshit thought that was about to spill out of those lips."

I glared at her.

"You guys done? Or you need me to leave so you can fuck it out?" the Kincaid asked, pretending to clean his fingernails on his shirt.

"Shut the fuck up," Ava growled at him. She threw me another glare then turned, stomping towards the door. "Let's get this the fuck over with."

Her scrap of a skirt barely covered her arse while that fucking top didn't leave anything to the imagination. I could see the shadows of her nipples, could trace the curve of her breasts with my eyes.

Mine. She's fucking mine.

Icy rage burned under my skin, cold fire licking at the edges of my soul.

She's your weak spot. Lock it down.

The fuck if I knew what to do with this rage. I'd felt nothing for decades, what use did I have for this shit?

I reached for the void, for the dark quiet that my trainers had beat into me decades before.

"Ah, Ava?" The Kincaid stopped her movement. "Aren't you forgetting something?"

He reached into his pocket pulling free the leather collar she'd discarded last night.

"Oh, fuck no." She shook her head. "I'm wearing ridiculous clothing without a bra. Over my dead body am I strapping a fucking collar around my neck as if I'm someone's little bitch."

Misty rose from her plush seat in the corner, moving to take the collar from Kincaid. She ran the leather through her fingers, making a tutting sound.

"Sean, you should know better than to use this." She looked around the room, spotting one of her bodyguards. "Tai, will you get me the collar box from upstairs please?"

Ava let out a strangled sound. "Collar box? You have a box of motherfucking collars?"

Misty nodded. "Of course. It's the only way to move around safely. Even a well-known woman like myself isn't safe without a collar."

Ava shook her head. "Sorry, you're gonna have to break this down for me. What the fuck is up with this shit?"

Sean shrugged, looking to Misty.

"The collars were introduced after the first wave." Misty ran the leather through her fingers, her gaze unfocussed. "The town lost nearly ninety-five percent of our women overnight. It felt as if our world were falling down around us. We were broken, heartsore, grieving." She fisted the leather. "And then we lost the children."

Ava sucked in a breath, her face stricken.

Fuck.

55

"Wave after wave of the virus affected our town—like so many others—until the only ones who remained were those who'd hidden away, or those who'd proved resistant." Misty's lips twisted into a bitter smile. "They called us the lucky ones. We weren't. No one left behind is."

Ava reached out, her hand sliding into mine.

I got you.

"The Dark came, and the world descended into chaos. I'd read the room after the first wave. Had known this was coming." Misty waved a hand around the room. "The Painted Lips became the last place women could be safe in this town."

"But it's a brothel."

"And the women get to choose. They choose who to take to their beds, they choose to work. To eat. To sleep. They are protected within these walls by men who have no interest in their bodies, only the gold and food they receive. There's a power here, Ava. These collars?" She tossed it on the table. "There's no one forcing us to wear it within these walls. But out there?" She pointed to the door. "Out there the monsters are waiting. And we women? Our only protection is a scrap of leather that declares us as a man's property."

Tai returned, a small box in his hands. Misty opened the lid, revealing fur-lined collars in a variety of colours. She considered them for a moment then removed a crimson collar, moving to stand before me.

"Here." She handed it to me. "Claim her. Out there you're her only protection."

Ava tilted her head back, her gaze searching as she studied me.

For a moment, no one in the room moved.

"I'll put this around her neck," I said, my gaze locked with

56

Ava's. "But she needs no protection. Ava's a she-devil. A viper. She's deadly. This?" I crushed the leather in my palm. "It's a symbol that they should fear *her*. You did right to choose one the colour of blood. It's a promise of the violence she'll spill if they touch her."

Ava's hand squeezed mine, her eyes full of an emotion I had no capacity to read.

"Ghost?"

I cocked an eyebrow.

"Just put the fucking thing on me."

With a small huff, I did as asked, relishing the feel of her warm skin, memorising the dance of her hair against my fingers.

"Ready?" Sean asked, holding the door open.

Ava sucked in a breath, letting it out slowly.

"Yep. Let's fucking do this."

Chapter Eleven

Ghost

The circus sat on a squat dirt plot adjacent to a section of the wall. A tent city had sprung up around it, filled with hawkers of food, purveyors of flesh, and the occasional weapons dealer.

Ava stopped in front of one such stall, perusing their wares. The guy watched her, sizing up her limbs with the eye of someone who knew a threat when he saw it.

"Not many places to hide a weapon in that outfit," he commented, chewing on some tobacco.

"No," Ava laughed, flicking at the hem of her skirt. "So you have anything that would work with it?"

The guy considered her for a moment then disappeared into his tent, returning with a lock box.

"This might work."

He spun the dial, opening a small sliding drawer in the box. A set of decorative wrist cuffs lay inside. The pieces of metal looked like two snakes intertwined, their heads pressing together to lay flat just above her knuckles.

"Silver?" Ava asked, raising her eyebrows.

"Titanium." He handed her one of the cuffs, showing her how to wear it.

"It's a pretty gaudy piece of jewellery," she said with a grin, swinging her arm around. "But might deliver a decent blow."

"Press the snake's eye with your thumb."

She did, grinning when a small dagger shot out of the snake's mouth. "Well, this is awesome."

I pulled a nugget of gold free, laying it on his table. "She'll take it."

The guy swept the nugget up, pocketing it. "For that you can have both."

Ava took the second cuff, clipping it into place and testing it before hiding the slip knives away.

"Anything else you need?" she asked as we continued on our way.

I shook my head, alert to the attention we were beginning to draw. "Just stay close."

She nodded, falling into step with me.

The looks continued as we moved closer to the heart of the circus, some becoming bold as they openly stared, catcalling as we passed. A few of the residents might have tried to make an approach—Ava's beauty hard to miss—if not for the death in my eyes.

I'll burn your fucking world down and relish every fucking minute of it.

"Which way?" she asked, pausing at a cross road.

I nodded to the left. "That one. Follow the blood."

The path cut through the final rows of tents, blood mixing with dust under our boots as we found our way into the circus.

The tent was silent, the stands empty, the festivities not expected until tomorrow evening. But a group of rough men sat behind a table, a line of equally rough men milling in front.

"Guess this is sign up," Ava muttered, glancing around. "Wonder where they keep the women during the day."

"Based on the population outside? I'd say somewhere really fucking secure. All it would take is one riot for this whole show to go to fuck."

Ava nodded, flicking a stray chunk of dark hair away from her cheek. The strands floated down, settling against her skin.

I had an overwhelming urge to tangle my fingers in her hair, tilt her head back and fuck her mouth with my tongue.

Not fucking now.

"She's a nice piece of gash."

I turned, watching one of the guys from the table rise and begin to stroll towards us. His gait was loose, his body relaxed as he openly appraised Ava.

A king in his domain.

The wolf in me rose from its slumber, scenting the air and finding its prey.

You'll be the first to die, motherfucker.

He circled Ava, his gaze possessive.

"How much she cost?"

I crossed my arms, choosing not to answer.

"Must be a pretty penny, she's barely marked."

He reached out but Ava caught his wrist, halting his movement.

"Uh-uh, no touching," she said with a polite smile that didn't reach her eyes. "Daddy over there wouldn't like it."

She let his hand go, stepping back and into me. I dropped an arm over her shoulders staking my claim.

The guy considered us for a long moment as I did the same.

Caucasian, mid-forties, brown eyes, bald, rough life but used to being in charge. Weakness is ego. Likely fucks with people for fun. Used to being the biggest dick in the room. Three visible weapons, four hidden, likely the kind of guy to bite you if you get him down.

Threat level: three of ten.

"You want in... Daddy?" the guy asked, a mocking smile on his lips.

I jerked my head up in acknowledgement.

"Mm." He crossed his arms. "You bartering her?"

"Me and this." Ava slid her hand along my chest, reaching into my jacket, lifting up on tip-toes to gently breath a warning against my ear as she did so.

"Guys on your three, eight, and eleven. Guns, knives and expressions that say life isn't worth living unless you're killing something."

I didn't react, all my focus remaining on the swinging dick across from us.

"This," Ava said, holding out the small pouch of gold. "When Daddy wins, he gets two."

The guy laughed. "Two? What's he gonna do with three women, little girl?"

She lifted one shoulder in a half-shrug. "Who says they're for him?"

Her comment broke the violent edge in the tent, shifting the energy to one of sexual tension.

Fuck, no.

I reached out, pulling her back against my front, wrapping one arm tight around her.

Mine.

"Alright. Be here by sundown tomorrow." He held out a hand. "Gold now. You?" He pointed to the cage in the corner. "You get to stay with the others until he wins you back."

A growl slipped free as I struggled to void the rage at his statement.

"No. She stays with me."

61

The dick shook his head. "No can do. She's collateral. Until you win her back...." He licked his lips. "She's ours."

Ava pressed back into me, her body warm and strong under mine.

Ava answered for me. "We'll be back tomorrow evening." She leaned into me. "You'll not get him to fight if you take me away before then."

The swinging dick glared for a moment then relaxed. "Fine." He offered Ava a lecherous grin. "See you then, hottie."

With a final warning glare, I turned us, escorting Ava from the tent. As we made our way outside, she tipped her head back, shooting me a grin.

"How many ways did you think to kill him?"

A tickle of something that felt like humour hit me.

"Five hundred and thirty-four."

With a laugh, she pressed into me, sending my body into overdrive. "That's what I thought."

Chapter Twelve

Ava

I lay in Misty's borrowed bed, my stomach full of another delicious meal, Ghost resting beside me. I should have been asleep an hour ago. Instead, my mind plagued me.

We hadn't spoken of the circus since returning. Hadn't touched each other. Hadn't done more than watch and listen as Misty and her household went about their business.

I knew Ghost needed rest before the fights began, but the way the douchebag at the circus had looked at me…. It'd triggered a memory I'd sooner forget.

"You're still awake."

Ghost's rough voice sounded loud in the dark of the room. I sighed, staring up at the shadowed ceiling.

"Yeah."

"Why?"

Truth or lie?

Tonight, the weight of my lies felt crushing.

"I didn't like the way he looked at me."

"The swinging dick?"

I huffed out a bitter laugh. "Yeah."

Ghost shifted, rolling to his side to watch me in the dark. "He'll be dead before the end of the week."

If I had been a normal person, the statement would have raised alarm bells. But I wasn't normal—not even close.

"Good." I twisted, offering him a small smile. "And thanks."

Ghost lifted one shoulder in a half shrug, as if offering to kill someone wasn't a big deal.

To a man like him, I guess it isn't.

"But that's not what's on your mind," he said, his voice low.

"I'm not sure I like that in addition to your powers of pervesion, you somehow get to add mindreading to that list."

Ghost reached out, his fingers tangling with the strands of my hair. He began to comb his fingers through them, the movement surprisingly gentle.

"Tell me."

I closed my eyes, grateful for the darkness.

"Not sure I want to. It's pretty fucking shameful."

He remained silent, allowing me to guide the conversation.

"I was on medical leave," I whispered, the words hard to find. "Sent back to Australia after a run in with an IED. Not badly injured, just fucked up my shoulder. Needed some surgery, a few months off to recover."

I swallowed, taking comfort in Ghost's touch.

"When?"

"Just before the first wave. Instead of allowing me home, they locked the borders and asked all personnel to stay on base. It's only me and Lottie, and she was safe down at her uni, so I stayed."

I opened my eyes, staring up at the dark ceiling, images of those days beginning to play like a montage in the dim light.

"The first wave wasn't so bad. Causalities, sure. I lost some good friends, but we all did. But the second?" I sucked in a breath. "That's when I knew shit was going to get bad."

"The women?" he asked, his voice low.

"Yeah. Of the women on the base, we lost eight—maybe eighty-five percent. When they realised how bad it was, they moved us remaining females to an outpost. Locked us in single rooms. We were penned in cells as if we were prisoners."

I choked on my words, the bitter impotent rage beginning to boil in my blood.

"I didn't care at first. Thought it wasn't so bad. Allowed them to do it because I trusted them. They were friends. I'd thought they were doing it for my own safety. Then they started the tests."

Ghost's hand paused. "Tests?"

"Vaccines. Or supposed vaccines."

I hadn't told anyone this. Hadn't even written it in that fucking history book Audrey wanted me to write. The truth was too horrifying. Too soul destroying to admit.

"The vaccines were biological warfare. They'd been tampered with during import by some country that hates our fucking guts, they created the first lot of bastards."

Ghost froze, his body tight. "What the fuck?"

"And then our own fucking government went and accidentally infected unwilling subjects." I closed my eyes, wishing I could forget the screams of the women who'd succumbed to the virus. "They'd thought it was doing its job. Spoiler, women shouldn't be turning into blood-thirsty animals after getting a vial of medicine."

"Fuck."

I blew out a breath. "But here's the kicker. They could have contained it if it had just been the women on the base. But you say to people there might be a vaccine and suddenly that shit goes missing. All it took was for three vials to be administered to two families for the mutation to spread."

"That means you knew about the mutation? But your women didn't. You kept it from them?"

"The mutation was the reason the world went dark. It spread too quickly to prevent. When the government made the choice to destroy the cities, I hoped... I...." I choked, my throat closing with bitter regret.

"How did you get out?"

This was the part of my story I hated the most.

"There were three healthy women left and we became a commodity. Women always are. Some of my own fucking team fought for the right to own me."

The memory of violence and blood, the rage and frustration churned in my gut.

Ghost's fingers tangled in my hair, gently stroking.

"So you escaped?"

"No. I killed them. All of them."

Chapter Thirteen

Ghost

Ava shuddered, her body tense as she waited for my judgement. Guilt hung like a cloud over her, its weight heavy.

I want to scrub their bloodlines from the face of the motherfucking earth.

"Good."

She started, her head lifting off the pillow, neck twisting as she stared at me in the dim light.

"Good? I killed them, Ghost. All of them."

"If you hadn't where would you be now?"

She flopped back on the bed, giving a shrug. "I don't know. Dead most likely. Sex slave maybe?"

"Better them than you."

She raised an eyebrow. "You can't know that."

"I fucking do. Back at the compound there are women. Some are old ladies. Some just kids. A few are sweet butts. Never once forced them. Never even been tempted. Not even when we realised that it was fucking likely the majority of us wouldn't get a future."

"That's because you're a machine." She poked me gently. "You don't break. You don't react. You don't feel emotions like the rest of us mere mortals. Desire? What's that to a machine like you."

That's because I hadn't tasted you.

My cock lengthened, my blood beginning to heat.

"Did they hurt you?"

"Not physically. I didn't give them a chance." Her face fell, her expression pure anguish."

"Ava, you did what you had to. I've been in some fucked up places. I've learned the hard way there are only two types of people—dicks and cowards." I reached out, running my fingers through her hair until I could fist it. "Then you came and fucked that all up."

Her eyes flashed in the dim light. "Which one am I?"

"The only one I'd never met."

"And that is?"

A partner.

The words caught in my throat, these fucking feelings threatening to overwhelm me.

You fucking pussy. Pull it the fuck together.

"A fighter," I said, voice rough.

Ava sucked in a breath. "You motherfucking charmer. Don't get sweet on me, Ghost. You and I both know there's no future between us."

Her words should have brought me back to reality. They should have thrown cold water over the heat of this moment, should have allowed me to shove everything that I felt back into the dark void that sat deep inside me.

They should have but didn't. They made me want to do something I'd never done before.

Prove her wrong.

An emotion quite unlike any I'd felt before burned in my gut, rolling its way through me like a motherfucking steam engine.

Hope. This is hope.

Fuck.

I despised this emotion. Despised the way I felt every time I looked at her. Despised the way I lost control every time I touched her.

I need more. I need forever.

I wasn't a forever kind of guy. I'd never be the prince in anyone's story.

But the way Ava looked at me? Fuck if she didn't make this dragon wanna try on a crown.

You fucking motherfucker. Monsters like you don't get the happy ending. They get a bullet to the head.

I pulled away from her, shoving up from the bed.

Ava rose to her elbows, watching me dress.

"Where are you going?"

"Out."

"Should I—"

I shook my head, cutting her off.

She watched me, her expression shutting down, becoming distant. "Will you be back?"

I shrugged.

"I see."

For a moment her words and the hurt behind them hovered in the dark room.

I snatched my jacket from the chair where I'd tossed it earlier.

"Ghost?"

I paused, one hand on the door, my back to the beautiful woman on the bed.

"Lock up after yourself."

I closed my eyes. Her words were delivered like a slap—cold, hard, and clinical.

Success. Just as you wanted.

I walked out into the hallway, closing and locking the door behind me then stopped, leaning against it for a moment.

You wanted this.

Yeah, I had. So why did it feel so fucking wrong?

Chapter Fourteen

Ava

I stared at the ceiling for the third hour post-Ghost's departure, my sleeplessness no longer caused by the memory of the men I'd killed but rather thoughts of the man who was killing me.

Killing me one fucking moment at a time.

He'd looked so dead as he'd dressed, his emotionless mask firmly in place. I'd have assumed he hated me if not for one thing.

He flinched.

When he'd called me a fighter his hand—which had been fisting my hair—had flinched. At first I hadn't noticed it, but he'd done it again after I'd told him there could be no future between us.

Why would he flinch? Unless...?

The thought was too incredible. Too fragile. Too unbelievable to even entertain.

He can't want a future. The man doesn't believe in anything except death.

But I couldn't get those two involuntary movements out of my head.

It doesn't mean anything, Ava.

But what if it does?

The door creaked, alerting me to Ghost's return even though I couldn't hear even the lightest footfall.

Motherfucker definitely needs a bell.

I snapped my eyes closed, forcing my breathing to even out, pretending to be asleep. Nervous butterflies took flight in my belly, a weird sense of anticipatory suspense hitting me.

He flinched.

A whisper of air brushed my skin a fraction before he touched me. His finger traced the curve of my cheek, down to the corner of my lips.

For a moment he paused there, his finger barely grazing my mouth.

What are you doing, Ghost?

I wondered if he could hear my heart. Wondered if he could see the pulse in my neck fluttering in the dark.

I wonder if he'll kiss me.

His touch retreated, the heat of him fading away. My eyes remained closed, my breathing even as I strained to hear him moving around the room.

The bed dipped, my body tipping slighting in his direction as he slipped under the blankets.

He reached out again, touching my hair.

"I lied," he murmured, breaking the silence. "When I look at you, I see something I've never seen before. I see hope. And it fucking terrifies me."

I didn't move. Didn't react. I just kept breathing as if I were sleeping beauty, and he an unwitting prince.

His fingers relaxed, still tangled in the strands of my hair.

"Good night, Ava."

And with that, we both finally slept.

Chapter Fifteen

Ava

Sweat ran down my back, the heavy material of my shirt sticking to me in ways that were distinctly unpleasant.

Next time, Ghost's wearing the lump.

After another delicious breakfast with Sean and Misty, Ghost and I decided to do a little recon, see if we could track down where they kept the women between fights.

He'd grunged himself up, somehow managing to look less intimidating.

"In my line of work, if you don't blend, you die."

I'd filed away that explanation for further examination.

While he might be comfortable strolling through the alleyways of the tent city, I was feeling a severe case of early heatstroke. The pile of rags tied to my back gave me a hunched look. It'd been Misty's idea, a way to blend in.

"No one cares about a dirty old man."

She'd been right. While Ghost still drew the occasional assessing eye, this little get-up had let me slip through almost unnoticed.

Well, except for the gang of street kids who'd marked me as an easy target. They'd learned the hard way not to fuck with grandpa.

"Dude, seriously, wait."

Ghost slowed, waiting for me to slip in beside him.

"This is useless, we need to try somewhere else."

We'd been at this for half the day, following dead lead after dead lead.

"Let's try this last lead."

I blew out a breath. "Fine, it's your gold to waste."

No matter how many palms we'd greased or threat's Ghost had tossed about, no one could give us even the slightest indication of where The Purge kept the women.

I don't even know if Jules and Lilith are alive.

My failure to protect burned like acid in my veins. The night The Purge had descended on the university had been a mix of darkness, blood, adrenaline, and fear. Every second played like a movie in my memories over and over.

If only I'd...

I could have...

I should have done...

Self-recrimination got me nowhere. Only action mattered. And action was why we were walking through a festering market in the summer sun towards a threadbare tent propped near the open-air lavatories.

"Fuck flies," I muttered, hunching over further as the fucking things swarmed around the cesspit. "And fuck men and their shitty planning."

Ghost shot me a raised eyebrow.

"If women were running this town, sanitation would have been sorted. This kind of open trench shitshow is how people end up with flesh eating bacteria."

His eyes flashed with amusement. "I'll remember that."

I note that not even one fly has dared to land on him.

Seriously, the guy isn't human.

"How are you not getting swarmed?" I asked, waving my hand, batting away around a million insects with that one move.

"Eucalyptus spray."

He said it as if I should have known.

"That shit actually works?"

He nodded, his hand moving to his pocket. "Gun, three o'clock."

I clocked the old guy as he watched us moving towards his lone tent. He held his pistol lightly, letting it rest on his knee, but I wasn't fooled, the old guy had the look of someone who'd used it more times that he could count. And in the After? The elderly rarely survived is they weren't prepared to do whatever it took to keep themselves alive.

"You two don't look like you're here for a shit," the old guy commented as we got close.

"We're looking for information." Ghost pulled up, holding his hands where the old guy could see them.

"So's a lot of people around these parts," the old guy said, his weathered face pinched. "Don't rightly know if I've got any to share with the likes of you two."

Ghost pulled a bag from his jacket, tossing it on the ground in front of the man. "This might help."

The old guy, gun still trained on us, leaned over, pulling the bag to him and peeking inside. He whistled softly.

"Someone's been talking."

"Or it was a good guess," Ghost said with a shrug. "Will that get us something?"

The old guy dropped the bag of ammunition beside him, leaning back on his chair. Flies buzzed around us, their numbers so great, it sounded as if someone had turned on a white noise machine.

"Depends on what you're looking for."

I stepped forward. "The women The Purge keep as prizes. Do you know where they keep them between fights?"

The man eyed me.

"Who'd they take from you?"

"Sisters," I said, my voice low and rough.

"A little old for The Purge, wouldn't they be?"

He'd seen through my disguise.

I shrugged, waiting him out.

Finally, he nodded, the hold on his gun easing. "Don't know their final destination, seems to change each night."

A heavy weight settled on my shoulders.

"But," the old guy said, pointing out towards the south-west. "There's been strange things happening at the zoo. I were you, I might be inclined to head out that way."

Ghost nodded. "Appreciate the info, old timer."

The man nodded. "You fighting tonight?"

Ghost lifted his chin in affirmation.

"Mm, might get me over to the circus then." He stared pointedly at Ghost's bicep. "Win me a new tent, mayhap."

I hid a grin.

We turned, walking away from him, the stench of shit clinging to our clothing.

"Zoo?" I asked, my voice low as we re-entered the tent city.

"No, it's too late in the day. We're due at the circus by sundown. Let's get back to the brothel and prepare"

We made our way through the market, down the streets and back to the Painted Lips.

"Oh, hell no." Misty shook her head, her fingers pinching

76

her nose. "Off, off with those clothes! Strip right here. You're not bringing that stench into *my* house."

We stripped, Misty sending us to the bathhouse to shower before allowing us inside.

Wrapped in a luxurious fluffy robe, I lazed in front of the empty fireplace, waiting for Ghost. He—as expected—arrived fully dressed.

"You can relax a little," I told him, poking my tongue out. "I could get used to living here."

"Don't." He took the settee across from me. "You'd have to fuck men for board."

I made a face. "I could be a bodyguard."

"The only value women have in this place is what's between their legs. Don't get attached to Misty. She's ruthless and doing whatever she can to survive."

I sobered.

"What's the plan?"

He laid the map on the coffee table between us.

"We're here," he placed a coin on where the Painted Lips sat. "Circus is here." Another coin.

"Zoo is here." A final coin.

"Which means they have to pass through these three areas to get the women back." I said, tracing my fingers over each of the routes.

"Unless they've got vehicles and some excess fuel. In which case they could be driving them any way to ensure they lose tails before heading back to their base."

I nodded. "Do you think the rumours of fuel drops are true?"

Ghost shrugged. "Not in the mission brief."

I looked back down at the map. "If Jules and Lilith are there, we should have a signal, so you know we're a go."

77

A muscle in his cheek jumped. "Agreed."

I raised my hands to my neck, pressing them there in a way that made it look as if I were uncertain or fearful. "This work for you?"

He grunted, head dropping to stare at the map, hair sliding forward to brush at his forehead.

He really is the most attractive of men. It's so fucking inconvenient.

"If they're there, let me recon. If you can find a way to get to me after your second match, by then I'll have a plan worked out."

He remained still, his gaze trained on the map.

"Ghost?"

"I don't like it."

"What?"

He looked up, his eyes bright with... *rage?*

"I don't fucking like it. I don't like separating. Don't like you putting yourself out there. I don't fucking like them taking you from me."

I reached out, sliding my hand against his. "It's only for a few nights."

"I. Don't. Care."

Anger vibrated off him in waves. I could feel his frustration, his impotent rage.

And it turned me the fuck on.

I want to harness him. I want him to unleash that on me. I want to feel this emotion as he fucks me deep, and hard, and rough as fuck.

I pressed my thighs together, trying to ignore the aching throb between my legs.

"Ghost, I—"

78

A knock at the door interrupted me. Misty poked her head in.

"Darlings, it's nearly sundown."

"Thanks, Misty."

I looked back at Ghost, silently sighing when I saw he'd extinguished the rage.

Maybe next time.

"Shall we?" I asked, pushing up from the arm chair.

Ghost watched me, his nostrils flaring.

"Ghost?"

"Yeah. Let's go."

Chapter Sixteen

Ava

There was an undercurrent to Dubbo that had been missing the last two nights. A strange feeling of electric violence danced in the air.

It's circus night.

The words were whispered around us as a crush of people pushed and shoved their way through the tent city towards the giant yellow marque.

It's circus night.

New meat.

New blood.

New rules.

Something had changed, I could sense it in the air.

Ghost's hand cupped the back of my neck, his touch possessive, marking me as his as we got lost in the crowd of men all headed to the circus.

"There's danger here," I muttered, not liking the glances sent my way.

Ghost grunted, shifting closer.

At the circus, men blocked the entry.

Gold exchanged hands, the crowd purchasing tickets to enter.

"Which way?" I asked, as men began to press against me, using the crush as an excuse to touch my body.

My hand shot out, catching one of the men, bending back his fingers until they snapped.

He swore, dropping to one knee as the crowd around us moved back, shifting to create a circle of space.

I let go of his hand, leaning down to grab his jaw, jerking his chin up, forcing him to look at me.

"See him?" I asked, jerking a thumb at Ghost. "You don't touch what's his. You think a few dislocated fingers are bad? Try it again and I'll let him finish you off."

The man jerked his face away, spitting on the ground at my feet. "Fucking cunt."

Ghost's movement was whip-fast. His boot shot out, landing a severe, bone-crunching injury to the man's face.

The guy fell back, screaming as his nose busted, blood spraying around the circle.

"Did I look like I needed your help?"

"No."

"Then was that absolutely necessary?" I asked, lifting an eyebrow at Ghost.

"Yes."

I sighed, rolling my eyes. "Well next time, maybe—"

"What the fuck is going on here?"

The swinging dick from yesterday shoved his way through the gathered crowd, his goons on his heels.

"I should have fucking known." He shook his head. "Now we're gonna have to get you two cleaned up. Fuck. Follow me and don't fucking touch another person."

Ghost wrapped an arm around my shoulders, his statement clear.

Touch and you're dead.

They took us to a small outbuilding at the back of the former playing fields.

"Get cleaned up," the main guy ordered. "And put on the fucking clothing. You're not here to have dinner. You're here to sell sex."

He turned to the guards. "Watch them. When she's ready, take her to the cage."

"On it, Ringo."

Ringo?

The remaining guard turned to us. "Tonight's not a normal night. The circus is moving tomorrow. We got orders. So it's four bouts in one night. You win—" he tilted his head towards me. "—you get to take her home. You lose?" He grinned. "She's ours."

"What the fuck? You can't do that. You motherfuckers should have told us before we bought in."

The guy shrugged. "You should have asked."

Ghost laid a hand on my shoulder. "Come."

With a last glare, I allowed him to guide me into the toilet block.

Inside there were three shower stalls, two low, long wooden benches, four toilet cubicles, and flickering fluoro lights that cast a poor pallor on the shitty setting.

"Is this what I'm meant to wear?" I held up the tiny G-string, giving it a sniff. "Oh, fuck off. This is used."

Ghost disappeared into a stall; the clothing they'd left for him bundled under one arm.

"And what's this?" I picked up the highest, most complicated looking heel I'd ever seen in my life. "Who wears this kind of stuff? Hookers?"

My only answer was the sound of water falling in Ghost's stall.

"Should have left the blood on your face," I muttered, beginning to change into the tiny skirt and push up bralette they'd left me. "Would have served as a warning to the rest of them."

The water shut off, silence descending as we changed. I avoided the underwear.

Bite me, Ringo, you fucking arsehole.

"How the fuck do I do this?" I grumbled, struggling with the buckle. Finally, I managed to work it out, wrapping the strap around my leg a few times then sealing it with the small clip.

"Honestly, I'm gonna kill that bastard just for forcing me into this bullshit."

Ghost exited the shower stall, coming to stand behind me. I was still fucking with my other stupid ass shoe.

"Ready?" he asked, his voice low.

I looked up, about to make another sarcastic comment about these fucking heels when my gaze stuttered to halt on his crotch.

Dear fucking God.

He wore only three items of clothing—a fucking frat boy cap, grey sweat pants, and a sleeveless zip hoodie that he'd left open.

His insane eight pack with just the right amount of chest hair might have been fucking impressive, but it was the outline of his cock against the grey material that killed me.

Oh God. Oh, my fucking God.

"Ava?"

I sucked in a breath, struggling, and failing to lift my gaze from the glorious outline of his dick.

"Ava."

My name was no longer a question but a growl. As I watched, his already generous size lengthened, growing thicker, more rigid.

Thank the good Lord for sweat pants.

"Eyes," Ghost barked and I snapped, looking up.

He watched me, his face—as always—carved from stone. But his eyes, oh his glorious eyes. They were hot and filled with filthy promises.

"I need to focus," he told me, his tone guttural. "They changed it up. Means I gotta win this tonight. Now."

I licked my lips, then bent, quickly tying the straps of the remaining heel then straightened to a stand. The heels gave me a few extra inches that brought me closer to his height.

I reached out, sliding my hand down his chest, fingers running across his pecs and down his stomach, following the goody trail to the waistband of his sweats.

Don't shut down. I need something from you. Anything. Just in case.

Ghost stood like a rock under my hand—motionless, as if craved from marble. Only the heat of his skin let me know he was a living, breathing man.

Well, that and his impressive dick.

My hand dropped further, cupping his cock through his sweats, the heavy weight hard and hot in my hand.

He growled, the rumble involuntary and delightfully animal-istic. I ignored the flood of moisture that slicked my pussy at the sound.

Needing to win this battle of wills that was being waged silently between us, I placed my free hand on his shoulder, boosting myself up until my lips could brush his ear, my words only for him.

"Survive, and I might let you fuck my mouth."

I pulled back but his hands shot out halting my retreat. One hand fisted my hair, the other pressing my hand back onto his thick cock, his body grinding against my palm.

I shuddered, wet heat drenching my underwear and thighs.

Ghost held me steady as he leaned in, his lips less than a hair's breadth from mine.

"And if I triumph? If I fuck those little boys up and win this fight? If I return your women to you tonight? Will you give me your cunt, Ava? Will you let me taste your cream?"

My legs clenched, my nipples responding to the harsh need in his voice.

"You sure you'd prefer that over a blow job?" I asked lightly, trying to sound casual even as I pressed closer, desperate to feel the rasp of my nipples against his chest. "You've already tasted me."

His hand let go of mine, shifting to my hip, pulling me closer then coasting over my side then down, lifting the hem of my skirt. His big, calloused hand slipped under to find my underwear, one finger rubbing against the material.

"Soaked," he growled, his breath rough against my cheek. "You want this."

"Maybe."

Fuck, he's like a addiction I can't shake.

His finger pulled my panties to the side, slipping between my lips to rub through my wet. I sucked in a breath at the intrusion. Blunt, rough and oh so fucking welcome, he rubbed my clit, teasing and stroking, his gaze electric.

So much emotion.

I shifted, swaying those two tiny breaths towards him,

closing the distance between us, desperate and needing release.

It's been so long. Too fucking long.

It'd been more than twenty-four hours since he'd last touched me like this, and I needed it like a druggy looking for their next fix.

Make me come.

Abruptly, Ghost pulled back, dropping his hands from my body, banking the heat in his eyes. I watched as he returned to that dead place inside him.

Fuck!

"Game time."

I took a second, reorientating myself, the heat from his touch still branded onto my skin. As I watched, he lifted his fingers to his mouth, licking my taste from them.

"You dirty fucker," I whispered, pressing my thighs together, hating and loving the way my body ached for him. "You better fucking win."

Fuck, Ava. Don't let him see how much you want this.

I straightened, fixed my skirt then stepped passed him, moving to lead us out of the room as I threw my parting words over my shoulder.

"You better be fucking worth it."

Chapter Seventeen

Ghost

You better be fucking worth it.

Ava's words were on repeat as I walked around the holding yard, sizing up my competition.

We'd been separated, Ava taken away to what they referred to as 'the cage.' It seemed to be a holding area for the prizes.

Prizes? They're fucking human beings.

The urge to burn this motherfucker to the ground was growing.

Focus.

I returned to assessing my competition.

There were a handful of guys—eight to be exact—who'd be knocked out first or second round. They'd entered because they had no other choice—either their women were collateral, or they were looking for a win to bring in some food. Either way, they were malnourished, and desperate—it'd be that desperation that would make them unpredictable but easy to break.

I dismissed them, turning my attention to the rest of the assembled crew. Two men looked to be brothers; their faces impassive as they ran through a patterned exercise together. They'd be harder to take down, their bodies honed and strong.

But the one on the left translated his movements with small flinches, while the one of the right appeared to be favouring his ribs, protecting them with a consistency that had me questioning why he was entering the ring.

No contest.

The final four were harder to read. At least one was ex-military, evident in his movement, his walk, his stance. I broke into a slow jog, beginning to warm up my muscles, paying attention to these four, watching them as they sized me up.

"All brawn, no brains. He'll make it to round three where one of us will take him."

The smallest of the four made the boast, his lips easy to read across the yard.

Idiot.

I continued to jog, loosening tight muscles, breathing steady, keeping them in my eyeline.

"I don't know," the tallest said. "There's something about him that's giving me the heebie-jeebies."

"Just remember the plan. Finals or we're all dead."

Now that's interesting.

I filed away that piece of intel.

Now, where's the champion?

A man entered the yard, a small box in one hand.

"Gather round, boys," he yelled, hoisting the box into the air. "The games are about to begin."

We circled in, standing around him as he held the box out, giving it a rough shake.

"Luck of the draw for round one and two. After that it's based on pairings and numbers. There's only four rounds tonight, so make the most of it, boys. You have good numbers, you get put with someone decent. We're fair like that."

He shoved the box into the face of the first guy—one of the desperados. The kid plunged his hand in, pulling a small white ball with the number five printed in black from the box.

"Your number matches, that's who you fight. Good luck."

Around the circle it went, one after another until they all had their numbers.

"Lucky last, big fella." He held out the box and I reached in, pulling the final number free.

Five.

I found my competitor—the young kid with a sickly complexion. He swallowed, fear flashing across his bare face, grim resignation settling on his features.

Well, fuck. This kid isn't even old enough to grow a ratty mo. He's got no business being here.

"Boys, heads up. You've got five minutes. The women will be paraded then we'll get down to business."

Paraded?

A howl went up from inside the circus tent, loud screams, whistles, and hoots spilled from under the canvas, thundering down to where we stood.

"What the fuck?" one of the brothers muttered.

"They're rowdy tonight. Looks like we might have some fresh meat."

I felt the shift as I glanced towards the tent, unable to see Ava. Ice began to flow through my veins, my body and mind zeroing in on one thought.

You better be fucking worth it.

I'd be more than worth it. I'd be the motherfucking champion.

A siren sounded followed by a roar of approval.

"That's your cue, kids." The guy held out the empty box

89

giving it a shake. "Go and give us a great show."

I trailed the other fighters, dropping my number in as I passed.

"Hey," the guy stopped me with a hand on my bicep. "You might want to have a word to your woman."

I cocked an eyebrow.

"She clocked one of our guys. Drew blood."

Good.

"He touch her?"

"Only to check over the merchandise."

"I said no touching."

The guy shrugged. "We gotta touch to ensure they're not damaged goods. Just tell her to rein it in. She might be fierce now but you lose and they'll rip her apart piece by piece."

"Good thing I'm not planning to lose."

The ice crashed through my veins, my vision narrowing as we walked towards the tent.

"This way," yelled a bored guard, waving us towards a metal grated door. "Don't dally, gentlemen."

Into the ring.

I'd travelled to Rome on a mission once, more than a decade ago now. Playing it up as a tourist to avoid detection, I'd booked a tour of the Colosseum, walking where gladiators had once fought. There was nothing separating this moment from that bloody history.

We walked the perimeter of the ring, hundreds of unwashed bodies piled inside. Drink and food spilled down on us, the only thing separating the bloodthirsty crowd from the men around me was a thin current of electrified wire.

Ava.

My gaze searched the stands, finding the cage. Guards stood

around smoking and looking generally bored as the girls inside watched the procession.

Ava had her arms up, her hands touching her neck, her cuffs glinting in the dim light.

They're here.

Anticipation simmered in my veins.

We'll get them out.

Her gaze met mine, her hands dropping as her eyebrow cocked in a taunting jest. Her body relaxed, leaning against a post in the cage as she watched me.

You better be fucking worth it.

I gave her a chin lift, giving into the ice.

Oh, I am.

Chapter Eighteen

Ava

The women were in a mustering yard in various states of undress. They'd sprayed them down with a hose, tossing them ratty rags to dry off with.

"You have showers over there but you keep them here like cattle?" I asked the guard.

"They're part of the show." He nodded towards the far end of the field where a mob of men were watching the women. "New fighters don't just appear overnight. Gotta give them a little incentive."

Fucking disgusting.

As we drew closer to the small group of women, I searched their faces, desperate for any signs of Lilith and Jules.

Come on. Come on. Come—There!

The weight on my shoulders lifted, my chest lightening as I stared hungrily at my girls, checking them over for signs of distress or weakness.

Thinner, bruising around their arms and legs. Otherwise look okay.

I knew better than to assume their emotional state. They'd experienced months in captivity—they were bound to be all sorts of fucked up.

Jules glanced up, her expression blank as she tugged underwear up her short legs. She glanced away then snapped back to me, her eyes widening, expression startled as she froze, staring at me as if I were a ghost.

Don't give us away.

I lifted my hand, making a subtle *be cool* gesture.

She jerked her head up, twisting to Lilith beside her. With a gentle bump, she leaned over, her lips barely moving as she spoke to Lilith. Lilith's neck twisted, her face frozen as she stared at me, shock written across her gorgeous face.

Hello, my sisters.

They were as different as two people could get. Lilith towered over most of the population at six foot, two inches, her body long, lean, and gorgeously made. Between her flawless skin and mesmerising near-amber eyes—the woman had the kind of stunning beauty that would have landed her a supermodel position in the Before.

She'd come to Australia eight years ago to study electrical engineering, expecting to take her degree back to her home country of Nigeria. When the virus had hit, she'd considered returning home, only to be told there was nothing left for her there—every member of her family had been lost in the first wave.

Jules could not have been more different. Short with a frizz of red-orange hair and a riot of freckles, she liked to joke that her most defining figure was her arse and boobs. But her pale blue eyes, coupled with her sensual lips lent her a soft, vulnerable look. A hydrologist, we'd joked that she'd been a mermaid in another life.

The guard stopped, turning to me. "Alright, let's see you."

I raised an eyebrow. "Excuse me?"

"Need to check you over." He pointed at my crotch. "Lift up your skirt, let's see the goods."

Over my fucking dead body.

"No."

"Look, bitch. Play nice or you'll get some."

I smirked. "Try it, dick."

He reached for me, his movements easy to predict. I easily shifted out of reach, my fist destroying his nose, blood gushing free.

"Fuck! You fucking bitch!" He made to grab me, a voice halting him.

"Stop! She's fucking merchandise, you idiot!"

The guard glared at me then jerked his head at the group. "Go and fucking join the rest of the cunts."

So lovely to have met you as well.

I made my way slowly to the still dressing women, forcing myself to set the tone for Lilith and Jules. As desperate as I was to rush to them, to hold them in my arms and reassure them that we were getting out of here—I couldn't. I had to be the one in control.

"Hey, fresh meat," one of the women called, tying her halter top at the back of her neck. "Welcome to the shittiest club in the world. You wagered or stolen?"

I tilted my head to one side. "Wagered."

She winced. "Damn girl. Your guy is either a cocky motherfucker or desperate for some new pussy. Good luck."

I crossed my arms. "What makes you think he's not going to win?"

"None of them ever win," another woman said with a shrug. "Not without Ringo's permission."

Something cold and sinister slithered down my back.

"What?"

Lilith and Jules slowly made their way closer, joining the gathered group.

"The ringmaster, they call him Ringo. He rigs the final matches. The reigning champion pays him off."

I gritted my teeth. "And you know this how?"

They all pointed at a small woman crouched on the ground.

"That's June," one whispered, stepping close to me. "She's been wagered and won more than any of us."

Ghost's words came back to haunt me.

"There's gonna be more girls there. More women than just your two."

"And?"

"We can't save them all."

I looked up, finding Jules and Lilith, their expressions a mix of hope and grim resignation. I looked at the women gathered around me—defeat easy to read on their faces.

Fuck. I can't leave them here.

I closed my eyes, sucking in a breath.

Ghost is gonna to kill me.

I opened my eyes, narrowing in on Jules and Lilith.

"Ladies, help is on the way. But first, I need you to tell me *everything.*"

Chapter Nineteen

Ghost

The ringmaster, the one they called Ringo, entered the tent. Arms spread wide, he walked around the edge of the rough ring, a megaphone in hand.

"Are you ready to see blood?" he roared, the crowd answering with a thunder of sound.

"Are you ready to see death!"

My gaze locked on two men towards the back of the circus tent. The violence in the air had overwhelmed them. They were throwing punches, the men around them on the verge of joining in.

Just what we need, a fucking riot.

Guards separated them quickly, tossing them off the raised seating. I lost sight as they fell.

"Are you ready for motherfucking fight night!"

The sound shook the earth under my feet, the electric wire surrounding the ring buzzing with the sound of men being pushed against it—a singed smell beginning to tint the air.

Ringo gestured for the crowd to settle, stalking around the ring until the men quietened.

"Tonight, is a special event. The circus is leaving town tomorrow—which means we need to crown a victor." He pointed at one of the four men I'd eyed off earlier. "Will our Champion reign supreme?"

He pointed to the tunnel from which we'd emerged earlier, a giant of a man stepping from the shadows, arms raised in triumph as the crowd roared its approval.

"Or," Ringo said, turning to the rest of us, a sardonic smile on his face. "Will a new victor emerge?"

Beer and garbage hit the wire, splashing the fighters inside.

"Well, this is one way to die," a young guy muttered beside me.

"Tonight, you're getting twice the blood, twice the fights, and twice the death! Unlike fight nights of the past, each battle is viewer's choice." Ringo pointed at a camera positioned above the ring. "Will our overlords be lenient?"

A big screen in the corner of the big top lit with a green square.

"Or will they show no mercy?"

The screen switched to red, the crowd screaming their approval.

"Without further ado...." The fucker ducked out of the ring, a gate slamming closed behind him. "Let the battle, commence!"

I paid no heed to my desperate competitor, I'd dealt with gnats more pesky than him. I easily parried and blocked the kid's wild swings, my focus on the actual threats—the four men I'd identified earlier, the two brothers, and the champion. Each fought with a ruthlessness and deliberation that indicated solid training. I marked them, turning my competitor this way and that as I studied their battles, picking their tells.

Shortie flinches before blocking.

Red beard favours an upper cut.

Camo likes to choke his competitors.

Tattoo enjoys round kicks.

The brothers are well matched but their weaknesses are clear.

The champion relies on brute strength.

Done with my observations, I looked at my competitor. The kid was flagging, hard core.

Something compelled me to engage with him. "What's your name?"

The kid threw a wild punch. "Your worst nightmare!"

I sighed, annoyed by the kid and even more annoyed by the fact I knew Ava would want me to try.

See? This is what I fucking get for allowing a woman in.

I took an opening, sweeping the kid off his feet and following him down into the dirt. He hit with an oof, the breath knocked out of him.

I pressed my forearm to his throat, applying gentle pressure.

"Breathe," I ordered. "Slowly."

The kid did as directed sucking in huge lungfuls of air.

"Are you trying to win a woman or food?"

"Sister," he coughed, his throat bobbing under my arm. "The one in the far corner."

I looked up, clocking her in the centre of a circle in which Ava appeared to be mustering the women.

Fuck. I fucking knew it. She's not gonna leave them behind.

Did you really expect she would? This mission was fucked before it even began.

"Is this your first time in the ring?"

"Third."

Fuck.

"What do they do when you lose?"

"Nothing. You get let go. They want you to re-enter. If they let you live, that is."

98

This kid had the potential to blow our plans to hell.

Didn't the change of schedule already do that?

"Tap," I told him, assessing my options.

He slapped the ground, his hand sending puffs of dust into the air. I watched the screen, waiting for the rich fucks to decide my next move.

The screen remained green.

I sighed, pulling back from the kid and holding out a hand to help him stand. "Go to the Painted Lips, tell 'em Ava sent you. They'll feed you and find a place for you to sleep."

The kid shoved me away. "No! I'm here for my sister."

I grabbed him by the throat, pulling him in, watching the fear of God appear in his eyes.

"Do as I say." I nodded towards the women. "I'll get your sister and deliver her to you."

The boy's gaze turned suspicious. "What do you want in exchange? She isn't gonna fuck you."

I let him go, turning away. "Not interested in fucking her."

"Well, I won't do it!"

I chuckled, dusting my sweats off. "Not interested in fucking you either."

The kid seemed confused as around us the crowd roared and the final battles were waged, some to the death as the screen turned red.

"Then what do you want?"

"Nothing you or your sister can give me."

I lifted my gaze, finding Ava watching me, a small smile playing on her lips.

Fuck she's gorgeous.

You owe me, I mouthed, glaring.

She opened her lips, attempting to pass me a message. I only caught snippets.

Deal... attention... you... water.

Something sinister hatched in my stomach, a deadly ice slipping under my skin.

The final two fighters finished, leaving one dead in the dirt. A group of men ran in, carrying the dead out and guiding the surviving losers from the ring. For Ava's sake, I hoped the kid did as I directed.

The guard from earlier entered the ring, the same box in his hand.

"Numbers, gentlemen. Take your number!"

I took it, barely glancing at the ball.

"Three! Oh, you're with the Champion."

I glanced at the guy, checking him out.

Brute force. Reliance on overpowering. Threat level: four out of ten.

I'd have him down in five moves.

Water was passed around, Ringo calling fight stats and results as we reset into our new pairs.

Across the ring I met the gaze of the champion—he grinned, revealing missing teeth and a violent smile.

"When I win, I'm gonna fuck your woman up her arse," the champion called, his tongue flicking out in an obscene gesture.

The ice called to me, inviting me to sink back into the void.

Just try it, motherfucker. I'm gonna gut you three ways to Sunday.

Ringo left the ring, every fighter tensing as we waited for his call.

"Fighters ready... go!"

Chapter Twenty

Ava

I watched Ghost open his arms up, wincing as he accepted a blow from the champion.

"Ouch," Jules winced, leaning into me. "He's really letting the guy beat on him."

Ghost embraced the punches like a lover, absorbing them as he led the champion around the ring.

"How you going back there, Lil?" I asked, shifting my body slightly to make sure she was fully blocked.

"Not—ouch—great. These wires are—fuck—corroded. They haven't used any kind of appropriate colour-coding. I'm not sure this is gonna work."

"Keep trying."

We were using our bodies to shield Lilith from view. In the field I'd outlined Ghost's plan to win the battle and get us home. But meeting these other women had thrown that plan into chaos. And the admission that Ringo rigged the finals had me worried.

Don't drink the water.

I didn't know if Ghost had understood my message, so I was doing the only thing I knew—coming up with a Plan B.

Lilith swore again, the slight smell of burning plastic wafting over my shoulder.

Jules sucked in a breath as Ghost took another punch, not even bothering to defend himself.

"Will the champion win?" one of the other women asked. "Your guy isn't looking too crash hot against him."

I grinned, anticipation pooling in my belly. "You'd think that, but just wait."

Sure enough, on the next overly cocky punch, Ghost used the momentum of the champion against him, twisting the guy and flipping him over. He sailed through the air to hit the side of the ring, electricity pulsing through him, frying his back.

The crowd roared its approval at the brutality of Ghost's actions, the platform seating shaking under the weight of their movement.

Come on, Lilith. Hurry up!

The champion scrambled to his feet as Ghost glided towards him, looking for all the world as if he were on a Sunday stroll.

Finish him!

The champion came in hard and fast, throwing punches at Ghost's head. True to his namesake, the man moved as if by magic, disappearing from under the fist before it could land. In return, he began to rain hellfire down upon the champion, breaking bones, dislocating limbs, crushing ligaments. Blood flowed from the champion's face, turning the dust of the ring floor into a bloody, muddy mess.

A chant struck up in the crowd.

"Finish him, finish him, finish him!"

Behind me I heard Lilith suck in a breath.

"Lil."

"Ava, I—I think I got it."

The women around us tensed, the hope they'd fought against

for so long finding new roots.

"Slowly we're going to swap positions. No one is going to react, no one is going to move. Got it?"

They all stayed still, pretending to watch the fight.

"Good girls."

I slipped back, dropping down beside Lilith.

"Talk to me quickly."

She pointed at the electrified gate. "The lock's disengaged. Anyone could open it now."

"Who normally does?"

"Only the ringmaster and his personal guards."

I glanced around, quickly assessing our risk factors.

Crowd, guards, fighters. The crowd is our biggest threat—if they think they have a chance to get a woman....

"How do they get you out?"

"They keep us in here and back the truck up. We climb in the back." She nodded at the open backed SUV a little distance away.

"And no one steals it?"

"They remove the battery."

Fuck.

"You know where they store it?"

She nodded, pointing across the ring to the fighter's entrance. "Ringo keeps it near him."

Fuck.

"What happens once you're in the back?"

"They drive us around for a while and then we stop, they blindfold us, and take us to the holding pen for the day."

"The zoo?"

She nodded. "They think they're smart but who can disguise the sound of a lion?"

103

"Thanks, Lil, go take my place."

She rose gracefully, stepping in beside Jules, their backs to me.

Shit. Okay, think Ava.

The guards were lax, most focussed on the violence on the floor. Which meant if I could track down a battery, we might be able to bail.

That's a big if.

With a quick glance around, I slipped off my heels, flicking my knife out of one of the cuffs to strip a piece of the leather strap from each shoe.

Maybe they'll come in useful after all.

I moved to the gate, casting a glance back at the ring where Ghost held the guy in a choke hold, the champion's face slowly turning a mottled purple.

The screen was red.

Shit. Just keep going, babe.

As the crowd roared, I pushed on the gate, letting out a silent prayer of thanks when it slid a tiny way open.

"Wait!" A young girl shoved through the assembled women, reaching for the gap. "Let me through!"

Fuck!

I slammed the door shut, snatching her before she could blow this for us.

"Let me go!" She struggled against me, fighting and clawing.

"Fuck! Settle down!"

"No! We could escape! We could—!"

"Oi!" One of the guards whacked a thick wooden batten on the cage fence. "Knock it off!"

We sat down, the girl tearful as we waited for the guard to turn back around, his attention drawn back to Ghost fucking up the champion.

"Fiona, what the fuck were you thinking?" one of the women hissed at the teenager. "You could blow this for all of us."

The girl shuddered, curling into herself. "I can't stay here. My brother needs me. I can't do this anymore. I just wanna go home."

One of the older women walked across the cage, bending down to slap the teen across her face.

I growled, springing to my feet and throwing myself between the two.

"What the fuck are you doing? She's a child."

"This *child* is gonna get us all killed," the woman hissed back, turning to flash a reassuring smile at the guard who'd twisted to glare at us again. "You're our hope of getting out of here. We can't afford for one little idiot to fuck this up for us."

I blew out a breath as the crowd roared its approval.

"Ladies, we're nearly two fights down. We only have a finite amount of time before someone figures out that the wires aren't live and the door's open." I thumbed my cuffs. "What's it gonna be Fiona?"

The girl curled in on herself, Jules wrapping arms around her.

"Go, Ava. We got this."

I nodded, gesturing for the other ladies to circle up.

"Here's the plan. I'm gonna go and try to get the SUV working. Once it's good, I'll push it back a few metres into position. If that works, and we go undetected then we'll start loading you one at a time."

I looked at the nervous faces of the women around me. "The next match will be when we do that. The attention will be on the death fights—not us. That means staying strong until then.

You guys okay with that?"

They all nodded.

"Good."

I glanced back at the ring, finding Ghost standing over the dead champion, his gaze locked on me.

I prayed like hell he could lip read as I delivered the same message.

Delay the fights. Attention on you. Don't drink the water.

This time, his chin lifted in acknowledgement.

Please God let this work.

Chapter Twenty-One

Ghost

There are two rounds left.

I surveyed the winners from round two, working out where I'd find allies. Shortie and the two brothers had made it through.

Shortie had death in his eye and vengeance in his stance. Despite the green screen, the fucker had killed his opponent.

No support there.

The brothers stood together, talking quietly.

What's the bet they pair them off against one another?

I made my approach, ignoring the catcalls and abuse being hauled by the crowd as they sought refreshments and exchanged bets between the rounds.

"Yo," I called, approaching. "Good fights."

The brothers watched me, twin expressions of wariness on their faces.

"Thanks," one said, sizing me up. "Pity we're all about to kill each other."

A perfect opening.

"About that, what are you fighting for? Women or gold?"

The wary expressions turned guarded.

My gut said to wait them out but Ava's voice had become an

annoying prompt in my head.

Give them a show of faith.

Fuck, I'm pussy whipped.

"I'm after two—friends of my woman." I nodded towards the cage. "She's in there right now, attempting to work out how to bust them free."

Both men stiffened.

"What the fuck?"

I leaned in. "Look, we all know what's about to go down. Even if you two make it through this match alive, one of you is gonna have to kill the other. It's too good a viewing for these sick fucks not to want it."

They both glanced over at the screen which had flicked to red.

"So, here's the deal. We need to delay this round, give my woman enough time to get all the women out. When it's clear, we end the fight and get out of here as fast as we fucking can—making as much of a distraction as possible to help them escape."

They looked sceptical.

"How the fuck as we supposed to do that?"

I jerked my head at Shortie who was sipping water near the exit.

"We kill him and pretend to kill one of you."

"And we just let you?" The talkative brother scoffed. "No thanks. Wasn't born yesterday."

I sucked in a breath. "Look, I'm only here for my woman. As soon as she gives the signal, I'm out. Don't care if you believe me or not. Just giving you the option." I looked between them. "I lost a brother back in the Before. I'm not above taking a life for the sake of my own, but this?" I pointed at the camera.

"This is fucked. They're gonna pit you two against each other eventually. Taking the life of someone you love? That's the kind of shit that stains your soul."

The brothers watched me; their expressions closed.

"If you're with me then delay your fight—make it look good but draw it out. After I kill Shortie, watch for my signal. You'll know it when you see it."

I turned on my heel, giving them my back.

"You'll let us have our woman?"

Woman? Just the one?

I glanced back. "If she wants you, then yeah. If she doesn't, then I'm not forcing her."

They exchanged a look. "You'll take her somewhere safe?"

I nodded.

Though what is safety in the After?

"We'll watch for your signal."

I looked to the cage, wanting to share this with Ava. The women were mustered in one corner, their bodies clustered tightly together.

No sign of Ava.

My gut clenched, ice beginning to freeze the blood in my veins.

You better be worth it.

Ava's tease settled on my shoulders, reminding me of the reward waiting at the other end of this mission.

Delay the fight. Kill Shortie. Kill Ringo. Get the women to safety. Find a bed, fuck Ava.

I welcomed the icy-fire freezing out all thoughts and feelings, embraced it like a lover until it narrowed my focus down to my first step.

Kill Shortie.

Ringo entered the ring, the megaphone in hand.

"Are we ready!"

The crowd roared their approval.

"Let's rumble!"

I can't wait to kill this fucker.

Ringo pointed at the big screen.

"Let's see what the stats say—who will be fighting this round?"

The screen flickered for a moment, then posted up the draw. As predicted, the brothers were pitted against one another.

I saw Shortie flinch, his shoulders straightening as he turned slowly, sizing me up. I met his gaze, watching as his hands turned into fists, his expression taking on a violent rage as he began to thump them against his chest, attempting to stare me down.

"You might be big," he taunted. "But I'm gonna fuck you up!"

Bring it, motherfucker.

Out of the corner of my eye I saw Ringo move to the edge of the ring.

"On my mark—one, two, three, fight!"

The crowd leapt to their collective feet, cursing and hollering as they caught a blood frenzy. My world narrowed in on the threat across from me, ignoring all motion, all distractions, all bullshit that would get me killed. All that matter was the man across from me and getting back to Ava.

You better be worth it.

Oh, baby. You better fucking believe I am.

110

Chapter Twenty-Two

Ava

Through Lilith's legs I saw the short fighter run at Ghost, throwing himself at my man.

Fuck. Him. Up.

I turned, focusing on my role in this escape. As much as I wanted to watch Ghost, I needed to trust he had his shit together.

He's trusted you. Now you need to trust him.

A howl came from the crowd, the platform rocking beneath my feet.

"Go!" Jules hissed, holding Fiona tight. "Hurry, Ava!"

I slowly inched the gate open, my body tense, hyper-aware of the vulnerable position I'd placed not only myself, but also the women behind me.

Shut it down, Ava. Channel your inner Ghost.

I sucked in a breath, letting it out slowly, finding a well of calm.

Under the cover of the dim lights and screaming crowd, I slipped through the entry, shutting it tight behind me and disappearing under the elevated platform. Flat on my belly, the wood only a whisper from my back, I crawled through filth consisting of God only knew what towards the far side of the tent.

I need a disguise

As if blessed by God himself, someone tripped off the side of the platform seating above me, falling with a crash to the ground.

"Fuck, Kev! You okay?"

I froze, body flat to the ground, praying the shadows hid me from the drunk.

"Yeah," Kev slurred, struggling like a turtle to roll over. "Jush fine. Keep your eyesh on the brute. I wanna make my moneysh back."

"Get your arse back up here then!"

Kev waved him off, rolling onto all fours as the crowd let out another roar.

I darted forward, leaping onto his back. My hands circled his neck, the leather pulling tight, cutting off his air supply as I bore down smashing his head into the ground, silently apologising to Kev as he flopped into an unconscious pile of drunken limbs. Just as quick, I yanked his arm, pulling him back into the dark underside of the pavilion seating, stripping him of hoodie, jeans and boots.

The skills you learn in the After.

Disguise in place, I crept out of the darkness, leaving Kev to sleep off his concussion.

The hoodie hid my shape, allowing me to pass through the crowd undetected.

Battery. I need a fucking battery.

The fight had drawn out, Ghost and the shorter fighter appearing well matched while the brothers traded blow for blow, the crowd screaming for more blood.

Battery. Battery. Battery.

112

I made my way around the outside of the tent, finding the entrance to the ring, a place where the losing fighters stood watching the death matches. A pile of the dead fighters dumped to one side.

A thin metal mesh separated me from the fighters—the battery sitting nearby.

Fuck!

Even if I dug under the wire, there was no way in fuck I'd be able to reach it.

If this were a movie, I'm sure the audience would expect me to look around in despair asking, 'what do we do now?' But I was made of sterner stuff.

I'm a woman. We fucking deal.

"Hey," I leaned against the metal, my hoodie pulled low. "Yo, kid!"

The kid Ghost had fought in the first round glanced my way, immediately turning back to the fight.

Ugh. Men.

"Yo," I reached down, scooping a small rock from the ground to throw at him. "Kid!"

"What?"

I cocked a finger at him, gesturing for him to come closer.

He sighed, obliging me. As soon as he was within arm's reach, I grabbed his shirt, jerking him into the metal.

"What the fu—"

"Shut the fuck up!" I barked, keeping him in place. "The guy in the ring said something to you, what was it?"

The kid stared at me, his eyes wide. "You're a woman."

"Jesus, keep it the fuck down. We've only got a few minutes. What did he say?"

The kid shook off his shock. "If I wanted to see my sister

113

again, I should go to the Painted Lips."

God love that man.

I relaxed my grip on his shirt. "He's right. But I need you to get me that battery." I nodded at the pack. "Get me that and then get the fuck out of here. Go to the Painted Lips. We'll be there in a few hours. Be ready to leave."

The kid swallowed. "Promise you'll get my sister out? Her name's Fiona. She's just a—"

"If I can, I will," I promised, no time to hear his pleas.

The kid hesitated, the sound of skin hitting skin cut through the crowd's noise.

"Alright."

I dropped, using the shadows to begin digging a hole large enough to slip the battery through.

Keep going, Ghost. Please, God just keep going.

The kid took the long way, pausing here and there to watch the fight. I couldn't fault him, I'd do the same thing—but fuck if it didn't shred my nerves.

Breathe, Ava. You've been in tougher situations than this.

Sure, there'd been bullets flying, people dying, and a shit ton of adrenaline pumping through my veins but somehow those moments paled in comparison to this one.

That's because you've never had anyone worth living for.

I shoved the thought away, needing to concentrate on the now. Dirt clung to my hands, the cuffs thick and heavy on my wrists as I waited for the kid to retrieve the battery.

Come on, come on, come on!

With a slow motion he bent, heaving the pack up and moving slowly back to where I crouched.

"Hurry," I whispered as he crouched, struggling to fit it through the hole. "Shit."

114

"Oi! What are you doing?"

The kid froze as I slowly twisted, looking over my shoulder.

"You don't have permission to be back here. Get up!"

I moved slowly, holding my hands up, my thumbs resting on the blade triggers.

Not yet. Get closer, Ava. One more step. Quick, silent, deadly. No room for mistakes.

"Come here—"

I struck, slashing at his throat, dropping him easily. He gurgled, his hands clutching at the wound, blood splattered, painting my face with hot droplets. I scooped up his gun, tucking it into my jeans as I twisted, hurrying back to the fence, heaving the battery into my arms.

"Remember, Painted Lips," I ordered. "Go!"

The kid nodded, his eyes wide circles of white as he stared at the body I'd dropped.

Fuck.

I didn't have time to say more, I could sense the crowd beginning to grow restless as the fight continued.

Hurry, kid! I don't have time to babysit your arse.

I turned and legged it back, moving as fast as I dared. The truck remained abandoned, the guards drawn into the fight. With fumbling fingers, I resecured the battery, connecting it up.

Please God, work.

I rounded the bonnet, sliding into the passenger seat and released the parking break. With strength born from desperation I pushed at the bonnet, shoving and heaving until the SUV began to rock, using its weight as momentum to roll it back towards the cage.

This is it. Fuck. Fuck. Fuck!

115

I jumped back in, pulling the hand break as I got it as close to the cage as I dared without drawing attention.

Okay. Slow. Breathe, Ava.

I reached down, pulling the under dash free and—with months of practice under my belt—I jimmied the wires, leaving one free for Lilith to connect once we were ready to get the fuck out of dodge.

Let's go!

I made my way back to the gate, pausing until the crowd roared their approval at something in the ring. I slipped back in, lying flat on the ground, protected from sight by the huddle of women.

"Okay," I said, my voice low. "One at a time we're gonna start moving out. I'll go last just in case. Lilith"—I pulled the gun from my jeans—"you're driving. You remember how to use one of these, right?"

She nodded, taking the gun.

"Good, you get settled. We'll give you ten seconds then send one out at a time. Get in the back, stay low, brace. It's gonna be a really fucking bumpy ride."

The women nodded as I peered out at the fight.

Ghost looked like an avenging angel, covered in blood and dirt, his face pure violence—I'd never wanted to fuck him as much as I did at that moment.

Pound him into the fucking ground, Ghost!

"Go!" I hissed, moving to allow Lilith to slip through.

One. Two. Three. Four.

I counted down then nodded at Fiona, allowing her to scramble through and into the back of the truck.

One. Two.

The crowd began to strike up a chant.

"Finish him! Finish him!"

Fuck!

"Alright, you two—" I pointed at the women. "—hurry!"

They slipped through the gate, darting across the dark area, and scrambling into the truck bed.

Four down eight to go.

Ghost began to chase the short guy around the ring, landing punch after brutal punch. He laid into him, cracking bones, and sending arcs of blood flying. The brothers had even stopped their fight, pausing to watch the brutal beauty of Ghost.

That's it, babe. Keep them distracted.

"Two more," I whispered, gesturing. "Go!"

As Ghost rode the guy down to the ground, laying punch after punch on him, the last of the women scrambled down, leaving only Jules and I in the cage.

"Ready?" I asked, watching the women scramble into the truck.

"Fuck yes."

I shoved the gate open, pushing her through as our plan went to shit.

I watched it happen as if in slow motion, Jules running in front of me, the truck bed so close and yet so *fucking* far.

An overly excited spectator chose that moment to slip, losing his grip on his beer bottle. It toppled, dropping to the ground near one of the guards. He turned, looking up at the excited spectator who was staring at the cage. The spectator lifted his hand, drunkenly pointing, his expression stunned. The guard turned, spotting Jules and I as we flew across the ground towards the vehicle.

We're not gonna make it.

117

"Go!" I screamed, shoving Jules forward. "Lilith! Go!"

The truck rumbled to life as I pivoted, the guard lifting his pistol to train on me.

This is gonna hurt.

Chapter Twenty-Three

Ava

The bullet bit my shoulder, tearing flesh from bone.

"Fuck!"

I ran at the guard, distantly aware of the crowd around us, their attention shifting from the fight, to the truck that had rumbled to life behind me.

Kill him. Get to the truck. Get to safety.

The guard fired another bullet, tearing a hole in my bicep. Pain flared, white-hot as he tore my body apart.

You're gonna die, motherfucker!

I hit him with force, taking him to the ground, my cuff blades ripping into his flesh. He struggled, fighting me as I hit an artery, my cuts perfectly positioned for maximum efficiency.

"It's the women! They're escaping!"

My head shot up, finding the spectator staring at the truck as it began to pull away, Jules hanging out the back, screaming my name.

Fuck!

I shoved to my feet, scooped the guard's gun from the ground, and sprinted towards the truck as it slowly gathered speed.

Faster, Ava! Faster!

I heard the thud of bodies as they dropped from the pavilion seating to the ground, the outraged cries of drunk men searching for violence.

Shit, shit, shit, fuck!

The truck bumped along, exiting the canvas tent, Lilith at the wheel as Jules crouched on the truck bed, her arms outstretched to me, two women anchoring her.

"Ava! Run!"

Jules' scream would haunt my nightmares. The horror and fear in it, her gaze full of terror as she tried desperately to reach me, our fingers brushing but not quite meeting.

Fuck!

"Ava!"

I felt something brush the back of my hoodie, the footsteps close—far too close.

If they get me down, I'm not getting back up.

Adrenaline punched through my veins, giving me strength.

I leaped, scrambling at the truck bed, clasping at Jules' arms, kicking at the hands that grasped my legs, attempting to prevent my escape.

Motherfucker!

Jules and the women heaved, pulling me and the man grasping my legs up and into the bed.

He fisted my hoodie, his mouth gasping for air, his hands brutal as he tried to wrestle me from the truck.

I pulled back my fists, pounding the cuff knife into him, over and over, seeing only red as blood splattered and flesh flew, the man's struggle slowing.

"Ava." Jules placed a hand on my shoulder. "Ava, leave him. Ava. Ava, he's dead."

Her words penetrated the haze of rage that had descended. I stopped, dimly aware of aching of my knuckles and the burning pain in my arm from the bullet wounds.

"Fuck." I blew out a breath, kicking his body from the back of the truck as I lifted my gaze to watch the crowd flooding from the now burning circus tent. "We gotta get out of Dubbo. It's gonna be a massacre tonight."

Jules nodded. "But where do we go?"

"The zoo," one of the girls whispered. "They have more fuel there. We can fuel the truck, travel."

I closed my eyes, sucking in a deep breath.

Ghost, you better be fucking alive.

I blinked open, doing what my training had taught me—looking at how we could stay alive for another five minutes.

"Let's hit the zoo. Then we're out."

The women nodded. Jules began to rip fabric from her excuse of a shirt, using the strips to begin binding my bullet wounds.

"Guards at the zoo?" I asked, gritting my teeth against the pain.

They shook their heads.

"Everyone's at fight night," one of the women said.

I nodded. "Right. Animals?"

"There are some loose ones, mostly the herbivores. They keep the dangerous ones caged."

I made a mental note to let them out. It'd add to the chaos.

"Jules, at the zoo we're gonna need to split."

"Split?"

I nodded, looking around. "I gotta get to the Painted Lips. Let them know what's going down."

Find Ghost.

"You can't. Ava—" She clasped my hand. "—we have to stick together."

121

The women all nodded, their expressions determined.

Fuck. Fuck. Fuck!

"Fine." I rapidly recalculated the plan. "We got a stop to make. Everyone get ready—it's gonna be a tight fucking fit."

Chapter Twenty-Four

Ghost

Ava.

Her name had become a mantra as I beat Shortie around the ring. Over and over, we traded blows turning bruises into blood.

Ava. Ava. Ava.

I turned Shortie, catching sight of the cage over his shoulder.

Four women left.

Ava was pressed to the floor, her back to me.

Three more minutes.

I leaped, wrapping legs around Shortie's hips, using the leverage to ride him to the ground, unleashing my full fury on him.

The bastard never stood a chance.

He put up a fight, his arms coming up to protect his face, desperate to hold me off, his body bucking as he tried to unseat me.

It's not personal.

"Finish him! Finish him!" I ignored the chanting crowd, concentrating on drawing this out, giving Ava all the time she needed.

I got your back.

A gunshot had my head lifting, whipping towards the sound. Another followed, a ripple of awareness passing through the drunk crowd.

The cage is empty.

Under my hands, Shortie breathed his last, his body collapsing into the dirt.

A cry went up, echoing urgently through the space.

"The women! They're escaping!"

Ava!

I surged to my feet, finding the brothers at the ready.

"I assume the plan is shot?" one yelled as the crowd began to riot, giving into the blood, violence and alcohol.

"On me. Stay close. Fight like fuck. You get lost, meet me at the Painted Lips."

"The what?"

"Just fucking stay close!"

I ran at the gate to the ring, slamming into it with force. The thing sizzled, electricity licking my skin. For all it was a flimsy design, the thing held.

Not for long.

Ringo twisted, still shouting orders as he looked our way.

"Stay in the goddamned ring!" he ordered. "You're not done yet!"

"Open it."

Ringo crossed his arms, attempting bravado in the face of the chaos around us. "Or what?"

"Or I rip your eyes from your fucking head before I kill you."

He laughed, gesturing at the gate. "Good luck. Looks like I have the power here."

I reached out, wrapping my fingers in the metal wire, my skin sizzling as I hauled back, the gate collapsing in on itself.

The electricity abruptly cut off, the wires that had been running from a small generator to the fence ripped apart.

How's that for being done, motherfucker?

I tossed it to the side, advancing on the rapidly retreating Ringo.

"Now boys, let's be reasonable. I can get you—"

I punched his stomach, relishing the pain in my knuckles as he doubled over.

"Stop, I—"

I struck him in the face, following as he tripped backwards, catching the back of his neck with one hand. With a practiced ease I gouged his eye socket, ripping his eyeballs from his head.

That's for looking at my woman.

I crushed his windpipe, regretting I didn't have more time to fuck him up.

That's for calling her a gash.

Around me, the brothers fought off guards and drunken rioters.

I reached for his neck, giving it a quick twist, watching as the life drained from his eyes.

And that's for me.

"Let's go," I barked, dropping the body into the dirt.

"Where?" one yelled, falling in behind, the other quickly following.

To Ava.

Chapter Twenty-Five

Ava

I slapped a hand on the cab of the truck.

"Here! Stop here."

Lilith slowed the vehicle, rumbling it to a halt. I handed my stolen pistol to Jules.

"Shoot first."

She nodded, checking the safety.

"Keep it running!" I yelled to Lilith as I leaped from the tray and dashed to the door of the Painted Lips. It opened easily, and I stepped into—

Nothing.

I blinked, staring at the now stripped parlour.

Where before the room had been filled with excesses of furniture, soft pillows, and decadent plush fabrics, now the place was only wood walls, hard tiles, and empty, echoing space.

What the actual fuck?

A small chest sat in the middle of the floor, a note pad and pen resting on it.

I snatched the pad, finding a letter written in feminine cursive.

My dearest Ava,

It was a pleasure to give you and your Ghost sanctuary for the short period we knew each other but as you can see, it is time for the Painted Lips to move on. We women can never be too cautious about our safety, and your warning of the risk of the bastards has been well heeded.

We're heading south, away from the bastards and towards those who may find some salvation in our loving arms during these trying times. I hope our paths may cross again one day.

Be kind to yourself, and look after your biker man. He needs you far more than you need him.

Until we meet again,

Misty

I crumbled the note, feeling relief and frustration in equal measures.

"Yo," a familiar voice called from the stairs. "This yours?"

Sean stepped from the dark, one hand fisting the scruff of the kid from the circus.

Thank Christ the kid is fast.

"Yes." I lifted the chest, turning on my heel. "Let's go."

"Go?" Sean echoed as I legged it back to the truck. "Go where?"

"Somewhere safe! Hurry!"

They followed me, scrambling into the tray as I tossed the chest into the back. Jules focussed on something behind me. I twisted, sensing the threat a moment before Jules drilled an effective if dirty shot into the guy's chest.

The club he'd lifted dropped to the ground, rolling away as he collapsed to his knees, a bellow of pain and rage ripping free from his chest—loud enough to draw unwanted attention.

Fuck!

"Go!" I shouted to Lilith, rounding the truck to slide into the

127

passenger seat as the sounds of the approaching crowd, and the movement of people in the shadows began to spill across the street. "Go, go, go!"

Tyres squealed, the truck letting out a tired groan as Lilith took off, navigating the debris-packed roads.

"We're not going to be able to circle back to the zoo," she said, her voice tight. "And this truck will only get us so far."

I clung to the oh-shit handle, grimacing as we began to ram through street carts, wares flying this way and that, the truck swaying as we crunched over obstacles.

"Agreed. Time for Plan C."

She arched an eyebrow in question.

"Drive like hell and hope no one can catch us."

I directed her towards the entrance to the Dubbo wall, unsure if the doors would be open at night.

This might get messy.

As my thought ended, my body did something weird, it lifted from the seat, the truck under me also lifting. I floated, suspended in some kind of strange nothing moment then the world snapped back into place, the truck and my body slamming back into the ground as the wave from the explosion passed us, fucking everything in its path.

Ghost!

"Fuck!"

I couldn't hear, the blast had taken out my hearing. Lilith glanced over, her eyes white circles of shock as she fought to keep the truck from hurtling across the road.

The tray!

I twisted, staring out the back window, counting heads and assessing for injuries.

We're okay.

128

The women were sprawled out at various angles, their expressions a mix of dazed shock. The kid and Sean were just as bad. Sean looked up, blood slicking across his face, lit by the glow of the gigantic fireball in the distance.

Ghost, what did you do?

The truck slowed under me, calling my attention back to our escape.

The explosion had toppled already flimsy buildings and unsettled some of the wall. One side of the two giant gates had fallen, people racing into the streets to stare at the giant fireball in our rear vision mirror.

Our hearing still shot, I made a judgement call. I tapped Lilith on the shoulder pointing at the gate.

Go! I mouthed. *Go!*

She nodded, tightening her grip on the steering wheel, her foot pressing to the floor. The truck bounced violently off the rubble, the right tyres spinning for a moment on air as we hit something, tilting the truck.

Dear God let this work!

Lilith held it steady as we shot across the road, men scattering to avoid the oncoming vehicle. She shot through the narrow gate, losing one side mirror in the process.

I twisted, double-checking our passengers who were clinging to the sides of the tray. Jules—gun gripped in one hand, the other white knuckling the side of the tray—shot me a grin. I returned it, twisting around as Lilith drove through the city, navigating the dead streets.

A ringing in my ears indicated the slow return of my hearing.

Behind us, flames licked the sky, smoke billowing high into the dark night as ash began to gently pepper the windscreen.

As my hearing returned, Lilith glanced over.

"Where to?" she asked, her voice overly loud in the dark cabin.

To Ghost.

I pointed into the dark night. "Somewhere safe."

"Safe?"

Her question hit me as hilarious. What was safety in the After?

"As safe as I can make us for now."

She nodded, accepting my answer. "Then lead on, fearless leader." She shot me a side-eye. "And start working out your story, 'cause Jules and I wanna know all about the hunk in the ring. Seems like a lot has changed since we've been gone."

More than you'll ever know.

Chapter Twenty-Six

Ghost

I'd led us to the zoo.

While my first reaction had been to get to the Painted Lips, the rapidly escalating riot and the lack of solid weapons was gonna work against me and the brothers.

We needed a distraction—and I needed to give Ava a signal to get the fuck out of town.

"Look for fuel," I ordered, as the brothers and I began to search the yard. "Anything we can blow up."

A growl halted my movement. In the dark of the night, two eyes glinted at me through mesh wire, the lion elegant but emaciated.

They didn't let them go?

He watched me, his expression hungry weariness, as if he knew I wasn't there to save him.

I closed my eyes, knowing exactly what Ava would do and resigning myself to my fate.

You better be worth it.

Those words were carved onto my soul, forcing me to be a better man. Even if she hadn't intended it—Ava had changed me.

And the fuck if it doesn't feel like hell.

131

"Open the cages."

"What?"

I sucked in a breath. "Open the cages. I'll deal with the fuel. These sorry animals don't deserve to be blown to kingdom fucking come. Let them out."

The brothers exchanged a look.

"Do it!" I roared, slamming a fist on an empty oil drum. "Or I'll fucking leave you here to rot."

They moved, scattering to unlock cages as I searched for fuel.

Come on you motherfuckers. I know you have a stash somewhere around here.

"Bingo," I muttered, sliding open a storage room door. The smell of gasoline hung in the air, the drums of oil stacked in neat piles, ready for use.

There's a treasure trove here. A fucking fortune. This shit could last the entire club—all three chapters—months. Fucking years if we conserved it.

I grinned.

This is gonna be a magnificent explosion.

In a corner of the mechanic's store room I found empty bottles, pliers, and exactly what I was hoping to find—a gas welder.

I rigged it up, waiting for the brothers to finish opening the cages.

"Ready?"

They nodded, keeping an eye on the lion as he sat watching us.

"Good," I switched on the welder.

"What's it gonna do?" one asked as I made sure it was tied in place.

"The flame will heat the small cannister of fuel," I said, testing the welder and nodding when it was secure. "Once that catches, the flame will race from this one to that—" I pointed at a turned over drum and the fuel line I'd created to connect the two.

"Then boom?"

I nodded, satisfied with my knot. "Then boom. Let's get the fuck outta here."

We bolted, running through the zoo, heading for a cluster of buildings in the distance.

One, two, three....

I counted it down. Knowing we needed to get out of the initial blast radius. The animals that had been caged near the storage facility were milling about—as if unsure if they were really free.

Run!

As if on cue, a horn sounded in the distance, startling the animals and sending them scattering.

The lion watched us for a moment, then took off at a run, heading for the open plains.

I kept running.

Thirty-three, thirty-four, thirty-five....

We dropped behind an outbuilding, pressing ourselves against the cool brick.

"Is it working?" one of the brothers asked.

Fifty-five, fifty-six, fifty-seven....

"What if it doesn't—"

The explosion hit before he could finish.

The blast force thumped into our bodies, hitting our chests. Windows above us blew out, showering us with glass as we fell backward, gasping for air. Heat raced across the grass, the punch of air from the explosion enough to singe the hair on my forearms—even through the brick.

Fuck, yeah!

I pushed to a stand, relishing the orange fireball as it ballooned into the sky, the glow the product of the now destroyed cache.

A hand landed on my shoulder—one of the brothers. He gestured at me, his lips moving but no words coming out. Blood flowed from his ears and nose, his face pale.

We need to go.

I nodded, acknowledging his concern. I gestured for them to follow me, keen to tick off the last item on my list.

Find a bed, fuck Ava.

I damn sure hoped no one had claimed the shitty mattress at the farm house.

Chapter Twenty-Seven

Ava

I woke with a start as a weight covered me, pegging my hands to the worn mattress. In the dark of the shed I couldn't make out anything beyond a large body, and a crop of dark hair.

What the fuck—?

I bucked, my leg coming up to knee whoever it was in the crotch.

"Stop."

Ghost's voice froze my movements. I blinked in the pitch dark of the shed, trying to make out his face. My body relaxed under his, relief making me snarky.

"Am I hallucinating? 'Cause I could have sworn I left you back in Dubbo, biker boy."

His teeth flashed white in the dark, his grin quick.

"Could have sworn I told you not to rescue the other women."

I tried for a casual shrug, barely shifting his body weight. "Shit happens."

His hands tightened around my wrists. "You could have died."

"But I didn't."

"You could have been captured."

"But I wasn't."

"You put other people in danger, Ava."

"They already were, more so if they'd stayed in the cage."

Ghost fell silent, his dark eyes inky black pools in the dim light. "You got shot."

I winced, hoping he hadn't noticed. "Yeah, well, that wasn't in the plan. Don't happen to have any more of those painkillers on you?"

He rocked up, reaching for his bag and digging through. A moment later he produced a small bottle and tipped a handful of pills into his palm. He sorted through them replacing most then handed me three small pills and a bottle of water.

"What are these?" I asked, shifting to sit up.

"Painkillers and antibiotics."

I popped them in my mouth, washing them down. "Thanks."

He reached for my arm and began to gently unwrap the makeshift bandage, checking over my wounds.

"Not bad."

"Thanks, Jules cleaned them up. Flesh wounds, thank God. They won't heal pretty but they'll suffice."

The two bullets had managed to hit me on my left arm—one to the curve of my shoulder, the other ripping flesh from my bicep. Adrenaline had kept me ticking along until about halfway to the farm house when the pain had sent me into shock.

Fucking body.

Ghost gently examined the torn flesh. "I can sew this."

I closed my eyes, knowing this was gonna hurt despite the painkillers. "If you have to."

He pulled a field kit from his bag, unwrapping fresh needles and thread, turning on a small camp lamp to better see.

"Ouch." I winced, reaching out a hand to touch his bruising

face. "I'd offer to kiss it better but I'm not sure it's worth the pain."

"It'd be worth it."

The words hung between us, shimmering in the air for a long moment.

Ghost broke eye contact, turning his head to reveal a bloody scab on the side of his cheek. "Give me your arm."

Battered, bloody and bruised, the man should not be this attractive.

With surprisingly gentle hands, he sewed the worst wound—the bicep tear.

"Was the explosion you?" I asked, as I watched his face in the light.

"Destroyed their fuel cache."

"Good."

He turned my arm slightly, giving himself better access to the wound.

"Misty left," I said, trying to fill the silence.

"I saw."

I searched for something to say, needing to hear his voice.

"You got our bags?"

"Mm."

"Why?"

He pulled the thread tight, my skin pinching. "Weapons. Clothes. Food. Figured your friends might need some of that shit."

I nodded.

"I found some allies in the ring. Brothers. They were fighting for a woman. They took her back tonight. They're already gone."

I sucked in a breath, trying to ignore the awful sensation of thread pulling through flesh. "Who?"

"The little scared one."

June.

"Did she go willingly?"

He nodded, his concentration trained on my arm. A drop of water landed on my skin.

"You showered."

"Don't make a habit of sleeping in another man's blood."

I chuckled, wincing as he dabbed at the wound which had begun bleeding.

"Sorry."

"Don't be." I gestured at the wound with my free hand. "Just make sure the scar looks good. Maybe add a little flourish—your signature perhaps?"

His hands stilled.

"What?"

"Nothing."

His face had shut down, something dark and ominous floated in the depth of his eyes.

I tilted my head to the side. "That's not a nothing expression."

He finished sewing me closed then checked the shoulder wound, choosing to only cover it in anti-bacterial gel before wrapping me in new bandages.

"Ghost?"

He packed away his things, methodically putting them in his bag.

"Ghost? Talk to me. Why are you shutting down? Did I say something wrong?"

He turned back to me.

"Lay down, you need rest."

I rolled my eyes. "Dude, I need answers. Rest is for the weak."

CHAPTER TWENTY-SEVEN

"Which you are."

"I take offence at that. I could still beat your arse."

"Ava, lay down."

"No."

"Ava—"

"For fucks sake! Just tell me what your problem is!"

"You!"

The word exploded from him, landing like a bomb between us.

"Me?"

"Yes, fucking you!" He plunged a hand into his hair. "You're fucking infuriating, woman."

"What?"

"You don't do what you're told. You're loud. You're fucking obnoxious. You don't fucking listen. And yet you want me to write my signature on you? To mark you? Fuck, Ava!"

I went to cross my arms dropping them when my wounds protested.

"And? Why do you even care?" I asked, frustrated by this damned man.

"I don't fucking know!"

The despair on his face gave me pause.

"Ghost... what are you saying?"

For a moment he seemed lost.

"I'm saying you're a fucking mess."

I chuckled. "Aren't we all?"

His lips twitched then his expression sobered. "You make me want things I have no business wanting, Ava."

I reached out a hand, touching his chest, my voice low as I asked, "Like what?"

"Like this."

He captured my hair in his big fist, forcing my head back, his lips crushing mine as he kissed me. No—scratch that. Kiss was too tame a word for what Ghost gave me.

The man kissed as if he wanted to possess me.

Oh.

Dear.

God.

Chapter Twenty-Eight

Ghost

She looks like sin and tastes like salvation.

I feasted on Ava's mouth, sliding my tongue along her lips, memorising the way she opened to me, her body softening against mine.

I want to possess her.

Her hand came up, pressing against my chest, pushing me back.

Fuck.

I lifted my head, banking my desire.

Ava blinked up at me, her eyes glazed with passion.

"You staying?"

Fuck yes.

"You want me to?" My hand slid up her long leg, resting on the inside of her thigh.

"We both know where this is going, Ghost. Don't fuck with me."

I grinned. "Here?"

She patted the musty mattress that she'd covered with a thin sheet and her sleeping bag. "Why not? It's better than some of the places I've slept."

I leaned in, crowding her, forcing her back until she lowered herself down onto the mattress.

"Why is it," she whispered, her tongue flicking out to taste my mouth. "I feel like I'm about to sell my soul to the devil?"

I slipped my hand under her shirt to cup her breast, teasing her nipple.

"Oh, fuck it," she groaned, her rough laugh brushing my mouth. "Where's the dotted line?"

Don't tempt a man searching for redemption.

You think you ever had a choice?

I caught her lips, tasting the lingering laughter on them, allowing it to spill into me and chase away the blackhole that had corroded my soul. With slow deliberation, I dragged my lips across her cheek and down the side of her neck, tasting her sensitive skin, relishing the goosebumps that prickled as I added teeth—nipping then sucking the sting away.

"You promised me something, Ava. Gonna deliver on it?"

Her head dropped back, her body arching as she sighed, opening herself to me. "Fine. Take what you want."

Want? No, baby. I'm gonna take what I need.

I pulled back, rocking up to my knees, surveying all the skin my mouth would touch.

She wore a thin shirt and underwear. The jeans she'd picked up somewhere along the way lay in a crumbled mess on the floor, her blood staining the fabric.

I rose to my feet, deliberately undressing for her, our gazes locked as I removed shirt, boots, socks, then pants—leaving me in only weapons.

"Wait," Ava said, as I reached to unstrap the knife at my ankle. "Leave it on."

Fucking perfect woman.

The rest of the women had bunked down at the house, piled

on top of each other as Sean and the kid patrolled the area, ensuring it remained safe.

I'd known Ava wouldn't be there. She didn't like being crowded, and wasn't one to display vulnerability in front of others. I'd showered, then searched the place, finding her asleep in the shed, those shitty bandages—stark even in the dim light—were a fucking knife to my gut.

I burned seeing them now, even knowing the wounds weren't severe, I fought against the urge to go back and raze the whole fucking town to the ground.

"Don't just look," Ava invited. "Touch."

I dropped back to my knees, my cock as hard as steel, my mouth watering for another taste of her spice.

With unworthy hands, I reached for the scrap of material that hid her sweet pussy from my gaze.

Mine.

I drew her underwear slowly down her body, relishing the reveal.

Ava wasn't sugar. She wasn't peaches or cream. She was spice and fire. Untamed lightning.

I pulled the underwear from her body, satisfaction weaving its way through me at the feel of the damp material in my palm.

"You want this, Ava?" I fisted my cock with her underwear, giving it a long, slow, pull.

For a second, she stared at my dick, her mouth parting to allow her little tongue to peek out and run over her lips.

Fuck.

Her gaze lifted, her eyes sparkling as she grinned at me.

"I believe you promised me something first."

She spread her legs wide, running a hand down her body to cup her mound, her fingers dancing in the curls that lay there.

143

"Mm," she sighed, tipping her head back. "So wet."

Her admission broke me.

I dropped, my mouth moving up her legs, alternatively kissing and tonguing her skin, fingers grazing, dragging, and brushing as I teased my way up to her curls. I hovered for a moment, sucking in a deep breath, nostrils flaring, dick jumping as I memorised the scent of her desire.

This won't last forever.

I knew eventually she'd turn away. If we ever made it back to my brothers, I knew she'd reject me. Ava wasn't the old lady type—and I'd never ask her to be. She wouldn't wear a patch that bore my name—it'd be like those fucking collars, an attempt to shackle a woman that embodied freedom. If she'd been born with a dick the brothers would have patched her in without a second thought. I'd never ask her to change. Couldn't. The she-devil under my hands made me feel something I'd never felt before.

Hope.

I'd do anything to keep her in my life. Even if it meant burning the fucking world down to protect her.

Even if it meant never having another taste.

My tongue and fingers slid through the wet heat of her desire. I found her rhythm, memorised the tenses and twitches, the moans and gasps that formed all the parts of this woman.

My woman.

If the devil granted me one wish, I'd have asked for this moment. For the feel of Ava's desire on my face, for the way she pressed against my mouth, greedy for her release. For the taste of her on my tongue, and the slick clutch of her flesh around my fingers.

I fucked her gently, pulling from her pleasure, building then

144

easing, building higher then easing again.

Don't let this end.

But it would. At some point Ava would leave and this heaven on earth would slam shut, returning me to the void—banishing me back into the shadows.

After experiencing the light, I didn't know if I'd survive the dark.

Mine.

I upped my game, pulling from her curses and praise in equal measure.

"Ghost!" She panted, her fingers now fisting my hair. "Fucking hurry!"

My fingers pressed up curling into her while my mouth feasted on her clit. Ava gasped out a ragged breath, a flood of desire coating my fingers, lips and tongue.

Mine.

My answering groan rumbled against her clit, driving her wild. Ava rode my face, mindless in her need as her body tensed then found its release in a glorious, gusty, wet fusion of unashamed passion.

I tasted her climax on my tongue, felt her flesh milk my fingers, watched her slump back to the mattress—her expression a mix of stunned disbelief and overwhelming pleasure.

"Holy shit," she panted. "That was...wow."

I needed to break the tension I felt inside—barely harnessed desire burned under my skin.

I want to fuck her until she begs me to stop.

Her fingers tightened in my hair, pulling my face back to her pussy.

"Wait, I'm not done with you yet."

I chuckled, desire building between us, my cock aching as I

returned to my newest pleasure. My fingers slipped into her as my lips pressed against the tip of her throbbing clit.

No mercy.

I went for hard and fast, forcing her to keep pace with me—never giving Ava a moment's reprieve. Her long limbs flushed, her chestnut hair slipped across the sleeping bag as she arched under my mouth, her body desperate for the relief only I could give.

Welcome to the club.

Ava broke under me, her body undulating as she came, her breath escaping in a lusty sigh.

"Ghost?"

I ignored her, continuing to tongue her flesh, greedy for more of her taste.

"Ghost."

I hooked arms under her legs, positioning her how I wanted.

"Ghost!"

I surged up, her knees sliding over my shoulders as I moved up her body, positioning myself so I could tease her clit with my cock.

"What?"

Her eyes drifted closed as I rubbed circles against her with the crown of my dick.

"Nothing. Please, continue."

A scratchy chuckle escaped me.

"You sure?" I asked, leaning down to capture one of her nipples in my mouth.

"Uh-huh," she murmured, her body curling to accommodate my movement.

I pulled back a little, moving to taste her other breast. "Absolutely sure?"

CHAPTER TWENTY-EIGHT

"Just fuck me already," she groaned.

I thrust into her, both of us cursing at my intrusion.

"Fuck, Ava…." My mouth hit her collarbone, nipping before I soothed the sting away with a kiss.

Ava shifted restlessly, her legs still wrapped around my shoulders.

"Move!"

I pulled back a little, feeding her just the tip. "Like this?"

Ava glared at me for a moment then sighed.

"Ugh. I can't believe I need to do everything myself."

Chapter Twenty-Nine

Ava

Fuck it.

I pressed against my elbows, using my legs to force him to the side, rolling us until he lay on the mattress, me straddling his chest.

I slipped back, settling on his thighs, hand fisting his spectacular cock.

Perfectly formed, deliciously veiny, he was built thick and long and heavy.

Just how I like it.

"If you're not prepared to get the job done," I said, my voice a low purr. "I guess I'll have to."

Ghost's eyes drifted to half-mast, a satisfied expression settling on his decadent lips. "Well, if you insist."

I adjusted my position, guiding his cock to me. For a moment I paused, my gaze locked with his.

Oh.

I was so used to his void, to the utter blank in his eyes that I couldn't handle this naked, desperate longing. He looked at me as if I were his last meal, his one desire, his—

Hope.

I broke our stare, unable and unwilling to deal with the

feelings between us.

It's just sex.

I thrust down, an involuntary whimper escaping me as I filled myself with him, stretched by his length and thickness. My hips shifted as I began to ride his cock.

And what a cock it is.

"Ava."

I blinked my eyes open, unsure of when they'd drifted shut. He met my gaze, his expression fierce as he stared at me, his hands sliding up my sides to settle on my hips.

"Yeah, Ava. That's it," he encouraged, hands guiding my ride. I ran fingers over his chest, one hand steadying me, the other pinching his nipple.

"Faster, babe. Harder. Fuck my cock." His voice was guttural; deep and dark—need threading through every word.

"Ghost," I gasped his name.

"No," he corrected, his hands flexing on my hips. "Grey."

Grey?

Before I could ask, Ghost surged up, holding my hips as he thrust into me, his lips finding my breast, his cock hitting me deep. I held his head to my chest moaning as I rocked into him, my climax hitting me like a freight train as I milked his thick, beautiful cock.

"Ava!"

Ghost fucked me—unrelenting in his brutality.

More.

A second orgasm hit me, stealing my breath.

"Fuck!" He roared his release, his cock thrusting into me one final time before he pulled me down onto him, both of us collapsing in a pile of sweaty limbs.

I rested my head on his chest, sucking in air as I tried to

process what had just occurred.

Only the best sex of my life.

He didn't offer me sweet kisses or murmured compliments. I didn't offer him praise or professions of love.

Silence hung like a cloud around us.

I peeked up at him, my mind turning back to the naked longing in his expression.

What do we do now?

Chapter Thirty

Ava

Ghost turned off the lamp, bathing the shed in darkness. For long moments he lay silent under me, his hand gently drawing words and pictures on my back, the tiny movements pleasurable but not sexual.

What do we do now? There's no future here. I'm just an itch for him to scratch—right?

"What did you mean, Grey?" I asked, breaking this strange tension between us.

His fingers paused on my skin, his body tensing under mine.

"You don't have to answer," I whispered, twisting to look up at him in the dark. "You don't owe me anything."

I couldn't make out his expression in the shadows.

"I've taken thousands of lives over the years—each for some bullshit reason." His voice sounded distant, pensive. As if he were telling a story involving someone else.

Goosebumps raised on my skin, the back of my neck prickling.

"But only three deaths haunt me."

My breath caught.

Am I ready for this?

"I was young. Too fucking young to be over in a godforsaken

country acting like a solider. But they'd trained me for it—and needed the kind of intel only young impressionable kids could get. My first assignment saw me infiltrate a terrorist cell operating out of Yemen. They'd been recruiting youngsters from the West, and my handlers had decided I was ready for the challenge."

"How old were you?"

He paused. "Thirteen, maybe? They never told us our age. By that stage I'd been in the program maybe five years. We were just kids trained to kill."

My gut clenched, bile burning the back of my throat.

"I was too fucking young and inexperienced to deal with the shit I saw. But I did it. I had to. I let a young girl—no more than eight or nine—be murdered in front of me. The bastards killed her because she wanted to go to school." He shook his head. "She wanted to read a fucking fairy tale book. Her dad had lost his sight in a bombing. All she wanted was to read to her siblings. I mean—fuck."

I pressed myself into his side, offering comfort that felt inadequate.

"The second was a woman in Moscow. I'd worked her for months. Played her like a fucking song. She fell in love with me. Thought I'd sweep her off her feet and take her away to beautiful places."

I braced, knowing how this was about to end.

"She died in front of me, shot in the fucking head for the information she'd inadvertently fed me."

"Ghost—"

He ignored me.

"Final is Blue." He stopped, sucking in a breath, his arm flinching on my back.

Oh, Ghost.

"Blue's the reason Hazard and I got out and joined the club. We're the reason the brothers never use first names—when you're patched in you relinquish who you were. Though I guess it doesn't matter what we go by much anymore."

I waited, my heart aching as he struggled against the memories.

"Before we were Ghost and Hazard, we were Red and Grey—callsigns given to us by trainers when they'd brought us in to the corps. We were new test subjects—a stream of kids no one wanted adopted by the government and pushed into a program designed to create super spies."

It sounded like something out of a thriller movie—something I would have watched and rolled my eyes at the entire time in the Before. But here, in the dark, listening to his pain as he described this life—it didn't sound like a movie. It sounded like a tragedy.

"They based it off the Russian program, a way to combat the intense training of our unspoken enemies overseas. There were four kids in our training group—Green, Blue, Red, and me—Grey. Green died first day out on his very first mission. Stupid fuck tripped on a fucking rifle strap and blew his brains out."

I winced.

"But Blue? He was good. They'd recruited him for his looks. Trained him up to be a honeypot—fucking men and women into giving him whatever information the government wanted." He huffed out a laugh. "Charming motherfucker—put Hazard to shame."

"Dude, having met Hazard," I said drolly, "I wouldn't call him charming."

Ghost grinned, his teeth flashing in the dim light. "Pretty sure he says the same about you."

I shoved him. "Get on with it."

The smile faded, his voice taking on an emotionless edge.

He's returning to the void.

"We were deployed on a mission that went… badly. We had one option—get to an extraction point a hundred click's away. We had to go on foot."

I sucked in a breath. "Damn."

"We made it out of the city but got caught in the foothills. Blue got injured taking a bullet meant for me. We managed to get out but he was in bad shape and we weren't much better. Hazard and I fucking carried and dragged him up the side of the mountain. Took us half a day to get to the extraction point, fighting every fucking moment for our lives. Got there with thirty minutes to spare."

His hand flinched on my back, his fingers digging into my skin as if he were looking for something to cling to.

Hold on to me. I got you.

"They cancelled the extraction. Said we were too compromised to pull out. Said it'd be too much of a risk."

"They left you?"

"They wrote our death sentence and sealed it with a fucking kiss."

Rage burned in my gut. "Fuck."

"Blue, he read the room. Knew we couldn't escape—not with all three of us. He was slowing us down. He did what we couldn't—he killed himself."

Breath caught in my lungs, my body flinching.

"Red and I, we found our way back to Australia. We killed everyone associated with the program—took four fucking years. Then we disappeared, becoming Hazard and Ghost, members of an outlaw motorcycle club."

Ghost fell silent.

"I'm sorry," I whispered. "Blue sounds like he was an amazing person."

"Yeah."

I placed a hand over his heart, resting it there.

He cupped my cheek. "You once asked why I follow you. It's because while those deaths haunt me—but yours, Ava? It'd destroy me."

"Grey, I—"

"Shh." He tucked me into him, holding me close. "Sleep."

"But—"

"Tomorrow is coming, Ava. Sleep."

I fell silent, focussing on the rise and fall of his chest. After a long time, he is breathing evened out as he finally drifted off.

What do I do now?

The night had no answers.

Chapter Thirty-One

Ava

We left in the early morning while mist still kissed the ground.

Piled into the truck, Ghost took the driver's seat, his void back in place as we began the long drive to Farmer's compound.

It was still before noon when the fuel light turned on, the gage hovering just above empty.

"Even with the siphoned fuel we won't make it, will we?" I asked softly, eyeing the dash.

Ghost shook his head. "We'll push as far as we can."

But then we'll have to walk.

"Shelter?" I asked, knowing that even if we managed to milk another twenty kilometres out of the truck, we wouldn't be anywhere close to making it to Farmer's by nightfall.

"We'll find something."

The women don't have any decent shoes.

I pulled the map from the glove compartment, attempting to do some rough calculations on our journey.

It's gotta be at least a three-day walk—and that's best-case scenario. Fuck.

I sighed, slumping in my seat and looking out the window,

watching the trees and fields as we drove by.

Well, this is gonna be shit.

Ghost reached over, laying a hand on my upper thigh.

"I'll relieve your tension later," he said, giving my thigh a squeeze.

That delicious little fizzle of awareness arched between us.

"Later?" I asked, leaning back on the bench seat.

He slid those big, blunt fingers up my leg, pressing them against the crotch of my jeans. "Later," he promised.

He withdrew his hand, correcting the truck as it bumped along the bitumen.

Well damn. Now I want sex.

I glanced out the rear window, checking on our passengers.

The women were in various states of dress, clothing cobbled together from finds in the farm house, and clothing Ghost and I had brought with us. They were hungry, tired, and traumatised.

Or at least some of them were. Jules—always a ray of sunshine and built like Teflon—shot me a thumbs up and a bright smile.

Love that girl.

"Gonna be a longer trek to Cunnamulla."

I turned back to Ghost. "Do you think they left us fuel?"

Ghost lifted one arm in a half shrug. "Either way, not sure we'll make it the full journey if we're carrying a load of women with us."

I worried my lip, considering our options.

"I think we should leave them at the farm," I finally said, my voice low even though there was no risk of the women in the back overhearing. "Jules and Lilith can come—need to come. They're part of our family. But the rest?" I glanced back over my shoulder. "They need a safe place to recover. Do you think Farmer will take them?"

"Likely. And he's the only one I'd trust around these parts."

The truck made a grinding sound under us, jerking on the road.

Please keep going.

"How long?" I asked.

Ghost's face tightened. "Not long enough."

True to his words within five minutes the engine sputtered and died, the truck immediately slowing as it lost all momentum.

Fuck, fuck, fuck!

Ghost steered her to the side of the road, keeping it going for as long as it continued to coast before finally rolling to a stop on the shoulder.

Silence descended.

"So," I sighed. "I guess that's it."

Ghost leaned forward, checking the sun. "Let's go. It's early but we gotta find some shelter before nightfall."

"Right."

"Are we walking?" Jules asked as I got out of the cab.

"Yep." I held out a hand, helping her jump off the back of the truck. "Let's wrap your feet, at least we can try and protect them from the rocks."

We found a few old towels in the back of the truck, ripping them up to bind the women's feet.

"This is about as good as it's going to get," Lilith said, rocking from heel to toe. "Let's just get started."

I searched for Ghost, finding him redistributing our packs into smaller bags.

"What are you doing?"

158

He lifted his head, nodding at Sean and the kid—whose name still hadn't been revealed.

"Apart from your women, they're the only two who can handle weapons. We're gonna need the others to carry this shit while the rest of us scout."

I absorbed his words. "You're worried about bastards."

"Bastards, militia, The Purge, and God knows what else."

My stomach clenched.

"What are our chances?"

He shrugged. "Fuck knows."

I huffed out a laugh. "You're less helpful than Audrey, at least she gives me a figure when I ask."

He tilted his head towards the small chest tucked in the back of the vehicle. "You gonna open that?"

I flushed, glancing away. "Anything of value I've already packed in my bag."

Ghost cocked an eyebrow. "Sure?"

"Yeah."

He rocked back on his heels. "You mind if I look inside?"

I swallowed. "Go ahead."

He reached for the chest, pulling it towards him as Sean began to muster the women.

With bated breath, I watched Ghost twist the latch, pulling it open. For a second he stared at the contents. He turned slightly, looking over his shoulder to give me a raised eyebrow.

Don't ask me, Misty's the one who gave it to me.

Ghost turned back, one hand shifting through the assorted sex toys, flimsy lingerie, and other adult paraphernalia to pull something free. He tucked it into his jacket, then scooped up the various clothing items before crawling out of the truck.

"They're not worth taking, surely," I said, my voice low.

He tucked the lace and silk into his bag, zipping it up. "Clothing is clothing, Ava."

I knew that. I did. It's just crotchless underwear hadn't struck me as particularly useful.

He handed me one of the bags. "Ready?"

I nodded.

"Choose someone to carry that. I'll take point. You take rear. Sean and the kid can take muster. Keep your women in with the rest of them." He glanced up at the sky. "Let's move."

With the sun beating down on us, we began our walk to safety.

Chapter Thirty-Two

Ghost

I fucking hated people, and this group was no different. They whinged and whined, bitching about the sun, the flies, the heat. They complained about their feet and their empty bellies, ignoring the fact Ava was not only helping them along but doing so with two bullet wounds.

I attempted to corral my temper, searching for the familiar void.

"How about," Jules asked, her voice strained. "Instead of complaining, we sing?"

God fucking help me.

The other women made various comments but Jules ignored them and behind me came a low rumble of a smoky voice. Not exactly on pitch but not exactly off it either, the girl began to sing "Numb" by Linkin Park.

I glanced back, my eyebrows rising as she hit the chorus, her voice taking on a rumble.

Well, that's unexpected.

As we walked, Jules continued to sing, making it part-way through Linkin Park's back list before pausing for a drink.

"Do you ever wonder what happened to the famous people of the world?" Lilith asked as Jules gulped from the water bottle.

"What do you mean?" one of the women asked.

"Do you think they lived? That they're like us now, fighting their way through the After?"

It started a conversation about which celebrity they thought would be best suited to survive.

Jesus Christ, save me from this shit.

Movement up ahead caught my attention.

I held up a hand, the group stumbling to a halt behind me, all conversation abruptly cut off.

I scanned the horizon, searching for whatever had caught my attention.

There.

I squinted, watching the shape as it shifted and moved.

Not a kangaroo. Not a cow. Can't be a horse.

It rose above the field, sniffing the air.

Fuck!

We were down wind of the bastard, but we'd have to keep moving to get past it.

Fuck.

I turned slowly, finding Ava watching me. She raised her rifle in a silent question.

Good girl.

I nodded, gesturing for her to come stand beside me.

She did, moving slowly, shooting the women reassuring smiles as she made her way to my side.

"Can you get it?" I asked, my voice low.

She settled the weapon on her uninjured shoulder, using the scope to track the bastard.

"Not yet," she murmured, the gun adjusting slightly. "Needs to be closer."

162

"See any others?"

"No. Doesn't mean they're not there, though."

And there's the fucking down side.

I considered our options.

"Take the shot."

"You sure?"

"What choice do we have?"

She made a sound of agreement in the back of her throat, the gun remaining trained on the bastard.

As it slowly stumbled closer her finger settled on the rifle.

One.

Two.

The gun went off, the crack loud in the quiet day. The bastard fell, body toppling into the field.

"Great shot."

She switched the safety back on, lowering the weapon. "Thanks, I—"

A growl sounded from somewhere nearby, a chorus starting up.

Oh, fuck no.

"Ava, what is—" one of the women began, immediately hushed by the others.

Too late.

A burst of movement came from a field to our left, the grass that had grown higher than our heads had hidden the horde from view.

"Run!"

163

Chapter Thirty-Three

Ava

The women took off, heading down the road, attempting to get in front of the moving horde—Jules and Lilith guiding them.

Sean, the kid, Ghost and I stood together, checking ammunition, watching as the seething beasts stirred up the grasses.

"Kid?" Ghost said, his voice low, gaze trained on the oncoming mass.

The young guy lifted his head, his expression one of terror. "Y-y-yeah?"

"Go with the women. Find a house or some high trees, get them up into it. These things can't climb. Get them higher than scratching distance."

"But—"

"Go!" Ghost snapped, raising his gun and taking out the first bastard to emerge from the field.

The kid turned on his heel, bolting after the straggling women.

"This isn't gonna be pretty," Sean said, his voice cheery. "But if we're lucky, maybe we won't end up as bastard food."

I resisted the urge to roll my eyes, pulling the trigger to take out a younger bastard—nothing more than a kid really,

164

her scraggly blonde hair falling off her in patches, her body covered in a ripped and bloody dress.

Rest in peace, darling.

As they pulled free of the grass, we took them out, picking them off like they were the machine ducks you shot at the fair.

Only here, the prize is life.

I frowned, hesitating on shooting one as it lurched free of the grass, another hot on his heels. They moved strangely, their walk jerky and less coordinated than the ones I'd met further south.

The heat affects them.

I raised my rifle, watching as Ghost and Sean took them out.

"What are you doing?" Sean asked, reloading his weapon.

"They're lethargic. I think…. I think they're dying."

"Of course, they're dying." He waved his gun around, then trained it on another bastard. "A bullet to the head does that."

"No." I placed a hand on his arm, stilling his shot. "Look."

Ghost paused, also observing as the middle of the horde emerged from the field. Decaying skin and rotting wounds, bodies emaciated and weakened by the disease.

"They look dehydrated." I gestured at the drought-stricken landscape. "The only nearby sources of water would be tanks—the creek is another few kilometres away—and they're no longer capable of working out how to get access."

Ghost watched them begin to stagger towards us, his expression grim.

"We need to save the ammunition."

I sighed, knowing where this was heading. "Fuck. Alright."

I pulled a machete free from my hip, Ghost doing the same as Sean watched, shaking his head.

"You're idiots. I'm not helping if you die."

165

"Never asked you to," I said, stretching my muscles. "Just keep an eye on our back."

As one, Ghost and I fell into step, approaching the poor creatures.

Let me end your suffering.

We whirled, stabbing and slashing, targeting heads and hearts in an effort to kill them quickly. We worked together as if we'd done this a million times before, an intricate dance of blood and gore.

They were slower than the ones we'd met down south, their bodies too far gone to do any real damage.

This feels wrong.

Ghost stabbed into the last one, pulling his blade free as the bastard choked, dropping to its knees and fading away.

"These were humans once," I said, my expression grim as we began to clean the weapons, careful not to get their blood on our skin. "But now it feels more like a massacre."

Ghost turned his blade, examining the weapon in the sunlight. "We just put down rabid dogs, Ava. They would have continued to suffer until they either starved or died of dehydration."

I nodded, using a rag to clean off a speck of blood I'd missed.

Sean lifted one of the bags. "I'll catch up to the group."

Ghost pulled his shirt off, turning around. "Check me."

I knew he meant for blood and injury—our clothes would need to be discarded if any blood had landed on us. But my mind went straight into the gutter.

Oh, Grey.

My gaze caressed his back, following the curve of his spine. From his thick neck, broad shoulders, and hefty torso, down to the tight butt encased in dark cargo pants—Grey had been crafted by the gods.

"Ava?"

My name rumbled out of him, his head twisting to look over his shoulder. A hunk of his too-long hair brushed his forehead, my fingers itching to tangle in the strands.

"You're fine." My voice sounded strange.

"Your turn."

I pulled the thin shirt over my head, holding my arms out by my sides. The bra I'd squeezed myself into hadn't been made for a woman with tits. But it'd been one of the only clean pieces of clothing left this morning, so I'd taken it. The black lace contrasted with the white bandages, both stark in the summer sun.

"Perfect."

His voice. His fucking voice.

If this had been the Before, and I'd been surrounded by blood and bodies, half-naked in the middle of nowhere with the sun beating down on me—I might have had a different response.

But this was the After—a time in history where love had learned to flourish between cracks in the pavement.

Love?

Ghost stepped closer, his eyes burning with an unholy light.

Love?

He cupped my jaw, simply holding my gaze for a long moment.

Well, fuck.

He bent, catching my lips and kissing me as if he hadn't been in me less than twelve hours ago. He kissed me as if I were water and he a desert. He kissed as if he wanted to capture my soul.

You've already got the heart, why not take it all?

I hated that I loved him. Hated that I knew he couldn't feel the same. Hated that these feelings that arched between us would be destroyed at some point in the future.

You know this can't last.

Nothing lasted in the After. We might convince ourselves otherwise. We might think we were capable of building futures or trusting someone. But I'd learned the hard way that the only person you could trust was yourself.

Don't fall in love with the devil. He'll burn you alive.

And with deliberate determination, I began to lay the foundations for the wall that would protect my heart.

Chapter Thirty-Four

Ghost

The kid did good.

We found the women hiding in trees along the side of the road. The kid and Sean were seated in the shade under the big gum trees.

"Are they gone?" one of the women asked from her perch on a branch about half-way up.

"Yeah, we're good." Ava leaned against one of the trunks, pulling out a flask and taking a long sip. "We should keep going."

"But I'm hungry," one of the women complained as she slid down the trunk to the ground. "And our feet are sore. Can't we stay here?"

And eat what exactly? Each other?

I eyed Ava, her taste lingering on my lips.

Actually, not a bad idea.

"I might have a few protein bars we can split. But until we find shelter for the night, we can't hunt any game. The faster we find shelter, the faster we can rest and eat."

The woman seemed dissatisfied with her answer.

"The Purge fed us."

"Amber!"

"What?" the woman asked, crossing her arms over her chest, her expression mulish. "I don't have shoes, I haven't eaten a proper meal, I'm hot, dirty and exhausted. At least with The Purge I never had to run from bastards."

Lilith reached over, slapping her across the face. Amber staggered back, her hand rising to her cheek.

"You ungrateful cow," Lilith said, advancing on her. "These people risked their lives to rescue us. The least you could do is shut up and keep walking."

"And what's the end game?" Amber demanded. "We just keep walking until we either get taken by bastards or picked up by The Purge again? Or someone worse?"

"We're going to a compound where women are free." Ava pulled the bars from her pack, handing them out to the gathered women. "A couple we know run a sanctuary. Anyone can join and you're protected there—the only provision is that you have to contribute to the compound."

"Sounds like paradise," one of the women remarked, accepting half a protein bar. "Never thought I'd value freedom so much."

Ava snapped one of the bars in half, holding the piece out to Amber. "Your choice. You can come with us, or you can head back towards Dubbo." Ava pointed down the highway. "Just keep following the road. It's an easy route."

Amber hesitated.

"I'll need an escort. And a gun. And shoes."

Ava shook her head, far more patient than I.

"No can do. We bought these with us and we're gonna need them to get to where we're going. You either make your own way back or continue with us. Your choice."

"You can't do that. You took me, you have to take me back!"

170

"Babe," Ava said, her tone droll. "At any time you could have said no. Last night you could have said no and stayed in the cage. This morning before getting in the truck, you could have said no and stayed at the farmhouse. Hell, we could have gotten half way and we would have stopped and let you out. We're not forcing you to be here. We'd never force any of you to do anything—there's enough idiots in the After trying to do that to us that I refuse to be another one." Ava shrugged. "You're saying no now and I respect that decision. That doesn't mean I'm gonna give in to what you want. We've got more people to look after than just you."

Amber looked around at the faces in the group, her chin lifting. "I wanna go back."

"Great." Ava reached down, scooping up her rifle, slipping the strap over her shoulder. "Good luck."

She began to walk away, leaving Amber staring after her.

"You can't do this!"

She ignored her.

"I mean it! Don't you know who I am?"

"This is the After," I told her. "No one gives a fuck."

I looked around at the others. "You either stay here with this one or you're with us. Your choice."

The women exchanged glances.

"We're with you."

They pushed up from the ground or scrambled down from the trees, each choosing to follow Ava as she picked her way along the road side.

Amber crossed her arms, glaring daggers at me. "Give me a gun."

"No."

"Food then."

"No."

"Water!"

I shook my head. "This is the After, little girl. You only get what you fought for." I pointed at Ava's back. "She fought for your freedom. Me? I'd have left you to rot in the cage."

I turned on my heel, following the group.

"What am I meant to do now?" she asked.

I shrugged. "Don't know, don't care. Either way, choice is yours."

For some reason those words stuck with me as we followed the silent road, trudging along the abandoned highway.

Either way, choice is yours.

Amber had chosen to turn back. Be it fear or stubbornness, the woman could be seen walking in the opposite direction—a lone figure in a dangerous landscape.

I looked to Ava, finding her at the front of our pack, her head raised, her hand gripping her rifle. The cuffs I'd given her glinted in the midday sun.

Either way, choice is yours.

I watched as Ava paused, checking over her rag-tag team of women, ensuring they drank water, stopping to check and retie Jules' rag shoe, joking with the kid when he stumbled.

And all the while, her gaze scanned the horizon, watching Amber get smaller and smaller, the light in her eyes fading.

She cares too much.

I sighed, resigned to my fate. I no longer had a choice—wherever she led I'd follow.

Someone needs to have her back.

I pulled a protein bar from my pocket, unwrapping the top and making my way to Ava's side. She looked up from where she'd stopped to secure another rag shoe.

"You're done." She patted the girl on the foot as she pushed to a stand.

"Thanks, Ava."

The girl walked away, shooting me nervous glances over her shoulder as she caught up to the group.

I held out the bar to Ava.

She looked down at it then up, tilting her head to one side, her hair falling across her shoulder.

"What's this?"

I didn't answer.

Finally, she took the bar, taking a bite as I continued to watch her.

"If you think this is getting you a blow job later, you are sadly mistaken, biker boy."

A twitch of a grin pulled at my lips. "Noted."

We fell in beside each other, following our pack as we walked along the road. Ava chewed off another bite, still considering me as we walked.

"What?"

She shrugged. "Nothing. I guess I just didn't expect that you'd be this kind of guy."

I cocked an eyebrow in question, waiting for her to explain. Ava took another bite, still watching me.

"What kind of guy?" I ground out, loathed to admit I wanted to know.

"The kind of guy who cares."

The words hung between us, hovering in the space.

Babe, I more than care.

"Ava, I—"

"Yo!" Sean called, interrupting the moment. "I think I found

173

us a place to crash for the night."

I gritted my teeth, turning to where he pointed. In the distance a small house sat up on a hill.

"Let's check it out," Ava said, tucking the rest of the protein bar in her pocket. With one final glance my way, she took off, threading through the women to lead the party.

I blew out a breath, adjusting my grip on my rifle.

Fuck.

And just as I'd sworn to do, I followed my woman.

Chapter Thirty-Five

Ava

I scrubbed a dirty hand across my face.

"Anyone got a set of pliers?"

We'd made it to the small shelter and begun the task of setting up camp for the night. The building had turned out to be an abandoned woolshed rather than a house. The place—like most everything in the After—had a thick layer of dust, and weeds growing up through cracks in the weatherboard walls.

The place wasn't plumbed to town water—not that it would do much good after the power grid had failed. But it did have three large rain water tanks out back. The only problem? Someone had stripped the fixtures from the building—including removing the old tap handles, leaving only a shaft.

"Pliers?" Jules asked, tucking hair behind her ears.

"If I can turn the shaft, I might be able to get us running water."

The woolshed had the kind of vintage features that led me to believe it had been built back in the early 1900s—including the original brass faucet. It wasn't a fancy tap by any stretch, built solely for a utilitarian purpose. But if I could find some pliers I might be able to loosen it enough to get us some free flowing water.

"Here," Ghost gently bumped me to the side. "I might have something."

From a pocket he pulled a tap handle, one of those old four-point ones with a hole in the middle for the shaft. I watched as he connected it, sliding the handle into place. He twisted, the handle slipping slightly without a tap cover to secure it but managing to stay mostly in place. The old pipes groaned in protest as they opened, carrying water from the gravity-fed water tanks down to splash into the sink.

I stuck my hands under the water, pleased to see it flowed mostly clear.

"Where on earth did you get that?" I asked, splashing my face, cleaning off the dust and grime that clung to my sticky skin. "Were you thinking of renovating a bathroom and hoping to find a matching set?"

Ghost shot me a look, his face void of emotion.

Uh-oh.

I braced.

"You gave it to me."

"What? When?"

"That night we climbed the wall."

I cast back, a vague memory of me throwing the handle at him tickling my brain.

Shit.

Jules cleared her throat. "I thought I saw a river outside. Come on girls, let's see if we can't cool off out there." With a bit of clucking, and gentle hand motions she cleared the room—casting a meaningful look my way before sliding the shed door shut, leaving me with the one man I didn't have a hope of figuring out.

He kept the tap. Why on earth would he keep a fucking tap?

176

I turned the water off—confused as hell and feeling nervous for some inexplicable reason. I didn't like the feeling.

Ghost watched me in the dim light, his arms crossing over his broad chest.

"You kept a tap handle?"

My voice sounded strange—soft and unsure. I cleared my throat.

He nodded once.

"Why?"

Ghost met my gaze, the blankness in his eyes retreating as we stared at each other.

"Don't you know?"

My breath caught, pain exploding in my chest at the raw emotion in his voice.

"Grey...."

Ghost's legendary control fractured, shattering into a million pieces. He reached out, gripping my neck, pulling me to him. I tumbled into his chest, tilting my head back, my lips parting as he leaned down, hovering for moment, his dark eyes searching mine.

"Only you can call me that," he growled, his expression feral. "Only you, Ava. And only when I'm about to fuck you."

I tried to nod, his hand still holding me prisoner.

"I'll only say this once," he continued, voice low and full of angry need. "You're mine. Don't care if you don't want me. Don't care if you let me fuck you for a day, or never again. You're mine and I'm yours. I'll follow you to hell if you ask. This—" He tapped his chest. "—is yours. You fucking own me, Ava. And I'm telling you right fucking now, I'd burn the motherfucking world down if you asked."

I sucked in a breath as the protective walls I'd been building around my heart crumbled; Ghost's next words crushing the remains into dust.

"Never knew I was capable of emotion until I met you. Love is a weak fucking word compared to the feelings burning in me." He searched my gaze—for what, I wasn't sure, but whatever it was he must have found it.

"I get you, Ava. I see you. You keep protecting everyone else—I'll focus on you."

Then he dropped his head, fisted my hair, and captured my mouth in a brutal kiss.

Don't fall in love with the devil? Oh, Ava. You're already burning.

Chapter Thirty-Six

Ava

Grey tasted like sweat and dust—the combination somehow feeding my desire. A liquid heat pooled low in my belly, a delicious tension spiralling out as he stepped closer, his hard body pressing against mine.

This shouldn't be this good. This should never be this good.

Grey's hands released my hair, slipping through the strands as he glided them down my back to grip my arse. In one smooth move, he lifted me—carrying me forward until my butt hit the sink.

"What are you—" I cut off my question as his hands dropped to my knees, gently prying my legs open. "Please continue."

He stepped forward, gorgeous dark eyes burning as he pressed his erection against my core. Grey captured the hungry little moan that slipping from between my lips—kissing me in a way I could only describe as feral.

More.

As if hearing my thought, he broke our kiss, his hands sliding up my legs to slip under the thin material of my shirt.

His greedy mouth returned to fuck mine as he slowly raised the fabric, revealing my sweaty skin.

"Wait," he ordered.

I blinked, confused as he moved to the faucet, turning on the water. In one smooth move he pulled off his own shirt, tossing them both in the sink, allowing the water to soak the dirty material.

"Grey, what are you doing?"

"Taking care of you." He reached for my belt, slowly undoing the buckle as our gazes held. "Let me do this for you."

A lump formed in my throat, my stupid heart giving a little tug.

"You don't have to. I'm more than capable of looking after myself."

"I know." He unzipped my jeans, one hand moving to cup my pussy. "But don't you remember? You promised to let me taste your cream if I won." He leaned in, sliding his nose along mine, dragging his scruff across my cheek until his lips could graze the shell of my ear.

"Time to pay up."

I swallowed, choking out the one thing that I seemed capable of saying. "I thought you did that last night?"

His chuckle was dark and dirty. "Not even close."

Grey twisted, one hand scooping water from the still flowing tap, his other arm wrapping around my body, pulling me tight against him. He tipped his palm over my breasts, watching as the water trickled down the valley between my breasts.

You're playing a deadly game.

I slipped my hands between us, cupping my breasts and pushing them up, offering my body like a sacrifice to this god of pleasure.

"You gonna clean that up?" I invited.

My personal demon stared at me for a moment.

"You're so fucking beautiful."

Before I could react, his head dipped, his tongue dragging along my skin as he followed the water droplets.

Oh, fuck.

My hands fell away, moving to my back to unclip my bra. In one easy, practiced movement, I slid it off, tossing it into the sink.

"Per-fucking-fection."

Grey's mouth caught my nipple, his eyes closing as he sucked on my rosy tip, my breasts heavy and aching for more.

The fucking hussies.

I arched my back, my hands slipping behind me to support my weight as Grey feasted, sucking one nipple then the other, his teeth grazing the sensitive skin in a way I knew would leave a mark.

"Grey…."

He growled against my skin, the rough noise that of a hungry predator.

Eat me, babe.

Instead, he stepped back, his hands sliding down my left leg to cup my ankle, lifting my foot to slowly untie my shoelace and pull my boot free.

A funny feeling began to duel with the rampant need surging through my body. It felt warm, a little like honey as it spread through my body, tiny flutters following.

I wasn't at all sure I liked it.

Grey peeled my sock from my foot, tossing the filthy thing in the sink pressing his fingers into the arch of my foot to give me a brief massage.

"Oh, fuck." I groaned, my head dropping back as he rubbed my aching sole. "You're fucking dangerous."

He chuckled, fanning the fires that threatened to burn me

181

alive.

I am so out of my depth. And I fucking love it.

"Next foot," he ordered, dropping my left to begin the same process on the right.

My pussy was a hot mess of delicious tension just waiting for the right guy to touch me.

The only guy.

My breath caught, the realisation slamming into me.

Fuck.

I'd worked so hard to protect my heart and yet here he was—already in my soul.

Fuck, that's terrifying.

"Pants," Grey ordered, hooking hands in my jeans and calling my attention back to him. "Off. Now."

I welcomed the distraction, arching my back and lifting my hips to allow him to pull the material from my body.

Down came my underwear and jeans, my butt now resting on the cool stainless-steel sink.

"Like what you see?" I asked, spreading my legs wide, offering him a world class view.

Grey stepped back, his expression shuttered as he watched me, a hand absently rubbing at his chest.

"No?" I asked, sliding a hand down my body to cup my pussy. Liquid heat coated my hand, my arousal perfuming the air around us.

"Grey?" I prompted, lifting my hand, and offering him a soaked finger.

His hand snaked out, wrapping around my wrist to hold me steady as his mouth encircled my finger, his tongue sliding slowly down its length, his gaze looked to mine as he searched for and savoured every lick of my cream.

CHAPTER THIRTY-SIX

"More?" I whispered, my voice thick.

He shook his head, pulling my finger free with a pop. "I believe you also promised *me* something."

I did?

He stepped back, crossing his arms. In that position, I couldn't help but noticed the enormous erection pressing against the crotch of his pants.

Fuck.

"Ava." He called my attention back to his face. As my gaze met his, goose pimples began to rise on my skin, my body awash with anticipation.

"You promised to suck my dick. It's time to deliver, woman."

Chapter Thirty-Seven

Ghost

I expected her to protest, or to at least take her sweet time. I should have known better.

Ava jumped off the sink, dropping to crouch on the ground, her knees resting in the dirt as she reached for my fly.

"Finally," she muttered, pulling down my zipper and yanking the material down my legs.

I kicked off my boots, allowing her to discard my socks, stepping free of my pants as she stared at my cock as if she'd never seen it before.

I reached down, catching her chin in my hand, tilting her head back until our gazes met.

"Fuck me or suck me. Either way, stop looking before I blow my load all over those pretty fucking tits."

She shivered, a full body shiver, her skin taking on a rosy hue.

"Yes, sir."

She meant it as a tease but my body didn't take it that way—my cock jumping at her words.

Ava's hand reached out, wrapping around my thick member. With a small, happy sigh, she leaned forward, her tongue darting out to catch the precum leaking from my tip.

Jesus fucking Christ.

I fisted her hair, pulling the strands back to give me visibility of her glorious face.

Fuck.

Her cheeks hallowed as she went to town, working me over, sucking my cock deep, her throat clenching around the crown before she pulled back and did it all again.

"Fuck, Ava." A sound ripped free from somewhere deep inside. "Keep going."

She redoubled her efforts, one hand tight around my shaft, the other cupping my balls as she sucked me like the fucking queen she was.

I'd never allowed myself to think beyond getting a taste of her. Never allowed myself to consider the possibility that she'd not only suck my cock, but get off doing it.

Yet here she was, losing her fucking mind as she swallowed my dick.

"Ava." I cupped her cheek, attempting to pull back.

She doubled down, protesting as I tried to draw away.

Fuck.

My control snapped at her whimpered protest, my arms reaching down to haul her up, turning her around, pressing her down until her hands braced on the sink, her arse tilted up for me.

Gonna fuck that arse first chance I get. But first....

I guided my cock to her, pressing my front to her back, one hand holding her in place, the other running my cock over her soaked slit.

"Ready?" I asked, my voice rough.

She arched back, her juices coating my dick.

"Bring it, biker boy."

185

I thrust—hard, fast, and rough as fuck—just the way she loved it.

"Gonna come in you," I told her, fucking into her tight cunt. "Gonna fuck this little snatch until you milk me dry."

She moaned, her hips pressing back against me, her body shifting with every thrust I made.

"Harder, Grey. Fuck me harder."

I slapped her arse, my teeth finding her shoulder, leaving a mark that I soothed away with a lick.

"You dirty girl," I whispered against her ear, my voice rough and low. "You want me to fuck your sweet pussy. You've been gagging for it for weeks."

Her answering pants were all I needed to know.

Mine.

I spanked her again, her inner muscles convulsing as her pussy flooded. I shifted one hand around her body to pinch her nipple, a dark chuckle escaping me at her whimpered moan.

"Shut the fuck up," she growled, pressing back. "Fuck me, Grey. Make me come!"

I let go of her breast, cupping her face and turning her head until I could capture her lips. My cock fucked into her, hitting deep as we kissed—our tongues fighting for dominance.

Mine.

She shattered under me, her mouth pulling free, her head tilting back, my name rasping from her throat as she came.

Fuck!

Control gone, I fucked her into the sink, marking her with another love bite as her pussy clenched, milking my cock. Three strokes and I was gone, filling her up with my cum, a violent need to mark her body inside and out hitting me.

I pumped into her, then pulled free, fisting my cock with a last splash of cum, marking the cheeks of her arse.

Mine.

Decorated in love bites and my seed, my woman slumped against the sink, fighting to catch her breath.

I pulled Ava into my body, gently turning her, wrapping her in my arms.

Naked, we stood in the hot woolshed, sweat trickling down our spines, our bodies cooling as she caught her breath.

For several long moments she remained silent, her body resting quietly against mine.

"I'm gonna have a hickey, aren't I?"

I glanced down at her shoulder, satisfied to see my handy work beginning to rise on her skin.

"Maybe."

"Do it again and I'll bite your dick instead of sucking it."

I leaned down, nipping at her bottom lip. "Threaten my dick and I'll spank that arse until it's pink then fuck it."

Ava's eyebrows lifted. "You really think I'd let you?"

My cock began to harden again, turned on by the challenge in her voice. I reached down, hauling her up against me, gratified when her legs wrapped around my waist, her arms around my neck, my cock pressing into the juncture of her thighs.

"Let? Ava, you'll beg me for it."

Before my maddening woman could protest, I captured her in a kiss and slid my cock home—standing still, my whole world held in my arms as she rode me, fucking herself on my cock until we both came.

"Next time," she murmured, resting her head on my shoulder. "You do all the work."

I grinned, cradling her in my arms. "Deal."

Chapter Thirty-Eight

Ava

I closed my eyes tilting my head back to enjoy the cool of the river water as it flowed over my heated skin.

A splash nearby interrupted my tranquillity.

"Fish!" Lilith screamed, holding up a soaked shirt bundle in one hand, the fabric bouncing as the fish slapped against the wet material. "I caught dinner!"

I laughed, watching her triumphantly carry the fish over to the small pile Ghost and Sean were beginning to amass.

"If I didn't know better, I'd almost think this were a normal day."

I looked over, finding a sunburnt Jules watching Lilith as Sean showed her how to kill the fish and thread it onto a stick to cook.

"Well—" she shot me a grin. "Except for escaping from slavers, surviving a zombie attack, making it through a mutiny, and at least one of us getting their rocks off."

"Yeah, so, about that…."

Lilith waded her way back over to us, dipping her makeshift fishing-net back into the water.

"Are we talking about Ava fucking the big man?"

"I don't know," Jules turned to me. "Are we?"

188

I glanced at Ghost, finding his dark gaze on me.

"Ava?" Lilith reached out, placing a hand on my arm.

"I'm good," I told them honestly. "He's...."

"Big, dangerous, scary?" Jules offered.

"A sexy protective alpha?" Lilith asked.

"All of the above?" I shook my head. "He's like this big lump of nothing emotion one minute and—"

"Fucking you raw with fire in his eyes the next?" Lilith asked, her grin wide.

"What?"

"Oh, she looked." Jules splashed her. "You dirty bird."

Lilith laughed, splashing her back. "Only for the tiniest minute. I swear. I just wanted to make sure you were okay."

I rolled my eyes, hands gliding through the water as I watched these women play.

"But seriously," Jules said, flicking water off her nose. "We've obviously missed a lot. What happened after The Purge?"

"Where do I start?"

"How about how you found us and work back from there? I mean—" She waved a hand around. "—this isn't exactly home."

I swallowed, a solid lump forming in my throat. "Lil, Jules... I'm sorry. I'm so fucking sorry that—"

Water hit me in the face.

"Shut up," Lilith said, rolling her eyes. "You did nothing wrong."

"Absolutely nothing," Jules agreed, crossing her arms.

"You taught us to fight and to survive. You taught us to adapt and to look for any opportunity to exploit."

"And we did." Jules reached out, threading her fingers with Lil's. "We made it through bastard infested territory in chains. We made it through threats of rape and violence. We made

189

it starving and with bloodied feet. We made it to here." She reached out capturing my hand, drawing me into their little circle. "We made it home."

I huffed out a broken breath. "Not exactly home. Not sure we even have one."

"Home isn't a place," Lilith reminded me. "It's a feeling. It's people—your people."

My gaze drifted across to where Ghost stood by the fire, his gaze locked on our little huddle.

"Ava," Jules called my attention back to her. "It's okay."

My heart broke, my stomach clenching. "No, it can't be. I—"

They cut me off by pulling me into their arms—wrapping me in a group hug.

"You were our home for a long time, Ava." Lil squeezed me tight. "But now it's time for our home to expand. And perhaps—" She glanced meaningfully at Ghost. "—there's already been room made for one more?"

Tears burned at the backs of my eyes.

"Don't worry." Jules patted my arm. "We won't make you say it. But that man over there with the deadly eyes—he might like to hear the words someday."

A wolf-whistle split the air, calling our attention to the fire.

"Grubs up," Sean yelled, holding up a stick with a spitted fish. "Come and get it!"

I met Ghost's gaze across the water, ignoring the muddling women as they made their way to the fire.

Jules was right, Ghost might like to hear the words that burned in my gut. But looking at him, trapped by his intensity, any words I might have said faded away—leaving only a certain truth.

I'm not getting out of this alive.

190

CHAPTER THIRTY-EIGHT

And for the first time in my life, that thought didn't scare me.

Chapter Thirty-Nine

Ava

We made it to Farmer's five days later. Hungry, sunburnt, tired, and stinking to high heaven—with more mosquito bites, blisters, and cuts than we knew what to do with. We trudged up the last hill, supporting each other as the gravel slipped under our feet. The gates in front of us opened, the late afternoon sun sending long shadows across our path.

"Well, fuck me dead" came a familiar voice. "You bloody well did it."

I looked up, finding Farmer standing in the middle of the giant gate, his arms crossed as he watched us struggle up the hill to his compound.

"Hello to you too, motherfucker." I raised my hand, flicking him the bird. "You wanna come down and help us?"

He grinned, turning around to let out an ear-splitting whistle. Within moments, men and women streamed from the compound, coming down the hill to help take bags and support the women to climb.

"What is this place?" Sean asked as we stepped through the towering gate and into the bustling compound.

"Heaven?" one of the women asked, staring around at the high walls, the fortified battlements, and the pens of livestock.

"They have hot showers," I said, shooting them a grin. "And fresh bread."

"We might even be able to find some mattresses for you all," one of the helpers said, laughing when a sigh escaped the woman she was assisting. "Come on, let's get you inside."

I'd once worked in a refugee camp supporting displaced people as they escaped war-torn cities. The compound felt a little like that, as they found blankets for the women, wrapping their wounds, handing out water, and producing toast with thick slathers of sweet jam.

"My sister?" I asked Farmer, finally taking a seat at his communal table, my women taken care of.

He handed me a cool glass of water. "Gone. They left a few days after you did."

Damn.

I'd expected it, but it hurt that Lottie wasn't here.

"Are they still headed to Cunnamulla?" I asked, referring to one of the three remaining Nameless Soul chapters.

"Last I heard." He took the seat beside me. "Your sister and the biker who lost his arm?"

"Zero."

Farmer nodded. "She managed to keep him alive."

"That's good. Did they leave you a phone?" I asked, referring to Audrey's latest invention. The woman had designed a communications network that used tiny relay towers to run what she referred to as the A-Network—the Audrey Network.

While the network was a success, the type of phone required to access it were few and far between.

"No. But we've now got all the parts. When your girl comes back through, we'll be ready for her to build one for us."

"Woman," I corrected absently, watching Ghost as he loaded

a plate with food across the room. "She's a woman, not a girl."

My man looked like an avenging angel as he strode towards me, a plate of food held in one hand, a glass of water in the other. Danger radiated from his every pore, people moving out of his way almost by instinct—the predator scaring the prey.

That's all mine.

My thighs pressed together, my inner muscles clenching in anticipation as I watched him cross the room.

"Here," he grunted, handing me the heaped plate. "Eat."

I laughed, rolling my eyes but taking the offering. "Ghost, I'm fine."

"Eat."

"I'll eat later."

He dropped into the seat beside me, giving me his *no prisoners* glare.

"I said, eat."

I blew out a sigh. "Fine."

I took a bite, quickly swallowing a moan as the raspberry flavoured jam burst across my tongue.

Oh, dear God.

Ghost relaxed, an amused smile playing at the corners of his mouth.

"Good?" he asked.

I sniffed, lifting one shoulder in a half shrug. "It'll do."

"I'll pass your crumb of a compliment to my wife." Farmer laughed, pushing to a stand. "We've got you all set up in the barracks. Take any room, my people are bunking down elsewhere for the night."

I reached out, stopping him with a hand. "Thank you. I know you'll do right by them."

CHAPTER THIRTY-NINE

"You're still determined to leave?"

I nodded. "We need to catch up with our people in Cunnamulla before they head to Queensland."

He shook his head. "You people have a fucking death wish. You need to pass through bastard hunting grounds."

"We've got vehicles. And weapons. We'll make it."

"Your choice." He looked to Ghost. "When will you leave?"

"The day after tomorrow."

My eyebrows lifted, my mouth full of toast.

"Not tomorrow?" Farmer asked.

Ghost looked at me, his expression heated. "No, we need... rest."

Oh, rest is it? I see you, Grey. Bring it, biker boy.

Farmer nodded. "I'll make sure your vehicles are ready for you." He moved to walk away then paused. "And Ghost?"

He lifted his head.

"Your kutte will be ready tomorrow."

Ghost nodded.

"What happened to your kutte?" I asked, scooping up a piece of melon with my fingers.

Ghost ignored me, watching the women over my shoulder.

"Oi, Mister silent treatment, what happened to your kutte?"

I knew he hadn't taken it with him to Dubbo—the risk of wearing it and being identified was too great. He hadn't been prepared for The Purge to blow back on the club, especially considering they were already facing issues with the local arm back in Adaminaby.

He shrugged. "Needed repairs."

I narrowed my eyes on him, taking a giant bite out of the melon piece. Ignoring me, Ghost stood, brushing off the dirt on his jeans.

195

"You nearly done?" he asked, looking pointedly at my now empty plate.

I shrugged. "Guess so."

He reached down, tugging it from me and laying it on the table, his other hand capturing mine and pulling me to my feet.

"Good."

"Good?" I asked, following as he led me out of the communal space. "Where are we going?"

He tossed a look over his shoulder, desire written on his face.

"Where do you think? To fuck."

Chapter Forty

Ghost

I stripped Ava, rough hands covering her skin, forcing her to look at me.

"Need you under me." I pushed her back on the bed, gratified when she fell with a grin.

I tore off my own clothing, near desperate to feel her body against mine.

A frown wrinkled her forehead as she watched me.

"What are you thinking about?"

The frown eased, a teasing smile replacing it. "Anal."

I groaned, my hand dropping to fist my cock, giving myself one rough stroke.

"Don't fucking tease me."

She chuckled, her hands sliding over her body, fingertips grazing skin—my mouth watered with the urge to taste.

"Not teasing. I just wondered how you'd feel buried balls deep inside my arse."

Fuck.

"As much as I wanna take you up on that offer, I'm gonna have to pass." I dropped to my knees beside the bed, hooking arms under her legs and dragging her to the edge of the bed. "I'm craving a taste of your sweet cream."

Ava arched as my mouth fell on her cunt, her body opening to me. Wet heat coated my face as I ate her—rough, sloppy and so fucking good I could drown in her.

I snaked one hand up her body to pinch her nipple, the other sliding through her juices, finding her entrance and slipping two fingers inside.

"Fuck!" She groaned as I worked her to the edge of her control. "God, I knew your lips were made for sex. I fucking—shit! Grey!"

My name on her lips had my cock thickening, lengthening, the fucker ready to blow his load at the first touch of her hand on me.

Fuck, she's beautiful.

I worked Ava hard, fucking and sucking her, determined to make this the longest orgasm of her life. Flushed and sweaty, her body in constant movement as she fought me for her release—Ava had to be the most stunning creature I'd ever had the privilege to see.

Now.

With a twist of my tongue she shattered, her hands clawing at my shoulders—their sharp bite welcome as she rode my face, flooding my skin with the evidence of her desire.

More.

I slid up her body, flipping her over, pressing her down and into the bed, my cock sliding between her slit, gathering the moisture and dragging over her sensitive flesh.

"I thought," she panted, pressing her arse up and into me. "This was meant to feel good."

Her playful ribbing unfurled something dark in me. A soul deep satisfaction.

"I can hold a whip in one hand and a feather in the other,

198

Ava." I leaned down, nipping at her shoulder then sucking the sting away. "Pleasure and pain aren't mutually exclusive."

Her body clenched at my words.

"Either fuck me, or let me ride you."

I rolled us until I was on my back on the mattress, Ava's back pressed to my chest, her body draped over mine.

"Do it."

In one move she impaled herself on my cock, both of us swearing as she took me deep.

"Fuck me, Ava. Ride me. Find our fucking release."

She shifted, her hips moving to take me deep. I gripped her, helping to guide her, helping to fuck her onto my aching dick.

"So fucking tight," I grunted, thrusting my hips up to meet her parry. "So fucking perfect for me, Ava. Take my dick. Fuck me, babe."

I watched her unravel, her body bowing back, her hair brushing my skin, fingernails creating little crescents in the muscles of my thighs as Ava's pussy spasmed around my cock.

Yes!

I roared my approval, holding her in place as I fucked her, my cock spilling inside her, marking Ava as mine.

We both collapsed on the bed, the explosive sex giving way to a new dimension between us—gentleness.

She cuddled into me, her body pressing to mine, her head resting on my chest as we caught our breaths. There was something so domestic about it, something that calmed and warmed me as she cuddled closer, murmuring a pleasant sound as I began to thread fingers through her hair.

"Grey?" she whispered some time later, her voice soft and sleepy.

"Mm?"

"Love you."

My body froze.

"What?"

She pressed a kiss to the skin above my heart. "I love you, biker boy."

There were only three things I'd ever loved in my life—Ava, Hazard, and Blue. I knew my brothers loved me—they'd had no choice. But Ava? Her words stirred shit inside me that I'd never fucking felt before.

Hope, you bastard. She's giving you hope for a fucking future.

With a sigh she rolled over, snuggling her arse into me. "Rest. You can fuck me more tomorrow."

Her breathing evened out, sleep taking her quickly. I curled around her, one hand cupping her breast, my cock pressed to the seam of her arse.

It didn't escape me that every single fucking thing I'd never dared to even dream lay in my arms. Blue's final words to Hazard and I came to me, the resignation in his eyes so clear it still felt like a punch in the gut.

"Boys, learn from my mistake. When you find the person whose death you fear more than your own." He'd looked from me to Hazard then raised the pistol to his temple. "Don't fucking let them go."

He'd pulled the trigger before we could stop him, his last words forever etched on my soul.

I pulled Ava closer, ignoring her sleepy huff of protest.

Never letting you go.

Chapter Forty-One

Ava

We spent the day in bed, Grey leaving to find food while I napped. He'd feed me in bed then make love to me until I felt as if I would shatter at the slightest breath.

I'd never wanted anyone as much as him. It was thrilling and terrifying and fucking horrible and magnificent all at once.

Or at least it had been, until this moment.

We'd showered and eaten, packing the car and double-checking the motorcycle that would carry us to Cunnamulla.

Lilith and Jules—outfitted in borrowed clothing and new shoes—handed me their packs.

"We ready?" I asked, glancing around.

"Yep." Jules opened the driver's door, sliding in behind the wheel. "We're ready when you are, my queen."

I shot her an eyeroll, glancing around for Ghost—spotting him chatting with Sean, Farmer, and Farmer's very pregnant wife beside his motorcycle.

"You got a map?" I asked, as Lilith settled in the passenger seat.

"Yes, mum."

I chuckled, shutting the door on her. "Alright. We'll just be a minute then we can head off."

They both gave me a salute, their identical grins full of mischief.

They're going to be fine.

I made my way over to Ghost, wrapping one arm around his waist and leaning into him as he finished his conversation.

"Thanks again." Ghost held out his big hand. "Appreciate all your assistance."

Farmer shook it. "You bring us more refugees, we'll take them." He dropped Ghost's hand, pressing a kiss to his wife's head. "We're committed to being a sanctuary."

His wife patted her extremely pregnant belly. "We'd want to be since we're beginning to expand."

I looked at Sean. "You absolutely sure you don't want to come?"

He nodded. "I got unfinished business in Adaminaby."

Mouse.

After his help, we'd felt obligated to give him the information he sought. Didn't mean I'd let him just go and fuck with someone in the club.

"You remember your promise?"

He rolled his eyes. "I'm not gonna hurt her, Ava. Swear."

It would have to do.

"Ready?" Ghost asked.

I nodded, allowing him to turn us.

"Wait!" A young woman ran across the courtyard, skidding to halt. "Here, your kutte."

She held it out to Ghost who took the worn leather and a small envelope from her. "Thanks."

She nodded, quickly ducking her head and darting away. Ghost pulled on the leather, the missing patches immediately drawing my eye.

"What the fuck? You removed your name?"

I stared at the space where his name patch had sat just above his heart. His title also missing.

"Yeah."

"Yeah?" I echoed, confused as fuck by his blasé tone. *"Yeah? What do you mean just yeah?"*

He glanced at me, that thick lock of hair falling across his forehead. "You gonna make a big deal out of this?"

I bristled, crossing my arms over my chest. "That depends on what *this* is."

He turned, presenting me with his back. My heart skipped, the bottom dropping out of my world as I stared at his kutte.

"Grey," I whispered, closing the distance between us. "What did you do?"

"What I had to."

I shook my head, fingers running up his back to his shoulders, helping him to remove the leather. I held it in my hands, staring at the stitching.

"But you earned this. It represents your place in the club." My breath caught, all too aware of how much the club meant to him. "What will they do if they see this?"

Ghost crossed his arms, widening his stance. "Who gives a fuck what they do?" He reached out, cupping my jaw. "You're my future, Ava. You're the only thing that fucking matters in this world."

I dropped my head, staring at the kutte in my hands. With trembling fingers, I traced the freshly sewn letters.

Property of Ava.

"You'd actually wear this?" I asked, my heart full.

"Every day."

"You're an idiot." My smile felt shaky.

203

He grinned. "I'm in fucking love."

I rolled my eyes. "And you sound thrilled about it."

His hand shot out cupping the back of my head and pulling me into him. His mouth descended, pausing for a second to whisper against my lips.

"Oh, I am."

Then he kissed me as if I really was the only thing in the world that mattered.

To him, you are.

And to me, he was too.

Reluctantly, I broke the kiss, leaning my forehead against his. "Grey, I'd never ask you to do this."

"And that's why I did it." He pulled back, tapping the kutte. "I'm not asking you to change—just to meet me halfway. I want your claim on me, Ava. I want your kiss on my lips and your name on my back."

I sucked in a breath. "They'll make your life hell. They might even kick you out of the club."

He snorted. "They can fucking try."

I looked down at the leather in my hands.

There's a future here. A 'til death do us part kind of love. If only you'd say yes.

"I want you to change it back," I said finally, handing him back the leather.

His eyes blanked, all the heat and hope wiped clean.

Oh, Grey.

"Instead, I want it tattooed here." I tapped his chest, right above his heart. "Property of Ava. Leather can be removed. It can be damaged or lost." I looked up, staring into his gorgeous dark eyes as I staked my claim. "I want my mark on you forever. Until we both turn to dust, Grey."

204

CHAPTER FORTY-ONE

His mask broke—the raw aching need shattering any barrier between us.

"I can do that."

We met halfway, our lips clashing together as we sealed our deal.

Until the end.

Epilogue One

Ava

"You're back!" Audrey screamed, rushing across the yard towards us.

"Jesus," Ghost muttered, waiting as I dismounted. "Someone turn her volume down."

"Hush," I told him. "She's just excited to see us."

" I can tell."

"You know, you're getting rather chatty in your old age."

He reached over, squeezing my thigh in a way I knew meant there would be retribution later.

"Did you find them?" Audrey demanded, wrapping me in a tight hug.

"Yeah, babe. They're in the car behind us."

She jumped back, staring at the truck that bumping along the long drive, her expression pure joy. "I knew you'd do it!"

I sucked in a breath, stunned by the certainty in her voice. "Well, shit. You could have told me that before I left."

Audrey laughed. "I have so much to tell you. Kate and Wrath are married—"

"Wow that's—"

"—and I had sex with a man. He's hot too."

"Pope finally pulled his finger out then?" I grinned, amused

206

by this new development.

"Oh no, Pope and I are just friends. I could never have sex with a friend."

My eyebrows shot up. "I'm sorry. What?"

"And my dog is pregnant. Do you guys want something to eat, we have—"

"Wait, Audrey. You had sex with someone who *isn't* Pope?"

She nodded, her dark hair swaying with her movement. "Yeah, is that a problem?"

"I mean…." I glanced at Ghost who looked as if he couldn't give a fuck. "No?"

"He's nice but bossy. I like it in the bedroom but in real life it's just annoying so we're on a break. He keeps telling me we're not but we are." With that said, she stepped around me dashing towards the SUV, Lilith and Jules screaming and crying as Audrey wrapped them in hugs.

People streamed out, watching our reunion. Kate, Ellie, and Jo appeared, all pulling me in for a tight group hug.

"How was it?"

"Tough," Jo admitted in a low voice as Kate and Ellie moved across to Lilith and Jules. "Shit went down, Ava. But we dealt. Like you'd taught us."

The normally restrained woman reached out, pulling me in for a second hug. "Fucking glad you're back."

This is home. Our people are home.

"Well, well, well, if it isn't the prodigal son and daughter, returned to our welcoming bosom."

I looked up, grinning as Pope strolled across the yard, arms stretched wide in welcome. Behind him trailed the rest of the Adaminaby crew, including Runner, Butcher, Wrath, Texas, Swift, and the now one-armed Zero.

We were greeted with hugs and news, and demands for us to retell our story over tonight's welcome feast.

"Where's Lottie?" I asked, searching for my sister amongst the crowd.

"In theatre. One of the guys had a run-in with a snake. They're everywhere around here, they tell me—" Pope broke off, his body frozen.

"Oh, fuck."

I twisted, catching sight of Jules as she stared at the young biker.

"It's you."

"Wait, you know each other?" Audrey asked, her head whipping from Jules to Pope and back.

"No."

"Yes."

"That is—"

"We don't really—"

They both fell silent, glaring at each other.

Audrey's head tilted to one side. "Is this a sex thing?"

Jules, already beet red from her sun burn, flushed magenta. "No, it's not a sex thing!"

Audrey shrugged. "Okay, whatever."

"Look, can someone take me to my—"

A familiar scream interrupted me.

My body went into high alert, my gaze scanning the crowded courtyard for a familiar head of wild hair.

Lottie.

My little sister with her riot of curls, sprinted across the compound—her arms held wide in welcome.

Lottie.

I moved, crashing into her halfway, wrapping her in a fierce, tight hug.

"You're home," she whispered, squeezing me tighter.

"Told you I'd come back."

She pulled back for a moment, her eyes glassy with unshed tears as she gave me a playful slap. "You're late."

"Sorry, I was busy trying to rescue people. And running out of fuel. Walking in this heat really takes it out of you."

Ghost caught my eye over her head, his eyebrow cocked in a teasing question.

And the never-ending desperate sex breaks didn't help.

"There's so much to tell you," Lottie said, pulling me back in a tight squeeze. "I've missed you."

I know. I missed you too.

I held her for a long minute, giving her reassurance and getting my own in return.

"Alright," she pulled back with a laugh, swiping at her eyes. "I know you don't do the mushy stuff so hit me. What do you want to know?"

"Um, how about we start with Audrey and Pope?" I linked my arm with hers, allowing her to escort us across the compound towards a large building from which delicious smells were wafting. "Not a thing?"

"Oh God, Ava. You've missed *so* much."

"Who is it? Do I know him?"

"It's—"

A voice interrupted Lottie.

"Ghost."

We stopped, turning to see a guy approaching.

Wow.

He was young—maybe mid-thirties, but he had the presence of a much older man. Grey touched the hair at his temples,

209

while wrinkles had begun to settle at the corners of his eyes. He wore responsibility like a cape and authority like a weapon—a king among men.

He expects people to follow.

"Shield," my man greeted, holding out a hand.

I started, blinking at the Nameless Souls National President. He clasped Ghost's hand, pulling him in for a backslapping hug.

"I thought they said he was in Queensland," I whispered to Lottie.

"Yeah, well, about that. So—"

"Good to see you, brother," the President rumbled, interrupting our whispered conversation. "Thought we might have lost you when you ran late."

Ghost shrugged. "Fuel ran out and we got sidetracked finding some more." He turned to me, reaching out to gently separate me from Lottie, wrapping an arm around my shoulder. "This is my woman, Ava."

I ignored Lottie's delighted gasp and I held out a hand. "Nice to meet you."

The President shook it, examining me with an expression that gave nothing away. "You're the ex-military girl."

"Woman," I corrected. "And yes."

He nodded. "Heard about you. Word is you're decent with a rifle."

I grinned. "I'm not bad."

"She's good," Ghost confirmed, his praise warming my insides.

Geez you're a lost cause.

"Good. We need more like you." He turned, searching the yard. "Who are the women with Audrey?"

210

"Jules and Lilith. They're mine," I stated firmly, claiming my sisters in heart.

He gave me a side-eye. "We're not in the habit of kicking people out, Ava."

I shrugged, crossing my arms. "After what we've been through you can never be too careful."

Audrey spotted Shield from where she'd remained with Jules and Lilith across the courtyard, pulling away from their group.

"Ava, have you met Shield?" she asked.

I nodded.

She gestured at him. "He's the guy who fucked me."

My head whipped from Audrey to Shield and back. *"Him?"*

She nodded, crossing her arms. "It was good. Not great. But good."

"Babe," Shield said with a sigh, pinching the bridge of his nose. "I already told you, five is unrealistic. Not with the amount of shit I have to do every fucking day."

Audrey rolled her eyes. "Kate said she and Wrath went five times without breaks."

Five times? Jesus.

I eyed Ghost. Being out on the road there'd only been finite snatches of time to get down and dirty between travelling, keeping watch for danger, and resting.

He looked down at me, his gaze heating.

"Is there a room for us around here?" I asked, a familiar heat beginning to pool in my belly.

"We set you up in the old barn. They've converted it into rooms. You're number four. Do you want me to show you—"

"I got it," Ghost rumbled, interrupting Audrey.

"Oh, I see. You want to fuck." She nodded wisely. "Ensure you do plenty of foreplay or try lube. I hear that helps. Not that I've needed it, but some people do. There should be some in each of the bedrooms—I made sure when we moved in."

I closed my eyes, laughter threatening to spill out. "Thanks, Audrey."

"Anytime. I'm quite good at giving sexual advice. Aren't I, Lottie?"

"Yeah, babe," my sister answered, her voice strained.

Ghost turned us, taking a step forward. I halted, knowing it would stir him up.

"Wait," I said, my expression remorseful. "We've only just gotten here. We should make sure everyone gets settled, give them a rundown of what's happened. Maybe—"

In a smooth move I could never hope to replicate, Ghost bent tossing me over his shoulder.

"No."

"But—" I protested, secretly delighted by this display of possessive need. "What about—"

"No."

"But—"

"Fucking, no." His hand slapped my ass as he carried me towards the barn.

I sighed dramatically. "Fine. But you're finding the lube."

"You won't need fucking lube."

"You'll for certain be using lube if you want my arse."

His body went tight under me. "Fuck, I love you."

I grinned, closing my eyes, loving this man with all my heart. "Oh, I know."

Epilogue Two

Ghost

Ava's fingers traced the outline of the tattoo that marked me as hers over my heart. She did this regularly, early in the morning before she thought I'd woken.

I never told her that I often faked sleep just to enjoy the feel of her fingers on my skin.

Ava's lips kissed my tattoo.

"I know you're awake."

I snorted, my eyes still closed.

"And I know you're wanting this."

Her hand snaked down to grip my cock.

I opened one eyes, giving her a lazy grin. "Good morning, Ava."

Her hair was a wild tangle around her head. She had a fading bruise on her cheek from a run in with a bastard, and a glint in her eyes that I had become all too familiar with.

My hand found the juncture of her thighs. My fingers caressed her curls, finding her wet, hot, and wanting.

"You know what I want?" I asked, rolling us so her back was to the mattress. "Or know what you want?"

She shrugged, her hand still fisting my cock. "Same, same, isn't it?"

With a rough tug, she stroked my cock, pleasure building at her touch.

I leaned down, nuzzling at her neck, kissing, and sucking at her sensitive skin, loving how her desire coated my fingers as I played her body to perfection.

"You started this," I reminded her as she began to squirm under me.

"Shh, less talk, more fuck."

I chuckled, catching her lips. For a moment she fought me, refusing to open her mouth. But one strategically placed finger had her gasping, allowing me to taste her sweet tongue.

Perfection.

A knock on our bedroom door interrupted us.

"Ava? Are you up?"

My woman sighed, pulling back from me to call, "yeah, I'm awake, Jules. What's up?"

"So... I don't mean to be alarmist but... Audrey's kind of...." she trailed off.

"Kind of?" Ava prompted giving me an amused eyeroll.

"Um... I think she's missing."

Under me, Ava went electric.

Fuck.

"What?" She scrambled, out from under me, my dick rapidly deflating.

She tugged the blanket along with her, leaving me naked as she walked across the small room to the door, throwing it open. "Talk to me."

I sighed, rolling out of bed to search for my pants.

I fucking hate people.

My cock agreed.

"Audrey's missing. Apparently, she got pissed at Shield last night and now no one can find her."

Jules hesitated, wringing her hands. "And Shield? He's kind of losing it."

I raised my eyebrow, tugging on my sweats.

"Losing it, how?" Ava asked, wrapping the blanket around her like a toga.

"Like about to murder someone if we can't find her."

Ava pinched the bridge of her nose. "So, this is a lovers spat?"

Jules nodded. "But of epic proportion."

Ava leaned forward looking right then left before stepping back to lay a hand on the door.

"Jules?"

"Yeah?"

"Did anyone send you here?"

She shook her head. "No. I just thought you'd like to know."

"Do we think Audrey—who is an actual genius—will leave the safety of the compound?"

Jules slowly shook her head, her hands stilling. "She's terrified of bastards."

"Right. And do we really think she'd put other people who have to go search for her at risk?"

Jules shook her head again.

"Good. Call off the search party, she'll reappear when she's ready." Ava made a move to close the door then paused. "And tell everyone else to leave me alone." She shot a look over her shoulder, sending me a wink. "I got something more important to do."

My cock responded, hardening as the door clicked shut.

Ava turned slightly towards me, a small smile playing on her lips as she fiddled with the top of the blanket, allowing it to slide down her perfect body.

My eyes followed its fall, caressing her newly naked skin, narrowing in on the tattoo she'd had along her side—two snakes intertwined to make the shape of a 'G'.

She told me it was for her Grey Ghost. It was her public declaration that she was mine.

"Ava," I barked, hands dropping to my sweats.

She looked over, cocking an eyebrow.

"I fucking love you."

She grinned, slowly making her way into my arms. With one hand resting on the tattoo across my heart, the other cupping my cheek, she met my gaze, her eyes shining.

"I love you too, Grey." Her hand slipped down my body to cup my cock as it tented the sweat pants. "And you."

I barked out a laugh, bending to lift her up, grinning as her hands wrapped around my neck, her legs tight around my waist.

"I think you deserve a little spanking for that," I told her, walking us back to the bed.

She kissed me, nipping at my bottom lip. "Can't wait."

* * *

Thank you so much for reading Ava and Ghost's story!
The Nameless Souls continues with Shield! I can't wait for you to read his story.
You can check out my website at www.EvieMitchell.com for more information on the
Nameless Souls series.

Books by Evie Mitchell

Nameless Souls MC Series
Runner
Wrath
Ghost
Shield

Elliot Security Series
Rough Edge
Bleeding Edge
Knife Edge

Capricorn Cove Series
Thunder Thighs
Double the D
Muffin Top
The Mrs. Clause
Beach Party
New Year Knew You
The Shake-Up
Double Breasted
As You Wish
You Sleigh Me
Resolution Revolution
Meat Load

Trunk Junk

Thor's Shipbuilding Series
Clean Sweep
The X-list
Reality Check
The Christmas Contract

Dogg Pack Series
Puppy Love
The Frock Up
Pier Pressure
Bad English

Archer Sibling Series
Just Joshing

Connect with Evie

Website
www.EvieMitchell.com

Newsletter
www.subscribepage.com/z2p2x3_copy

Amazon
www.amazon.com/author/eviemitchell

Bookbub, Instagram and Facebook
@EvieMitchellAuthor

Facebook Group
Evie Mitchell's Greedy Reader Book Club